POWER ALWAYS COMES WITH A PRICE

DEATH & DIVINATION

JADIS MOON

CRANTHORPE
MILLNER
PUBLISHERS

Character artwork by Kristina Pidpalova
Social media: @ikrississ
Contact via krispdplv@gmail.com

First published by Cranthorpe Millner Publishers (2025)

ISBN 978-1-80378-294-2 (Paperback)

www.cranthorpemillner.com

Cranthorpe Millner Publishers

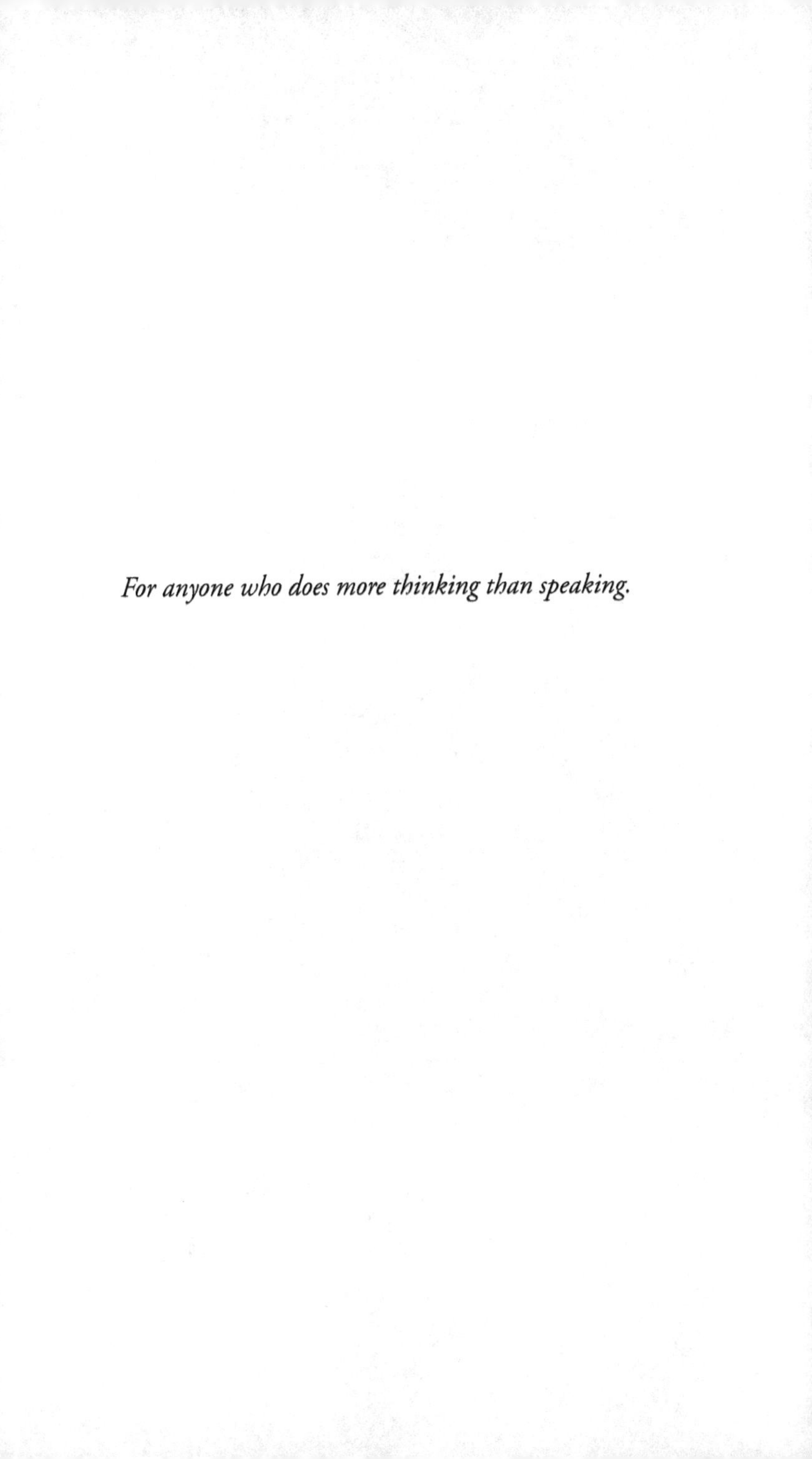

For anyone who does more thinking than speaking.

EDESSA
Itharene
Kaedia
Elirede
Thelassan
The Hatchery
The Serpents Sea
The Obsidian Bay
The Wastes
Ossory
Vesuryn
Cenna
Dreka
The Bones
The Arcane Pocket
Ethil
Newrath
Athria
Astela
Mushroom Forest
The Hollow Hills
Galvaria
Pallum
The Prison Isle

PROLOGUE

I didn't mean to kill my lover.

He was a kind man. Being in his presence had always reminded me of sitting in the sun. He had the kind of warmth that heated my skin until it burned. We met years ago, under the two moons of Kaedia. He'd asked for my hand, and when he smiled at me, I'd given it without a second thought. He was beautiful; no one could blame me for falling for a mortal.

I didn't *mean* to kill my lover.

We had spent hours in the very same cottage where I stood now. I'd explored more than his body; I knew his mind. That was how I knew he was kind; he was good. He was to be trusted.

My heart wrenched at the thought.

I didn't mean to *kill* my lover.

When I had arrived at the cottage in the early morning, the sun was barely peeking through the arcane trees that covered the mountains. I hadn't expected to find my lover in the arms of another. I'd been angry; I'd wanted to scare him. How dare a mortal cross me? How could he break my heart?

Still, I hadn't meant to murder him.

I didn't mean to kill *my* lover.

No, I'd wanted to kill his. The woman was pretty, with flushed skin and a shine to her long hair that I would never achieve. Had his betrayal been about beauty? It didn't matter now; she was hardly beautiful anymore—her skin was mangled and covered with the red blood only mortals could bleed.

I didn't mean to kill my *lover*.

Yet his body lay crumpled at my feet, his once handsome face permanently contorted in horror at my hand. I couldn't remember how it happened; it had been so fast. I still stood in the exact place where I'd frozen when I first saw them together, their limbs intertwined with frenzied lovemaking. I hadn't moved, yet they'd been brutally destroyed in a flash of darkness.

It couldn't have been me; I didn't have power like that. Gods, I didn't have power at all. I was as useless as a mortal when it came to arcane, yet I couldn't deny that the darkness that enveloped the room before their screams felt familiar.

My hands… my hands were covered in blood. Fresh petals lay scattered at my feet, slowly being drowned in the red liquid that oozed from my lover's body. An hour ago, I'd been picking flowers to bring to him.

I wanted to laugh, but the movement brought bile up my throat. I turned and vomited as the room filled with static electricity.

The dracon was here. I could feel it.

Sure enough, when I looked up, she stood in the center of the destruction. Her bright blue eyes were wide with shock as she surveyed the scene. When her gaze met mine, I saw the horror they had held before now drowned by confusion. She didn't understand how *I* could have created the bloody scene we stood in. I didn't have an explanation for it either.

Her mouth moved, but I never heard the words. My head was buzzing, and the sticky blood on my hands was driving me crazy. I wiped my palms on my dress over and over and over, but the feeling didn't go away, it just left streaks of red on the pale lavender dress that had been one of my favorites before this moment.

I didn't see her move, but then her hands were clenched around my wrists, pulling my hands away. They were rubbed raw now, my own blood seeping through the cracks. She was still trying to talk to me, but I couldn't hear anything over the whispers in my ears.

I didn't mean to kill my lover.

Did I say that out loud?

CHAPTER ONE

The Edessa Empire, Year 1499

"You frighten them, you know," Sarya whispered to me.

"I'm well aware."

She straightened as another group of soldiers approached the dais, an empathetic smile naturally finding its way to her lips.

Three stood before her with weary frames, dirt and grime coating their faces. Their armor was ill-fitting and tarnished, discolored by time and lack of care. With gaunt faces that only came from slow starvation, they basked in Sarya's warmth; the kindness with which she handed them a handful of rations and painted sigils on their foreheads. She sent them on their way with a whispered blessing from the Light.

None of them dared to meet my eyes.

It had always been this way—mortals and ethereals alike struggled to meet my gaze. There was no gods' known explanation for why I was so unsettling to look at, but I'd once been told I made a young fae's skin crawl.

It wasn't exactly flattering.

It was that less-than-stellar impression general society had of me that made it difficult to understand why the priestess had chosen me for this particular assignment. I would have been perfectly content to spend my day cataloging the dusty scrolls in the library like usual, but instead, I was sent to the outskirts of Dreka to distribute rations.

And blessings. The priestess would argue that was more

important than food.

As thick smoke from the incense in the corner burned my lungs, I wondered if we were doing more harm than good. The Temple of Light was filled with the impoverished folk of Dreka, their mud-caked shoes and worn bags dragging across the luxurious rugs strewn about. They waited in long lines, winding through the sandstone pillars of the temple and across the manicured lawns surrounding it. We would be able to help more of them if we could use the temples of the other realms—Elemental, Arcane, and Night—but the king of Kaedia had outlawed worshipping gods outside of the Light decades ago. The three temples were abandoned, ghosts of what they used to be, offering no solace to the grumbling people impatiently waiting for their turn. Apologies danced on the tip of my tongue with each scowl from them, but I didn't know what I would even begin to say.

That was why Sarya was here—to do the socializing. She had more practice, after all, as a prophet. She wore a tiny gold circlet to signify the fact—as if the ornamental white robes weren't clear enough. The late afternoon sun glinted off her skirt's gold trimming and cast a warm glow on the temple floors.

She embodied the gods of Light she worshiped. Most of the prophets did.

Not like me.

Little was known about us seers. The title had been cast upon me when it became clear that though I had the sight, I did not share any similarities with the prophets the kingdom loved. Prophets were good omens, messengers of the gods who delivered news of peace and abundance.

I saw death.

The nobles loathed my appearance in the council chambers. I could hardly blame them. Every time I closed my eyes, dark visions were waiting to play out. Conveying their messages to the kingdom was almost harder than seeing them in the first place.

There used to be more of us, those with the cursed sight, blessed by the Night Realm the same way prophets were said to be gifted by the Light. The priestess never talked about the rarity of seers, even when I pushed, so the burden of the gift was mine alone to bear.

So I did, as was my duty. Perhaps it was my sole purpose, my reason for existence? Though that thought did make the air feel a little thinner in the temple.

More soldiers and townspeople filtered through the overdressed receiving room, waiting for their blessing from Sarya and avoiding eye contact with me as I handed them their tiny satchels of rations. It was strange to be in a temple decorated with such opulent furnishings while handing out rations to the starving, but the orders from the priestess had been clear. Still, the gold accents in every floor tile seemed to be almost mocking the townspeople, but Sarya appeared unfazed.

By dusk, we'd run out of supplies and were forced to send the rest of the needy away.

"Tolith will come to collect us," Sarya said as she gathered the empty baskets we'd brought the rations in. "The priestess warned against being out alone with all the attacks lately."

Tolith was one of our little circle of four. Sarya, Tolith, his twin brother, Haryk, and I had spent most of our time together on temple grounds for the last few centuries. I was older than them, but my friends were far and few between, so I didn't complain.

"Those are still going on?" I asked.

It'd been weeks since I'd heard of another one, and I hadn't seen any in my visions lately. I found our discarded cloaks by the door and handed Sarya's to her. It was brown, nearly the same shade as her eyes, and complemented the tan of her skin from too many afternoons lounging in the courtyard. She swung it over her shoulders and tied it in one fluid motion.

"Two elves in the square last night," she confirmed, a frown pulling at her lips. She clutched the amber stone that hung around her neck.

"The square? That's bold."

I wondered how they had been killed, but I knew better than to ask. Sarya was the type to care far too much about people she didn't know. She would tear up at the death of a fly.

Before she could answer, a curly mop of green hair appeared between a pair of columns.

"I heard you two lovely ladies needed an escort?" Tolith smiled cheekily as he waltzed into the temple. He wore the same robes as Sarya, though his were a little grass-stained around the knees.

I sighed. "Pity. I was hoping for Haryk."

Tolith feigned hurt at the mention of his twin. "Good to know the murders haven't changed your sunny disposition, Asteria."

"Don't act so surprised," Sarya muttered, bending to scoop up the tomes of Light Realm prayers she'd insisted on lugging here this morning.

We hadn't cracked them open all day, but I chose not to point that out.

Tucking away the cloth bag of oils and tinctures I was responsible for, I followed behind Tolith and Sarya as she looped her arm through his.

"Let's go," she groaned. "It's a long walk across the grounds."

Tolith's brows knotted. "Oh, you haven't heard? We're going a lot further than the grounds—the king is making some speech."

Sarya stopped dead in her tracks. "You're joking."

Tolith shook his head.

"Gods, I needed to go down to the market still. Now I'm never going to make it."

Tolith patted her arm consolingly, ushering her down the winding paths toward the city square once more.

I floated behind, ever the observer.

"How did it go today? The young faerie sprites took *all* my energy," Tolith complained. He'd been assigned to a different kind of blessing, one that took place on the outskirts of Dreka, honoring Elirede, home of the fae.

Sarya laughed, her annoyance briefly forgotten. "We had an easy time—besides Asteria scaring off half the soldiers."

Tolith turned around with a scandalized expression. "What did you do to those poor boys?"

Sarya answered before I got the chance. "It's the eyes, obviously."

Tolith laughed. "You're right, of course! When I'm talking to her, I just stare at the center of her forehead."

"I can hear you, you know," I grumbled. I hated it when they talked about me like I wasn't there. Unfortunately, it was one of Tolith's favorite jokes.

"As long as you don't make eye contact, I'll be fine," he teased, offering a warm smile.

It was hard to be mad at them; they didn't mean any harm. I was just… different from the rest of them. My sight was one thing, but my appearance was an entirely different issue, one the priestess had spent years trying to tackle. With unruly waves of white hair, pale, scarred skin, and eerie eyes the shade of lilacs, I was like a ghost that Drekkan sprites were told scary stories about.

"It's so crowded," Sarya moaned as we neared the city streets.

Dreka was bustling tonight, despite the attacks that had been occurring exclusively after the sun went down over the capital city of Kaedia. I suppose the townspeople were willing to risk being out late if it meant hearing news from the king directly. The street merchants weren't wasting the opportunity to attract customers, hollering at passersby and offering samples of their latest wares. Musicians were posted on every corner, playing dancing tunes that enamored the citizens who crowded the brick streets. In between the blocks, the overlapping songs created a dissonance that made me grind my teeth.

It was too *loud* in the city.

I'd nearly forgotten how overwhelming it could be. The temple grounds and the dorms where we lived were in the sprawling gardens on the outskirts of the inner ring. It was much quieter out there, where our only neighbors were shrubs, instead of the sprawling stone structures that lined the streets here.

Thankfully, Tolith spent most of his nights prowling these streets, searching for wherever the best party was. He led the way through the crowds, stopping every so often to make sure he hadn't left us behind. There were drunk townspeople on every street we turned down. They parted for the prophets, their white robes commanding respect. When *I* passed through their circles though, they paid no mind to my black attire, despite the stitched emblem that showed my status as a seer. They knocked into my shoulders and pressed in too tightly. It was a fight to make it to the square.

Even though the rest of the city was laid out in circles, the king's first order of his reign had been to expand the castle territory well into the city. In the process, they'd ripped an entire orchard out, creating the square. It was a sandstone courtyard, accented with gold, just like the Temple of Light, though this area was never meant for commoners. Even now, it was filled to the brim with royal guards, standing to attention below an empty balcony.

"I swear they multiply every time I walk by here," Tolith muttered, eyeing the guards with suspicion.

I'd never pried, but I knew he had his reasons for disliking the king. In his defense, most fae weren't fond of him, and Tolith, with his predominantly fae blood, was no exception. He was just more brazen about it than his brother.

"Of course there are more of them—these attacks are getting out of hand," Sarya said, craning her neck to try and catch a glimpse of the king as the lush curtains on the balcony swished in the breeze.

She had never quite understood the twins' frustrations with the king. Her parents were nobles in his court, and she'd lived quite a plush life before joining the temples. She was the youngest of us, so she didn't remember what life was like before Orien.

I had plenty of grievances of my own against the great King Orien, but it was treason to speak of such things.

Or at least, that's what Verena always said when I complained to her. My half-sister served on the Draconian council, a collection of representatives from each dracon bloodline that advised the king. As the sole stormkeeper, Verena had been appointed almost immediately after graduating from the protector program. I'd been naive enough to think she would use her newfound position to change the things that were broken in Kaedia. Instead, she'd played the political game, but to what end, I wasn't sure.

"Where's Haryk?" I leaned over to ask Tolith, unable to spot his brother's navy curls in the crowd.

He scanned the area around us and shrugged.

Suddenly, the curtains parted on the balcony, and two trumpeters stepped out to announce the king's arrival. The rumbling tune of their brass instruments incited gasps of excitement through the crowd. Had they forgotten we were here because people were dying in the streets of our city?

The council filed out onto the balcony first. Seven of them, each in a different colored robe, signifying their bloodline. Verena stood at the very end, dressed in cobalt blue. Her face, like the others, was schooled into a perfect, emotionless mask, as was their duty. The dracons, above all, were the peacekeepers of the Edessa Empire. They were born protectors, and from the moment they could shift into their beastly forms, they were whisked away to the Arcane Isle to study and train with the greatest of them all—the Broodmother.

I'd always thought Verena and I would make that trip together, but when the time came, she'd shifted, and I hadn't. Our mother hadn't given me enough of her blood, I suppose.

We hadn't been close since.

If we didn't share the same last name, the public would never know we were tied together. Verena looked more like her father, with bronze skin, dark hair, and bright blue eyes. We couldn't have been more different.

"So much fanfare," Tolith yawned, pulling my focus back to the crowd.

"Always," I muttered back.

His original plans for the evening had probably been much more exciting than this.

As the king finally graced us with his presence, his golden crown coming into view, the crowd erupted in applause. Well, those at the front, that is. The others, the faeries and impoverished, lurked at the back with scowls even deeper than my own.

King Orien smiled brightly at his adoring fans, his gaze sweeping over the rest of us briefly before returning to his devoted. "My dear Kaedians…"

His voice dripped from his lips like honey. It sent a chill down my spine.

Tolith crossed his arms. "Here we go."

"Believe me when I say that the events of the last few cycles have disturbed me greatly." Orien's voice boomed over the crowd, his words emphasized with a flourish of hand movements. "I have heard your pleas, and can assure you that my royal guards and the draconian protectors are doing everything they can to solve this heinous crime."

It was unfortunate that the king was devilishly handsome. With golden brown hair that curled away from his face, a warrior's frame, and warm amber eyes, he'd charmed his way into the highest tiers of Drekkan nobility. If only the elven women in front of me knew what a snake he was, they wouldn't be fawning over him.

"However," he continued with a frown, "until this matter is resolved, there are certain security measures we must put in place for the wellbeing of this kingdom. Starting this evening, there will be a city-wide curfew. All beings must be in their homes by the time the moons rise."

"*No,*" Tolith whispered, horrified as his social life died before his eyes.

My stomach turned at the thought of being trapped on temple grounds after work hours. I lived for my secret escapades into the forests on the edge of the farmlands that surrounded the city.

But the king wasn't done.

"Those caught out after hours will be assumed to be involved in these attacks and will be arrested by the guard for questioning. As your king, I must keep this kingdom safe, and I take that duty seriously. These rules may seem strict, but this is a matter of life and death."

Sarya nodded emphatically, as though he would notice her devotion above all the other elves with weak knees. Tolith and I shared a pointed look.

"Now, I recommend you all return to your homes. In half an hour, my guards will begin sweeping the city for stragglers." King Orien's voice was firm as he completed his address to the city. Then, he placed a hand over his heart and bowed his head ever so slightly, playing the humble king. In the next breath, he had slipped past the council, back through the curtains to the safety of his sprawling castle.

It was quiet until the council disappeared from view. With no greater beings to ogle at, the crowd dissolved immediately. Merchants and musicians resumed their noise with little concern for the king's warnings, but most people rushed by, not willing to be caught out past curfew.

I was grateful for the quiet by the time we made it back to the dormitories. Breathing deeply, I made a vow never to take personal space for granted again as Sarya started toward the rooms.

"I'll see you guys later—I *had* a date with a *very* eligible bachelor I have to cancel," Tolith grumbled, not bothering to stick around for our response as he slipped back into the twilight.

I followed Sarya through the dormitory doors, but that was where we split ways. She was immediately absorbed into a group of prophets, raving about the king's speech, the day's work, and whatever they'd seen in their most recent visions. I turned in the opposite direction and headed for the dark corridor that ended in my room. The dorms weren't run down by any means, but they didn't have the luxuries I knew the draconian whelps enjoyed. The floors were made of sturdy dark wood harvested from the arcane trees that surrounded the mountains and acted as an outer shell for Dreka. There were some uneven boards, even some wobbly ones, but they were solid enough for the most part. The navy wall paint wasn't more than two turns old, though I supposed in mortal time that *was* quite a while. Two hundred years passed by so slowly for humans. It was strange to think that, whilst the faeries, dracons and other ethereals of Dreka remained, the mortal residents were constantly changing.

Unlike us prophets, the royals were used to a whole other breed of extravagance, judging by the limited chambers I'd seen on my trips to the castle to report visions. Verena had lived there for as long as I could remember. Her chambers were likely much better decorated than my shabby dorm room. The floors were arcane wood like the hallway, but the walls were painted dark gray instead of patchy navy. Spiderweb cracks were running up the plaster in a few places, but I couldn't be bothered to fix them. I had a bookshelf in one corner, and a desk littered with empty vials and parchment covered in botanical sketches beside it. Across the room was a bed, large enough for me alone, which was fine. I didn't get visitors very often.

It wasn't much, but the room was warm and the water in my bathing chambers was hot. That was enough for me.

Despite how soothing it sounded, I didn't pour myself a bath or climb into bed. Instead, I stripped my thick robes off, tossing them to the side, before rooting around the chest at the foot of my bed for a pair of pants and a tunic I could move around in. Once I'd changed and donned a pair of thick socks, I pulled my leather boots on, lacing them up my shins. Retrieving the satchel from my desk drawer that held a small sketchbook, charcoal, quills, and vials, I secured it over my shoulder and tied my cloak.

I was ready to venture into the Bones.

I moved quietly through the halls, careful not to disturb anyone. I didn't want to get caught heading out just before curfew. That would result in a whole slew of unnecessary questions.

When I made it onto the streets without being spotted, I forced some of the tension out of my shoulders. Despite being in an empty alley, the feeling of being watched stuck with me. I looked over my shoulder, seeing nothing but the gray bricks that made up most of the buildings on the Edge.

The Edge was the ring that separated the inner city from the outer city. King Orien said it was to keep citizens on both sides of Dreka safe, but we all knew it was just so the nobles didn't have to interact with the poorer townspeople.

There was a stark contrast between the inner and outer city. While the inner city partied, the outer city was dark and quiet. Squat buildings lined dirt roads, barren farms tucked away on neglected plots. Lavender bushes were planted every few paces or so, but the floral scent did little to cover the smell of filth and disease. It was like a different world.

I followed the rough road out of the furthest reaches of the city and through the mountain pass that separated Dreka from the rest of the world. Some might think one road in and out of the capital was inefficient, but most believed the city was crafted by the elemental god, Zenir, as the cradle of dracons. Either way, it led me straight to the Bones, a grove of dead trees within the Silent Forest that surrounded the cradle. Affectionately named after the spindly appearance of the foliage that grew within its ashy borders, the broad trunks of the trees within the Bones were bleached white from their roots to the tips of the sparse leaves that covered their thin, twisting branches. Nothing grew in the Bones anymore, not since the day the stars fell, and the ground was littered with dead leaves, brittle twigs, and bones from the animals that used to call this part of the forest home.

The rest of the Silent Forest remained unaffected by whatever had destroyed the life in this grove, but no one in Kaedia could explain why, just like no one could explain why the stars had fallen on that fateful day so many turns ago. Countless lives were lost when the world was plunged into an all-consuming darkness that lasted hours. Some thought it was an act of wrath from the gods, others feared dark magick.

I pushed the thoughts out of my mind as twigs crunched and rustled in the distance. There were rumors of monsters lurking in this stretch of woods, but in all my time traveling through here, I'd never seen another living being, besides the mushrooms I came to harvest.

Crystal lycarrea.

They grew in patches by the roots of dead arcane trees and upon animal carcasses, making the Bones my own personal gold mine. *Crystal lycarrea* was the key ingredient in an elixir I made regularly; one that inspired psychedelic visions and thinned the veil between worlds. It wasn't unheard of to use such tinctures for magick purposes, but under King Orien's rule it was strongly discouraged, so few learned the practice of alchemy these days. Thankfully, back when I was but a sprite, I'd found a teacher who was willing to educate me.

I prowled through the forest, on the hunt for the iridescent caps of the strange little mushrooms I'd grown dependent on. The Bones seemed to stretch on and on as I hiked, but eventually I found a little patch of *lycarrea* resting in a tangle of tree roots. The light from the two moons overhead glinted off their caps—a telltale sign I'd found the right fungi.

This particular mushroom was beyond the normal definition of fragile. If too much pressure is placed on the stem, the entire thing disintegrated. I'd lost my fair share of mushrooms during the trip back to my dorm, and there was nothing more infuriating than a wasted journey.

Nowadays, I came prepared.

I pulled one of the glass vials from my bag, crouching near the patch of fungi.

"Easy, Asteria," I muttered to myself, working up the courage to pluck the mushroom from the earth.

I pinched at the stalk, careful not to touch the head too much, and carefully secured it in the vial. I repeated the process until there were only a few mushrooms left at the base of the tree. I didn't like to take more than I needed, especially not from an ecosystem as fragile as this one.

I took longer than I needed to on the hike back, sketching anything that caught my eye. I spent most of my waking days working in the temples or the libraries, so I savored the opportunity to just… exist. Every part of me felt liberated outside of the city limits of Dreka, even the magick that fueled my sight. It lurked in the back of my mind, almost a creature of its own, watching and whispering from the darkness. It was louder in the Bones, more urgent. It spoke of secrets and warnings and death. I tried not to listen too closely—it never said anything coherent.

When the two moons shone directly overhead, I hurried a little more through the trees. It was rare for someone to come looking for me after working hours, but it wasn't impossible. I didn't want to be caught out after dark and be imprisoned under suspicion of murder. The priestess would be mortified, and staying on her good side was always best.

The Edge was in sight when a cloaked figure slipped from the alleyway, blocking my path.

"I can't believe you're out here right now."

Sucking a breath through my teeth, I looked up at my half-sister Verena.

"I can't believe you're outside of the castle."

She scoffed. "Don't deflect. What are you doing out right

after the king implemented a curfew?"

Summoning every bit of subtlety I had, I shifted the bag of illegal ingredients under my cloak and prayed to the gods she didn't notice. I wasn't foolish enough to think Verena would be loyal to me over her king. Duty above all—that was Verena's way.

"I could ask you the same thing," I sniffed. "You don't look like you're on watch."

No, she'd traded blue robes for flight leathers at this late hour.

"I'm not here on official business."

"I didn't know you had any other kind."

"Asteria, this is serious." She frowned, crossing her arms. "You can't be caught out."

"Look around, Verena, you're the only other one out here." I huffed. The longer we argued in the streets, the less time I had to use the *lycarrea* before it decayed.

"Because I knew *you* would be," she hissed.

My brows knotted. In what world was Verena aware enough of my existence to know I'd be out here tonight?

"Are you following me?" It was the only explanation—familial concern didn't apply here.

She pinched the bridge of her nose. "Listen to me. Whatever this is—this rebellion—it has to stop. You can't openly defy the king, especially not now. They're looking for someone to blame, and they'd be all too happy to pin it on you."

"What? That doesn't make any sense. Why me?"

She shook her head. "You wouldn't understand. Just… remember that we share a name. Your actions reflect on more than just you, Asteria."

Ah, this was about her reputation. She was right, it *would* look bad for the sister of a councilmember to be arrested in connection with a string of gruesome murders. I just hadn't thought she would seek me out to remind me of that.

I laughed dryly. "Message received, Verena. You know, you might as well save yourself the trouble and change your name. Then you wouldn't have to pretend to worry about me."

My older sister scowled as dark clouds formed overhead. "That's not fair."

"Save the theatrics," I retorted, brushing past her with faux confidence. She didn't know me well enough to know the difference.

Verena didn't follow me. I only knew she was gone when the smell of rain filled the streets and arcane surged in the distance. Heartbeats later, a great, scaled beast soared through the skies.

Show off.

Seething, I stuck to the shadows for the rest of the journey back. Once I reached my room, I wasted no time in locking the door and setting up my desk with the freshly gathered mushrooms. I rummaged through the drawers for the remaining ingredients of the elixir and found the bowl I normally used to mix these kinds of concoctions. After combining the ingredients in the correct order—mugwort, arcane-blessed oil, *crystal lycarrea* caps, amethyst buds, and water from a northern stream—I mixed thoroughly, then took a deep breath before drinking the contents of the bowl in several disgustingly sweet gulps. I only had minutes before the brew would take effect, so I settled into the nook of my window, curling up on the cushion and focusing on the stars above as I tried to find my target.

It didn't take long. His aura was different from all the others that swarmed the inbetween where magick lived. His essence was shrouded, covered in gauzy darkness that seemed to dissipate as I got closer to it. I envisioned myself connecting to it, letting it pull me to him—to his mind. I was seeing the world through his eyes in a matter of minutes.

"Stea," he uttered, though he didn't turn toward his

accomplice.

He never did.

He was walking through a town I'd only ever seen through his eyes. It was dark there too, so I assumed he lived in same half of the world as I did. Other than that general notion, I had no clue where my mystery target was.

His footsteps echoed off the stone path until he came to the edge of a forest. Then, without warning, he raised one tattooed arm and snapped his fingers. He blinked, and opened his eyes in an entirely different place. Watching someone use magick without feeling it was disorienting, but after years of visiting this man, I'd grown used to it.

He'd transported himself to a seaside town—or maybe village was more accurate. It was small and in disrepair, save for one large stone fortress at the top of the hill.

I caught a glimpse of the heavy black boots he wore as he marched up the incline to the front doors of the stone building. He didn't knock; with a wave of his ring-adorned hand, they opened, slamming into the walls with force.

Then came the slaughter.

As the inhabitants of the stronghold came to the front hall to investigate the noise, the man whose eyes I lived through raised his hands and bloodied them. Some, he killed with magick. For others, he used his hands. I felt it all. Every snap of bone, every slice of his blade.

I wasn't sure what drew me back to the savage scenes night after night, but it had become a bit of a ritual. I would enter his mind as he made his way to wherever he deemed his targets to be, and I would watch as he killed. I should have felt shame, maybe disgust or fear, but I felt nothing as I watched their bodies fall. No regret for the lives cut short or contempt for the man who held the blade.

Perhaps it was the fact he seemed to take no satisfaction in his killing that interested the sentient magick in my mind. At least, none I could sense. The sight was fickle sometimes, but strong emotions tended to make their way through. He wasn't excited by the bloodshed. It felt… routine.

He used the hem of his cloak to wipe the blood from his dagger, but he didn't bother to clean his hands. Blood remained caked under his fingernails and caught in the creases of his skin as he swept through the rest of the fortress, making sure he had collected every last soul.

When it was done, he made his way back to the grassy hill he'd transported himself to earlier. He stared out at the sea for a long moment, the waves lapping against the shore. His heart seemed to beat in time with the pulse of the ocean. I could feel his chest rising and falling with the water as if it were my own heart beating there. The gentleness of this moment seemed dreamlike compared to the gruesomeness of before.

Then, with a snap of his fingers, it was all gone.

CHAPTER TWO

My heart beat wildly in my chest as I sat up, back in my room in the dormitories. Walls spinning around me, I forced myself to breathe deeply, resting my head against the chilled glass of the windowpane. The cold seeped into my skin, then my bones. It calmed my frenzied nerves before I stood, removing the tunic and pants that suddenly felt suffocating. Moving across the room to the sink, I turned the faucet on, dousing my face in freezing water.

It was always hard to reorient myself after waking from the sight. I wasn't sure if it was the lingering elixir or the effect of my mind traveling to gods-knew-where, but I always felt foggy for a while. Unfortunately, I had responsibilities to attend to before I could rest. Recalling the faces of the fallen from my vision, I made use of the parchment and charcoal on my desk, drawing as many details about them, their fortress, and the surrounding land as possible. Then, I passed the report off to the half-asleep messenger who was slumped in a chair in the corridor outside my room.

It was a nightly ritual—one I dreaded. Years ago, when these visions had started, I'd hoped the protectors would find and save the victims I drew in time.

During the last two turns, I hadn't saved a single soul. It made me wonder what the point of my sight was if I couldn't do anything useful with it, but that thought was for the morning.

Thankfully, the sky was still dark. There was time to sleep

before I was expected at the temples.

Cleaning up the mess from my little alchemy session earlier, I sat at my desk and wrote down everything I remembered from the evening in a leather-bound journal I kept in the bottom drawer. Once I'd finished scratching every detail into the parchment, I climbed into bed and finally let myself rest.

Or tried to, at least.

The man's voice haunted me.

It was rich and deep; smooth, like silk on my skin. Not that I'd had many silk garments in my life, but I imagined it felt similar.

Rolling over, I squished my pillow into place. My bed didn't usually feel this lumpy.

I wished he would talk more on our nightly outings. Surely the companion he traveled with wished for something to fill the silence between seemingly endless bloodshed? There were a million questions I wanted to ask him; I needed to understand why he killed so ruthlessly. At least if this mysterious 'Stea' started speaking to him, I might be able to learn something from their discussions.

Agitated and too hot under my blankets, I pushed them away, sitting up in bed.

I longed to see his tattoos in their entirety. I'd only ever seen glimpses where they peeked out from beneath his sleeves, but I'd memorized the swirling patterns that wrapped around his wrists all the same.

There were strange sigils on his rings too, ones I didn't recognize.

Sighing, I fished my journal from the desk drawer and began to draw the familiar shape of his hands, the tattoos that decorated them, and the runes on his rings. There were hundreds of sketches like this one shoved in my bookcase. I couldn't help but focus on this one identifying part of the killer I had watched for so long. Maybe it was some desperate attempt by my subconscious to find him.

Curiosity was my biggest weakness, or so Verena had always told me. She'd warned me that one day I'd ask the wrong person a question and learn something I didn't want to, but I couldn't contain myself sometimes. The longer I saw visions of the killer, the more I needed to know.

"Tolith didn't slink in until well after moonrise last night," Haryk grumbled to me as we stood in line for breakfast. He was the quieter of the twins and studied arcane instead of prophecy.

He was also handsome. Like Tolith, he had curly hair, but Haryk's was a stunning shade of deep blue, complementing the pale bone color of the tiny horns that sprouted from the top of his head. He was of fae heritage, so most avoided him. Associating with fae required careful words that most didn't have the patience or intelligence to string together.

"He did mention an eligible bachelor," I said pointedly, accepting a sack of fruit and a piece of bread from the cooks as I passed.

"Not the first," Haryk sighed, leading the way through the doors to the courtyard. "Certainly won't be the last."

"I'm surprised he broke curfew," I murmured. Prophets were notoriously nosy.

Haryk scoffed. "Are we talking about the same Tolith?"

I snorted. "Fair enough."

The air was warm and thick today. After a few moments, my skin started tingling, burning beneath the sun's rays. I found a spot in the shade to sit and Haryk followed.

"Where are you assigned today?" I asked as he produced a small gold knife from his pocket and began to cut his arcane fruit into bite-sized chunks.

He gave me a strange look. "You haven't heard?"

I frowned. "Apparently not. What's going on?"

"Two more elves were killed last night. We're all working on the grounds today—the priestess and archmage agree that it isn't safe for us to leave."

Great. My nightly escapades to the Bones would be even harder to accomplish now. I sighed. Why hadn't I seen the attacks? My sight had insisted on showing me the strange man and his murders all the way across the empire, but I couldn't see what was happening in my own city. I bit back a curse as I stole a piece of Haryk's cut fruit.

"It must be serious if those two managed to agree on something."

Haryk hummed. "Still, the archmage wasn't happy this morning."

"These attacks are getting out of hand. What are the protectors doing about it?"

Haryk shrugged, taking another bite. "Gods know," he said through a mouthful. "Something, I hope. The king made a big enough show of it last night."

"We didn't see you in the crowd, I wasn't sure you saw his performance."

He waved a hand. "Our test subjects were antsy; it made me late."

Haryk studied magick with the other arcanists under the archmage's tutelage. Usually, their experiments involved whatever unfortunate creature they were able to catch in the fields outside of the city. Haryk didn't want anyone to know, but he was soft at heart and often late to dinner because he stayed afterwards to care for them.

"And how is little Tolith junior?" I asked, referring to a particularly ugly beast Haryk had grown too fond of over the last cycle.

He snorted. "If my brother ever hears you say that he'll have a fit."

"Good thing he isn't here then," I retorted, earning a chuckle from my fae companion.

Out of the four of us, Haryk and I spent the most time together. We shared a similar temperament and didn't bother with the drama that filled our days on temple grounds. He was my closest friend, though I'd never utter those words aloud. That would be mortifying.

Haryk pulled a timepiece from his pocket, flipping open the silver cover to reveal the ticking hands beneath.

I raised a brow. "Somewhere to be?"

"Unfortunately," he sighed. "They've got me cleaning out the old storerooms."

I grimaced. "Good luck."

"Thanks." He stood, dusting the grass from his pants. "I'll come find you for lunch."

"See you then."

He looked over his shoulder, offering me a half-smile before starting across the manicured lawn toward the arcanists' quarters. Once he was out of sight, I laid back against the grass, staring at the tree branches above.

There was probably a long list of chores waiting for me if we were all stuck here today, but I couldn't find the will to get up. My world was infinitely smaller now that it was confined to the temple grounds, and that fact didn't sit right with me. My stomach knotted at the thought of spending night after night here until they caught the killer roaming our streets.

Who was talented enough to evade the dracons? I didn't think such a being existed—at least, not in the Mortal world. Beings from the Immortal world rarely bothered with petty affairs across the veil, so I doubted the involvement of the gods.

There was no point in playing detective, especially if my turns-old obsession with the murderer from my visions was any indicator of my investigative skills.

Still, I couldn't help but wonder why I hadn't seen last night's attacks. Why hadn't the sight given me a warning? Maybe I could have saved someone.

The wind blowing through the courtyard suddenly ran cold, despite the sun shining overhead. The chill seeped through my robes and into my skin as the trees above were replaced with a starry darkness that meant the sight had taken hold.

In my vision, the sun had just started to disappear over the horizon, bathing the city in a dusky orange glow. With the newly imposed curfew fast approaching, the streets were practically empty—save for the blonde elven male striding across the bricks with purpose. The darkness that lived in the back of my mind hovered around him like an aura. He was the focus of this message.

Dressed in golden yellow robes, his eyes were bright and familiar. I'd seen him before, I was sure of it.

As he passed by, the fading glow of the sun glinted off a golden pin on his chest: the crest of the dracon council.

Ah, of course. I must have spoken to him dozens of times in the briefing rooms of the castle. But that was beside the point. What business did he have in the city after curfew? Anyone he met out here would be imprisoned if caught. Surely if he was visiting with the other dracons he would do so on castle grounds?

I would never get the answer to that question. As he reached the next block, a figure in dark robes stepped from the shadows of the alley. He stabbed the councilmember in one smooth, practiced motion.

The councilman bled out in minutes.

The attacker waited for him to take his last breath, then turned to make his escape, an oily grin plastered on his face.

My next breath felt like ice in my lungs. A heartbeat later, the tree branches were swaying above me, the air warm and the sun high in the sky once again.

I didn't bother waiting for the dizziness to pass. I needed to see the priestess.

I didn't visit this part of the temple grounds very often, but that was for good reason. Although the priestess cared about our well-being as prophets under her care, she wasn't particularly kind. She didn't tolerate wasting time, especially hers. I swallowed my nervousness as I approached the gold gilded doors that she was likely on the other side of. Breathing deeply, I raised my fist and knocked twice.

They swung open mere seconds later, revealing the priestess in all her glory. She stared at me with liquid amber eyes, annoyance already apparent on her perfectly symmetrical features.

"Are you going to linger in the doorway all day?" she asked, her tone icy.

I took a quick step into the room, and the doors swung shut behind me.

We were alone.

She tapped a filed nail against her desk in irritation. Her hair was straight and smooth, the red color almost resembling Sarya's auburn locks. She was beautiful, which combined with the intensity of her gaze made her extremely intimidating.

"What do you need?" she asked flatly.

"I had a vision. I believe a councilman will be killed this evening."

Her tapping ceased as she stared me down, assessing my words. "You're sure, seer?"

I nodded.

"Then we'll send word to the castle."

"I can be there within the hour," I offered, making to bow and exit as quickly as possible, but her eyes flashed to mine, an incredulous look on her face.

"You cannot leave the temple grounds. We'll have a messenger go," she insisted, though her seriousness was muted as she looked away, unable to take the weight of my stare.

"I *need* to go," I insisted. The thought of being locked in the dormitory every night for the foreseeable future was nauseating. I needed to know what Verena and the others were doing about the attacks.

The priestess raised an eyebrow. "Unless you know the identity of the attacker, you'll remain here, seer. Have you had a vision of such details?

I faltered.

"No? Then I refuse to grant you permission." She gestured toward the doors, insinuating that I should already be gone.

In her mind, I probably should never have come in the first place.

I bowed my head to her as custom demanded before turning on my heel and leaving. The doors slammed shut behind me.

Back to square one.

The priestess wouldn't give me her blessing until I could produce a vision that required attention from the council. My cheeks were hot with embarrassment, but I was still determined to talk to Verena. Anything to protect my freedom.

And to prevent more attacks, of course.

It wasn't that I didn't trust Verena and her peers to apprehend the killer, but since she'd moved to Castle Dreka her time had been spent with gallons of arcwine instead of fieldwork. Before her most recent visit, it had been months since I'd seen her. Though I was hopeful they would resolve the situation without prompting, I was not naive.

I made my way back to my room where I gathered supplies for an elixir, mixing it quickly in the bowl I'd used just last night. When it was finished, I funneled it into a vial, placing a cork in the top before slipping it into my satchel.

The main temple buildings were usually flooded with citizens of Dreka, but since the grounds were on lockdown, it was like walking through a ghost town. The rest of the prophets and acolytes were busy with their duties, like I should have been. Instead, I began prepping a temple for meditation.

The obsidian finishes sparkled like black glass in the sun and drew me to the Temple of Night. There were rugs strewn across the floor despite the fact this temple was rarely used anymore. It had once been popular, or at least that was what the scrolls in the library said. The Kingdom of Kaedia used to worship the gods of the Night Realm, but ever since King Orien came into power, there'd been a new narrative. Now, the prophets and citizens alike flooded the Temple of Light in favor of its shadowy counterpart.

I didn't mind—it meant the room was all mine today.

I quickly lit the candles that rested in the sconces on the walls and burned incense near the altar at the front of the room. Usually, there wasn't this much preparation involved in the sight. Images and omens would come to me without warning at any given time. It was an art, not a science, so I didn't try to force visions often, but this was a special occasion. It demanded a bit of manipulation.

Sitting cross-legged on the rug at the center of the room, I closed my eyes. Breathing was difficult with the haze of herbs and incense in the air, making it harder to focus on my intention. I tried to find the center of my being, the calm that the priestess had described when the sight was young in me. It always seemed to evade when called, as if it too preferred spontaneous messages over being prompted.

"Come on," I muttered under my breath, tapping my fingers on my knees.

I had the draught in my bag, but I didn't want to use it if I didn't have to. I was far more likely to be discovered avoiding my work duty if I was passed out on psychedelics in the Temple of Night. At least when I was meditating, I was conscious.

Though I *was* at risk of falling asleep the longer I sat and saw nothing. I hummed, trying to recenter my thoughts on my breathing and the dark being that always lingered at the back of my mind—the source of my sight. It sometimes whispered rumors of the future and showed me what was to come. It could be terrifying, but I almost wanted it to wake now. Anything to save me from fruitless labor.

"*Focus*," I whispered, willing myself to get back on track.

I thought of the elves that had been murdered, their images plastered across the papers circulated by Dreka citizens before the Royal Guard collected them as contraband. I willed the sight to show me how they'd died, and whoever's hands were responsible. I needed *something* to give me the grounds to go to Castle Dreka.

As if hearing my silent plea, the being that lurked in my mind came to life. My vision went black as a gust of wind tore through the temple. I waited, my muscles tense, as shapes started to form in front of me, their outlines fuzzy. As the shadows cleared, two figures came into view.

A man and a woman, maybe a couple. They were arguing in the street, two moons shining high above them. The woman was pale, her hair the color of straw in the low light. The man tangled his hands in it before he pulled her into a passionate kiss.

Perhaps they weren't arguing after all.

They became so enamored with each other that they didn't notice the being lurking in the darkness of the city. I made out the shape of their attacker as he lurched forward, a silver blade glinting dangerously.

The couple finally noticed him, jumping apart and raising their hands in surrender. The man stepped in front of the woman in an attempt to protect her, but the attacker's blade cut through him like he was parchment. His blood pooled out into the street, and the woman screamed.

She didn't stand a chance. The attacker killed her just as swiftly as he had the man, that much was a blessing. I couldn't see his face, but his figure was undoubtedly male. He was tall and broad, like the draconians I'd met at Castle Dreka. Even if he didn't have his blade, he could have overpowered both of them with his hands alone.

I watched, powerless to change anything, as he ran away into the night. I expected the vision to end there, but my focus kept being drawn back to the fallen bodies. The woman.

Her hair was splayed around her like a halo, even though she lay face down. That wasn't what caught my eye though. No, my gaze was fixed on the dark circle of ink that stained the back of her neck.

She was Marked.

With that realization, I returned to my body with a jolt. The temple came back into focus around me, and the wind I had felt so strongly before was gone. The incense had burned to ash, and the scent of herbs in the air was faint.

How long had I been gone?

My body hadn't left, of course. The spot I occupied on the rug was warm, but my mind had been elsewhere. The sun was still shining overhead, so there was a good chance the other prophets were still working.

Not bothering to clean up my mess, I ran out of the Temple of Night, back toward the extravagant building that held the offices of the priestess and the archmage. I stopped outside of her office, my heart pounding in my chest.

The doors swung open as soon as I knocked. Glaring amber eyes landed on me.

"Priestess," I huffed, out of breath after running across the temple grounds. "It's the Marked."

"Compose yourself, seer," she said, though at least she now seemed more willing to listen. The doors to her office closed behind me just as they had this morning. "What is going on?"

"It's not just elves—the Marked are being killed," I gasped.

She frowned. "Marks aren't due to start appearing for another…" She leaned across to look at the lunar calendar posted on the wall next to her desk and the crease between her brows deepened. "I'll request an audience with the Dracon Council. You need to share this information with them at once."

It wasn't the attacker's identity, but it was just as important.

"Yes, Priestess." I bowed. "Of course."

She waved her hand to dismiss me. Worry lingered in her features as I left, and I wondered just how grave this news was.

The Marked were an elite few, treated as nobles and celebrated with every luxury in the kingdom. They were sacrifices to be given to the Immortal world when the veil between worlds was thin. It only happened once every five turns, and lasted a few months, leading up to the night when gods walked among ethereals and mortals. In preparation for the event, Marks appeared, always in the same spot—the back of the neck. It made them easy to spot. Maybe that was what had called the attacker to them?

But *why?*

Why would someone target sacrifices?

Did they not fear the wrath of the gods?

That little voice in the back of my mind warned me that they should.

CHAPTER THREE

"Stop fidgeting," the priestess hissed under her breath.

I'd forgotten how tall she was. She towered over me in her golden heels. Her straight, sleek red hair draped elegantly over her shoulders, held in place with a more extravagant version of the golden circlets the prophets wore. Her robes were white like theirs, too, but with more ornamentation. They had clearly been pressed; there wasn't a wrinkle in sight.

She was nervous. I could see it in the way she glanced around the corridor as we waited for the council to be ready to receive us. I was almost certain she'd picked at my appearance to satiate the anxiety bubbling in her chest.

Still, I stopped picking at the skin around my nails, even if just to appease her. Under her assessing stare I had the urge to check my own robes and circlet, but I didn't. I knew the black robes were stiff and straight, as they always were, and the silver circlet that set me apart from the rest of the prophets was positioned as expected on top of the unruly waves of my hair.

"Priestess, Seer Taranis, the council will see you now," a man dressed in court finery announced, reading from a scroll that I doubted contained any words at all. He likely spent all day facilitating audiences with the council.

I didn't envy him.

Two members of the Royal Guard who lined the halls opened the grand double doors, revealing the council chambers.

I'd only been here a handful of times, but the opulence always stunned me. The room was dome-shaped, with dark wood stretching to the ceilings in extravagant arches. The windows were paned with stained glass, each depicting a different tale from the lore of the dracons. They cast colorful beams of light across the room, painting the stone floors in bright tones. At the center of the room was a dais, and on it, a long table with seven chairs—one for each draconian school of magick.

At the center sat my half-sister, Verena. Her electric blue stare found me in the doorway before I'd even taken a step.

The priestess entered the room, her heels clicking on the floor and echoing off the walls. When she stood before the council, she bowed. I followed closely behind like a lost pet, mimicking her movements.

"It is an honor," the priestess said in greeting.

A blonde man with age lines around his mouth waved a hand. "Enough niceties," he grunted. "We understand there was a vision." Despite the weariness of his tone, his eyes were bright—just like in my vision.

He was the victim.

He wore yellow robes, the color of the lifebinders, the draconian faction of healers. Their power as a group had only grown in the last few turns, now that one of their own was on the throne of Kaedia. This man must be powerful if he represented them on the council, but he wasn't who I remembered sitting in that chair on my last visit.

Then again… that *was* well over a century ago. Things could have changed.

He eyed me with suspicion. I didn't look like the normal prophets who came to tell them the future. I was enough of a bad omen that the rest of the council frowned when I stepped forward.

"The deaths in Dreka—the elves being murdered. I have

reason to believe they are Marked," I informed the council.

"What reason?" Verena asked. She was the only woman on the council, and sat straighter in her chair than anyone else.

"I had a vision this afternoon. It was clear that the woman who was struck down bore a Mark on the back of her neck," I explained.

"Did you see the killer?" the blonde man from before asked.

"No," I replied. "His face was obscured, either by a mask or magick."

A man in green—from the poison brood—cleared his throat. His strong jaw and dark hair were familiar: Councilmember Arrais.

"You've only seen one of these… attacks?" he clarified.

I stiffened. "The most recent murder, and the death of one of your own, as I'm sure the messengers have reported."

They argued amongst themselves then, whispering as they took in my words. The priestess shifted from one foot to the other beside me. I swallowed the urge to tell her to stop fidgeting. Finally, after much deliberation, a man in red—Councilmember Yelnan, of the evocationists—spoke.

"How are you certain this assailant is targeting the Marked?" he asked. "You've only witnessed one death where that is the case, yes? Perhaps she just *happened* to be Marked."

"You're chalking this up to coincidence?" The words were out of my mouth before I could stop them.

The priestess let out a hiss, glaring at me with every bit of disdain she could muster. I winced under the weight of it, looking to the council to find that they didn't seem to appreciate my input either.

"Until we have reason to believe otherwise, it would be foolish to act on this *short-sighted* message," Councilmember Yelnan said, waving a dismissive hand in my direction.

Short-sighted? What was the point of enlisting seers and prophets if the council didn't heed our warnings? How many more would die before they trusted what I had told them? I knew in my gut this was no mere coincidence.

I opened my mouth to voice those thoughts, but the priestess spoke first.

"We understand," she said through clenched teeth. "We apologize for the interruption." She turned on a pointed heel, clicking her way toward the door. I turned to follow, stopping only at the sound of another voice.

"If you see anything further that supports your theory, do be sure to return."

Looking over my shoulder, I spied a man in purple robes. He was young, like Verena, and I didn't recognize him. He must have been a new addition, like the lifebinder.

"I won't hesitate," I confirmed, following the priestess into the corridor.

The doors slammed shut behind us, and guards escorted us from the castle grounds seconds later. Anger radiated from the priestess, matching the gaping chasm in my chest. They had been fools to disregard us, and they would learn so sooner rather than later, especially if the gods realized what was happening to the Marked right under the council's noses.

"They dismissed you?" Tolith asked through a mouth full of food.

The twins had that habit in common.

I'd spent the last hour filling them in on everything that had happened: my visions of the attacks, the priestess, and our trip to the Dracon Council. The late afternoon sun moved through the sky, casting shadows from the trees across the grass we sat on. I lurked in the shade while Sarya sunbathed.

I nodded, cringing. "It was quick."

"Close your mouth, you slob," Haryk grumbled, pushing his brother's shoulder.

Sarya frowned. "It sounds like they didn't want to hear your vision in the first place."

"They never do." I shrugged, earning three confused stares. "Don't look at me like that. I'm not like the rest of you—I only come to them with bad news. Of course they're more excited to hear from Sarya than they are from me."

She shook her head, auburn strands falling over her shoulder. "Your sight is just as important."

"Sure, but it is *significantly* less fun to hear about," I reasoned, though I did appreciate her effort to console me.

"Something about it seems strange," Haryk continued, circling back.

I shrugged. "Maybe they're distracted by the thinning veil. It's happening early this year."

Tolith rolled his eyes. "They say that every time."

"No, I'm talking about your sight, Asteria," Haryk clarified. "Did you say you *forced* yourself to have a vision?"

"Forced is a strong word. I meditated and burned some herbs. Don't you guys do that?"

Tolith and Sarya stared blankly at me.

"The priestess always told us we couldn't manifest the sight on our own. It chooses when to show us the Light," Sarya recited the familiar words from one of the many lessons prophets were forced to endure when they were younger.

Despite how often I'd heard that particular line, I'd forgotten it over the years.

"Who taught you to force visions?" Haryk asked.

I shook my head. "I wasn't taught."

"Ugh, we get it!" Tolith exclaimed. "She's different, she's a freak, blah, blah, blah."

Evidently, he was bored with the subject, but I was grateful to have everyone's focus shifted elsewhere.

"Have you started thinking about what you're going to wear to the ball?" Tolith asked, shifting the topic away from me. "The shops in the city are already almost out of fabric."

Sarya jumped at the chance to describe the gown she'd picked out to an excited Tolith, who responded with the exact shades of green he had selected for his suit. I hadn't even begun to plan for the Veiled Night; I'd been so wrapped up in other things. I should have known Tolith would be excited, though. Who wouldn't love the chance to attend a ball? Especially one that only happened every five hundred years.

"What about you, Asteria? Please tell me you're going to wear something not... *black*." Tolith shuddered.

I winced. "I haven't settled on anything yet."

"That means she hasn't started looking," Sarya whispered to Tolith.

He raised an eyebrow. "You're going to end up in a potato sack if you don't start soon."

I raised my hands up in surrender. "I'm working on it," I insisted. He didn't need to know that Sarya was right.

Tolith hummed like he didn't really believe me, but relented nonetheless, shifting his focus to his twin brother.

"I could go with you to the city when the lockdown lifts if you want some help," Sarya offered, playing with a blade of grass she'd plucked from the soil.

"Sure, when the lockdown is over," I agreed, though my words were somewhat hollow.

If my instincts were right, the lockdown wasn't going to end any time soon.

Later that night, in the comfort of my room, I stared into an empty bowl.

I'd just swallowed the remnants of an elixir, and the usual fuzziness was working its way through my body, tugging my eyelids closed and forcing my muscles to relax. I ended most nights this way, but it was different this time.

I was nervous.

The feeling knotted my chest, fighting against the effects of the elixir. For the first time since I'd found him, I didn't want to visit the killer I observed night after night. I thought of the attacker I'd seen in my more recent vision—his tall, broad frame, and the practiced manner in which he murdered. I couldn't help but wonder if he was the same man who I saw in my nightly visions.

If it was him, I didn't know how I would manage the dissonance in my mind. I didn't want to report this man to the priestess, and yet if he was the one killing the Marked... Not that I was sure how I would identify him in the first place, but I knew I wouldn't be able to keep any discoveries a secret.

The complexity of my feelings had anxiety swirling in my stomach, but I was out of time to ponder it further. Darkness crept into the edges of my vision and my body no longer belonged to me. I was floating, disappearing into the inbetween. My surroundings were familiar, the same vast gray nothing, but I shook as I found the string coiled in shadows. It practically called out to me, its energy drawing me in. It surrounded me, easing my nerves with the familiarity of its hold.

I prayed to the gods that he wasn't the attacker.

My world grew darker as I followed the thread into his mind, like I had thousands of times before, until I could see through his eyes.

He sat with one leg folded over his knee in front of a dwindling fire. His pants were dark, perfectly creased at the seams like the finely-pressed clothes nobles in Kaedia often wore. In one hand he held a crystal glass with remnants of a red liquid swimming at the bottom. His sleeves were rolled up, revealing more of the dark ink that covered his tanned skin.

I drank the image in, absorbing every detail of the room as he finished his wine. There were velvet chairs on either side of the fireplace, and I assumed he was seated in a third. Beneath his polished shoes—for once, he wasn't dressed in blood-spattered boots—there was a dark rug, patterned with different shades of green and blue. Sprouting from the tall walls were bookshelves filled with tomes bound in leather. Half of them seemed to have a coat of dust on their spines; others were nudged forward, suggesting they were pulled down often. Was this a library?

"You're late, Stea," his deep voice rumbled. There was a hint of amusement in his tone.

His accomplice didn't respond.

Eventually, he sighed and stood, leaving his glass on a table filled with decanters of various shapes and sizes.

"We have a busy night ahead of us," he stated, lifting his hand and snapping his fingers, jolting us away from the cozy library.

Arcane travel was said to be dizzying, at least for those who weren't strong enough to withstand the magick required to do so. But the man cloaked in shadows never faltered, landing graciously in a forested area, evidently familiar with the toll of such power.

He looked down, revealing the dark boots and pants I was

familiar with. How had he changed out of his noble's clothes? Not that it mattered. I knew what the new clothes meant.

Death was coming.

Fallen leaves crunched beneath his boots as he started through the woods, specks of light sparkling through the gaps in the foliage.

When he broke through the tree line, my stomach hollowed.

I was staring at Dreka.

He didn't falter at my revelation—why would he? I was a silent observer, unseen and unfelt. He had no idea that this place was significant to me.

He ventured on, through the farms at the edge of the city and past the Edge, into the heart of Dreka. The alleys were quiet, but the streets were crowded. Both moons shone brightly overhead, and citizens partied in the streets to celebrate the fact, brazen in their dismissal of the curfew. The rich could afford to be.

Besides, Drekkans would use any excuse to drink arcwine until they were sick.

If the crowds bothered my mystery target, he didn't show it. He made his way through the city, following some internal compass to his destination. Despite not being able to feel my body, I was tense—paranoid that I would either know whoever he was going to hurt, or that they would be Marked.

He stopped outside of a townhouse on the outskirts of The Ring, the neighborhood of noble homes just outside of the castle. Built to surround Castle Dreka, only the richest occupied them. I'd never stepped foot in one myself, but it seemed that was going to change momentarily.

Unlike every other night, he didn't storm inside, murdering everyone in sight. Instead, he knocked on the door.

A servant appeared in the doorway, looking up at the man with a curious glance. I would have given anything to see through their eyes right now—to know what my mystery target looked like.

The servant was a faerie, evident by the anxiously swishing wiry tail that curled and uncurled around their leg. All fae had some indicator of their heritage, whether it be horns, tails, odd-colored hair or skin, wings… the list went on.

The man reached a hand out toward the faerie, but instead of striking them down, he summoned a surge of arcane. The faerie slumped down the wall, unconscious, but very much alive.

In all my time visiting this man, he had never shown anyone mercy. I wondered what made the faerie different.

He moved through the townhouse like a shadow, his boots making no sound against the polished tile floors. Every servant he came into contact with was incapacitated, but not killed.

The bloodshed began in the master suite.

There was a couple sleeping in bed. The woman woke first, though she didn't have time to panic or warn her lover. Her throat was cut and she fell to the floor, bleeding out on the clean tiles. At the sound of her body hitting the ground, the man jolted awake. I caught sight of his pointed ears before he joined her in the land of the dead.

The gory scene should have made me halt the vision, but I couldn't stop staring at the bodies through the mystery man's eyes. One question repeated in my mind, echoing over and over.

Were they Marked?

As if he heard my thoughts, he moved to the man with pointed ears. Nudging his body so it turned over, he revealed nothing but pale skin on his back. Then, he went to the woman and repeated the movement. She wasn't Marked either.

This man was a killer, but he wasn't *the* killer. I wouldn't have to report him.

My breaths came easier.

Leaving the townhouse without a word, he snapped his fingers, transporting us to streets of gold. We were in Thelassan, the kingdom to the southwest. As I looked around through his eyes, every fixture shimmered in the moonlight, but though it should have been beautiful, it looked gaudy. An opulence that bordered on gluttony.

Two more died at his hand in Thelassan, though they were mere mortals. The city was quiet when he moved on, the sun just barely peeking through the tops of the trees. He visited three more villages, reaping souls and carrying on without much acknowledgment of the blood spilled.

He hadn't lied earlier; this *was* a busy night, even for him.

My mystery target had just returned to the manor I assumed was his home when a sharp pain started behind my eyes; piercing, white-hot pain that spotted my vision. My connection to him grew weak, the view from his eyes fuzzy. I was being pulled out of my vision.

"Stea?" I heard him call out from far away, but I was back in the inbetween before I could hear anything more.

The spots across my eyes grew larger and darker, and I was swallowed by a familiar sensation. The sight took over my senses, showing me the message it deemed urgent enough to overpower the elixir that coursed through my system.

The streets of Dreka appeared before me, occupied by a broad man with a shining blade beneath the two moons. Three bodies littered the stone, swimming in a pool of crimson. The man's blade dripped with the same color. I didn't need to look closer to know they were Marked, but I did anyway.

The wind blew as I stepped forward, carrying the metallic scent of blood and... citrus.

Odd.

Once I confirmed that there were dark swirls on the corpses,

I turned to get a better look at the attacker, but his features were distorted.

As quickly as it had come, my sight retreated, taking the vision and the sharp pain with it.

I blinked, back in my room in the dormitories.

Thankfully, I'd left the draught bowl on my nightstand, else the contents of my stomach would have ended up all over the floor.

Shaking and tired, I got to my feet.

I needed to see the priestess.

CHAPTER FOUR

The sun shone brightly over Kaedia as morning arrived. I'd likely hear birds singing if the windows were open. For a moment, I could forget that Marked ones were being murdered in the streets every night after the moonrise. Everything felt almost normal.

Except for the fact that I was packing all my belongings into tiny bags. It would seem I'd accumulated far too many things over the centuries. I was debating throwing out the fiftieth tunic I'd folded when there was a knock on my open door.

"Here's another if you need it, Asteria. I had an extra." Sarya leaned into the doorway of my room and dropped a canvas bag onto the now empty desk.

"Thanks." I couldn't imagine how she had got her hands on an extra, but I wasn't going to complain. "Is Tolith still mad at me?"

Sarya rolled her eyes, a rare gesture. "He's just pouting."

I hummed noncommittally. She was just trying to be reassuring—Tolith had all but wailed last night when the news came. It had arrived with the latest paper, the bright-eyed councilmember's body splayed across the front page.

All prophets, arcanists, and healers are to be housed in Castle Dreka, effective immediately.

Signed,

King Orien, Ruler of Kaedia and the Draconian People

It was all thanks to me, of course. Or my visions, at least.

We had been hopeful the lockdown would end, but the move to the castle almost guaranteed matters were becoming worse. There would be no more sneaking out after hours to visit the city, or the river, or the Bones. Tolith would never forgive me for ruining his social life.

"If it helps, I'm actually a little excited about all of this," Sarya said conspiratorially.

I raised an eyebrow. "Really?"

"Think about it." She grinned. "Nobles, princes, balls, feasts… what's not to be excited about? Tolith will realize sooner or later."

"I don't think there are any princes in Kaedia."

She scoffed. "Don't be such a slug."

"I am not being a slug, you're being overly optimistic."

"I don't know, you sound pretty slimy to me!" She crossed her arms.

"Gods," I grumbled, but she just grinned before disappearing into the corridor again.

By early afternoon, the Royal Guard had arrived at the dormitories to escort us to the castle. I had half a mind to remind them the attacks only happened after dark, but I was sure the knights sweating under all that metal wouldn't be too pleased to hear it. They surrounded us, encasing us in walls of silver armor as we made our way through the city to Castle Dreka.

It was quite the spectacle—all the prophets and arcanists in their robes and jewelry being paraded down the streets with the Royal Guard. Citizens of Dreka came out of their homes and shops, stopping to watch us go by. It was like we were the rare creatures the arcanists kept in cages to study day in and day out.

The council waited for us at the Great Entrance, solemn

expressions on their faces. They all looked the same, as though they had rehearsed in a mirror together. Verena's expression was a little tighter than the others. Her eyes searched the crowd of prophets, her eyebrows creasing with each person she assessed until they landed on me. She eased then, nodding at me before shifting her gaze away.

Councilmember Yelnan stepped forward, the red of his robes a little too bright under the afternoon sun.

"The council is honored to welcome all of you into the king's humble home." His words were no doubt meant to be friendly, but the look in his eyes put me on edge.

I didn't trust him, but perhaps I was just holding a grudge after his dismissal of me.

"Please, allow the servants to show you to your rooms. We'll see all of you this evening for a celebratory feast," Yelnan continued, offering another tight smile before the council dispersed and a handful of beings dressed in rags took their places.

It felt wrong to host a feast when this move was due to savage murders in the city, but there wasn't time to ponder that thought. The servants started guiding groups of us into the castle, leading the way down winding corridors I would need a map to make sense of.

The fae woman who led my group had light blue skin and curling ram's horns that stuck out from her tangled blonde hair. All the servants were faeries, I realized, as I took stock of the other groups. I swallowed hard and kept my head down as the first from my group filtered into their new chambers.

Unfortunately, the blonde faerie picked me out of the crowd. "Seer, yes?" she asked with an odd accent.

It reminded me of my father's.

I tried to look into her eyes, but she avoided my gaze. "Yes," I replied.

"Welcome home. I'll show you to your room," she said, gesturing for me to follow her as she started in the opposite direction.

I frowned. "Home?"

I'd never expected to live in the castle, and unlike Sarya, my stomach was twisting at the thought. I met the woman's eyes with a grimace. Nevertheless, the faerie woman smiled and nodded as we left the rest of my group behind and entered a separate corridor. Unlike where the rest of the prophets were residing, the stone floors and walls here were lined with rugs and tapestries, and tall windows stretched toward the ceiling, letting in a warm glow that was near impossible to get in my south-facing room at the dormitories.

I should have reveled in it, but I clung to the comfort of the shadows, avoiding the beams of light.

The woman stopped outside an arched doorway, the stone around it trimmed in black.

"This is yours," she said, opening the door with a large, rusted key, and gesturing for me to enter.

I took two steps into the room before I sneezed, overcome by the layers of dust covering every surface.

"It's been many years since your kind occupied this room. I'll be by to clean up later," she said apologetically.

The disastrous state of my chambers could wait. "My kind?" I echoed.

Did she know I was fae? How?

She nodded, an odd look in her eye. "Cursed ones."

Deflating, I fought the urge to sigh. This kingdom put far too much stock in silly superstitions. I was tired of hearing that my sight was cursed. I started to dispute her words, but she moved toward the door.

"I'll be back later," she repeated, not waiting for my response as she slipped out of the room and closed the door behind her.

"Perfect," I grumbled. "Just leave me alone with my thoughts and this… *grime.*"

I dropped my bags, desperately trying to ignore the stains on the rug that looked to be a familiar rusty shade. There was only one window in this room. It was small, only a half circle, and far too high off the ground for me to see out of. I didn't mind the darkness, but it would drive anyone else mad, I was sure. The bed was bare and pushed into the corner of the room, and it too needed a good clean.

Perhaps I shouldn't have made the mistake of assuming that quarters in the castle would be in good shape. This certainly felt like a punishment.

I had the strong urge to mix an elixir and forget I was here in the first place, but I had to be sparing with my ingredients. We wouldn't be allowed to leave the grounds very often if my assumptions proved true. I would have to cut back on my usage, though just the thought soured my mood.

Too antsy to stand here and do nothing, I picked through the scraps of fabric in the corner of the room to find a cloth and tried not to wonder what it had been used for before. I ran it along the top of the rickety desk, against the wall opposite the bed, the bookshelf in the corner, and the nightstand, before tossing it back into the pile it had come from and flopping onto the bed. The stiff fabric of the cot scratched my skin, but I couldn't be bothered to hunt down any linens. The faerie woman had said she would return later. I could be patient until then.

Besides, I was exhausted. Last night had been nothing but chaotic, and I'd barely gotten a second of rest in the last two days.

"Asteria."

I jolted awake to the sound of my name whispered in a hiss. The source was obvious—Verena—who stood upright in shock at my rapid waking. I'd always been a light sleeper. I was surprised she didn't remember that.

"Verena? What are you doing?" I asked, my voice thick with slumber. There was no sun streaming in through the tiny window—it must have set while I was napping.

"You missed the feast; I was worried," she said with a crease in her brows that meant she was telling the truth.

As concerned as she might have been, though, she still couldn't meet my eyes. She stared intently at the wall behind me instead.

"It's not like you to worry," I replied over my growling stomach. It was upset at Verena's reminder of a missed meal.

Suddenly stoic, she shifted on her feet. "Things have changed lately."

"Oh?"

What could possibly make Verena turn her attention to *me?* She had barely visited in the last four turns.

"There are whispers among the nobles," she said conspiratorially.

"Are you going to make me beg for every detail?"

She furrowed her brows. "This is serious, Asteria."

"I'm sure."

"They're talking about *you.*"

That caught my attention. "What could they possibly know of me?" I'd only visited the castle a handful of times; there hadn't been much opportunity for rumors to start.

She looked at the floor. "Only what they fear. I just wanted to warn you."

I hadn't slept long enough to deal with this. My head was still foggy and the emptiness of my stomach was starting to make me nauseous.

I frowned at my sister. "Your warning is that nobles are starting rumors about me?" I reiterated, rubbing my eyes.

"My warning is that they fear you, Asteria. I would keep the fact that you're the one who had the vision of the Marked quiet. Do not trust anyone and don't venture off alone. The man who rules this castle is twisted, and he won't hesitate if you give him an opening."

Something in her tone unsettled me. "I hear you, Verena."

"Good." She reached into the pocket of her robe, producing a bundle wrapped in a cloth napkin. She pressed it into my hand. "It's all I could take."

I unraveled the package. Inside was the heel of a loaf of bread and a few pieces of arcane fruit.

"This is plenty. Thank you." I popped one of the small violet fruits into my mouth. The sugary sweet flavor exploded over my tongue as I bit down. The other two were eaten in quick succession.

She watched me for a moment, before heading toward the door. "I'll have a servant fetch your linens. Come find me if anything feels awry."

"I will," I promised, even though I had no idea how to find her in this maze of a castle.

Verena gave me a tight-lipped smile and then she was gone, leaving nothing but the faint feeling of static behind. Back when we were sprites, she would make my hair stand on end for fun. Things had changed when her true power started to show. She was whisked away from the little cottage we'd grown up in and brought to the castle to serve the former queen.

Queen Eletha had been... different. There had been no

division in the city when she was queen, no distrust between the fae and the elves. My father—a full blooded fae—had admired her greatly for that alone. It was his intense admiration that had pushed our mother out, away from the cottage we'd shared on the edge of the city. Verena had stayed, despite having no connection to my father. She'd worked with Queen Eletha and the other dracons to keep the peace between the four kingdoms of Edessa.

Those had been the good years between us. Now, under the king's rule, I hardly knew my sister. Whether that was his doing or hers, I would never know. I wasn't sure that I wanted to.

Right now, all I really wanted was sleep, but there were too many questions plaguing me. The talk of curses and rumors made my stomach churn. I drew my knees into my chest and tried to take a deep breath. It felt sharp, like the air was poking at the inside of my ribs and ripping at my chest. The vials I knew lay in the bags on the floor seemed appealing right about now, but I knew my elixirs wouldn't solve anything. I needed answers, not an escape. For the first night in years, I would have to skip my visit to the harbinger of death.

Dragging myself off the cot, I moved to the floor to rifle through my bags, looking for one item in particular. Beneath the vials and clothes, I found the amethyst dagger I'd been gifted nearly three centuries ago. It had almost been left behind in the dormitories, but after hearing Verena's warning, I was glad I'd packed it. It had only been used for rituals up until now, but I'd seen my mystery man wield his blade enough that I felt prepared to mimic the movements if I needed to.

Gods, I hoped I didn't need to.

Verena's warning was making me paranoid; I needed air. Surely I could seek out the castle library without fear of being attacked? I tucked the blade into the deep pocket of my robes, hoping it wasn't sharp enough to cut through the fabric. It would be difficult to explain to the Royal Guard why daggers were falling from beneath my skirts.

My door opened with a squeak, and I glared at it as though that would silence the sound. Thankfully, the corridor seemed to be empty for the moment. I crept into the darkness, clinging to the shadows and corners when I heard footsteps or the clanging of armor. The air in the castle was thick with arcane energy, more so than I had ever felt on temple grounds. The consequence of housing hundreds of powerful beings, no doubt.

I made it down two of the twisting hallways before I realized I had no idea where I was going. I'd only been inside the castle a handful of times, and during visits I'd never left the council chambers. What were the odds that I could traverse the entire castle without being seen? I doubted they had helpful maps lying around.

I was taking a moment to breathe and consider my options when I heard it—quiet sniffling, and the kind of shaky breaths that accompanied crying.

Oh gods. This was not my area of expertise—Sarya was the comforting one. I wanted to turn, to run back to my chambers so I wouldn't have to face whoever was in distress, but my feet carried me toward the sound instead. When I rounded the corner, I found Tolith, his face buried in his hands and his knees pulled to his chest.

He was the one crying.

"Tolith?" My voice was shaky—tentative.

"Oh gods," he groaned, wiping his face furiously. "I knew I should have found a better place than this."

"Perhaps your room?" I offered, sinking to the floor next to him.

At least Tolith wasn't the type to want comfort. He had a

sharper tongue than his brother and much thicker skin.

He rolled his bloodshot eyes. "And have my new roommate witness it all? No, thank you."

The others had roommates? Should I mention the quiet, empty chambers I'd been assigned to?

"What happened?" I asked instead.

"*This* happened. The move. This is the worst thing that has happened to me in the last two centuries."

"You're only two turns old," I reminded him.

"Exactly!" He sighed. "This place is horrid."

"The castle?"

"Yes. And I'm still angry with you for making all of us live here," Tolith grumbled. Fresh tears flowed down his cheeks.

Guilt panged through my chest. I swallowed the urge to remind him it was the king's decree, not my decision.

"I'm sorry, Tolith."

He shook his head. "I'm fae, you know."

I looked at him, confused. "I'm aware." The horns peeking out from his curls all but announced the fact every time he entered a room.

"Look around," he snapped, though the hallway was empty. "Every servant here is fae. I know what they think of my people, and now I'm expected to grace their halls and smile when they speak to me?"

"You *do* have a lovely smile," I joked, desperate to make him feel better.

"My mother lived here, you know? Not by choice," he explained, smiling weakly. "She was a servant under King Orien. Haryk and I spent our younger years here with her. I don't remember much other than being locked away, out of sight. We were a disgrace to the elves, she'd told us. I didn't understand why. I still don't." He took a shaky breath. "She passed a turn ago, but these halls feel haunted. I remember the scornful looks and feeling like I was always in the way. I don't want to live through that again."

"Tolith, I— I'm so sorry. I can't imagine how hard this is for you." My words sounded rehearsed, but in a way, they were. They were words I'd heard Sarya spout countless times over the years, but they seemed to fit now.

He scoffed. "Of course not! You're an elf. It's different when you're something the kingdom adores."

I faltered. "I'm not an elf."

He frowned. "What? How do you explain those, then?" He flicked the tip of my pointed ear.

I made a stupid decision then, one that went against everything my father had ever taught me. Maybe it was Tolith's tears that compelled me to grab his hand and run his fingers over the sharp points that hid beneath the wavy mess of hair I hadn't bothered to tame when I'd woken from my nap.

His eyes wide went in disbelief. "Horns?" He didn't wait for my answer, jumping to his feet and parting my hair to get a look for himself.

"Easy!" I griped, swatting his hands away with no real effort.

"Why didn't you tell me you were fae?" he asked, plopping down next to me again.

At least he'd stopped crying now.

I shrugged. "I was told to keep it to myself when I was young."

"You pass as an elf well."

"I was taught to. I'm pretty unnoticeable, except for the eyes," I said, gesturing to the lavender irises that sent people running for the hills.

Tolith nodded, letting out a brief chuckle, though it lacked his usual levity. "Well, it's not what they look like that's important—

it's how they make you *feel.*"

I couldn't stop the question that poured from my mouth. "What does it feel like to you? My stare?"

He shuddered. "I can't describe it." His eyes were still lingering on the spot where he now knew my horns lay.

"Try," I urged.

I'd received different answers from everyone I'd ever asked this question to, but it didn't matter. The symptoms differed, but the end result was always the same: hysteria.

He sighed. His shoulders sagged. "It starts with this... *whistling* sound. Like a ringing in my ears that I can't make go away. If I keep looking at you—at your eyes—I hear whispers."

I hung onto his every word. "What do they say?"

"Nothing I can discern. They all speak at the same time, interrupting each other. I can never quite tell what words are coming out. It gets louder the longer I look. It fills my mind and it's all I can think. It's... consuming." He shook his head. "I don't ever look longer than that."

I squirmed, suddenly uncomfortable. "It sounds like I'm driving you mad," I muttered, horror clawing at the edge of my mind.

He laughed, properly this time. "You do that well enough without the freaky eyes, Asteria."

He's trying to take the edge off, to lighten the mood, but I couldn't join him in his jokes. I wanted to know *why.* Why did my stare unsettle everyone? What was it about my eyes that caused such an effect on the mind? What if I was never able to look *anyone* in the eyes?

It felt like some kind of... *curse.*

I wanted to be sick.

"Are you okay? You look pale—err, more pale than usual." Tolith put his hand on my shoulder, but I scrambled to my feet.

"Sorry, lost in thought. Are you alright?" I took a step toward the end of the corridor that would lead back to my room.

"Yeah, I'll be fine," he said, rubbing his eyes before getting to his feet. "I'm sure my roommate is wondering where I've gone. I'll see you in the morning. Thanks, Asteria."

"Of course." I gave him a halfhearted smile before turning the corner and rushing back to my room.

I'd hoped to catch the woman there, perhaps bringing the linens I'd been promised, but when I arrived, the room was empty—save for the dust, of course.

With nothing but my thoughts to keep me company, I laid on the cot, but I knew sleep would be impossible.

Instead, I started to make a plan.

CHAPTER FIVE

Verena answered her door with bleary eyes the next morning.

I'd knocked on twelve chamber doors before this one, and the occupants were no happier to see me than I was to see them. Thankfully, I'd finally found my sister's room.

It was extravagant, at least from what I could see. A large four-poster bed sat in the middle of the room, with an ornate desk and overstuffed chair on the opposite wall. There was a fireplace made of dark stone and etched with a deep blue that almost matched the robes she wore during council meetings, signifying her ties to the storm. Her walls, unlike the ones in my chamber, were in impeccable shape. No signs of peeling or decay, and no dust either.

"Gods, it's early," she grumbled. She didn't seem surprised to see me as she waved for me to enter.

I closed the door behind me. "I didn't sleep much."

Verena wrapped her dressing robe around her a little tighter. Her dark hair was sleek and straight even though she'd just woken up. Mine was a nest of unruly white waves. I tried to keep my jealousy at bay.

"What's on your mind?" she asked, perching on the edge of her bed. The covers looked to be made of silk.

My mystery target flashed across my mind, but I forced the thought of him away. I couldn't afford distractions right now.

"So much," I began. "Your warning, of course, but I'm not here for that. I wanted to ask you about something before I go to the priestess."

Verena paled but waved her hand anyway. "I'm listening."

"The servant who showed me to my room mentioned that there have been others like me—seers—here at the castle. She called us 'cursed ones'. Have you ever heard of anything like that? A curse that only affects seers?" I spoke quickly but Verena didn't flinch.

"Mags," she muttered under her breath. "Yes, I've heard."

Verena was only a century older than I was, ringing in five hundred and fifty years this spring. She had been around for the last Veiled Night; I'd been born just after. Still, I was shocked there was such a knowledge gap between us. Though perhaps that had more to do with the fact that she had served under Queen Eletha for two full centuries before King Orien came into power.

"Seers are rare; you know that already," she explained. "They don't live very long, and there has never been more than one alive at any given time, so somewhere along the line, a rumor began that this particular kind of sight is cursed. *You* are not cursed, Asteria."

"But my sight is?"

She sighed. "There's no proof of that."

"How did the other seers die?" I asked. She wasn't giving me enough details to satiate the savage curiosity that gnawed at my bones.

Verena shook her head. "I don't know about all of them. The one before you had a tragic accident near the astronomy tower."

"An accident?"

"He fell. Or jumped. We couldn't figure out which." She rubbed a hand across her face. "This is quite a morbid discussion to have before I've even eaten breakfast."

"You'll have to forgive me," I said dryly. She was crazy if she thought I would leave something like this be. I needed to know the truth, and the priestess was next on my list to visit.

◊ ◊ ◊ ◊ ◊

"A curse? Please, seer, don't tell me you're listening to castle gossip." The priestess sighed, taking a long pull on her herbal cigarillo. She had once told us that they helped with her migraines, but I wasn't convinced that was the case.

Bewildered by her calm, I sank into one of the cushioned chairs in front of her desk.

"Who told you about this?" she asked, peering over her gold-rimmed glasses.

"A faerie mentioned it in passing. She said I was cursed."

She rolled her eyes. "Leave it to the fae to spill centuries-old secrets. They can't lie, you know. It pains them if they do."

I was intimately familiar with the fact, but I did my best to make it look like this was a new revelation. It wasn't that faeries couldn't lie at all, it was that the pain that accompanied a lie was too much to bear. I'd heard tales of some who had managed to master the pain, but I couldn't imagine how anyone could withstand the sensation of their very skin being flayed from their body, their bones cracking, their insides twisting and contorting, with nothing more than a slight wince on their face. I had long since disregarded such fantasy.

"So, there *is* a curse?" I prompted. I was nearly on the edge of my seat, waiting for some kind of explanation.

"Yes," she said, pinning me with a disdainful look. "Your gift is a curse, just like all of us, seer. Many have lost their way when the visions become too much. It just happens more often with those of you touched by the Night. There have been six before you, though they usually pass just after their hundredth birthday."

"When they reach arcane maturity?"

She nodded. "The power becomes too much. You are the first to break the pattern, though I've never been able to understand why. Perhaps it is simply because you joined us much later in life. Maybe you have a higher tolerance for the arcane than others." The priestess slid her glasses down her nose, folding them and dropping them onto her desk. "I knew the last three before you. They were all driven mad by a voice in their mind. Does that sound familiar?"

It *sounded* like the dark thing that lurked in the back of my thoughts at every waking moment.

"Yes," I croaked.

"Your sight does not come from the Well like the prophets'," the priestess explained. "The being that speaks to you is older. We know very little about it."

"Naturally," I muttered.

The Well was said to be the source of all arcane power. Its energy ebbed and flowed with the cycles of the moons, and mortal souls were rumored to feed its power. It was a holy grail for everyone in the Edessa Empire. We held tens of rituals throughout the cycles, honoring the ancient host.

"The ones in contact haven't been very useful in learning more, on account of the madness and all," the priestess continued, ignoring my snarky comment. "Haven't you ever wondered why the others find you so strange? Why they can't look at you?"

I wasn't in the mood to entertain her dramatic reveal. "Why didn't you tell me all of this centuries ago?"

"I didn't think you were going to live this long," she explained flatly. "Why ruin the few years you did have with worry?"

"And when I didn't show any signs of madness?"

"It was clear you were different from the others. I was

observing."

My hands shook and my face grew hot. She simply raised her eyebrows. It was a challenge, or maybe a reminder of my station. I couldn't have an outburst at the priestess without losing everything I'd earned over the last four hundred years. She would make sure of it.

I pressed my nails into my palms, willing the frustration away. No matter how I felt, I needed to appear calm. It was the only way she would give me more information.

"What happens now that I know?"

She cocked her head to the side. "Nothing."

"What?"

"Nothing changes. You will continue having visions when the gods intend it, and you will continue to report them to me. Should the voices in your mind get too loud, take a sleeping draught. Otherwise, carry on, seer." She said all this as if it was simple, as if the terrifying truth of my sight hadn't just been revealed to me. She wanted me to continue as normal, as though the fact that my visions came from an unsettling source wasn't important.

No, I knew in my chest it meant *something*. Perhaps the priestess just didn't know what.

But I would figure it out.

"Thank you for your time," I said stiffly, standing and moving toward the door.

She hummed, but said nothing more as I left, taking my rage and my curiosity with me.

The fae woman did not reappear by the time the moons rose over Kaedia. I could just barely see their glow through the tiny window in my room. It illuminated the desk I was working at, mixing a psychedelic elixir to take my mind off what I'd learned today. I'd only skipped one night… my plan to conserve my resources wasn't going very well.

I reached for the bottle of stream water, scowling when it felt too light. I peered into the opening.

Empty.

Groaning, I tugged at the roots of my hair in frustration. Nothing was easy lately.

I pulled on the thin slippers most of the prophets wore before sneaking into the corridors. It was well past the curfew the priestess had enforced when we lived in the dormitories. Perhaps there was a different rule within the castle? It would only be logical to assume we were safer here, and the curfew was no longer necessary.

At least, that was the line I would spit out if I was caught.

Now, if I were alchemy supplies, where would I be?

There was an atrium somewhere in the castle; I just had to find it. The halls were quiet at this time of night, thank the gods. This would be infinitely harder if I had to dodge members of the guard every time I turned a corner. It was dark, as if the entire castle was asleep. My footsteps were light on the stone, but the sound still echoed enough to make me cringe.

I'd hit the third dead end of the evening when I felt it; a presence at my back. A piercing stare, intense. The energy around the being buzzed ominously—an enemy.

Breathing deeply, I turned toward the source.

The man had hair the color of wet sand. Almost brown, but not quite. Amber stones appeared to rest in the facets of his eyes, and his jaw was square; his skin tanned. He was handsome, yet something in his features was undeniably cold.

And incredibly familiar.

I didn't register the golden crown resting on his head until I had been staring for an inexcusable length of time.

"King Orien." I lowered myself into a bow, despite the voice at the back of my mind that warned me not to take my eyes off him.

He stared at me for a moment too long before acknowledging my words. "Please, no need for such formalities, *Lady...?*" His voice was sultry—smug. Natural charisma poured out with every word.

Should I give him my true name? He was the king; he could find such information if he truly wanted to. There didn't seem to be much point in concealing the fact. Besides, with the disdain he had for the fae, I doubted he was one. There was no power to gain by knowing my name.

"Taranis. Asteria Taranis."

"Lady Taranis," he purred. "Related to the infamous councilmember Taranis."

"She is my half-sister."

He smiled at that. "On the elven or draconian side?"

"Draconian," I told him, though I had never claimed that part of my heritage. I hadn't been gifted a dracon form like the others, my bloodline apparently too weak.

"You share a mother," he mused, the gears turning in his mind.

We did, but she rarely made appearances in Edessa. Verena didn't talk about her, and I had never known her well enough to seek her out.

I nodded, keeping the details to myself.

He hummed, a finger on his chin. "Dare I ask what you're doing in the corridors so long after moonrise?"

'Trying to find the atrium,' I wanted to say, on the off chance he would be helpful and lead the way. But then I remembered that this was the king who had practically outlawed recreational elixirs.

"I just wanted some peace and quiet," I said, hoping he didn't see through my roundabout line. "My quarters are quite… confining."

His eyes lit up in a way that made my stomach turn. "Yes. You're the oracle, the one who saw the attacks."

It wasn't a question.

Verena's words echoed in my mind, and suddenly I didn't want to confirm his theory. "I came to the castle with the prophets."

He tilted his head, suspicion clear on his features. "You have a particular way of speaking, don't you?"

Did he know I was part fae? He certainly knew plenty about Verena's heritage—was it ridiculous to assume he might know mine? We had never met before this moment; I couldn't imagine a reason why he would have done his research on me before now.

Unless he already knew I was the seer.

Did that explain the sinister aura radiating from him? Or was this what Verena had meant when she said he was 'twisted'? A million questions raced through my mind, but one thing was certain. I needed to get away from this man.

We were *very* alone in the dark hallway.

My breaths were shallow as I considered my options. I could run, but he was a dracon and much stronger, more agile, than I was. Even if I managed to escape, he was a king—*the* king. I wouldn't make it far without a member of the guard apprehending me. His orders were law.

"You could say that," I replied when I realized I had been silent for a moment too long.

He was studying me; I could see it in his measured stare and in the way he assessed every word that left my mouth. I was slipping, and he was catching every mistake.

"Lady Taranis, are you a faerie?" he asked, a smirk playing on his lips. He already knew the answer. "What did you see in your visions of the attacks? What do you know of the assailant?" With the newfound knowledge that I could not lie, he asked question after question, stepping forward with each query.

"I—" I swallowed. This was the man who had killed Queen Eletha. The same man who had driven my father's people out of the kingdom. He was dangerous. "I know that the victims are Marked."

Displeasure flashed in his eyes. It wasn't a good look for the kingdom, or its king, that sacrifices to the gods were being murdered under his watch.

"Do you know the assailant's identity?" he pushed.

"No," I answered immediately.

He smiled. A cold, oily smile.

The vision flashed in my mind, evidence side by side with the real thing. The attacker... his smile as he'd cut the Marked down... it was the same as the king's before me.

The *king* was killing the Marked.

He watched as the realization washed over me, his brow pinching with malice. He cocked his head at me.

"What if I were to ask you that question again, Asteria?"

I was trapped. The weight of his gaze pinned me in place, though I did not meet his eyes.

Except... I *could* meet his eyes. Would he experience the same thing the prophets did? Would it be enough for him to leave me be?

"I've learned from the faerie people over the years. I know that silence speaks quite loudly, don't you agree?"

I blinked. Then, I was staring at him. Into the molten ochre pits that were filled with thinly layered malice. Into his power, the swirling golden warmth of a lifebinder, corrupted by whatever darkness tainted him.

I stared into his soul.

The being at the back of my mind throbbed, and my thoughts grew fuzzy. Was this what *power* felt like?

His mouth was slightly agape, his brows furrowed angrily. I took a step forward, and he didn't move to stop me. Had I incapacitated him enough to get away? There was only one way to find out.

"Your Highness." I nodded my head once, and scurried past him, back down the hall I'd come from.

He didn't move—perhaps he couldn't. How long until the effects wore off? Would he come charging after me?

I didn't have the answers, but in that moment, I didn't care.

CHAPTER SIX

The sky was dark, void of the two moons, and the air was cold.

I didn't recognize the buildings around me. They were made of strange stone, dark and shimmering. In the cluster's center was an obelisk, tall enough to pierce the night sky and wide enough to contain Castle Dreka three times over. Judging by the lines of people milling about, the central obelisk was a temple. They were all dressed in ragged clothes, their faces gaunt. They were on the brink of death, every last one of them.

Curiosity carried me forward, or maybe it was the nudging from the being at the back of my mind. I fell in line with the strange people, biding my time until I passed through the silver engraved doorway at the temple's base. It was hazy inside, as if the air was filled with dark smoke. There were no lanterns to light our path. Arcane was thick in the air, clinging to my skin, to every fiber of my being.

The people around me moved their lips, but no words came out. It was silent, but not still. Shadowed men ushered us through a short hall and into a receiving room.

There, on a raised dais at the center of the darkness, sat a solitary being.

He was enshrouded in the same shadows that surrounded us, but on him, they belonged. He lounged on a throne adorned with twisting spires, dark fabric draped over his broad frame. He watched over the room with a sharp gaze and a bored expression.

His presence didn't stop the people from piling in. They

filled the room, pressing against the walls and knocking into my shoulders. My chest grew tight as I felt them on all sides. The room spun, but no one else seemed to notice. When we were packed in tighter than prophets at the rite, the man on the dais stood.

He was tall, his head adorned with a dark crown of twisted points that matched his throne, and a heavy, dark cloak hung over his shoulders, pooling at his feet. The arcane in the room seemed to radiate from him. It shimmered in the air, potent and dangerous. A lingering threat of what he was capable of.

I was in the presence of a god.

His lips parted, revealing pointed incisors. "You have been found guilty of irredeemable crimes. Your souls are tarnished, unable to be restored. For that, you are condemned."

His voice rumbled through the room, piercing the silence. It was deep, with a scratch that reminded me of someone; I just couldn't pinpoint who. There wasn't time to try and place it— the floor beneath me was crumbling, falling away, and revealing nothing but swirling darkness. Its presence repelled the souls standing in the room, but it was no use. The ones in the center fell first, and I could finally hear them.

Their screams.

The wails pierced my ears, and the floor disintegrated beneath me.

I plummeted into the depths with the condemned souls, destroyed by shadow and fire.

"Wake up, girl!"

A choked breath left my lips as someone swatted my arm. Shooting upright as best I could in my makeshift hammock, I found a faerie woman staring at me.

Not just any faerie woman—the servant from two days ago.

"Mags?" I asked, unsure whether that was actually her name.

She scowled. "We are not that familiar, cursed girl. What are you doing down here?"

I blinked, bleary-eyed and stuck beneath the fog of my dreams. They had been beyond strange last night, though perhaps that was due to the stressful evening before—not to mention the odd place I'd chosen to settle in. Countless fae bumbled around the run-down quarters, waking and dressing quickly before descending the stretching corridors that connected them to the rest of Castle Dreka. The room buzzed with anxiety, adding another layer of distress to the poorly maintained sleeping rooms. Despite King Orien's access to the kingdom's gold, he obviously wasn't spending it here.

"Sleeping," I managed to mutter, dropping from the hammock as gracefully as I could. I stumbled when my feet hit the ground, still laced into the leather boots I'd neglected to remove before I'd fallen asleep. I'd wanted to be prepared to run in case Orien came for me.

Perhaps I was being paranoid, but that voice in the back of my mind validated my suspicion. Maybe it knew something I didn't.

"Do I look like a fool to you?" Mags asked.

No, she didn't. With her shiny gold ringlets and pale blue skin, I might've mistaken her for Elirede royalty if she were wearing anything other than a smock. The lines on her face aged her, but she was beautiful.

"What are you doing in the servants' quarters?" she pushed, when I took too long to answer.

"*Hiding*," I hissed under my breath. It was far too early for her tone, and I hadn't slept well wrapped in the knotted hammock.

"From what?" She squinted. "Or whom?"

I carefully glanced over my shoulder, checking for prying eyes before I whispered my answer. "*King Orien.*"

She hissed in distaste. It was a common reaction from faeries in Dreka.

Kaedia used to be a sanctuary for all beings touched by the arcane—it was the epicenter of magick. But that all changed when the brood of lifebinders took the throne some centuries ago. Faeries lived in fear now. King Orien was just one of many in a line of twisted rulers wreaking havoc on the kingdom.

"He's after you," Mags muttered, shaking her head.

"Because I'm a seer." She didn't need to know the whole story. I barely believed it myself.

"*The* seer," she corrected. "Here, put these on." She thrust a pair of dingy pants and a smock into my hands. They were the same color as the clothes the rest of the servants were wearing—a beige that looked as though it hadn't always been that shade.

I pulled them on slowly, noting the strong mothball scent wafting from them.

"Nothing will make you invisible, but being a faerie here is as close as you can get. Tie your hair back," she instructed, her voice clipped.

The worn scrap of leather that she produced from the pocket of her apron wouldn't be enough to tame the silvery white waves of unruly hair, but I humored her regardless. For once, I didn't check to make sure my horns were covered.

"Stay away from the Great Hall—it's getting far too close to the Veiled Night. There'll be plenty of his dracons lurking around waiting to sniff you out."

With those final words of advice, Mags disappeared, leaving me with nothing but my thoughts.

I breathed until the whirlwind in my head became static, my

mind numb and hands calm. Then, I fell into line with a group of fae that seemed to be heading in the opposite direction to the throne room.

I would be safe here, for a while. Not for long, but hopefully long enough.

Days passed.

Verena had shown her face once, tracking me by my arcane signature—or at least that's what she'd said. My half-sister had been pale and feverish, though she had insisted she wasn't ill. I knew the look on her face. It was not the plague, but rather the look of someone plagued by their thoughts. I hadn't pried; I doubted she would have shared.

The Veiled Night was approaching. I could feel it. The air in the castle buzzed with magick, filled to the brim with arcane, and the gods hadn't even arrived yet. Every arcane being was at its strongest when the veil between realms was thin.

Myself included.

The visions—the whispers—had grown more frequent and much more intense as of late. I spent my nights in the knotted, swinging hammocks of the servants' quarters, though the dank room was never what I saw. Every night, images of a man— the same man who had occupied the throne in that cold, dark room with the twisted souls—came to me in a rush. They were overwhelming and full of power.

However powerful, the visions made little sense. Scenes played out before me, but I couldn't understand what I was being shown. The man, the realm he occupied, it was dark. Dangerous. Cold.

Why was this god plaguing my thoughts? Was Verena

experiencing something similar? Was that why she looked so sick?

Finishing making the bed I'd been working on, I fluffed the pillows and headed out of whichever noble's room I'd been cleaning, trying to convince myself that my strange visons and Verena's pallor were nothing to worry about. I'd always hated chores, but I would take mindless tasks over certain death any day.

The seeming success of my evasion made me wonder whether the king wasn't even trying to find me. Had I been deemed unworthy of his attention, what with the Veiled Night on the horizon? Had I ever been in danger at all? Maybe I had overreacted that night.

The corridors were quiet this evening. It was surprising, considering the fast-approaching event that left the air humming with power. I'd expected tens of dracons to be milling about, or even a few elves here and there, yet the stone halls were empty, void of life.

I missed my friends more than I cared to admit.

Sarya might be young, but she was warm-hearted and wise beyond her years. Tolith, though dramatic, was witty and sharp-minded, more than most gave him credit for. Haryk, though he'd never admit it, was compassionate at his core. I'd caught him mourning the death of one of the beings the acolytes had been experimenting with one late afternoon centuries ago. He'd made me promise to tell no one of the tears that had stained his cheeks.

They were an odd group, but they were mine.

Missing them left an odd ache in my chest, a feeling almost entirely foreign. Maybe I'd felt this way as a sprite when my father had left the little cottage we'd shared at the edge of the city for days at a time on business trips. Or perhaps when Verena had first moved to Castle Dreka. Regardless, it had been centuries since I'd felt it this strongly.

Driven by the ache, and against my better judgment, I sought them out.

I knew where Tolith's chambers were, so I decided to start with him, keeping my gaze on the stone floor of the corridors as I made my way through the castle to the prophets' wing. It was ridiculous how donning servants' garb could make you entirely invisible to the ethereals milling about. No one stopped me as I meandered through the halls.

Tolith's door was indistinguishable from the others and I wouldn't have found it had his roommate not exited the very moment I turned the corner into the wing. There was a glimpse of green curls and white horns that I recognized, and that was enough for me to slip my hand into the crack just before the door clicked shut again.

"Tolith!" I hissed, and his eyes snapped up to meet mine.

"Asteria? What are you doing here? Where have you been?" he asked, one question coming quickly after another. The shock was clear on his features. "What are you *wearing?*"

I waved him off. "Don't get me started. I've just been avoiding someone, everything's fine. How are you? How are Sarya and Haryk?"

His eyes narrowed at my vague response to his question, but he closed the book in his lap nonetheless, making room for me on his cot. I dropped onto the space next to him, pulling my knees into my chest. It was comforting to be close to someone safe after days spent looking over my shoulder at every turn.

"The priestess has been… *intense* lately. She's got that look in her eyes… remember the Fire Festival a turn ago? It's just like that."

The Fire Festival happened every century. It was a massive

event to honor the gods of the Elemental Realm. The last one had been a nightmare for the priestess after the Flame Devotees went missing just before the ritual sacrifice. There was a panicked flurry to find other eligible sacrifices at such short notice, but she'd managed.

All of Edessa had been sure we'd face the wrath of the gods until she'd found suitable replacements. Tolith was barely a century old; it had been a spectacle for one of his first festivals.

"What's got her so worked up?" I asked, though I strongly suspected it had to do with the missing Marked.

He shrugged. "She's keeping quiet about it. Sarya asks every now and then, but she usually gets scolded and sent on her way."

A knock on the door pulled our attention to the sound.

"Tolith, open up!" a feminine voice called through the wood.

"It's like we summoned her," Tolith teased, looking at me with mocking eyes before sliding from the cot to open the door.

Sarya stood on the other side, her auburn hair pulled back into a neat braid that curled around the crown of her head, the folded circlet nestled into her plaits. She still wore her neatly pressed white robes, despite the late hour.

"Asteria!" she exclaimed in shock once her eyes landed on me. Whatever she'd needed from Tolith was forgotten as she rushed forward to embrace me. "We've been worried!"

"Worried? Why?" I asked, frowning.

She pulled back. "Your sister warned us not to tell anyone we knew you, and then you were gone. No one knew where you were or if you'd be back."

I glared at Tolith. "That would have been a good thing to mention when I asked how things were."

He shrugged. "I was getting to it."

Sarya reached back blindly to swat his arm. "So, what's going on? Why all the secrecy? You know I can't stand secrets."

That was something we had in common—hating the unknown. Not knowing was my least favorite thing. I felt bad that I couldn't give her the answers she obviously wanted.

"Hold on, let me get Haryk so we don't have to do this a million times. He should be in his room down the wing," Tolith said, holding up a finger before disappearing into the hall. He returned shortly with the navy-haired fae in tow.

"Asteria!" Haryk breathed a sigh of relief as he entered the room.

"Yeah, yeah, she's back, it's exciting—moving on!" Tolith brushed off his brother's excitement, earning a scowl from his twin. "Tell us what's going on."

I shook my head. "It's not safe."

Three faces frowned back at me.

"Are you doubting us?" Tolith asked, crossing his arms. "I was sure you thought better of us than that."

"We can handle it," Sarya urged.

"I'm not risking your lives for this—it's nothing that concerns you," I said sternly.

They were quiet for a moment, then Haryk spoke. "If it concerns you, it concerns us. Tell us what's going on."

His steady words struck a foreign chord in my chest that brought tears to my eyes. They would risk their lives for an unknown cause? Simply because it pertained to me?

I'd been wrong all those years, thinking we were just friends. These people were my family, my chosen family. They'd been with me through thick and thin; this time would be no different.

I took a deep breath and told them everything.

CHAPTER SEVEN

"Three more."

The words came out of my mouth without me willing them to.

The vision still played on a loop in my mind. Three sprites, less than a turn old, all bearing the dark inky Mark on the back of their necks. Cut down. Bleeding out onto the floor of their family home.

Their attacker had smiled. A flash of blindingly white teeth. A cold grin. His features were hazy, covered in a blur that made it impossible to see who was responsible for the gore, but I knew.

The priestess needed to know too, but I couldn't accuse the king without evidence.

Verena's warning echoed in my mind. I'd been living by her words lately. Save for last night. Regret rumbled up my throat in the form of bile at the thought of Tolith, Sarya, and Haryk. I shouldn't have told them what I knew, what I had seen. They had no part in this; it wasn't worth the risk. I'd let my affection for them cloud my judgment, and with the images of the three sprites fresh in my mind, I couldn't stop myself from replacing their faces with the ones of my friends—my family.

No, I couldn't tell the priestess. I needed to keep my head down, if not for my sake, then for the others who now knew of the terrible king and his hatred for my visions.

I'd been standing outside a pair of chamber doors for an unnatural amount of time. I knocked twice on the dark wood before slipping into the noble's chamber.

"It's about time! My room is a mess and I've been waiting for one of you to fix it." The woman's voice was harsh, even as she slurred her words.

I didn't look in her direction—she wasn't the first entitled being to complain about the servants here. I'd encountered more than a few during my week of hiding. I couldn't imagine what Mags and the others had dealt with during their lifespans.

"Apologies," I muttered under my breath. It was usually enough to be dismissed. I just wanted to change the sheets and get out of this room; it smelled of stale arcwine and sick.

She hadn't been lying—it was a mess. If I were the kind to bet, I'd say it was her own creation. How could someone of her status live this way? I thought nobles were supposed to show some decorum. Perhaps the nearing of the Veiled Night enabled their bad habits. Many ethereals spent this time partying into oblivion, though that hardly seemed wise just before coming into contact with the gods. Surely, they commanded more respect than that?

Or not. I'd never met one. How was I to know?

While my thoughts raced, I cleaned. I tidied the woman's chamber, mopped up several piles of sick, and rid the room of the empty bottles of arcwine. Nearly an hour later, it was as if she had never been there. The snoring from the bedroom meant I didn't have to announce my departure, so I slipped through her doors without a word, craving a bath and a sleeping draught.

Unfortunately, this was just the start of my day.

Several more rooms were cleaned before I earned a break. Mags was waiting in the servants' quarters with a chunk of bread and a slice of melon that was a bit too soft. It was probably on its way out, but that was what the servants at Castle Dreka ate—the scraps.

"Thank you," I murmured as I accepted the food. There was an old rule that you should never accept gifts from faeries, otherwise you'd end up in horrible debt, but I was sure Mags had no poor intentions.

She nodded once. "I heard you ended up in Lady Archibold's chambers this morning."

I winced. "You heard true."

"Then the thanks are mine. That woman is horrid." Mags laughed. I hadn't been aware of her reputation, but it seemed the fae were more than familiar with the noble who reeked of liquor.

"She was hardly conscious when I arrived," I said, and the expression on Mags's face indicated that was the favorable scenario. I wondered what servicing Lady Archibold usually looked like if what I had seen was a good day.

"Consider yourself lucky," she grumbled. Then her eyes darkened, a serious expression overtaking her face. "I have bad news for you, cursed girl."

My blood ran cold at her words. "Go on."

"Some of the others say the king's attendants have been sniffing around here for you."

"When?"

"This morning. Asking all kinds of questions. Seems they know you've been living down here." Mags shook her head. "My girls tried to mislead them, but they couldn't risk their lives."

"Of course not." I wouldn't expect them to. I wouldn't *want* them to. It was dangerous enough being a faerie in this place.

Still, panic flooded my veins. Had one of my friends ratted me out to the royals? It hardly seemed like a coincidence that the very next morning after I had seen them, the king's lapdogs were searching for me.

It was more than suspicious, but I didn't want to doubt them. I didn't want to believe they'd betray me.

"What are you going to do?" Mags asked, more out of curiosity than concern. I never mistook her small acts of kindness for compassion—no, to her, I was like an exciting creature in a cage. She just wanted to know what move I'd make next.

I didn't have an answer. I wanted to ask Verena if she'd heard anything from the council, but I would have to be cautious if I were to approach her rooms. She wouldn't be pleased to see me, but I had no one else to turn to.

My sister was my only lifeline.

Her office was unlocked.

Considering how paranoid she'd been the last time I saw her, it was strange to say the least.

Quickly, I slipped into the room before any of the patrolling guards spotted me.

The room was empty, void of my sister's presence. It was messier than the last time I was here. Parchment littered her desk and her furniture was all askew. Her walls, which had previously been covered in framed art, were bare. If I didn't know better, I'd assume she was moving.

But I did know better. Verena was planning for something. Perhaps she was going to flee Castle Dreka, though, as a councilmember, that task would be infinitely more complex. A councilmember abandoning their post wouldn't just be seen as a crime against Kaedia, it would be considered treason against Edessa. The dracons served as protectors of the empire, and the council ruled over them. Verena was in no position to jump ship.

I checked that the door was locked behind me and made my way to her desk. I wasn't sure if Verena had visitors often, but I couldn't afford to be caught nosing through her documents. Not that the prospect of being caught would stop me from looking at the neatly written parchment—nothing could satiate my curiosity quite like snooping.

I picked up the first piece of neatly pressed paper.

Royal Decree 57

Faeries residing in Kaedia will have the option to return to Elirede, Home of the Fae. Those wishing to migrate will be offered escort by the Protectors of Edessa to ensure a safe pilgrimage.

—By the order of Queen Verena

I blinked.

Had I read that right?

Queen Verena?

The next piece of parchment was written in the same penmanship.

Royal Decree 29

The temples of Dreka will be reverted to their former status as Temples of Night with the New Moons. The Kingdom of Kaedia was founded by the Gods of the Night and it is due time to honor them.

—By the order of Queen Verena

What was Verena planning? Surely, she wasn't going to marry Orien? She obviously despised him.

But that meant...

No, there was no way. The throne of Kaedia hadn't been challenged in centuries.

Although… that would explain her odd behavior. She always seemed anxious and paranoid these days, constantly looking over her shoulder. If her plan was discovered, Orien wouldn't hesitate to kill her before she got the chance to issue a formal challenge.

"What are you doing!"

I jumped at the sound of my sister's voice, dropping the parchment as I met her panicked stare. I hadn't even heard her rattle the doorknob, let alone enter the room.

"What is this, Verena? Are you planning a coup?" I shot back. "Or should I say *Queen* Verena?"

Her lips pressed into a thin line. "Don't say another word. There are ears everywhere, Asteria. You'll get us both killed."

"Are you actually considering challenging Orien? Do you know what will happen if you lose?"

Death. That's what. A challenge for the throne meant a fight to the death between the current ruler and the challenger. Verena was strong, but so was Orien. If she lost, it would mean more than just a hit to her ego.

"I'm well aware of the risks, sister," she hissed. "There is much more to this than you understand."

I crossed my arms. "Enlighten me, then."

She stared at me for a moment, her electric blue gaze full of the storm that lurked just beneath her skin. She was still wearing her council robes; she must have just come from a meeting.

"I'm not the only one involved; I can't put the others at risk."

"You're the only one challenging the king, Verena. You're risking your life. Damn their risk."

"It's not that simple." She sighed, sinking into a chair opposite me. "He's ruining this kingdom, you know."

I did know. Between the mistreatment of mortals and ethereals, the desecration of the Temples of Night, and the preferential treatment of lifebinders, there was plenty King

Orien was doing to corrupt Kaedia.

Still, the idea of Verena being the one to challenge him made my skin crawl.

"And you're going to fix it?" I asked, my eyebrows raised.

"Are you saying you wouldn't try if you had the choice?"

If I had the power, she meant. There was always a choice, but I wasn't strong enough to fight him. I was just a seer.

"You know I would," I admitted, running a hand over the tiny points of the horns that rested just below my crown of unruly waves.

"I have to, Asteria. Surely you can see that? There hasn't been a dracon as strong as me in centuries. This is the best chance to change things for the good of the people."

"You don't need to convince me, Verena." I shook my head. "I'm not your keeper."

"No, but you are my *sister*. I want you in my corner."

"I'll always be in your corner." That wasn't up for debate.

There was a sobering silence as her words sunk into my bones. These decrees were her ideas for the kingdom, her plan to make things better. If she could survive challenging Orien, she would have the power to reshape Kaedia—to fix what was broken. There was a flicker of hope in my chest, but more potent than that was the heavy dread that seeped into every muscle in my body. The fear that she would not win; that I would lose my older sister.

I had to trust her. Her power. She was strong, that much I knew. I had to believe she was strong enough to beat him.

"What did you come here for?" her voice wavered.

I didn't need to look to know that her eyes were full of tears. She was worried about this too, but dwelling on it wouldn't change the outcome.

Mags's warning came rushing back to me, temporarily

forgotten.

"The king has his guards looking for me. They know where I've been hiding; it's not safe for me with the fae any longer."

The blood drained from her face. "He knows. Gods, he knows," she muttered under her breath.

"About me? I'm well aware." That was the reason I'd been hiding.

"No, he knows I'm going to challenge him. Why else would he start looking for you now? He's going to use you as leverage against me."

"I'm certain it's worse," I breathed, the weight of the accusation heavy on my tongue, begging to be spoken.

I caved to its desire.

"I believe Orien is connected to the Marked murders."

Verena inhaled sharply. "How?"

"I don't know for certain. My visions aren't clear, but I think he has something to do with it. And worse, he knows that I suspect him."

She paled, taking several shaky breaths as she absorbed my words. "You cannot be found, Asteria. The future of the kingdom relies on it."

"It is the last thing I want, believe me." I was sure he'd already had a mount for my head made up. "But where am I to go? I don't know this castle the way you do."

She pondered that for a moment, wringing her hands. "There's the old astronomy tower. It hasn't been used in decades; the servants don't even venture that far."

It sounded like an ideal solution. The fewer eyes that spotted me, the better. "Point me there and I'll go."

"It's at the end of the south wing, a bookcase half covers it. You should be able to slip inside. I'll make sure you have food and water for the next few days."

"A few days? What am I to do after?" Surely she didn't expect me to fend for myself?

"I'll be the queen after the Veiled Night. You won't need to hide anymore." Verena's unwavering tone almost made me believe her words.

"I suppose it's a good thing you're confident." I sighed, trying to keep the nerves out of my voice. She didn't need my doubt right now, she needed support.

"I have to be. Now hurry, you should get going. It's well past moonrise; the guards will only get more alert as the night goes on."

Nodding, I rose from my chair. "Pray to the gods that I make it."

I slipped out of her office before she could respond. It wasn't often that we shared niceties, and this kind of conversation was even rarer. It left me feeling strangely comforted, though I knew it was likely a fleeting sensation. Verena wasn't the type of sister to take care of me. She'd never tried. I wanted to believe this was a new version of her, but I knew better. She needed allies right now. It wasn't easy to overthrow a king.

The corridors were bustling with servants, but no guards. Light from the two moons shone through the many windows that lined the halls, illuminating the space in pale light. I'd always found more beauty in the moons than in the sun. Sarya had called me odd more than once for it, usually when she was sunbathing on temple grounds. Even now, as servants bumped into my shoulders, I wasn't bothered. The white glow had me mesmerized.

So much so that I didn't notice the line of guards waiting for me as I rounded the corridor to the south wing.

"Seer Taranis," a man with a wolfish grin sneered. "We've been waiting for you."

Ice filled my veins, making my limbs sluggish. Their eyes were covered. Every guard wore an opaque visor, radiating so much arcane that I knew they must be enchanted. They could look at me. I had no power. Orien had warned them. He knew I'd done something to him the night he'd cornered me in the halls.

"Nothing to say?" the same man said. He was taunting me; he knew I was caught.

He gave a single hand motion and two guards surged toward me, grabbing my arms with their harsh metal-plated hands and tugging me forward. I thrashed against their hold, but it was no use.

"It's rude to fight us, you know. We're just here to give you a gift."

"I want nothing from you," I spat, jerking against my captors. They lifted me so that my feet weren't touching the ground, taking away any leverage I had left.

The man laughed. "I wouldn't give a damn thing to your kind. This gift is from the king."

My kind? Orien had told them even more than I thought. If these measly guards knew I was fae, did the council? Did the priestess?

There was no time to wonder. The guards were carrying me down the corridors toward the Great Hall. I struggled against their hold as much as I could, realizing that Orien was likely waiting there for me. His gift was death, I was sure of it.

As they opened the doors to the Great Hall and dropped me, I realized I was right. My knees cracked against the stone floor, but the pain was nothing compared to the overwhelming grief that threatened to shred me to pieces.

Orien's gift *was* death. Just not my own.

Three bodies hung from the ceiling, swinging as if their

necks had broken only moments ago. Screams echoed off the walls, but they didn't belong to the corpses.

They were my own.

Twisted laughter came from the guards behind me, but I couldn't take my eyes off my friends.

Tolith, Sarya, and Haryk stared blankly back at me, their eyes forever unseeing.

CHAPTER EIGHT

"Did you really think you'd get away with your little trick, witch?"

Orien's voice broke through the ringing in my ears, his sneer piercing the fog of grief that had settled over me.

I clawed at the ground, desperate to find some purchase as my entire world died with my friends hanging above. Face wet with tears and snot, throat raw from screaming, I sobbed for them, for what I had caused.

"Did you think you could entrance, let alone *accuse* a king with no consequences? Surely you aren't that dim."

I was no witch, though I doubted he wanted to hear that. There hadn't been stories of witches on the Isle of Edessa for several turns now.

His golden eyes stared into mine, smug and brimming with challenge. The smile he wore was blinding... and sickeningly familiar.

Orien wanted me to fight back, to push, so that he had an excuse to kill me where I stood. To add my body to the three swinging above us. But my knowledge of his intentions did nothing to dampen the rage that swirled in my chest, leaving an inky void where my soul should have been. I wanted to destroy him, to sink him into the same nothingness that consumed me.

"You are a *monster!*" The words ripped their way out of my throat as I met his gaze with every ounce of hatred I could muster.

He flinched. "That is no way to speak to your king, now,

is it?" Orien mused, as if the weight of my stare wasn't pinning him down.

"You will never be *my* king," I spat.

The thing that lived in the back of my mind purred in approval.

Orien didn't appreciate the comment. He stalked forward, his boots thundering on the tiled floor. Arcane surged and filled the room. The bright light emanating from him burned my skin. I squinted against it, failing to see his hand until he was striking me, white-hot pain streaking across my cheek.

I crashed to my knees before him, knocked off balance from the weight of his blow. The light subsided enough to see the arrogance on his face. My skin stung, every muscle in my body twitching with the urge to fight back.

Gritting my teeth, I glared back at him, willing whatever sensation had left him paralyzed the last time we met to work against him now.

He grimaced, a snarl coming from deep in his throat, and with the incredible speed only a dracon could possess, he flitted toward me unseen, twisting his hands into my hair and yanking me forward. Pain pulsed through my skull, and I threw my arms out to stop myself from hitting the ground. My elbows slammed into the stone floor, but he didn't release me.

"I'll kill you right here, Taranis," he said, so close I could feel his mouth moving against the side of my face.

There was a collective gasp from the guards as I was forced to the ground. My knees throbbed and my hair felt as though it was being ripped from my skull as he shoved my head against the stone. My skin burned with fury, but I was out of options. Orien was in control now.

"My lord," one of the guards interrupted hesitantly, though I couldn't see who from my position on the floor. "She... she is

Marked."

Time stopped.

Marked?

Me?

My heartbeat pounded in my ears as Orien pulled my hair higher, twisting my head at an unnatural angle to look for himself.

He stiffened, then scoffed. "And? It matters not whether the witch is Marked—she is still a witch."

I barely held back my gasp. The guard had spoken the truth. But how? Since *when?*

There was an uncomfortable silence as the guards shifted on their feet, their metal armor creaking as they moved.

"You cannot kill a Marked, Your Highness," a brave soul finally spoke up. "The gods will dispense their wrath upon any involved in such an act."

A long, torturous moment passed.

Then Orien cursed, releasing me as if I were diseased.

"You live on borrowed time, Taranis," he whispered through clenched teeth. "You are only breathing because your life will end in mere days."

"How gracious," I managed to wheeze out.

Anger flashed through his eyes, bright and full of murderous intent, but he could do nothing with witnesses surrounding us. Harming a Marked was like spitting at the gods' feet. Even he wasn't foolish enough to commit such a crime when people were watching.

"Take her to the dungeons. I don't want to see her until the Veiled Night," Orien commanded, his voice ringing with authority that left no room for questions.

The Veiled Night.

The night I would be sacrificed to the gods.

The guards flanked me, two of them hooking their metal-plated hands under my arms, lifting my limp body and dragging me down the stone stairs to the damp, dark underground of the castle.

Time passed slowly.

The dungeons were one of the few areas of the castle Orien hadn't renovated. Blood, pus, and sick covered the floors in a sticky grime that coated every prisoner in the filthy cells lining the walls. It clung to me, to the rags I'd been left in for days, caking under my fingernails and soaking into my pores. I'd never feel clean again.

But I didn't have the worst of it. The dungeon was full of moaning beings, praying for their ends to come. The ones I could see were fae, though I'd seen ethereal beings of every variety carted in over the last few days. The faerie in the neighboring cell was delirious, rambling about gods-knew-what with clouded eyes and gnarled fingers. She had a long tail that swished anxiously every time the doors to the outside opened.

Guards came every few hours to walk the stretch of cells, all the way down to mine at the end of the hall, before turning back without a word. I hadn't seen anyone receive a food delivery yet.

No one complained to the guards though. A large, spiked torture rack that had obviously been well-used, judging by the bloodstained surface and torn restraints, stood at the end of the cells as a constant threat. More than a few of the imprisoned bore marks of torture.

My days were spent pacing my cell, willing the ache in my body to vanish. On the fourth morning of my captivity, my muscles still screamed when stretched a certain way, thanks to

Orien's heavy hand. The understanding that he would have murdered me had the guards not been present weighed heavily on my mind. Had he won, I would no longer exist. I was sure he felt a certain smug satisfaction at the knowledge that the Mark on my neck guaranteed my death merely a few hours from now. Or perhaps he remained bitter that my death would not be at his hand?

I tried not to think about it. My impending death, or the inky Mark on my neck.

It was like none other I'd seen in my four turns of life; a perfect circle, void of the intricate swirls and patterns the other Marked sported. Mine was entirely black. No indication of which realm my soul would be sacrificed to for eternal servitude.

I hated not knowing. It ate away at me, so I pushed it to the back of my mind. I'd wanted to spend my days drowning in elixirs, but had I even been able to access them, my supplies would have run dry long before now.

I wondered what my mystery target was up to. Was he continuing to spend his evenings covered in blood? I missed seeing the world through his eyes, despite his murderous tendencies. I tried to find shame at that thought, but none came.

What did come was the sharp slam of the metal door that kept us captive. Two of the larger guards who usually kept watch stalked through the doorway. The imprisoned around me backed away into the corners of their cells, fear alight in their eyes. The delirious fae in the cell next to me started backing away too, until she spotted the faerie woman who was following behind the guards, her hands clasped in front of her.

Mags. She scanned the cells with emotionless eyes, stopping when her gaze settled on me. How many of these people did she know? Were they her friends? Family?

The faerie next to me certainly seemed to know her. For

the first time since my capture, her eyes were clear and bright, focused on Mags.

"Taranis," the larger guard grunted as he fiddled with the lock keeping me contained.

"What's going on?" I asked, my knees buckling even as I forced my voice to come out even. Were they taking me to my execution?

Suddenly, the faerie prisoner turned to me, something sharp in her gaze that made me wince.

"What are you doing back here?" she hissed, launching toward the bars that separated our cells, her knuckles turning white as she gripped the iron. It sizzled against her skin, but she didn't react. She was focused on me.

"*Dalia*," Mags warned, and the faerie blinked as if she had just come out of a trance. She jumped away from the bars again, cradling her blistered hands.

"Enough," the other guard snapped, clanging the hilt of his sword against the posts.

The prisoners whimpered at the sound.

"You." He pointed to me. "Come here."

With the silhouette of the torture rack looming over me, I obeyed, shuffling forward on bare, dirty feet. As soon as I was in reach, the guard grabbed my wrists, clasping them in harsh iron chains as he yanked me forward. The iron stung, but didn't outright burn, and in that moment I thanked the gods for my mixed blood.

Once I was secured like the dangerous criminal they believed me to be, they opened the cell doors, tugging me along by the chain that swung between my hands.

"What's going on?" I asked again as they led me toward the metal door.

They didn't answer. Neither said a word as they ushered me

through the halls, blocking me from view when we encountered any of the visiting ethereals. My chest heaved with relief when they dumped me in front of the doors to my room instead of an executioner's block.

"These damn keys," the larger guard grumbled, fumbling with several gold keys on a ring.

After a moment of no progress, the stockier guard cursed and snatched the keys away, selecting the correct one and inserting it into the door in a matter of seconds. Then, he undid the bracers around my wrists. The skin beneath was bright red and starting to swell.

"Go," he commanded to both me and Mags.

I opened my mouth to ask what was happening for the third time, but Mags hooked her hand around my elbow and pulled me into the room before I had the chance. The door closed behind us immediately, the lock clicking into place.

"You look terrible, girl," Mags grunted as she swept into the center of the room, producing a long thin box in one hand and a small pouch in the other. "You need a bath."

"What are you doing here?"

She paid my words no mind, stepping forward and sniffing sharply. Her nose wrinkled in disgust. "Have you no pride? Fill the tub before you make my eyes water," she griped. "There's a ball to prepare for, you know."

I grimaced, fully aware that the cesspool of a dungeon had infiltrated its stench into my skin, not that I had been able to do anything about it whilst I was trapped down there.

"The veil has thinned?" I asked, though I hardly needed her confirmation. The arcane humming in the air was potent, almost tangible now.

"The castle is teeming with dracons and elves, so you tell me," Mags replied in a huff, starting toward the bathing chambers.

The faucet squeaked as she turned it, and soon the water was gushing into the dingy tub. "Come, girl. I don't have time to dote on you."

I sighed. Even as disgusting as I felt, the bath was less than appealing, given what I knew would come afterwards. All I wanted was to curl up in a soft bed and grieve the deaths of my friends, not bathe and dress and decorate myself in preparation for a ball that would end in my own demise.

"I don't want to die tonight," I murmured as I began to undress, knowing Mags would do it for me if I didn't hurry up.

The faerie snorted. "That Mark on your neck says it doesn't matter what you want."

She was right, of course. Now that I was Marked, my choices were no longer my own. But that didn't mean I had to like it.

As I sank into the lukewarm water, she handed me a bar of lavender-scented soap, oddly similar to what I had used back in the temple dorms. That bar had been gifted to me by Sarya, and the reminder made my chest constrict painfully.

I pushed the memory away as I lathered the soap.

"What's in the box?" I asked, changing the subject.

Mags shrugged. "Arcane knows. Councilmember Taranis insisted I bring it here before tonight." She placed a towel on a rusted stool in the corner of the bathroom, moving toward the doorway. "You've got an hour. Don't be late, or it's my hide," she warned, giving me one last stern look before disappearing into my bedchamber. There was a knock on the door; it creaked open, then shut again.

I was alone once more.

The pressure in my chest was building, clawing at me from the inside out. I sank under the soapy water, relishing in the silence that came with it. When my lungs screamed for air and I could no longer deny the stars on my eyelids, I resurfaced.

I made quick work of washing my hair, despite the ungodly amount of tangles that had formed over the last few days.

The towel Mags had left was scratchy, but functional, protecting my skin from the cool air. With curiosity blazing at the front of my mind, I made my way to the desk in my bed chamber, eyeing the thin box Mags had left behind. She'd set the small cloth pouch on top of it, so I opened that first.

The rough canvas fabric unfolded easily to reveal a few pieces of arcane fruit. My stomach growled as if just realizing it had been days since its last meal. To satiate the beast, I popped one of the fruits into my mouth, letting the almost-too-sweet flavor burst over my tongue as I moved on to the box.

It was white, with sharp corners, and clean enough that it couldn't have been stored in Verena's chambers for long. I was fond of my sister, but I knew she was quite the slob in her private quarters. At least, she used to be—back when we were sprites and spent far more of our days together. A thin, pale green ribbon looped over the top of the box, securing the lid tightly in place. Tucked under the knot was a small slip of parchment. I tried desperately to still the shaking in my hands as I took in the familiar penmanship.

Tolith's handwriting.

Asteria,

I know that as much as Sarya tries, she'll never get you into a dress that isn't black. I hope this one is to your liking—if it isn't, wear it anyway. Gods know you won't have started shopping for one yourself.

Tolith

Wetness dripped onto the parchment.

I wiped at my eyes furiously, willing the tears away. It was just like Tolith to do this. He knew me well, more so than I'd ever admitted to myself. He and Haryk were my oldest friends. My heart squeezed, full of grief; heavy like lead. I'd gotten them killed. If not for me, they'd be dressing for this event, too. I'd stolen this moment and thousands of others from them.

And Sarya…

What had her gown looked like? I remembered sitting on the temple lawns discussing that very fact, but I'd been too preoccupied to listen. I'd give anything to go back to that moment and absorb every word of her thoughts on lace, but it was too late. She had been the youngest of us; far too young for her life to have ended. She was always so full of Light. The real kind, not the magick Orien claimed had blessed him.

Swallowing the lump in my throat, I untied the ribbon. Had Tolith's suit been the same green?

The lid was snug; I had to pry it from the box. When it finally opened, my breath caught. Inside lay a dress of black velvet that must have cost a fortune. I lifted it delicately from the package, holding it up by the thin straps. It *wasn't* my style, but Tolith had impeccable taste. The top of the bodice was trimmed with lace, in a way that would highlight the curve of my breasts. At the sternum, the fabric disappeared, displaying enough skin that I would have left the dress on the rack had I seen it in a store. Tolith had always been more adventurous than I was. The velvet skirt flared out at the waist, the fabric extending far enough that I was sure it would ghost the floor when I put it on.

A clock chimed outside in the hall, pulling me from my admiration. The ball was starting, the fact confirmed by the hum of chatter filtering through the hall and the buzz of music. The sky was dark, at least the parts I could see through the small window in my chamber. With Mags's warning in my mind, I started to dress quickly, but carefully. I couldn't bear for one of

Tolith's last acts to go to waste.

The gown fit perfectly, so much so that I wondered when Tolith had snuck in to get my measurements. It was snug but not tight, and the velvet was smooth and soft against my skin. At the bottom of the box, there was a pair of silk slippers and a thin silver wristlet to match. He'd truly thought of everything. Tears pricked my eyes again, but I blinked them back. There was no time to wallow.

I left my white hair in its unruly waves. I had no energy to do much else with it, and I needed the coverage. Though it was beautiful, the dress did leave me feeling exposed to all the prying eyes I knew would be waiting in the Great Hall. This way, the Mark on my neck was hidden—though I knew that wouldn't spare me from my fate.

With one last shaky breath, I started toward the door. The handle was cool and turned without hesitation. I was no longer locked inside, but my freedom would be short-lived. I glanced over my temporary chambers, soaking in every last detail, then started down the corridor.

It was time to face my death.

CHAPTER NINE

The Great Hall was packed.

Arcane beings filled the room, crowding the dancefloor and sneaking off to the shadowy alcoves that pressed into the walls. Lilting tunes from a string quintet filled the air, guiding partygoers to an enchanting rhythm. The Veiled Night was an event that welcomed all ethereal beings, and that sentiment held true tonight. Elves, dragons, nymphs, gorgons and more milled about.

The gods wouldn't arrive until later.

At least, that was what Verena had told me years ago when I'd asked a hundred questions about this event. Back when it had interested me.

Now it just filled me with dread.

"Ah, Asteria, there you are."

Verena broke through a throng of drinking elves, stepping toward me. Arcwine wafted from her breath, but she looked beautiful. Her long crimson gown was silky and sleek, clinging to her curves in a way that had eyes following her every move. She looked… *regal*.

She grabbed my arm as she neared. "Is it true?" she whispered, her eyes suddenly too clear for someone who had been drinking as much as she seemed to have been. "Is there a Mark?"

I frowned. "Yes."

Her lips pressed into a thin line, her mind swimming with words she wouldn't say. "I'm sorry, Asteria."

There was more that remained unspoken between us; a brief moment of grief for the years we would lose as sisters, sorrow for the friends she must have known I'd lost, and anxiety that I wouldn't be here as her support when she challenged the king.

"It will be how it is meant. The gods' will, as the priestess would say," I replied, trying to keep my tone as detached and even as possible.

I knew she saw through it.

Verena cleared her throat. "The other Marked are gathered." She gestured toward a group of elves in cloaks colored for each realm of the Immortal world.

Well, all but one.

"No Night Realm sacrifices this year?" I asked, my brows furrowed. There were always more than a handful, according to the texts. Kaedia was the mortal kingdom founded by Night, after all. It was more than strange that there was not a single Marked draped in a midnight blue cloak.

"Odd, isn't it?" Verena replied, though she wasn't looking at the Marked. She stared straight at Orien.

The king lazed upon his throne with an aura of arrogance. His gold crown sat atop brunette curls, tightly coiled and neatly styled. He wore a finely pressed suit trimmed in gold that matched his royal jewelry. He looked more like a king of Thelassan, not Kaedia.

"Very," I murmured.

Verena blinked, turning back to me as if a haze had cleared. "Which realm are you dedicated to, sister?"

I winced. "So you haven't heard the whispers. I was sure news would travel fast through the guard."

I turned my back to her, lifting the hair to reveal my neck. She sucked in a sharp breath, and I knew she'd seen enough. I let my unruly white waves fall back into place.

"Just… take a black cloak for now. I'm sure when the rulers arrive they will have answers," Verena suggested, assuring herself more than me.

"The rulers of the realms actually attend?"

She cocked her head. "Some of them. It is the entire purpose of this night."

At least the strongest beings in the Immortal world would be the ones to reap my soul. There was a small amount of satisfaction in that thought, but it was quickly smothered by the anxiety that thrummed beneath my skin.

Verena left me for a moment, returning with a black cloak almost as velvety as my gown. She didn't place it in my hands, instead taking it upon herself to tie it around my neck.

"Enjoy this night, Asteria," she said.

I heard the part she didn't.

Enjoy this night, because it would be my last.

The air left the room when the gods arrived.

Conversation quieted, bodies stilled, and even the musicians faltered as the feeling of immense arcane power swept over us. Eyes drifted to the entryway, taking in each god as they appeared, assessing whether their actions were acceptable to be witnessed by the immortals entering the room.

Had there not been a growing pit of nausea in my stomach, the sight would have made me laugh. Hundreds of the most powerful beings in the Mortal world gathered here, but they were reduced to nervous partygoers the moment a god arrived.

More continued to filter in; minor gods from the Light Realm being the most common. I'd planted myself near one of the unoccupied alcoves, where I had a clear view of the doorway and where Orien's gaze could not reach me. I'd felt his stare all night, and if looks could kill, I'd have stopped breathing already. He was undoubtedly counting down the moments to my death, ticking them off on his fingers—which were adorned with the gaudiest gold rings I'd ever seen.

Verena flitted between groups of people. She had always been the one with charisma. She laughed, smiled, and made witty comments to whoever she was entertaining, and then moved on to the next group. How many of these people did she consider friends? How many were pawns in her political game?

In Kaedia, one didn't need support from the public in order to rule, but it helped. All Verena had to do was kill Orien and the throne would be hers—but the throne meant very little when the council was against you. She was smart to lay her groundwork before dethroning Orien, but that didn't make it any less dangerous.

Willing the worry to leave my mind, I focused on the tune coming from the stringed instruments nearby. Verena's problems would be none of my concern in a matter of hours. I would cease to exist here before the sun rose over Edessa. The thought was oddly calming. Serenity washed over me as I leaned against the cold stone walls, watching the party rage on before me.

It was much, much later when I felt it—when the whole room felt it. Power that was nearly suffocating. Arcane replaced air, pressing into my skin and filling my lungs. It was almost a real, physical thing, nearly tangible. Even Orien sat up straighter in his throne.

A sinister figure darkened the entryway of the Great Hall. He was tall; broad shouldered with muscled arms that indicated he wasn't just a warrior—he'd won every fight he'd ever been involved in. Dark, harshly chopped curls brushed his brow, giving him a rugged look, and beneath the black strands were a pair of piercing green eyes. The disinterested mask he wore couldn't hide the menacing edge in his stare.

The Great Hall fell silent.

All eyes were on him.

There was no doubt in my mind that he was one of the four rulers of the Immortal world. It wasn't hard to guess which— as if he didn't already scream danger, shadows seemed to cling to him, darkening the air around him. The perfectly tailored black suit he wore only confirmed what we all knew—we were in the presence of Nox. God of Death and Darkness, the Reaper, and Ruler of the Night Realm.

He stepped into the room, and it was like the spell that had fallen over the party vanished. The music returned, guests resumed their idle chatter, and the dancing couples began to sway once more in the center of the floor.

My eyes didn't leave the god—they *couldn't*. I was in the presence of the ruler of the most bloodthirsty realm of the four. The Night Realm housed gods of murder, despair, disease— anything dark or unsavory. It all lived there.

He was… beautiful, considering.

So entrancing, in fact, that it had taken me a while to notice the brunet god who had arrived with him. The man was tall, though shorter than the ruler of the Night Realm. Chocolate hair fell to just above his ears in waves, slicked away from his face. His deep navy suit complemented icy blue eyes. He, like Nox, was handsome, but that was a typical trait of immortals.

The pair moved to the edge of the room opposite me, and anyone paying attention would notice the way they spoke in quiet voices. The brunet man's gaze was tense, sweeping over the room as he listened to Nox speak, only stopping when his eyes landed on me.

I froze.

A god had caught me staring.

He paused for only a moment before continuing his assessment of the room, and I let out the breath I was holding.

I should have learned from my mistake, but I couldn't bear to look away, however pathetic I must have seemed to the other partygoers. They were all-consuming, these gods.

I was so caught up that I hadn't noticed Orien descending from his throne, his presence going undetected until he stood between me and the gods, cutting off my line of sight.

Glancing up, I met his rage-filled stare, no doubt heightened by the fact that I hadn't been paying attention to him. He likely believed he was the greatest threat in the room.

I knew better.

"Seer," the king hissed, grimacing as though the word left a bad taste in his mouth. "Enjoying yourself?"

I looked at him with disinterest. "I *was*."

His calm from earlier had long disappeared, and I relished in his souring expression.

"You should enjoy breathing while you still can," he taunted, a smug smirk finding its way to his lips.

He was trying to rile me, but I refused to rise to it.

"I plan to," I replied noncommittally.

His fists clenched at his side, and then he moved with draconian speed. His rough grip encircled my wrist, dragging me toward the dance floor with no room for argument. If I pulled away, he would most likely have broken my arm. Perhaps I should have humored his remarks.

"To properly enjoy yourself at a ball, you must dance, no?" he exclaimed with false enthusiasm, only just covering the rage that had him vibrating as he pulled my body closer to his.

I couldn't keep the cringe off my lips as his hand found my waist. My skin crawled as his gaze looked over me, lingering on the bare skin exposed by my gown.

"Pity," was all he muttered.

Then we were dancing.

Or rather, he was dancing, dragging me along with him. I wrenched away from his hold as he pulled me closer, and he didn't hesitate to tighten his crushing grip on my hand as he guided my tense frame around the floor. Darkness filled my mind as Orien touched the fabric of my gown.

How dare he touch me with the same hands that had murdered Tolith.

Noticing their king had joined the fun, the citizens of Kaedia gave us space to dance, clearing to the edge of the room. I longed for one of them to notice how hard he was squeezing me, or the look of disgust on my face. If anyone did, though, they did not interfere. It was foolish to think anyone would be brave enough to oppose their king.

As the music reached its halfway mark, Orien froze.

Gauzy shadows filled the space around us, an overwhelming presence at my back. I didn't have to turn to know who it was.

Orien's grip tightened. I was sure to have a bruise now.

"I'll be cutting in."

The god's voice was deep and smooth.

Familiar.

Orien didn't release me. "The song hasn't finished," he objected.

It took courage to argue with a god, that much was certain, but the feeling of pure arcane rolling off the immortal meant Orien was a fool for doing so.

I still hadn't turned to face the god. I couldn't with Orien keeping me in place, so I didn't see what he did to get the quintet to screech to a halt at the edge of the dancefloor.

"It has," the god replied simply. "Now go. I will deal with

you later."

Orien paled and opened his mouth to argue once more, but the god's shadows grew denser around the king's figure and he thought better of it. Another second ticked by before I was free from his hands.

I needed another bath.

Relishing in the fact that the king was no longer touching me, I'd missed the part where a *god* had asked to cut in. He intended to take Orien's place. The blood drained from my face as I turned toward the god cloaked in darkness.

"May I?" Nox asked, holding his hand out to me.

He was close now—close enough that I could see the angles of his features. The fullness of his lips, his straight nose, sharp jawline, and his *eyes*. They were beyond piercing, they stared into my very soul.

When I met his gaze, he didn't flinch.

Swallowing hard, I nodded and placed my hand in his. Arcane sparked when we touched. Was this the effect of a god as powerful as he?

He was patient, waiting for me to come closer. A stark contrast to Orien's demanding pushes and pulls.

I stepped toward him, feeling the heat radiating from his body. Nox, the God of Death and Darkness, was careful as he placed the hand that wasn't holding mine on my waist.

He held me as though I was fragile. I had a strange urge to assure him I wasn't.

The strings started again, hesitant in their waltzing tune. The rhythm flowed through my bones, heightened by the intensity of the attention the god was giving me as he began to guide me through our dance.

It was strange having someone look me in my eyes. Most were uncomfortable with the briefest shared glance, but not

Nox. He held my gaze unwaveringly.

Only when his eyes shifted to survey the rest of my face did I avert my gaze from his. I'd already noticed he was tall, but standing this close offered a new perspective. My head barely met his shoulder. Dark black hair brushed the back of his neck, and I resisted the urge to touch it. He wore a charcoal shirt under his black jacket, and dark swirls on his chest peeked through the undone buttons near his collarbone. He was muscular—I could feel that much from where our bodies connected.

Nox pulled back, extending his arm as he spun me. It was then that his sleeve slid up, revealing more of the inky pattern that decorated his chest.

I recognized the marks on his arms as soon as they were revealed.

I'd drawn them hundreds of times.

Freezing in the center of the dancefloor, I found myself unable to move.

Nox frowned as he moved to pull me back in, but was met with resistance.

"*You?*" my voice was no more than a whisper. "It was you all this time."

He sighed, and that was all the confirmation I needed.

My mystery murderer, the man I'd visited over countless nights, the being whose eyes I had watched the world through, was Nox, God of Death and Darkness, the Reaper, Ruler of the Night Realm.

"Hello, Stea."

CHAPTER
TEN

"Your voice is lovely," Nox continued when I said nothing. "You never spoke on our outings."

A new thought crossed my mind, freeing me from the stunned silence that had paralyzed me.

"What do you mean *outings*? I saw you in my visions."

He cocked his head, and amused look on his face. "You projected yourself into my mind. Do you mean to tell me you did so unknowingly?"

My jaw dropped, my mouth opening and closing as I tried to find an explanation that would please an all-powerful god.

"I— I made elixirs... to thin the veil, so I could have clearer visions."

"Ah. Perhaps they were a little *too* effective. You thinned the veil enough to see into my mind."

"You knew I was there?"

The corner of his mouth tilted up. "Of course. You know who I am, yes? *What* I am?"

I nodded shakily.

It was foolish to think I had entered his mind undetected— though, in my defense, I hadn't known whose mind I was occupying at the time. Gods know I would have never followed that shadowy thread in the inbetween if I'd known it led to Nox.

His hands made their way back to my waist, but his touch didn't repulse me like Orien's had. I barely registered it amid the shock echoing through my body. The god guided me as we swayed to the music, his eyes searching mine. I wasn't sure what he was looking for.

"I didn't know," I finally managed to get out. "Who you were, I mean."

He nodded. "I see that now. In the beginning, I wondered whether you were just incredibly brave… or incredibly foolish."

A shaky exhale left my lips. "The latter, it seems."

Again, he offered a small smile. "I'm not sure I would agree."

"You don't know me very well," I retorted, and his head tilted.

"I've seen through your eyes, just as you have seen through mine. I find that provides a unique view of a person." Nox stared at me intently. "Don't you think?"

"What—?"

Suddenly the music stopped, and the sound of metal screeching against stone filled the air. It seemed I would never have the chance to ask him the burning questions on the tip of my tongue.

"Enough dawdling! It is time for the main event!" Orien's booming voice cried out.

Nox's lips pressed into a line, irritation flashing across his face. For some reason, it amused me to see the god show such disdain for the king of Kaedia. He released me from his hold, turning to the dais where Orien stood.

The king's face was red with anger—why, I couldn't tell. He was about to get exactly what he wanted: the kingdom would gain another five turns of favor with the four Immortal realms, and I would die. Yet, his eyes burned as he regarded the god standing at my side.

"Marked ones!" His voice boomed with the authority only a king could possess. "It is time to experience the greatest honor of your lives—the ultimate sacrifice to strengthen your kingdoms.

Please take your places before the throne."

Cloaked figures separated from the crowd, moving to the front of the ballroom. They stood in a line, three colors of fabric present. Two in violet for Arcane, three in red for Elemental, and the largest group for Light. There were at least seven beings dressed in yellow cloaks who stood before Orien, as he regarded them with a satisfaction barely shy of smugness. He looked down the row, counting them off one by one before stopping, his features pinched.

Orien's eyes found mine, and he cleared his throat pointedly. I closed my eyes, hoping the room might disappear. When I opened them again, the king was still in front of the throne, staring me down. Breathing deeply, I moved forward to take my spot at the end of the line.

I was out of place and everyone knew it. There had never been a black cloak involved in this ceremony, at least not in the recorded history of the Mortal world. I had earned the bewildered stares that pierced my skin.

Pleased with my compliance, Orien moved on. "Will a god from each realm represented here step forward to claim these Marked souls?"

A thin, frail man came to stand behind the group. His eyes glinted with something more, something strong. His looks were deceiving—he was from the Arcane Realm. They were gifted with deception.

Another god, this one a woman, stepped forward. Her hair fell in golden waves over her shoulder. Orien smiled warmly at her. She must be from the Light Realm.

The last god to approach was a man with hair that was dark and peppered with gray. His hands seemed to be stained with soot. Clearly Elemental.

Nox remained in the center of the floor. I could feel the

weight of his stare even now. He hadn't moved from where we'd been dancing.

"Kneel," Orien commanded, and the Marked dropped to their knees.

I followed a beat later. I couldn't will the blind obedience the others had into my bones. My hatred for Orien ran far too deep.

The Dracon Council filed into the space in front of the dais, staring at the gods on the other side of the Marked as though they could not bear to acknowledge the beings that would be killed like cattle at their feet.

"To the Arcane Realm, I offer the sacrifice of two souls," a young councilmember in violet robes announced.

Without another word, the frail god, the deceptive one, raised his hand. With a flick of his wrist, the violet-cloaked Marked ones' necks snapped in unison, their bodies slumping forward until they fell unceremoniously to the floor. The others in the row flinched, now violently aware of their fate.

Who would be the one to kill me, I wondered? I belonged to no realm, according to the inky Mark on my neck.

The council moved on. I noticed Verena was not standing with them.

"To the Elemental Realm, I offer the sacrifice of three souls," Councilmember Yelnan's scratchy voice uttered.

The god with stained hands raised them. Three bodies crashed to the ground seconds later.

The next group would be the worst. Orien cleared his throat once more, and the council dispersed. Then the blonde god nodded to him in acknowledgment. He smiled like they had shared secret words.

"It is my immense pleasure to offer a sacrifice of seven souls to the Light Realm. This will be the largest number of Marked sacrificed to the god-king Lux in the history of Kaedia."

Genuine pride was clear in his tone, but all I felt was disgust at how pleased he was that so many were dying in the name of sacrifice.

The God of the Light Realm raised her hand, and it was then that one of the Marked lunged forward, falling out of line.

"Wait! Please—" the girl cried, but it was too late. The god flicked her wrist. Seven necks snapped. Seven bodies hit the floor.

The girl's pleas meant nothing.

Would I be given the chance for last words? Did I have anything to say?

I could tell the nobles of Kaedia that their king was an evil, twisted man. How much of my story would I get out, though, before my neck was snapped?

"Thank you for honoring us with your presence." Orien nodded to the three gods, and they fell back into the crowd.

He lifted his gaze to the rest of the people in the room. I knew they stared at me, wondering why I was different, why I still lived.

"We have an anomaly tonight, as I'm sure you've all noticed. Our beloved seer, sister of Councilmember Taranis, has been blessed with an unspecified Mark," he explained to the room. "Be a dear and show them, seer." He nodded toward me.

When I didn't move to obey, he sighed, then stalked forward. He stopped before me, reaching out to grab my hair in his fist, but before he could, dense shadows swept over me, surrounding Orien.

Gasps and murmurs started in the crowd. Orien faltered, lowered his hands, and backed away from me, returning to his throne. He cleared his throat nervously. "Trust me when I say she is different from the others. Given this extraordinary occurrence, I have chosen to take the honor of her sacrifice into my own hands. I will be the one to send her soul to the Immortal world, where she will be dealt with properly."

Orien was going to kill me.

There was ringing around me, and a pounding in my ears. Of all the hands by which to die, his were surely the worst. The swirling void in my chest called out for violence, for the king's blood, but there was nothing I could do. I wouldn't make it a step, surrounded by so many arcane-imbued beings.

The room was quiet, the faces I could see painted with a mix of shock and apprehension. From what I knew, the killing of the Marked was an honor given only to the gods. Orien taking this task upon himself was beyond arrogant.

He raised his hand nonetheless, unconcerned by the impending wrath of the gods. He was blinded by his hatred for me. His magick surged around me, wrapping me in a suffocating cocoon, pressing against my windpipe.

From behind me, someone cleared their throat.

Orien faltered.

"I believe my presence is deserving of sacrifice, no? Considering you didn't manage to produce a single soul for the Night Realm?"

Orien's features tightened in frustration at Nox's words. He couldn't say no to the ruler of the Night Realm, but he wanted more than anything to kill me. He was caught.

"Do you need time to consider?" a new voice entered the conversation. A glance over my shoulder revealed the brunet god, who had moved to Nox's side. Though his words posed a question, it wasn't genuine. Every syllable was laced with threat.

Orien knew the consequences of denying a god.

"Of course," the king spoke through gritted teeth. "You may sacrifice her soul." He lowered his arm reluctantly, and his magick subsided.

My breath came easily again, though I knew it wouldn't last long.

"I requested *a* soul," Nox said, stepping forward. His steps echoed off the floor until he stood a few paces in front of me. Then, he raised his arm. "Yours will do."

The crowd gasped as Nox gripped Orien with his arcane. The king's hands flew to his throat, sensing what was to come.

"Did you really think I wasn't aware of what you were up to? Your late-night trips into the city?" Nox took another step forward.

Orien's eyes widened in fear.

"I know what you have been doing to the Marked of the Night Realm. To *my* people."

Confused whispers broke out across the ballroom as the pieces clicked into place for the citizens of Dreka. The arcane rolling off Nox made it clear Orien would pay for his crimes here and now.

The God of Death and Darkness turned toward the crowd. "Your king is a false one. He is a murderer, a corrupt man, and a coward. He has dedicated this kingdom to the Light, though your ancestors knew to honor the Night. He will die by my hand, and you will all bear witness. Watch and remember what becomes of those who forsake the Night Realm." His voice rang through the Great Hall, full of anger and intent. It was nothing like Orien's petty rage—this fury was overwhelming.

Nox's hand closed into a fist, and Orien's face began to turn red. He was suffocating.

"Wait!" a voice I recognized all too well called out.

Verena burst through the front of the crowd.

Nox turned, but did not release his hold. "You dare defend a corrupt king? One who has forsaken the gods who built this kingdom?"

Verena swallowed, her bronze skin much paler than usual. "No," she managed, shaking her head. "I wish to challenge him for the throne. I wish to rule Kaedia and to right the wrongs he has committed. I wish to dedicate this land to the gods of Night, the way it was intended."

Nox considered her words, mulling them over with raised eyebrows. He looked to the brunet god who lingered somewhere behind me. They shared unspoken words, and when Nox turned back to Verena, he lowered the arm pinning Orien in place.

The corrupt king of Kaedia fell to his knees and took several gasping breaths as Nox spoke.

"Very well. You may issue your challenge—but be warned, if you do not fulfil the claims made here, you will face his fate."

My heart squeezed at the thought of Verena in Orien's place, but I had seen her plans myself. They were already in writing. She could fix this kingdom.

Verena hesitated, looking between Nox and Orien before stepping toward the latter.

"Orien Nozac, Lifebinder and King of Kaedia. I, Verena Taranis, Keeper of the Storm, challenge you for the throne and the crown of Kaedia. This challenge shall be a fight to the death, and the winner will emerge a royal." Her voice was strong despite the hesitance in her stance.

Orien glared at her with pure malice as he clambered to his feet. "You will regret this, Councilmember," he swore. He intended to win.

Verena's gaze was full of thunder. She wouldn't go down as easily as he assumed.

"Orien." Nox's voice silenced the king's furious cursing. "No matter the results of this challenge, you will not leave this room alive."

The king's mouth tightened, but he said nothing as Nox

moved away from the dais, stopping in front of me where I kneeled on the floor. He held out his hand.

A hand that had killed thousands.

"Come with me," he commanded, and I couldn't find an acceptable reason to object.

I placed my hand in his, letting him pull me up from the floor and back to the edge of the crowd where the brunet god was waiting.

The rest of the party guests pressed back as far as possible, lining the walls. I wasn't sure how much space would be needed for a fight between two dracons, but I knew these people shouldn't be anywhere close.

I didn't want to watch, but I couldn't bear to look away. Verena's life was in the balance.

"Carry on," the brunet god stated, his tone filled with boredom as if a challenge for the throne happened every other day in the Night Realm.

"It's a shame your sister won't live long enough to arrange a service for you, Councilmember," Orien taunted Verena, moving to stand across from her in the center of the room.

Verena regarded him coolly. "They will call me Queen when this is done," she retorted, a sureness in her tone that should have shaken Orien to his core.

There were no more words. A crack of thunder rumbled through the Great Hall.

The challenge had commenced.

Verena had begun the fight for her life, and the future of Kaedia.

CHAPTER ELEVEN

"Lifebinders are pesky," Nox said quietly, his eyes glued to the deadly dance happening in the center of the room. "Because of their healing abilities, any blows have to be fatal. If they aren't, the lifebinder wins in a game of endurance. Your sister is learning that lesson now."

I looked at the God of Death with a questioning stare. Why was he giving me a combat lecture?

He held my gaze. "This is important. Pay attention."

Given that he was an all-powerful god, I obeyed, turning back to the battle.

Still, it didn't make sense why he would bother explaining these things to me. I was destined for death regardless of whether or not Orien died. There was no need to teach me anything further. My curiosity had finally died, and I would soon follow.

I almost laughed.

"We won't be home until sunrise at this rate," the brunet god grumbled from Nox's left. "Can't you interfere? You're going to kill the lifebinder anyway."

Nox waved him off. "Not until the stormkeeper proves herself worthy. I won't let just anyone take the throne. Didn't you learn your lesson from last time?" He gestured toward Orien, who laughed maniacally every time he evaded one of Verena's attacks. He was a man on the brink of death regardless of whether he beat my sister, so this effort was for his pride. That made him all the more dangerous.

"He's sloppy," I mumbled, watching Verena land a severe kick to his side. Orien coughed, but seconds later, it was as if the hit never happened. "If not for his healing, he would be dead."

I wasn't sure what had allowed me to be in a position to have a casual conversation with one of the rulers of the realms, but I wasn't going to question it. Nox had brought me to his side, and I would be a fool to object. Besides, I'd spent years of my life with this man, however one-sided the company had been. Maybe that was why he felt so familiar, so comfortable to be around. I didn't fear him the way I should a god of his status, or a killer of his practice.

Nox's lips kicked up just a fraction. "Good. A lifebinder as strong as he is can afford to neglect their form and defenses. The stormkeeper is no threat until she does irreversible damage."

"She's capable. Verena is one of the strongest draconians of our time," I assured him, though as a god, I was sure he could already sense that much.

"There hasn't been a stormkeeper in several turns now. I wouldn't be surprised if she does manage to beat him," he mused, crossing his arms over his chest as he watched. "But you should never underestimate your opponent."

I tried to turn my focus back to Orien and Verena, but it was nearly impossible to ignore the way Nox towered over everyone in the ballroom. At least if things did go poorly for Verena, he would be able to stop Orien before too many lives were lost. His appearance made me question why a god as skilled in magick as he was needed to be so... *strong?*

Thinking back to the nights had spent watching the world through his eyes, I found my answer.

He used his hands for his reaping.

Come to think of it, he didn't seem to rely much on his arcane at all, from what I'd seen, the gauzy darkness that cloaked him being the exception. The shadows were ever-present, and they moved with a mind of their own. They swarmed me too, bleeding over from Nox's form. I glanced at the brunet god to see if he too was shrouded, but he seemed to be free of them.

Glass shattered, pulling me back to the matter at hand. Kaedians screamed.

Verena fell to the floor on the other side of the Great Hall, just below the arcing stained-glass window that was now nothing but shards. The storm raging outside burst into the room, taking advantage of the enclosed space. Everyone beneath the broken window was pelted with rain, and harsh winds tore through the air.

I didn't have time to worry about Verena. She was already getting to her feet, huffing and staring Orien down. The king was smug, standing with his hands on his hips in the center of the ballroom. It was clear Verena wasn't a concern to him.

"Enough of this. I want a real fight!" she declared.

Lightning struck a tree just outside, leaving it scorched and smoking.

Orien laughed. "As you wish, Councilmember."

Arcane exploded through the room, blinding and hot. The remaining partygoers rushed toward the doors, desperate to escape the sensation. They were smart to do so; there would be no room for observation once two dracons filled the space. Only the council remained to witness the results of the challenge, though I suspected that was more out of a sense of duty than any desire to be in attendance.

Nox didn't move. His eyes were alight with amusement, as though this was what he had been waiting for. When the light dimmed, we were met with two beasts, battling before us with claws and fangs. In this form, their arcane was even more potent. Orien could heal faster, and Verena's storm was uncontainable.

Verena's dracon was beautiful. I'd always been jealous of her ability to shift, and the fact that her form was so entrancing stoked the flame. Her scales were electric blue, the same shade as her eyes. They seemed to ripple as she moved, mimicking the storm she controlled. Rigid spines ran along her back, leading to a deadly spiked tail. She was using it now to rip into Orien's flesh with every chance she got.

Orien's beast was like that of every lifebinder I'd seen before, bedecked in shimmering gold scales that reflected the sunlight when they soared through the sky. Now, under the cover of Verena's storm, his scales looked dull. The fangs in his mouth were still long and deadly, though, and he didn't hesitate to slash at her when she got close.

"This may be the most boring fight I've ever been forced to watch," the brunet god all but yawned.

Nox tilted his head. "They're still on the ground. Dracons do their best fighting in the sky."

As if Verena had heard him, she released a ground-shaking roar, extending her wings as far as possible in the confined space. Her legs tensed, then she launched, breaking through the glass-domed ceiling. Shards rained down, but they never made contact with my skin. Nox's shadows stretched, covering the area over the three of us until the rubble stilled. Orien responded to her movement immediately, huffing in annoyance and taking flight after her. She was leading him into the eye of her storm.

My stomach turned as they flew higher, out of sight. Nox and the brunet god had their eyes trained on the dark clouds. Perhaps they could see further than I with their immortal eyes. The rain stung my face, and the wind lifted and twisted my hair as it whipped through the room. There was no safety from the elements Verena had manipulated. I stared upwards, waiting for the moment when one of their bodies would plummet to the earth.

I nearly jumped out of my skin when my cloak moved, the hood coming up over my head to protect me from the weather. Nox's hand returned to his side, and I tried to stifle the strange feeling that blossomed in my chest; the warmth that filled the space so often reserved for the raging void that lived there. His help felt oddly intimate, like when Verena had tied the cloak around my neck. Perhaps our time spent together was what had promoted him to take such measures?

The foreign feeling was overpowered by the turning of my stomach the longer Verena stayed out of sight. I'd never wished for access to my dracon form more than now. I was utterly helpless, stuck on the ground with no way to protect her. Lightning crackled through the sky as if reminding me she needed no protection. Still, I wrung my hands tighter with each passing moment.

"She is doing fine, don't fret," Nox murmured, in a voice low enough that only I could hear.

I glanced at him briefly, putting in real effort not to linger too long. "I can't help but worry."

He hummed. "It'll be over soon."

How could he be so sure?

It felt like hours ticked by. The rain never stopped, and neither did the howling wind. Lightning flashed and thunder rolled, but the unease filling my bones didn't lessen. I wouldn't feel right again until Verena was standing in front of me.

Nox was entertained by whatever he saw in the sky, though the brunet god seemed to grow more bored as time passed. It was as he opened his mouth to say something—likely to complain about how long this was taking—that the atmosphere shifted.

Clouds parted, and the rain dried up. The moons were visible once again.

And a dracon was falling to the earth.

"No," I whispered, terror flooding my veins. I couldn't lose anyone else.

The dracon moved too fast to see, nothing more than a blur in the sky. The ground cracked on impact, shaking the castle. A tree splintered, shards spraying into the air. The body landed just outside the Great Hall, in the courtyard. My legs were moving before I'd told them to, running toward the spot. My gown snagged under my feet and I bunched it up in my fists as I ran.

There was no time to go through the castle. I climbed through one of the shattered windows instead. My skin burned as I pulled myself through—maybe I hadn't been as careful with the glass sticking out of the frame as I should have, but there was no time to inspect the wound.

"Verena?" I cried as I neared the hulking mass in the dirt.

The fear that she would respond was greater than the fear that she wouldn't. If she was still in the sky, she was alive. I had little hope for that if she was the one lying here.

The body was covered in the remains of an arcane tree. I dropped to my knees, pulling branches and wood away from the beast. Splinters dug their way into my fingers, but I didn't stop. Not until I saw the glint of bloodied golden scales beneath the rubble.

All the air left me in a rush. Relief flooded my body until my limbs shook.

Verena had won.

I buried my face in my hands, desperately trying to control the heaving breaths that ravaged my lungs.

"I told you she was fine." Nox stood a few paces behind me, a smirk on his face.

I shook my head. "I can't believe she killed him."

"You have such little faith in me, sister." At the sound of

Verena's voice, I shot to my feet, searching for her form. When had she returned?

She was making her way to us, holding her side and moving slowly. Her naked body was bruised and battered, but the discarded cloak she'd wrapped around herself masked the severity. She was injured, but she still lived—that was what was important. I rushed toward her, throwing my arms around her for the first time in Gods knew how long. She returned my hold, squeezing me as I shook.

"It's okay, Asteria," she whispered against my hair. She'd always stood a few inches taller than me, even when we were sprites. "I won. It's over."

"It has only just begun, Queen Verena."

She pulled away from me at Nox's words, wiping tears from her cheeks. "Thank you for allowing this challenge, my lord," she said, bowing her head.

"Be better than he was," Nox warned, gesturing toward the unbreathing mass of scales. "Or you too will end up slain by one of your subjects."

She paled, but nodded nonetheless. Verena had to know ruling a kingdom wasn't an easy job, but she was strong.

"Taranis? Is that you standing upright?" Councilmember Yelnan called out from behind the broken windows.

"Yes, Councilmember," she answered. The council dissolved into whispers of disbelief, shaking their heads as they spoke to one another in hushed tones.

"You have work to do," Nox instructed as the brunet god came to his side. "And we must return to the Immortal world."

Verena nodded, bowing once more to the ruler of the Night Realm. "Thank you for your presence, it is truly an honor. I am... *sorry*, for what Orien has done. Though that word does not seem strong enough to atone for his crimes."

"You are not responsible for his actions. You have punished him for me, and for that, you and this kingdom are cleared," Nox assured her, his voice full of order and authority.

The change in him was almost jarring.

"Thank you," Verena repeated. Then, she turned to me. "Let's get inside. I'm sure the council have questions."

I nodded, stepping forward, until Nox's hand stretched out in front of me.

"Your sister will be coming with us."

Verena and I balked. "What?"

"You took Orien's soul—was that not enough?" my sister added.

Nox frowned. "I will not be reaping her soul." He turned to meet my confused gaze. "You will return to the Immortal world, as you are destined to. You are still Marked."

"You aren't going to kill me?" I clarified. I wasn't aware of any other way to get to the Immortal world if you weren't a god.

"Unfortunately not," the brunet god sighed.

Nox glared at him over his shoulder. "I can promise you won't die by my hand," he swore, a hand over his heart.

Did gods have beating hearts? Did blood flow through their veins?

Verena's features tightened as she regarded me with something weighty in her eyes. "I don't have a say in the matter, do I?"

Nox shook his head.

"It will be as it should be," I repeated the words the priestess had so often spoken to me. I had no control over my fate now, and though I wanted to believe Nox, I'd seen him take countless lives—why would my fate be any different?

Verena looked like she wanted to argue further, but there was nothing she could do to oppose the gods. Nothing that would keep her from ending up like Orien, at least.

Besides, she had a kingdom to run. The last thing she needed was her younger sister riding her coattails.

She threw her arms around me one last time, and when she pulled back, her cheeks were red.

"I will see you again," she insisted, resigned yet determined.

"You will," I promised. Then, I turned to the gods. "I am ready."

Nox smiled. "I hope that is true."

CHAPTER TWELVE

"We'll use arcane travel to get out of the city. Are you familiar with the sensation?" Nox asked, looking down at me as we walked through the castle grounds.

The brunet god led the way, walking a few paces ahead of us. The God of Death and Darkness lingered at my side, perhaps to make sure I didn't bolt. There wouldn't be much point in trying—they would catch me before I made it a pace.

They'd been kind enough to let me gather a few things from my room, namely the amethyst dagger I had stored away, my botany journals, and several items of clothing. I'd changed into something more appropriate for the journey too, but I couldn't bear to leave the gown behind. Though it made the bag slung over my shoulder much heavier, I kept telling myself it was worth it.

The gods had changed too, swapping finely tailored suits for tunics and pants that were much more comfortable looking. Nox had told me we would be walking for at least two days, and that some of the hike might be strenuous. Our evening attire would have been unsuitable to say the least.

I'd never left Dreka in the four hundred and ninety-two years I'd been breathing, other than in my visions. That fact left my chest feeling hollow. Had I really spent so much time here and experienced so little?

I shook my head in response to Nox's question, though in a way, I supposed I was somewhat familiar with arcane travel. I'd just never travelled that way in my own body. "What do I need to do?"

"You don't have to do anything, I'll take care of it. You just hold on. It will feel a little strange." He held out his arm out to me.

I hesitated, but when he nodded in encouragement, I decided to trust him, wrapping my hand around the crook of his elbow. After all, it wasn't like I had a choice.

His eyes met mine. "Ready?" he asked.

"I suppose so," I breathed.

There was a surge of arcane, and then it happened. My body was pushed and pulled in a hundred different directions, smoke filling my mouth and lungs as I was turned inside out and then right again. My feet found solid ground what felt like hours later, but in reality, it was only a few seconds. I let go of Nox's arm, my stomach still doing flips.

The brunet god wrinkled his nose. "Are you going to be sick?"

The room—no, not room—*trees* were spinning around me, but I gathered enough focus to scowl back at him.

Nox chuckled, giving our companion an exasperated look. "Don't let Drystan bother you; he's not our friendliest face."

I grumbled, squinting at the god—Drystan—who led the way, walking forward through the dead trees surrounding us. We were in the Bones, the two moons looming overhead.

"He grows on you after five centuries or so," Nox added.

It was clear they were friends, maybe even lifelong if they'd spent so many turns together.

I focused on putting one foot in front of the other as we walked through the forest under the cover of darkness. The trees were all bare, but no leaves were coating the ground. They'd been dead for much longer than a season.

There were stories about this forest; none of them good. It was rumored that monsters lurked here, waiting for some foolish mortal to venture into the dead depths. I'd never seen another living creature in all my evenings spent prowling the Bones, but that didn't mean they didn't exist. Perhaps they were all hiding in the presence of a being as powerful as Nox? Even the beasts could sense arcane like his.

Other stories said the miles of forest were cursed to be barren after the royals affronted the gods—a punishment from the God of Death himself. I could ask, but the silence that settled over the three of us was thick and suffocating. It didn't feel like the right time.

Still, I could find truth in the story, especially after the atrocities Orien had committed.

We carried on, Drystan pointing out fallen trees and gnarled roots to keep an eye out for as we walked. Eventually, the forest floor turned to ash. The black, sand-like substance clung to my boots, leaving me wishing for a stream to clean up in, but Drystan showed no signs of slowing. Not until he reached the darkest point—the Scorch.

This was where the death emanated from, the spot from which the once lush grove had been poisoned.

"Through here," Drystan said, peering into the ash. "This is the way to the Night Realm."

I stepped forward, apprehensive, until I saw what he did; glittering darkness at the very center of the Scorch.

I'd never been this close to a portal before, let alone one that crossed worlds.

"Let's get you home," Nox said softly.

Kaedia had been my home for the last four turns. I had never loved it the way Verena did, but could I really leave it behind? The Night Realm would eat me alive.

Still… there wasn't anything—anyone—left in Dreka for me, other than Verena. The people that had tied me to this kingdom were all gone.

Home.

The word echoed around my mind as I took a step and plunged into darkness.

The sky was alive in the Night Realm.

The bright flecks of light that embroidered the darkness seemed to shine brighter than any other stars I'd seen in the Mortal world, though the absence of the moons was unsettling. I'd lived my entire life underneath the orbit of those two moons.

"What's on your mind?" Nox's deep voice asked from behind me as Drystan marched ahead, crunching leaves under his boots.

I couldn't get a read on him. He spoke to me as if we were friends, yet throughout all the time we'd spent together, we had never shared any conversation. He seemed so casual for a god, especially one of his status. It was easy to forget he was one of the four.

"There are no moons," I explained.

A pause. "Were you fond of them?"

I shrugged. "You could say that."

Draconians were born of the Arcane Well, the second moon in the sky. It felt strange to be disconnected from it, regardless of the fact I'd never accessed that side of my heritage. I'd always carried mixed feelings toward that second moon.

"Your homesickness will fade after your induction," Nox continued, like his words were supposed to ease my mind.

Instead, they only sparked questions.

"Induction?"

"Your official welcome," he explained, "where you'll be sworn in to the Immortal world as a godling."

I froze, my blood suddenly cold, moving through my veins like shards of ice. My legs wouldn't move, and my mind couldn't tell them to. There was only one word circulating on repeat in my head.

Godling.

Nox had misspoken, surely? Me, destined to be a god? That was impossible.

"Why are we stopping?"

Drystan's grumbling pulled me out of my spiraling thoughts. I realized then that Nox remained beside me, an uncharacteristically concerned expression on his face.

"*Godling?*" The word came out in a croak.

Nox frowned. "Do you not know the history of the realms, Stea?"

"Of course I do." I'd read up on the subject extensively during my time as a seer at the temples. My visions had always been rarer during times of prosperity, which was when the prophets were at their busiest, so I'd had many hours to myself. Such was the blessing of only seeing death.

"Ah, but you only know the Mortal world history, don't you? My apologies, I had forgotten." He paused, running a hand through his dark hair.

"A long time ago, the rulers of the four realms closed off access to the Immortal world. You had to be of godly descent to travel across the veil."

This much I knew. Though he seemed to be missing the detail that stated even gods could not pass between the worlds freely; only when the veil was at its thinnest could they cross over.

"Over time, mortals and ethereals confused what the

sacrifice of the Marked really meant, believing it to be a simple transaction—the lives of the Marked in exchange for the favor of the gods. Of course, that belief still allows the transportation of the Marked to the Immortal world, but most of the gods would be more than willing to collect their Marked ones without needless bloodshed."

Drystan groaned. "The Marked are godlings, for arcane's sake, catch up. And stop taking so long to fill her in."

I gaped at him. The Marked were godlings? Did that mean they were all still alive? Questions whirled in my head, and I cleared my throat, intending to make a retort about how my whole life had been thrown on its head in the last few days, so *excuse me* for taking a while to get used to it, but Nox spoke before I had the chance.

"*Easy.*" The word seemed simple enough, but it was spoken like a command.

Drystan frowned, turning back in the direction we'd been travelling. "Can we continue?"

Nox returned to stand close to my side, giving Drystan a sharp nod as he turned back to look at us, before gesturing for me to keep walking. I felt his stare, but I couldn't meet his eyes. Funny that *I* was now the one having a hard time looking someone in the eye.

"Where are we?" I asked in an attempt to ease the tension that lingered between us.

"The forest at the edge of the Night Realm. We're a couple of days away from the Onyx City." His ring-adorned fingers lifted once more, this time to pull his shaggy dark hair back, tying it with a dark scrap of leather he had produced from the pocket of his pants. My eyes followed the movement against my will.

I didn't want to ask what the Onyx City was, but I did anyway. Curiosity would always be my downfall.

"You're quite inquisitive," Nox commented, his head tilted to the side as his lips kicked up into a smirk.

"Is that your way of saying you're annoyed with my questions?" I asked. It wouldn't be the first time I'd met someone with limited patience.

"Not in the slightest," Nox assured me. "The Onyx City is the closest thing to a capital the Night Realm has. Most of the citizens of the realm live there or on the outskirts."

"Most?"

Even with his reassurance, I felt like I was pushing my luck with each query. I couldn't let myself forget what he was capable of.

"Some of the gods reside in their domains, of course," he clarified, as though it was a simple fact of life.

I suppose, to him, it was.

"Don't make me ask."

He smiled, the brightness contrasting against the shadows that swarmed him. "A god's domain is created from the essence of what they rule over. It exists and it doesn't at the god's will."

"Sounds fickle," I muttered.

"It can be," he conceded. "Will you answer one of my questions?"

What could an immortal god possibly want to know from me? "It would only be fair," I answered regardless.

He hesitated. "You are different from the other prophets, yes? Through your eyes, I have seen their white robes, their golden adornments. Yet you were always clothed and jeweled in other colors?"

"Yes."

"Why?" He searched my face, and I met his intense stare. As had been the case earlier in the night, he didn't react to meeting my eyes.

Was he immune? I supposed it made sense that if anyone was going to be immune to my gaze it would be a ruler of the realms. Looking into his eyes, *I* felt strange. Like he could read my thoughts with a single glance.

I looked away. "They are prophets, I am a seer. Their visions come from the Light, and are usually positive, showing good news for the kingdom. My sight is… darker. The council always dreaded my visits. I imagine that's why they ignored my warnings about the Marked being killed. They didn't want to entertain such horrific visions."

His eyes widened ever so slightly. "You saw the murders?"

"After they happened. And never the assailant— Orien," I corrected myself. "The council turned me away, said there wasn't enough proof."

He shook his head. "Corrupt. Your sister shall have to weed them out, or they will be her downfall."

"Verena is strong-willed, and she already has plans for the kingdom. She won't let them hinder her."

Nox hummed, seemingly out of questions for the moment. We trudged through the foreign forest wordlessly, following Drystan's lead.

What had I done to make the brunet god dislike me so much? It wasn't like me to worry about how others felt when it concerned their opinions of me, but if we were to spend eternity together in the Immortal world, chances were we would run into each other.

Perhaps our shaky start was something I could fix once things had settled. I could barely contemplate just how much there was to figure out. I was in a new world, with people—gods—I didn't truly know, and there were customs and expectations I'd have to uphold as a godling. That title still didn't ring true to me. I was a seer. There was nothing powerful about me; I wasn't like Verena.

I wasn't strong enough to one day become a god.

The hours ticked on, the forest floor beneath my feet stretching beyond my sight. Though the stars were vibrant here, there was no morning sun. I was certain it must be peeking above the horizon in Kaedia by now.

Stifling thoughts of home, I focused on the moonless sky above, trying to outline the constellations I knew, but it was useless. Even the stars aligned differently in this world.

The Immortal world.

I should have spent more time reading the texts on the subject. It had seemed pointless to study the home of the gods, since I wasn't supposed to ever see it, yet now, Nox kept calling it *my* home.

Hindsight was a cruel beast.

The walk turned into a hike as we continued in silence, stretches of time that felt like days, but with the unmoving sky, I had no clue how many hours had passed. The forest was dense, and thick patches of black-petaled flowers coated sections of the mossy floor. In the distance, a stream gurgled.

For a realm that was known for its brutality, it was remarkably peaceful.

I spent the next few hours admiring the different patterns of leaves on the shrubbery we passed, cataloging every possible detail I could remember before Nox began to disappear from view. I kept jogging to catch up, only to end up crouched beside another plant with markings I'd never seen before.

Eventually, Drystan circled back to us.

"There's a good spot to camp just ahead. I'll start setting up."

"We're camping?" I asked, unable to keep the question from leaving my tongue, despite knowing the brunet god would likely have a snarky response for me. "I thought you said we would reach your home by sunrise?"

"The Night Realm is my home," Drystan replied dryly. "It takes days of hiking to reach the Onyx City."

Perhaps Nox's earlier warning had worked, for his words had far less bite than I had anticipated. I shouldn't have been so surprised; if a god as powerful as Nox spoke, most would listen.

"I'll ward the area," Nox informed his friend, heading in the opposite direction before pausing and looking at me over his shoulder. "Don't stray too far, Stea. It's dangerous out here."

I nodded, unsure what else I could say, when Drystan started barking out orders.

"Godling, grab that bag and follow me." He pointed at the black canvas bag he had been carrying since we left Kaedia. It was packed to the brim, bulging with whatever he had deemed necessary for this trip. I clamped my lips together to prevent a groan from escaping as I lifted it.

It was *heavy*.

Drystan must have been well aware of that fact, considering the smirk on his lips as I trudged my way over to the spot he'd pointed out. It was an opening in a wall of oddly colored trees, which formed a circle around the makeshift camp. It seemed like a popular spot for travelers to rest.

"You can leave it here. Now go gather up some kindling; it gets cold at night."

"This isn't night?" I asked, looking up at the dark, starry sky again to make sure I wasn't hallucinating.

"No," Drystan replied, like it should have been obvious. I decided to save my questions for Nox; he at least seemed more willing to answer them.

"Is there any special place to look—?"

"Sticks. Off the ground. It isn't hard, godling," Drystan grunted, pulling bedrolls out of his pack and barely sparing me a second glance.

Right. I could collect kindling. Never mind the fact that I was in a forest surrounded by beings I knew nothing about and magick I couldn't fathom. I left the circle of trees Drystan occupied and searched through the beds of leaves for twigs and sticks that would help to get a fire started.

I didn't have much experience camping. It was a tradition for draconian whelps to spend time in the wilderness to learn how to survive, but since I'd never shifted, I had been excluded from many of their rituals and outings. Orien had made sure of that.

Orien.

That was a name I wanted to forget.

I barely had enough kindling to make a spark. I needed to focus on the task at hand; I could figure out the rest of my life later.

Looking up, I startled.

Where was I?

I turned in a full circle, finding no signs of the camp that must have been fully set up by now. I'd gotten myself lost in a realm that was notorious for housing the deadliest creatures in the Immortal world.

Drystan had been right to doubt me.

Normally, I'd turn to the stars for the answers, but they kept their secrets where they sat in the sky, arranged in unfamiliar patterns that would be no help to me now. I shifted the bundle of sticks in my hand, hissing when one of them scraped across my skin, the thorns adorning it leaving a long, bloody gash on the palm of my hand. Between that and the slice on my arm from the broken window in the Great Hall, I was sticky with blood, new and old.

"Perfect," I grumbled. Drystan was already going to make fun of me for getting lost, but hurting myself on a twig was bound to lead to relentless jokes at my expense.

If I could even find my way back to the camp.

As I tried to orient myself, I realized the sky had grown even darker. Maybe that should have been obvious, considering this was the Night Realm, but the endless blackness around me made me grateful for all the nights I'd spent wandering the temple grounds in search of supplies for my draughts and elixirs. I wasn't sure I would be stomaching this so well if I hadn't. Closing my eyes, I listened for any sounds that would lead me where I needed to be.

The wind whistled through the trees, rusting the oddly colored leaves. In one direction there was rushing water, in the other, crackling wood—a fire. Surely that was the camp; Drystan *had* wanted to start a fire. The water was good too, maybe a river or creek where I could wash the blood off my hands so the gods I was traveling with didn't take note of the injury. I headed in the direction of the water, making haste. I'd already been gone too long.

I arrived at a river with ash-colored sand lining the banks, sinking beneath my leather boots with every step. The tree branches seemed to bend away from the steady flow of water, allowing the stars to peek through.

The water itself was foreign to me. Shimmering iridescence danced in the river, the colors muted without sunlight to show off every swatch. Smooth stones lay beneath the water, flattened by time.

Untying my cloak and tossing it onto a nearby rock, I crouched by the edge. Blood smudged the area around the cut and stained the torn edges of my gloves. The wound itself was puckered and angry; slightly swollen. As I pressed on it, a searing heat shot through my fingers. Spots danced in my vision as I dipped one hand into the water, sighing at the soothing cool stream that wove around me.

I considered soaking my entire body in the icy water. Maybe it would shock my system and wake me up from this bizarre dream? I'd had a long day—I was sure I could use a bath. Mags's voice seemed to hum in approval in the back of my mind.

With that thought, I looked over my shoulder for prying eyes before slipping my tunic over my head, following shortly after with my socks, boots, and pants. The water was colder than it had originally felt on my hands, and a shiver rocked through my bones. I clenched my jaw to stop the chattering and quickly rinsed my wounds before scrubbing the dirt from the rest of my body. When the shimmering water ran clear again, no longer swirling with the blood from my skin, I pulled myself out of the water, redressing as quickly as my near-frozen limbs would allow.

My breath came out in white clouds, and my fingers were numb, completely unfeeling. Perhaps a dip in the river wasn't the best idea with the quickly dropping temperature of the night. Infection would be worse than freezing though, or at least, that was what I told myself as I gathered the kindling I'd abandoned by the river's edge. A plume of gray smoke filtered upwards through the trees to my left, so I headed in that direction.

Scarlett spotted mushrooms grew at the base of the unusually large trees that made up the forest, and their stems were striped in a way I'd never seen on the fungi in the Mortal world. I longed for the botany journals that were in my bag at the campsite. I'd have to come back and sketch them later.

As I walked toward the smoke, the trees began to bend over the path, making an archway I was sure hadn't been part of the landscape near our camp. Branches intertwined with one another, beckoning me forwards. My feet moved without a thought, following a distant rhythm.

Buhm-Buhm-Buhm.

Leaves rustled above me, but I couldn't find the source of the sound. The treetops were empty.

The smoke ahead wavered, filling my vision with intricate whisps of color. The brightest shades of violets and greens danced before me as I neared the fire. A haunting song floated through the air, a cry of sorrow. I felt its notes in my chest, beating alongside the strange rhythm.

The flames grew larger, stoked by my presence. They were dark, burning hot, and higher than my head. The heat licked over my skin, and suddenly, I was burning up. My tunic was suffocating—it had to come off.

I ripped the fabric over my head, paying no mind to the protest of my long-forgotten wounds. My pants followed shortly after, and I swayed in just my underthings, influenced by something other than myself. The voice in the back of my mind reminded me that this wasn't normal, but I couldn't stop.

The sorrowful song grew louder, and my legs followed their unspoken command, carrying me around the fire in time to its cries.

Buhm-Buhm-Buhm.

Buhm-Buhm-Buhm.

Buhm-Buhm-Buhm.

The spires of color curled around the fire and arced again, the flames growing higher and higher. I was sure they would touch the leaves on the too-tall trees, but I couldn't focus on the canopy above me, not when the dark flames in front of me began to take shape.

The heat was frenzied, nearly exploding when two black eyes appeared in the fire. They watched me, watched the frantic movements my limbs made, desperate to keep up with the deafening tune in my ears. Their gaze pierced me, my blood going cold despite the inferno nearby. Sweat glowed on my skin and terror settled into my bones, but my body couldn't stop moving, even if I wanted it to.

Something about its stare made my very insides freeze. I needed to get away from this thing. My instincts screamed *run, run, RUN!*

Sweat dripped down my neck. The eyes in the fire never wavered, even as the outline of clawed fingers reached through the flames toward my body.

I tried to move away from the reaching talons, but I wasn't in control of myself. Violet and green filled my vision and the sorrowful song was too loud, far too loud. The *thing* in the fire was too close.

I could only watch as it made contact with the bare skin of my scarred stomach, its talons sickeningly sharp.

Pure agony burned through my chest, white-hot. Hotter than the fire in front of me. A guttural scream tore its way through my lips and spots filled my vision, pushing out the swirls of color.

My cries echoed off the trees, unheard, and darkness filled my vision. There was nothing.

Nothing but those bottomless black eyes.

CHAPTER THIRTEEN

My breaths wouldn't come. Warmth poured over my hips and pain followed seconds later.

I was going to die here.

The pressure of it all built, rising in mass and temperature beneath my skin, ready to explode.

Then it all stopped.

The ground came rushing to meet me, the pointed ends of sticks biting into my blood-slicked skin.

It was dark.

The fire was gone, and I was freezing.

It was *so* dark.

"Stay awake, Asteria. I mean it." The words were sharp, the tone low.

I *was* awake. My eyes were open.

Oh… perhaps they weren't.

They weighed twice my body weight each, but with great effort, I pried them open, the haze of the smoky forest greeting me once again. My skin wasn't visible under the blood that coated me, still pumping steadily in places where that… *creature* had torn into me. Bile rose in my throat.

"That's it, keep them open." His voice was much softer now that I was following his directions.

His?

Messy hair, inked skin.

Nox.

My body burned in embarrassment as I realized who was inspecting my wounds. I moved to sit up, but the forest spun and nausea washed over me in waves. Warm fingers pushed my shoulders back until I was horizontal again.

My body felt light, maybe too much so, as his hands glided over my stomach. He mumbled something, but I couldn't understand the words. I tried to bat his fingers away from my wounds, but he pushed my hands away.

I was too tired to fight. The dirt underneath me felt soft as a feather pillow, and I let my eyes close. They were so heavy.

"Good to know you aren't capable of following orders," Nox said, taking a break from his mumbling.

"What?" I asked hoarsely, my throat oddly sore.

His voice came from somewhere above me. "I told you not to stray too far. Now look what's happened."

I just wanted to sleep.

"Hey." Rough fingers prodded my cheek. "Keep your eyes open."

"Tired," I mumbled, my lips refusing to speak any more words than necessary.

The calloused caress became a solid grip on my jaw.

"I don't care if you're tired, you cannot sleep now." He sounded stressed; frantic.

What could possibly be terrible enough to frighten the God of Death?

He released me after a moment, going back to prodding my wounds and mumbling in that strange tongue.

Footsteps and a low curse from nearby alerted me to Drystan's presence.

Great. Even more witnesses.

"Don't just stand there, help me," Nox snapped.

Fingers poked and prodded, but I hardly felt it, my skin

numb. It was so cold out here. I thought I heard Nox tell me to open my eyes again, but the call of sleep was stronger.

As his frantic voice echoed in my head, I succumbed to the darkness.

When I woke, it was to flames.

I'd had enough of fire to last a lifetime. Thankfully, these blazing tendrils were orange, not the cursed black that had called to me like a lost moth.

The worn, velvety fabric of my cloak lay beneath me like a makeshift blanket. It smelled of lavender and blood. My head ached, pounding in time with my heart. I ran my fingers over my side, trying to assess the damage left behind, but all I could feel were the torn shreds of my tunic and slightly raised skin.

That couldn't be right.

I sat up quickly—too quickly, I realized, as the trees spun around me. Lifting the edge of my shirt, I tried to see the wounds for myself. I'd been practically swimming in blood, they had to be there somewhere.

Speaking of which, everything looked suspiciously clean.

As I ran my hands over the ghosts of my wounds, Drystan appeared, squinting at me.

"What is it?" I asked, unable to contain myself.

His jaw clenched. "You should be dead right now." He said it like an accusation, crossing his arms.

Suddenly, I felt very small, like a sprite caught doing something they shouldn't. "I'm sorry?"

"You should be," he repeated, in exasperation. "But you aren't. This *fool* made sure of that." He gestured angrily toward a figure on the ground.

Long legs and arms covered in intricate patterns of dark ink stuck out from under a charcoal gray cloak. Black shaggy hair poked out of the top of the garment, and long, wheezing breaths came from the mass underneath.

Nox.

I knew in my gut that it was he who had saved me, seemingly at his own expense.

But why? He was the ruler of the Night Realm—there was no good reason for him to take a risk like this. Judging by his labored breathing, he was hurt.

Because of me.

"Is he alright?" I asked, my voice coming out smaller than intended.

Drystan's angry features loosened just a bit. He sighed. "I don't know. He had to use a *lot* of arcane to heal you."

Using magick outside of your specialism always took a toll, even on gods. Some sorcerers thought it simply damaged the physical body; others believed such an action tarnished the soul. No one truly knew for certain. It was a known fact that healers were rare in the Night Realm—any god here would pay a heavy price to heal, especially to heal the kind of wounds I had sustained.

Nox was no exception.

I'd heard that some never recovered from magickal overload, dying in a comatose state. My chest felt hollow at the thought of Nox meeting that fate. How many more had to die because of me?

Drystan crouched by his unconscious figure, his fingers resting on the other god's neck for a long moment. When he stood again, he looked tired.

"You two are close?" The question tumbled from my lips before I had time to consider my words. Perhaps I should gag

without the help of an elixir, but I found it was easy to get lost studying the markings that trailed up and down Nox's arms. There wasn't a pattern to the shapes, but they still had a sense of fluidity. Dark ink swirled from his elbow to his wrist, tanned skin showing in the gaps between artwork. It was strange studying them in person instead of through his eyes.

Had it hurt? There were a few elves that had been marked with ink, but nothing like his designs. They had come home to the dormitories complaining about how sore they were, and how much they'd bled.

Corded muscles flexed in the arm I was studying. His fingers twitched and relaxed in an alternating rhythm.

I breathed in deeply once, then again, rolling away from him. Curling into my right side, I relaxed into the earth as much as I could. Wishing away the cold, I found sleep some odd hours later.

When I woke next, Nox was gone.

The only evidence he had ever lain nearby was the indent in the dead grass.

Sitting up, I searched the area for signs of Drystan. Surely they hadn't abandoned me? Drystan *had* been angry with me for that mess with the wraith, but would he really leave me here?

I wouldn't last. Last night was proof of that.

The spot where Drystan had taken up watch was empty, and there were no other makeshift blankets lying around, so I doubted he had slept. My stomach hollowed, my theories of abandonment ringing truer as I took in the empty campsite.

I was smart and resourceful, but that meant nothing in a strange realm with creatures and spirits I'd never even heard of. I couldn't risk losing my guides. I'd have to search for them.

My bag was splayed out haphazardly near the dwindling fire, and my dagger lay in the dirt a few feet from it. I was working on fastening the old, worn sheath I'd found in a bin of guards' gear back in Castle Dreka when the figure of a man appeared between the trees circling the camp.

"Just where do you think you're running off to?" Drystan enquired as he meandered into view.

I glared at him in annoyance, but I couldn't deny the relief that flooded through me. They hadn't left me behind. "I'm not running. I assumed we were going to keep making our way toward the Onyx City."

Drystan plopped down onto an overturned log. "If Nox is up for travel, we will be."

Right. The god had been close to death the last time I saw him. He must have recovered, considering how calm Drystan now seemed. Yet again, I wondered what their connection was. Maybe Drystan was a guard of sorts?

"How is he?" I couldn't help but ask. The question was heavy on my tongue as I sat beside Drystan on the log.

He snorted. "Arcane knows."

He said that quite a bit. Did he know *anything* useful? Then again, there was always the possibility that he was brushing me off because I was an outsider. Up until yesterday, I had been a citizen of Dreka, the capital of Kaedia, a kingdom that had been corrupted by the lifebinders. Of course he wouldn't consider me an ally.

"He's quite angry with you, you know," Drystan added.

For the first time, I wished he'd kept his information to himself.

"Oh?" I asked hesitantly. It didn't seem wise to get on Nox's bad side.

"You should be concerned. He's terrifying when he's angry. Cold, calculating, and patient. I've seen him skin someone alive and rip their—"

"That's enough." Nox's stern voice came from the tree line.

Drystan tensed, his mouth clamping shut.

The atmosphere changed then, and for a moment, the arcane felt suffocating. Then, as quickly, the pressure in the air was gone, and Drystan slipped back into simple conversation with the god.

They had their own flow, an obvious bond that had formed over years of working together. I was nearly invisible when I wasn't causing problems, but I didn't mind that. At least it was reminiscent of my life in Dreka.

"Do you feel well enough to travel?" Drystan asked.

"We should continue," Nox replied, though it wasn't much of an answer.

Drystan didn't argue, simply moving around our makeshift campsite and collecting the things we'd unpacked. Before long, we were trekking through the forest again, the timeless sky revealing nothing above us.

I missed the stars—my stars. It was all I thought about for hours as we walked. Drystan occasionally tried to fill the silence with comments about the passing scenery, but Nox stayed quiet. Perhaps yesterday's conversation had been an anomaly.

Nox led the group today, Drystan following behind me. Either they were worried I was going to make a run for it, or—more likely—they were making sure I didn't get myself into any more trouble.

I had no concept of the passing time, but after what felt like an eternity of walking through the same foliage and too large trees, there was something new to look at.

Rolling hills covered in tall, swaying grasses and wildflowers stretched on for miles, blooming in shades of white, silver, and navy. I touched a petal as we started through the prairie, surprised by the velvety texture of the wispy flower.

"What is this place?"

Nox looked over his shoulder at my question. We locked eyes for a brief moment, green on violet, before he turned away.

"The Meadow," he said simply.

"It's beautiful." I couldn't stop the wonder from creeping into my tone. I bent to touch another flower. "What are these called?"

"Streya blooms."

I memorized the word, mumbling it a few times under my breath to feel it on my tongue. Their petals funneled together into trumpet shapes, drooping toward the ground. I wondered what effects they had when ingested.

"They look like…" The word was on the tip of my tongue, but I was struggling to place it.

"They resemble shooting stars," Nox filled the silence, reaching one tattooed arm out to brush against a blossoming bud.

He ran his finger down the curved, thin bell shape of the flower and I realized he was right. They did look like shooting stars, arcing across the sky.

Drystan cleared his throat. "We should keep moving."

His words broke the comfortable feeling that had settled over us, and Nox stiffened once more, continuing. I swallowed my disappointment that the soft moment had gone so quickly, shaking the thought away as I trudged after the god.

After another hour of travel through the Meadow, I finally saw it. A shimmering obsidian pillar rose into the sky, larger than any spire I'd seen in Kaedia. Despite the lack of sunlight, the whole building sparkled, and appeared to be surrounded by iridescent glass orbs, though from this far away, I couldn't tell what filled them or what their purpose was.

I was certain of one thing though—we had reached the Onyx City, and this colossal structure was the Temple of Night. My suspicions were confirmed as Drystan cleared his throat, gesturing toward the structure with a sweeping motion of his hand.

"Welcome to our home, godling."

CHAPTER FOURTEEN

The Onyx City was not at all what I had expected from the Night Realm's capital. Citizens bustled around the streets, chattering cheerfully; colorful stalls were set up with their vendors posted out front, offering samples to passersby; musicians played on various street corners, weaving lively tunes with their stringed instruments. It reminded me of Dreka, back when the city had thrived.

"It's so vibrant here." I didn't want to sound naive in my amazement, but I couldn't stop the awe from creeping into my voice.

Neither of the gods acknowledged me, but I paid them little mind. I'd already moved on to the next stall, examining the nymph's selection of bizarre, glowing mushrooms. There were spindly purple ones that glowed eerily, and bright blue ones with big, rounded tops that nearly covered their stalks entirely. In jars, she displayed green and yellow toadstools in neon shades, encased in thick liquid.

I'd never seen anything like it. How did they glow? *Why* did they glow? I would be willing to bet they were seven different types of dangerous. I was about to ask the seller some of my questions when a warm hand hooked around my elbow, tugging me away from the stall.

I instinctively tried to wrench my arm away, but their grip didn't loosen. I looked up to find Nox was holding onto me, his eyes focused on a distant point ahead of us.

"Come, Stea. There's no time to browse," he said, his voice firm as he weaved through the crowd with me in tow.

It seemed Drystan had been telling the truth. The God of Death and Darkness was *definitely* angry with me. I looked around for the brunet god, but I couldn't find him in the crowd.

"Can we stop for a moment? There's so much to see." I hated that my voice sounded like a plea, but I couldn't help it. There were tens of stalls and hundreds of oddities I'd never heard of. The curiosity nearly had me vibrating.

Nox frowned, shaking his head. "It isn't safe for you here. Not yet."

I wanted to ask why, but before I could get the words out, a man stumbled into me, spilling the contents of his cup all over my front. The impact jostled me enough that I fell out of Nox's hold, causing the god to turn sharply.

"Oh, sorry! It's so busy today… Wait, I don't recognize you," the man started, staring down at me with squinting red eyes.

Was it so unusual not to know someone in this realm?

The stranger hissed. "You smell like the Mortal world." His lips pulled back, revealing sharp incisors.

Nox stepped forward then, a force of Night that would make even the bravest man flinch. His eyes had turned fully black— all-consuming and intoxicating. They brimmed with violence and rage. Shadowy tendrils licked at the edge of his figure, responding to his every movement. Arcane pulsed from him, emanating power and danger. It made my hair stand on end.

This was his godly form.

My heart raced under his murderous glare. I hated how much I liked the weight of it.

"Move along." The words were a growl—a warning.

The man had no choice but to obey. He disappeared into the crowd without another word, and soon, Nox's aura calmed.

He gave me a pointed look. "Let's get out of here. I'll explain everything once we're somewhere safe."

This time, I listened without argument, following him through the sea of people to the edge of the city square. Further out, the houses started resembling family homes. Most were built from stone and rippling panes of glass, as if they'd been blown by hand. It was calmer here, the streets quieter.

"Good to see you made it through the market," Drystan drawled from a few feet away.

My head snapped toward the sound, finding him leaning against a stone wall, one leg crossed in front of the other.

"Where'd you disappear to?"

His lips tilted up in a smirk. "Mind your tone," he warned, before turning to Nox and speaking in a tone low enough that I couldn't hear.

I crossed my arms, glaring at them like a petulant sprite. I hated being left out of the loop.

At least we had made it to the Onyx City. Surely this would be where we parted ways? I was itching to be alone again. I needed to sit in silence and convince myself everything that had happened in the last day or so was real. Part of me was still convinced I was experiencing some sort of elaborate hallucination from ingesting too much dream draught.

The gods ended their quiet discussion, and Nox turned to me, meeting my eyes. I was relieved to see a familiar mossy green color looking back at me, nothing like the endless black I'd seen earlier. They swam with a confusing mix of emotions, quelled too quickly for me to place.

"You will come with me for now. We'll make proper arrangements for you once you've been inducted by the council."

I had only one thought—I was going with Nox, the God of Death and Darkness… alone?

"Come with you? Where?" I asked, not bothering to hide my hesitance.

He frowned. "My estate."

I shifted on my feet. "There's nowhere else? Drystan can't house me? I wouldn't want to be an inconvenience."

The other god didn't really seem to like me, but I would take it over the one made of darkness that made the thing in the back of my mind swirl dangerously. The one I'd seen end hundreds, if not thousands, of lives. The one who was currently angry with me.

Drystan opened his mouth, but Nox didn't give him a chance to speak.

"He doesn't have room." His tone was final.

Something heavy filled my chest, and I had to look away from the gods to stop my emotions from overflowing. Staring at the stone wall some way down the street, I focused on the gray bricks until they all blurred together and nothing felt real.

It would be fine. It was always fine. I took another shallow breath, swallowing my emotions, and meeting Nox's tense stare once more.

"Lead the way."

He regarded me for a moment longer before turning down the path to our right. Drystan disappeared as Nox led me back to his 'estate', as he'd referred to it. The actual building resembled a castle, but I wasn't going to correct him.

Despite my inner turmoil, astonishment swelled in me as I looked over the immaculate gardens and sculpted topiary that outlined a paved pathway that seemed to loop around the estate. The main building was fitting for the god made of Night. Cold stone and obsidian features made up the exterior of the structure, and the three dagger-sharp spires gave it a sinister feel, yet it was strangely beautiful, much like the god himself. The obsidian reflected the lights from the Onyx City, even, but it was removed from the bustling crowds. The blackness of the stone against the permanently starry skies painted a striking image.

I nearly complimented Nox on his home, but the tension between us made me think better of it. He opened the massive, ornate double doors that must have served as the grand entrance.

"Do you house godlings often?" It was a stupid question, I realized. According to Drystan, there hadn't been a godling here in at least five turns.

Still, Nox answered, "No. Never."

He started down a dimly lit corridor and I followed, admiring the interior of his castle as we went. It was similar to Castle Dreka, but Nox's home was more elegant. Simple details decorated the corridors, and smooth black stone made up at least one surface in every room we passed.

I had counted nearly twelve as we walked, but I had yet to see another soul in the building.

"Do you live here alone?" I asked, my hands clasped together behind my back. I matched his stride as best as I could, but he was so tall that he kept outpacing me.

"Mostly."

It seemed he was a fan of one-word answers today. He'd soon grow tired of my endless questions, just like everyone else did, but I refused to let that stop me.

"Mostly?"

"Yes. I rarely have guests. I prefer to be alone."

Great. Now I felt like even more of a burden. I would have been perfectly content in a hut on the edge of town. The ruler of the realm didn't need to house me.

Nox stopped in front of a door made from dark wood. There was a complicated design carved into it, but he turned the handle and pushed it open before I had the chance to study it.

"Your room." He gestured inside the space. It was at least five degrees colder than the corridor had been.

There was a simple, yet regal chamber before me, much larger than the one I'd occupied in the temple dormitories. I stood in a small sitting room, with a burning fireplace made from the same black stone that decorated the rest of the estate, and two overstuffed velvet chairs before it. On the opposite wall was an empty desk near a not-so-empty bookcase. The shelves were stuffed with books and journals, some shoved into the space above the rows to accommodate the large collection. To the right, an open arch revealed a vast bed, easily large enough for four people, clothed in gray linens and a dark charcoal blanket over the top. There was a door in the bed chamber—it must lead to the bathroom.

"I assume this will be fitting, *your godliness?*"

I whirled around, my cheeks burning. "Drystan," I muttered, cursing him under my breath.

Nox chuckled, and a shiver skittered across my skin at the sound. It was not one I had expected to hear from him.

His eyes searched mine, looking for something. He was difficult to read, but I got the sense that was something he'd worked hard to achieve.

I shook my head, summoning all the courage I possessed. "I'm… sorry, about yesterday. The attack. You shouldn't have had to risk your life for some godling you just met."

"We've known each other for years," was all he said.

I swallowed hard, dropping the one small bag I had brought onto the floor. My boot toed the ground. "Still… thank you," I added, before turning away toward the bedroom so I didn't have to observe his reaction to the sentiment.

My words left an awkward pang in the air—I wasn't the most socially adept. A lifetime of my peers being unable to even look into my eyes meant I hadn't had the chance to socialize much outside of…

Well, I didn't want to think of them.

I was grateful when Nox said nothing in response, leaving only the click of the door to signal his absence.

When I woke the following morning, my room was silent. The nothingness covered me, bringing comfort with it. I was used to being alone, and when Nox's estate had appeared empty during our brief walk to my temporary chambers, I'd felt waves of relief.

This whole situation was strange enough to begin with; I didn't think I could handle meeting dozens of new faces too. Especially not when these were the people I would be spending the rest of my immortal existence with.

It was an odd notion, that *I* would experience immortality. But would I? Could I trust what Nox and Drystan had promised? That I would not be slaughtered like cattle in the coming days? I repeated that promise in my mind, as though the act would make me believe I was safe. I was staying in an estate owned by a god, a god that I had believed would siphon my soul for power without a thought, up until a few nights ago.

I expected to feel the cold grip of fear in my chest at the thought of Nox, but none came.

I'd spent the last hour or so combing through the overloaded bookshelf that sat in the corner of the sitting room. I'd found nothing interesting, just dusty novels that hadn't seen the light in years. My fingers had just closed around the spine of what I assumed was a leatherbound journal when two sharp raps on the door interrupted me. There was only one person who would be waiting on the other side.

I crossed the room to let him in.

"Ah, glad to see you made it through the night," Nox said as soon as he saw me on the other side of the doorway. He was dressed in dark trousers and a gray tunic that was tight enough to show off the corded muscles in his arms.

"How are you sure it's night when the sky never changes?" I asked, gesturing to the stars through the high-arched windows.

He tilted his head, a smirk tugging at the corner of his lips. "You'll grow fond of its consistency." His words sounded like a promise.

"We'll see." I shrugged, leaning against one hip. "What can I do for you this *morning?*"

"I came to see if you were hungry. It was quite the journey here, and you never did eat much," Nox commented, his eyes scanning the room behind me. Perhaps he was assessing the damage I'd done to the previously untouched suite?

It was true, I'd barely eaten in days. I'd long grown numb to the hollowness in my stomach.

"I could eat," I replied, earning a hint of a smile from the god leaning against the doorframe.

He straightened, stepping back into the corridor once more. "Allow me to cook for you," he proposed as I followed him into the obsidian-accented hall. The ceilings were high, speckled with skylights that illuminated the stretching corridors in starlight.

I nearly balked. A god? Cooking for *me?* "I'm sure I can manage."

"I wasn't asking, Stea." He seemed pleased by my reluctance, almost amused, even.

"Why do you call me that? Stea?" He'd used the name for years, but I'd always assumed he was speaking to an accomplice to his crimes. I'd only recently realized that he had always been referring to me.

"It means star," Nox replied. "Celestial." He offered no explanation as to why he would use such a term, and I decided not to press, a difficult choice given my natural inclination to pester.

Instead, I changed the subject. "You cook for yourself? I assumed all of the gods kept servants."

He scoffed. "It'd do you well not to assume things."

I supposed he was right about that. After all, I'd been entirely blindsided by the truth behind the Marked—what else was I wrong about?

"Does that mean you have no help? None at all?"

"No. I prefer to keep my home private." His amusement was gone now, replaced by a burning stare I couldn't hold for long.

Message received. I wouldn't be a guest here longer than I needed to be. It was clear Nox valued his privacy, and I was getting in the way.

I didn't respond to his comment, and we spent the rest of the walk to the kitchen in uncomfortable silence.

The kitchen was huge, but that shouldn't have been a surprise. Black marble countertops formed a U-shape with an island of the same material in the center. Glass-fronted cabinets held more dishware than we had ever needed at Castle Dreka, and I found myself wondering who Nox entertained here, given his insistence that he preferred his own company.

"Have a seat." He gestured toward a row of black stools tucked under the edge of the island. I followed his instructions, sitting on the chair closest to me. "Now, tell me what you normally eat," he prompted as he moved toward what I guessed was the pantry.

I was slightly taken aback by his question. No one had ever bothered to ask, and I had always been too grateful for food to complain when it was something I didn't enjoy.

"I'm not picky." I didn't want to burden the god further, besides, it was the truth. Not that I could lie, even if I wanted to. I had my faerie heritage to thank for that.

Nox turned to look at me, raising one eyebrow as if he didn't believe me.

"I'm not!"

"Whatever you say," he conceded, shaking his head as he pulled a mix of ingredients from the fully stocked shelves.

I watched wordlessly as he moved over to a wood-burning stove, stoked the flames, and started combining ingredients in a pan.

"Did you sleep well?" he asked casually as he pushed the sizzling food around.

Amused by his sudden interest in small talk, I decided to play him at his own game.

"I slept," I answered.

He tensed for a moment before lifting the pan, shimmying the food around, and placing it back on the burner.

"You have a way of avoiding my questions," he noted, leaning against the counter as he looked at me with those intense green eyes.

I smiled. "It's a practiced skill."

"You'll open up to me eventually, Stea. I can promise you that."

CHAPTER FIFTEEN

By my second afternoon at Nox's estate, I was restless. My godly host disappeared often, for hours at a time, leaving me to entertain myself. After spending hours in the maze of corridors Nox called home, I was attempting to make a mental map of the place so that I wouldn't have to ask for his help when I needed something. I didn't like being dependent on people.

Starting at my chambers, I retraced our steps to the kitchen, though I did make a wrong turn and ended up in a hall filled with odd paintings. I didn't recognize any of the artwork, but I *did* recognize the god they depicted. Nox stood in an ornately decorated room. The artist had captured the eerie glow of his green eyes that tilted up at the ends and his sharp, angular jaw. This painted version of him captured my attention just as much as the real-life one did.

He stood in a row with three other gods. All men, but distinctly different. One with honey blond hair, neatly trimmed on the sides and golden cuffs wrapped around his bulging biceps. Another with an angry red glare that reminded me of the volcanic mounds in Itharene. The last was impish, his mischief palpable through the canvas. These must be the rulers of the realms.

The idea of the four of them in the same room left my hair standing on end. The arcane would be overwhelming, especially if they were all as strong as Nox. I stared for a moment longer, trying to absorb every detail, before I moved on, returning to the path I'd followed before ending up in this hall.

The corridors were empty, barren of a single soul. What did Nox do here that made him so against having people in his home?

My train of thought was completely abandoned when I turned the corner to reveal an obsidian arch that led to a library grander than even the king of Kaedia had possessed.

Close your mouth, I had to remind myself as I stepped into the domed room. It would be quite embarrassing if I drooled on Nox's floor.

Shelves made of the same black stone that decorated the castle stretched from the floor to the ceiling. Glass orbs floated at regular intervals around the room, containing a flickering fire that bathed everything in a warm glow. The ceiling was painted black, forming a kind of bottomless void that it would be so easy to disappear into, were it not speckled with pinpricks of starlight, organized in constellations across the library. I'd seen this room hundreds of times through Nox's eyes, but it was breathtaking to say the least, and I hadn't even gotten to the books yet.

As I ventured into the room, the smell of pine and smoke enveloped me. I couldn't quite place it, but it was enticing nonetheless. Past endless rows of shelves, I found an extravagantly carved fireplace, with an active flame eating up several logs. In front of it were two lush chairs and a bench off to the side. To the left of the chairs stood a small bar with a number of oddly shaped bottles, housing gods-knew-what-kind of concoctions. They were likely intoxicating at minimum.

The whole room had a completely different atmosphere than the rest of the castle. Did Nox spend a lot of time here? There wasn't a single speck of dust in the entire room. I didn't understand how it could be so sterile and so cozy at the same time.

I was supposed to be mapping out the castle, but the chairs looked so comfortable. I could return to my mapmaking later—thousands of books were calling my name.

The shelves were endless, the top five out of reach to me. Maybe Nox had a ladder hidden somewhere around here? Or, more likely, he just used his magick to reach whatever he needed.

It must be nice to call on such abilities at whim. Something acidic hit the back of my throat at the thought, and I had to swallow hard to get rid of it. I would never know what that felt like—there was no point in dwelling on it now.

Surely there were answers to my questions about the Night Realm in the books, or what it meant to be a godling? I walked along row after row, trying to decide where to start, but truthfully, it was overwhelming. There were no labels or indications of what subjects the books covered besides the titles neatly pressed into their leatherbound spines. I'd have to leaf through them by hand.

This would take forever. It would be much faster to ask the god in question, but what was immortality for if not avoiding unnecessary encounters?

I walked back to the sitting area I'd found earlier, tossing a log into the dwindling fire before venturing towards the closest shelf. I had to start somewhere, and since Nox apparently didn't believe in helpful guides, I'd have to dive in blind.

The first three books I flipped through weren't helpful—just texts on rituals used to honor the gods. I'd read through manifestos like those hundreds of times. I needed information on the Immortal world.

I was luckier with the next one. It was leatherbound like the rest, but the cover was embossed with silver writing declaring it an early history of the Night Realm. This was exactly what I needed, especially if Nox was as old a god as I assumed he was.

Tucking the book under my arm and making my way back to

the chairs I was dying to sink into, it hit me again just how quiet this place really was. I'd craved silence my entire life, and now I had it. It felt… bittersweet.

The velvet of the overstuffed chair was plush under my fingers, and the cushion melted around me as I sat, tucking my legs up with me. I was suddenly grateful that I'd dressed the way I had this morning: a simple black cloth dress, thin enough to allow ease of movement, but long sleeved to keep me warm in the stone castle that wasn't very good at holding heat. The skirt covered my legs like a blanket, and an involuntary sigh escaped my lips as I got comfortable.

I could get used to this.

Of course, the library belonged to a violent god who was clearly all kinds of twisted given how easily he killed. I'd witnessed hundreds of his murders, so I shouldn't feel as comfortable as I did. I pushed that thought away—I had research to do.

"I should have known you would find your way here."

The low rumble made me jump, losing my place in the pages I'd started to read.

I looked up to find Nox leaning against a shelf across from my seat. His shaggy hair was messier than usual, and he wore dark trousers and a black tunic that was undone just enough to reveal inked, smooth skin. His wrists were sprayed with crimson, and his chest heaved ever so slightly.

I swallowed, glancing back at my pages before I zeroed in on his smirk. "Are you a seer?"

My dry response didn't make him laugh. He shook his head as he moved to the bar. My eyes didn't leave him as he poured some red liquid into a crystal glass.

"You're too curious to pass this place up," he explained, though I hadn't asked.

I turned back to the book once again.

"You disagree?"

I looked back at him. "Is it a problem that I'm here?" I asked directly, gripping the cover of the book with clenched fingers. I hated being interrupted while I was reading, even if it was by an entrancing god covered in blood.

An amused half-smile graced his lips. "If it were, you would have known the moment you stepped into the room."

I could understand why he was feared; his vague words held the whisper of a threat, the kind that sent a shiver down someone's spine. If I were smarter, I'd be among the terrified, but the darkness that lived in the back of my mind called out to that fear, to the sinister energy he carried. I didn't like it, but at the same time, it was comfortable.

Familiar.

"Do you practice these lines in a mirror or does Drystan stand in for authenticity?" I deadpanned, though I regretted the words as soon as they left my mouth. He'd been patient so far, but my reflexes were to push him away. Not just him—anyone who had the misfortune of crossing my path. It'd taken Tolith and Haryk years to wear down the barrier I'd so carefully built.

Unbothered by my rudeness, Nox rolled his eyes, stepping further into the sitting area to perch on the tufted bench in front of the fire. "Not your favorite, I take it?"

"Not your best work," I said, turning the page even though I'd barely skimmed it since he had appeared.

"I'll have to fix that," he murmured, like he was truly upset about it. "What are you reading?"

"Early history of the Night Realm."

"Are you finding it interesting?" he asked, genuinely curious.

I sighed. "Not particularly. I'm trying, but the words are all blurring together."

He chuckled. "Have you always been a poor student?"

"I've *never* been a poor student," I replied, offended he would make such a claim. "Perhaps you should acquire some more interesting reading materials."

He tilted his head, looking at me in a way that made me squirm. "Perhaps I should. Why don't you take a break?"

"I've barely started." I held up the book with the pages pinned so he could see how much progress I'd made.

"Tell me about your life in Kaedia," he suggested, moving from his spot on the bench to the seat next to mine. He sat with one leg crossed over the other, his glass resting on his knee.

I closed the book. "There isn't much to tell. I spent most of my days on temple grounds working with the prophets and sorcerers. There were nights spent with elixirs and... *you*, but you're well aware of that."

"You're an alchemist," he prompted, though there was a hint of a question in his tone.

A breathless laugh leaves my lips. "Definitely not. Botany interests me, and I've dabbled in elixirs, but I am no alchemist."

"Is that because you don't want to be or because you haven't been given the chance?"

The question left me speechless. In Kaedia, when your sight manifested, you were sent to the priestess to serve the temples. There was no question, no choice. I couldn't have decided to pursue alchemy instead, but would I have wanted to? Was making my draughts more about the desired effect than the process? I'd found joy in both. Discovering new plants had been the part of the journey through the Night Realm I'd been most interested in. I'd kept botany journals for almost four turns. Maybe there *was* some interest there?

"The latter, I suppose," I said, my voice softer than intended.

"How much of your life has been decided for you?"

I didn't like that question. Mostly because I didn't like the answer. "Most of it," I whispered.

Nox frowned. "I want you to have choices here, Stea. You've spent far too long at the whims of others."

I didn't know how to respond, so I didn't. Even if I'd tried, the words wouldn't have made it past the warmth in my chest. It was thick and all-consuming, matching the flush on my cheeks. I wanted to believe him, but I'd lived far too long in a kingdom with a ruler who made false promises. Doubt lingered in the back of my mind.

"There is one thing that is non-negotiable," he added.

"Oh?" I asked, though I wasn't surprised. I was here for a purpose—what that purpose was, I wasn't sure yet.

He nodded. "You'll begin training with Drystan and myself. You need to be able to defend yourself until your induction."

"From what? I'm still waiting on an explanation about what happened in the city."

He held his hands up in defense. "I haven't forgotten, I was just giving you time to settle in."

"I'm settled," I replied, gesturing to the camp I'd set up in his library.

"I see that." He tilted his empty glass back and forth before standing to refill it. His rings clinked against the decanter as he poured.

"So?" I prompted, as he returned to his chair.

"Where to begin," he mused. "You know that the four realms are only inhabited by immortal beings, yes?"

I nodded.

"Good. Normally, when a godling is brought over the veil, they are inducted into their realm rather quickly, ascending soon after. The induction ritual does more than secure your place in the Immortal world. It provides a kind of separation from the Mortal world and the status you held there. Until that happens, you have a target on your back."

I frowned as I mulled over his words. "Why are they so concerned with godlings in the first place?"

He smiled darkly. "Fresh blood, of course."

"Right. I nearly forgot Night's reputation."

Nox's smile widened, amusement dancing across his features as he leaned back in his seat.

"You believe that we're all monsters? Murderers?"

I moved the tome from my lap to the pile in front of me, crossing my arms over my chest. "I've seen you kill countless times—you have blood on your cuffs right now."

He barked out a laugh, lifting his arm to inspect the crimson stained cuffs of his shirt.

"You're laughing at mass murder?"

Nox pinned me with a pointed stare. "I am the Reaper, Asteria. It is my job to remove souls from the Mortal world when their time is done."

That... should have been obvious the moment I realized who he was.

"It is my role in the world, my duty, and my sworn responsibility as the God of Death."

My eyes met his, pleasantly surprised and relieved to have an answer to a turns-old mystery. Suddenly, the dark aura he possessed lost some of its edge.

"I suppose that's fair enough. It must be difficult."

He looked away. "It can be."

A moment passed, and the air grew too thick for comfort.

I cleared my throat, changing the subject. "When is my induction?"

He shifted. "That's still being decided. You're a special case because of your Mark. Most godlings are clearly dedicated to a specific realm. You aren't," he explained, before taking another sip from his glass.

Strange disappointment flooded me. "Then why am I here? You seemed sure that I belonged in the Night Realm. You called it my home."

"Selfishly, I want that to be the case. The truth is that you could belong to any of the four realms," he admitted, somewhat sheepishly considering he was a powerful, ancient god.

The burning returned to my cheeks with a vengeance as his words sank in. Nox wanted me here? I couldn't imagine a world where I was significant enough to the god that he cared whether I stayed or left.

"I see," I mumbled.

"Word travels fast in the Immortal world. Rumors of a godling with an ambiguous Mark have already made it to the other rulers. I imagine they'll be sending messengers with invitations soon. I'm sure quite a few are angry that I've made a claim on you."

"You've *claimed* me?"

His eyes burned into mine. "You are in my realm, are you not? In my home?"

"I suppose that's true. And you think the other rulers are upset?" I was desperately trying to understand the dynamic between Nox and the others. It didn't sound as if they ruled the Immortal world in peace, but I'd never heard of a war between realms.

He tilted his head, considering. A wry smile lay on his lips. "Lux most likely will be. He has always been one to hoard novelties. To him, you are another rare trinket for his collection."

A shiver ran down my spine. An image of butterflies with pins through their wings crossed my thoughts. Lux was not a god I wanted to be left alone with, I decided. Or maybe this was Nox's strategy to ensure I stayed in the Night Realm? He *had* said that was what he wanted. Could I trust him to guide me without bias? I wanted to think so, but how well did I truly know him?

"Will I be meeting him? And the others?"

"When you're ready. There is no rush. You have an eternity ahead of you."

The tension in my shoulders eased and I nodded, unable to form words. My head was swimming with new information and plans. I was doing my best not to drown.

Nox stood, moving to the bar to set his empty glass down. "One thing we can't wait on is your training. Take today to rest and read, if you wish. Tomorrow morning, we begin."

CHAPTER SIXTEEN

When the morning actually rolled around—not that I could tell with the midnight sky that gave away nothing—I was woken by several loud knocks on my door. I stifled a yawn and debated whether or not I wanted to get out of bed. I could always pretend I hadn't heard and get a few more moments of sleep.

Curiosity got the best of me, though, and I was soon shuffling across the room. I didn't make it to the door before it swung open, revealing the brunet god who had proven already to have a lack of manners and boundaries.

"Drystan," I groaned, a yawn escaping my lips shortly after. "What are you doing?"

"Good morning, sunshine," he trilled. "Didn't you hear? You're starting training today."

"It's a little early, isn't it?"

Drystan rolled his eyes, exasperated. "No, it's not. Can't you tell?" He gestured to the window as if I was supposed to see a difference in the sky. "Quick, get dressed! You'll need to be able to move, and I'd bring some bandages if you have any."

He disappeared through the doorway, slamming it behind him. At least he was giving me the privacy to get dressed without his pressing stare. I could hear him humming impatiently through the wood, and I was almost positive that if I took too long he would make me go in my nightgown.

I got dressed into a loose tunic and thick woolen leggings that allowed me my full range of motion. I was running out of clothes though; I'd need to visit the city soon to do some shopping.

When Drystan burst through the doors again with a scowl on his face, I was finishing the laces on my trusty leather boots.

"Oh, good, I thought I was going to have to drag you there in your nightclothes." He held the crook of his elbow out to me. "Let's get going."

I slipped my hand into his arm, praying to the gods that he wasn't going to make us arcane travel. Much to my relief, he guided me out of my chambers and down the winding corridors of Nox's estate. No portals or arcane necessary.

We walked through the immaculately groomed grounds in silence until I could no longer stand it.

"I read about Nox last night," I blurted out. I'd lingered in the library for a few hours after the God of Death and Darkness had left me alone, and I'd managed to make a dent in a few different texts.

"Oh?" Drystan prompted.

"The book I was reading went into great detail about his murderous activities in Edessa. The slaughter of mortals and whatnot," I responded casually, as if it were normal for a god to murder thousands of innocents. Sure, he was the Reaper, but the events described in the history books were far outside of his duties. The deaths had been triggered by pure wrath.

I did have to admit, the act he put on was convincing. I'd almost begun to believe the rumors about the Night Realm might be misleading before last night.

Drystan smirked, looking almost amused.

"What? You don't have anything to say?" I was curious to know what Nox's close friend thought of his crimes.

He smiled. "It might be helpful for you to keep in mind that every story has multiple perspectives."

"What do you mean?" I asked, but he didn't answer as we stopped in front of a large stone building just outside of the city.

Drystan opened the heavy wooden doors with no explanation, gesturing for me to enter.

The floors and walls were made of stone, though a thin layer of padding covered most of the floor in the expansive room. Along one wall, weapons of every kind were hung neatly, and on the opposite wall, mirrors covered every available inch.

In the corner of the room, the god covered in shadows stood, his green eyes trained on my own from the moment we walked in. Nox's intense gaze pinned me in place.

"Are you ready?" Drystan asked from behind me.

"For what?"

"We're going to make you strong."

"Here."

Nox walked over to where I was slouching in a rigid chair in his kitchen. He was holding a tightly wrapped bag of ice.

"It'll help with the..." He gestured to my shoulder, where Drystan had slammed me into the floor of the training room countless times earlier in the day.

"Thanks." I grimaced, taking the freezing bag from him and holding it against the muscle that was already sore.

There hadn't been much training. It had felt more like I was Drystan's personal punching bag for the morning. Every single time I'd annoyed him since we'd met was channeled into the severe beating he'd given me. Every time I'd been laid out on the mat and he retreated, I thought it was over, but it never lasted. He was right back with a new maneuver that left me gasping for air. No wonder he had been so cheerful this morning.

"It'll get easier," Nox promised.

I raised my eyebrows. "Taking a beating?"

He chuckled, shaking his head. "*Avoiding* the beating."

I scoffed. I wasn't so sure. The pain in my body agreed with the doubt.

"What else did you have on the schedule today?" Nox asked, changing the subject.

"Well." I had to come up with something to say. I wasn't used to dictating my daily activities. "I need more clothes. I didn't get to pack much before we left Kaedia. There are shops in the city, right?"

Nox nodded. "Plenty."

"But now that I've been thoroughly battered and bruised I'm not sure I'm up to doing much," I added, groaning as I shifted in the chair.

"No, you should keep moving," he protested immediately. "It'll be worse if you get stiff."

I sighed. "Okay, fine. I'll head into town." I moved slowly as I got up from the chair. I'd already been still for too long if what Nox had said was true.

He stood too. "I'll accompany you."

"Nox, it's really fine—"

"Call me Waelyn here," he interrupted, "when we're alone."

Something swirled in my chest, reminding me of the tales my father had told me about the full-blooded fae. With someone's true name, they could bend them to their will. It was incredibly foolish to give a full-blooded faerie your true name. Luckily for Nox—*Waelyn*—fae blood was only half of my composition.

"The others don't know your true name?"

He regarded me with a strange look in his eyes. "Only Drystan. Are you a faerie, Asteria?"

I swallowed. "Half. How could you tell?"

There was a small smile on his lips. "Besides the comment you just made? You keep avoiding my questions. Not to mention *these*," he poked the tip of one of the short horns that were hidden beneath the waves of my hair.

How had he spotted them?

"You sound quite knowledgeable in the way of the fae," I said, trying to keep the shock from my face.

He shrugged. "When something is part of your identity, you tend to become familiar with it."

I balked. "*You're* a faerie?"

"I am."

I shook my head. "I can't imagine… how can you possibly hold the position you do and not tell a single lie?"

"It *should* be impossible. But, I can't avoid lying here and there. I have had to learn to control the pain."

Control the pain? There were fae who had torn their own tongues from their mouths to cease the pain lying caused.

"But… *how?*"

He smiled sadly, uncomfortably. "Years of practice. Years of enduring it. I don't necessarily recommend this path."

Once I'd moved past the surprise, it was almost comforting to know that Waelyn was fae. He might be able to control the pain, but if I looked closely enough, I should be able to tell if he was lying. He had certainly been telling the truth when he'd warned me about Lux.

And when he had spoken of his *wants*.

Waelyn hummed. "Let's get going. I don't want you out in the city too late."

He led the way through his estate, pointing out plants in his gardens that he thought might interest me. He was patient when I stopped to inspect each one, stroking their leaves and asking a million questions. It seemed his anger at my foolishness during our journey here had eased over the days we'd spent in his castle.

When I was satisfied, we ventured further into the Onyx City. The streets were busy, the same as they'd been when I had first arrived in the realm. Music poured out of the square, citizens dancing to the thrumming beat. Most held glasses filled with intoxicating liquids despite the fact that it was early in the day.

"What do they celebrate so endlessly?" I asked, looking up at the god who walked wordlessly at my side.

He glanced at the crowd, stepping in closer to me. "It's tradition when the realm receives new godlings."

"Even though I am not dedicated to this realm?"

A frown tugged at his lips. "They, like me, are hopeful that this will be your home, Stea."

I couldn't form a response, and Waelyn didn't ask for one, he just led me to a shop on the corner of the closest block. It was a squat building, made of gray stone like most of the others on this street. There were mannequins in the front window draped in gowns and neatly pressed tunics. A gray cat lay curled up in front of them, napping on a folded fabric swatch.

The ring of a bell signaled our entry into the shop. The air was sweet like the perfume nobles wore in Dreka. Verena probably had a bottle or two of a similar scent on her dresser. Racks of clothes lined the walls, and there was a pedestal in the center of the room with mirrors surrounding it.

"Hello! Welcome to— Oh my gods, Lord Nox, please, come in!" A woman with copper hair appeared from a doorway in the back of the room.

"Hello, Cara," Waelyn responded, somewhat amused with her fumbling.

She was an older woman with laugh lines clear on her face. Her eyes were warm, a brown so light that they were like tree sap in the sun. Despite the extravagant items she sold in her shop, she was dressed simply in a plain dress with a pin cushion wrapped around her wrist.

"What brings you in today. Who's this?" she asked as her eyes finally landed on me.

"This is Lady Aura; we'll be shopping for her today," he said, introducing me with a name I'd never heard before.

I made a note to ask about that later, and reminded myself to respond to the name he'd given. I cursed the fact I had been too focused on Cara to study Waelyn's face for his tells. I would just have to be patient; catch him in another lie.

"I see."

Cara sounded disappointed, and I couldn't blame her; Waelyn was beautiful. I imagined a seamstress could get quite close under the guise of taking measurements. Acid hit the back of my throat at the thought. I swallowed it away.

"What are you looking for?" she asked.

"Tunics, pants—"

"I have a list," Waelyn interrupted, handing over a slip of parchment. "You can take her measurements and we'll be on our way."

"Of course, my lord. Lady Aura, if you could step up here." Cara gestured to the pedestal, offering a half-hearted smile.

"Thanks," I replied, moving to stand where she was waiting with a measuring tape.

Waelyn stared as I had my measurements taken. Every time Cara asked me to move into a new odd position or stretch a certain way, I felt the pressure of his eyes. It wasn't the heavy gaze that the nobles had when they had one too many glasses of ale. This was different. Curious. Assessing.

Cara finished before the hour was over, Waelyn paid in advance for the garments from his list, and then we were making our way through the streets once again.

"Lady Aura?" I asked once we were walking through the immaculate gardens of his estate.

He smiled. "I thought you would ask. I didn't want to give your true name to Cara without your permission. And it's close enough to your true name, just a different language. An ancient one."

My chest warmed. He hadn't lied on my behalf, just bent the truth. The true faerie way. "That's considerate. Why not use Stea?"

We were approaching my chambers now, which I was grateful for. My legs were screaming at me to rest.

"That is *my* name for you. It's not for anyone else to use."

My mouth opened and closed, searching for a proper response. "I— I see."

His smile brightened. "I'm sure you're exhausted. I'll see you tomorrow for training."

"Right. Goodnight," I mumbled, my eyes stuck on his until he opened the door behind me.

"Goodnight, Stea," Waelyn murmured, his gaze following me as I entered my room.

I couldn't explain why it was so difficult to close the door, but it seemed nearly impossible to sever the eye contact between us. In the end, he was the one to pull my door shut, the click ringing in my ears.

All the air left my lungs as Drystan slammed me into the training mats for the seventh time. I'd lost count of how many times I'd begged him to stop so I could catch my breath, but he only laughed and charged me again.

I was weak, and it was growing more obvious with the

passing minutes. A sharp pain had bloomed in my chest, and I must have looked miserable enough to earn some pity because Drystan left the mat to drink some water. I gasped for air, unable to draw a satisfying breath.

I may not have been able to access my dracon form, but I should at least have inherited the stamina and agility.

Waelyn stood to the side, his arms crossed and brow furrowed as he watched me wheeze.

"Why aren't you training with us?" I asked, stalling as Drystan approached the mat.

Waelyn chuckled dryly. "When you beat Drystan, I'll consider it."

Why was he watching? It was embarrassing to know that he had seen every failure.

"That's enough for today," he added.

Did he think I was too weak to keep going? "No!" I argued. I wouldn't give up. I had to be good at this.

"You won't be able to start again tomorrow if you push yourself too hard," he countered, his voice tinged with something like concern.

Drystan smirked as he spoke. "I don't mind throwing her around some more."

The shadows that festered around Waelyn seemed to expand, growing agitated and restless as he turned to the brunet god.

"I don't remember asking you," he said darkly.

Drystan laughed, holding his hands up in surrender. "All right, easy, easy. I'll see you tomorrow, *your godliness*," he teased, disappearing with the scent of cinnamon before Waelyn could say another word.

The god stared after the brunet long after he disappeared, taking deep breaths with a scowl on his face. Eventually, I grew too tired to stay upright, flopping backward onto the mat and unwrapping the thick bandages around my wrists that Drystan had tied on far too tightly this morning. I rubbed my aching arms, stretching my legs out as much as I could considering my muscles were already locking up. I hadn't trained this hard since Verena had tried to keep me in line with the dracons—until it became painfully obvious that I was different from the others.

"We can get some ice back at the estate." Waelyn's voice cut through the memories and echoed off the hard floors.

I shook my head. "Do I look that miserable already?"

"I just know what this feels like."

"Training? I'd hope so," I scoffed, making a great effort to stand without groaning.

"The adjustment," he corrected me. "It took me months to find a routine here, to find my purpose."

I nodded noncommittally. I couldn't tell him how my bones screamed for something *more*. I had no plans and no answers, but I yearned for something to feel right. I doubted this silly training would give me that, but I appreciated the god for trying. At the very least, it was a distraction from the ache in my chest that hadn't lessened since we left Kaedia.

A stretching moment of silence hung in the air between us. I toed the mat with my boot, a sign of nervousness the priestess would have snapped me out of at first sight. I waited for Waelyn to speak, or even to leave.

"I'll walk you back," he finally said, pulling his cloak around his shoulders from where it had been discarded to the side when he'd arrived early this morning.

I moved to the corner where my dagger and its holster lay, quickly snapping the piece of fabric around my leg where it lived before reaching for my cloak. Warm fingers brushed mine as the thick cloth was pulled from my hands, the smell of smoke filling my senses. Waelyn draped the cloak around my shoulders, before expertly tying the ribbon to keep it closed. I tried to keep the surprise from my face.

A difficult task, given how close the god stood to me.

Warmth radiated from his impossibly large frame, and the dark patterns of ink that were just barely visible under his tunic were on full display now. I longed to run my fingers along the intricate lines, to trace every detail, but that was hardly appropriate. Instead, I focused on putting one foot in front of the other as he tugged my hood up over my head and led the way down the stone path back to the estate.

CHAPTER SEVENTEEN

My training days continued for weeks, maybe even months. I still hadn't gotten the hang of tracking the passing time with the sky of stars overhead.

I had assumed my induction would happen soon after I arrived, but that was not to be the case. Instead, I woke each morning at Waelyn's estate, forced down whatever breakfast was prepared by him or Drystan, and headed to the training grounds. Drystan would then beat me to a pulp over and over again until Waelyn called him off.

Once, I'd passed out after a particularly rough attack, and woke to Waelyn kneeling over me, murmuring words in a tongue I didn't understand. When I'd opened my eyes, he'd immediately switched to reprimanding Drystan with a wave of anger I didn't ever want to be on the receiving end of.

They told me I was making progress, but the constant soreness in my limbs and the bruises on my body suggested otherwise. Every night, Waelyn walked me back to the estate. Sometimes he'd cook dinner and answer my questions about the Night Realm. Other times, he'd be quiet and withdrawn, meeting my questions with short answers before disappearing from the estate for hours. When he returned, it was with bags under his eyes and blood staining his clothes. Those were the nights I spent in the library, searching through old tomes for my answers.

Despite the temperamental god, I was learning.

The Night Realm had a rich history, and while it was true that it was violent, it was full of culture too. Full of life. I could see the similarities between Onyx City and Dreka—or at least, the stripped-down version of Dreka that Orien had created.

There were a large pantheon of gods that called the Night Realm home, and their domains were spread far and wide. Nox, the God of Death and Darkness, the Reaper, ruled them all.

I hadn't feared much in the Mortal world, but here I feared plenty. It was natural to fear that which I didn't understand. Or at least, that was what I told myself on nights I couldn't sleep because I was plagued with questions and incoherent whispers from the thing in the back of my mind. There were some evenings I had to talk myself out of knocking on the green-eyed god's door to ask about all the things I still didn't know.

Tonight was one of those nights.

I'd paced the lengths of my chambers over a hundred times. My legs were screaming to rest, to sleep before Drystan beat me into the ground tomorrow, but I did not listen.

I entered the hall and approached the large, black door to Waelyn's chambers. I tried to calm the hammering in my chest as I raised my hand to knock. Why was I so nervous? In the time I hesitated, the door swung open to reveal a squinty-eyed Waelyn. His hair was disheveled and he blinked at the light flooding his doorway.

Had my presence alone woken him? Surely not.

He stared down at me. "Are you well?" His voice was raspy and thick with sleep. "Do you need something?"

"No. I mean, yes. But it's not important." I lost my nerve as his eyes traced over my frame in that assessing way of his. I cursed myself for it.

"It seems pretty important if you're standing outside of my door in the middle of the night." Waelyn tilted his head to the side, the edges of a smile on his lips. It seemed he was in a good mood.

"I was going to knock. Besides, isn't it always the middle of the night?" I retorted, raising my eyebrows at him. I pulled my robe tighter around my body, wishing I was wearing more than the thin silk nightgown beneath. His burning stare was going right through me.

"Tell me what's on your mind, Stea," his low voice rumbled out of his chest, which I could very clearly see through the gap in his shirt.

"I have a lot of questions."

"And that's different from every other day?"

"I can't sleep," I added, as if that explained everything.

Still, he seemed to understand. Waelyn took a step back, opening his door a little wider and inviting me into the darkness that smelled like smoke and pine. Against my better judgment, I stepped into his room.

Waelyn closed the door behind me and crossed the floor to light a lamp. I was sure he could achieve the same thing with a wave of his hand given the level of arcane he possessed, but I noticed he still did things by hand that most gods wouldn't bother with.

Once a warm glow of light blanketed the room, I sat in one of the black velvety armchairs that rested by his obsidian stone fireplace. The fire within was only embers now, but it provided enough heat for me.

"So," Waelyn prompted as he stood in front of the small bar in the corner of the room, pouring two glasses of dark red liquid. "Tell me what's troubling you. I'll try and put your mind at ease."

"You can hardly be the one to ease my worries when you are half of them," I grumbled.

"Not wasting any time, are you?" Waelyn chuckled, an amused look on his face as he handed me one of the glasses and planted himself in the seat opposite mine.

"I'm not used to having time to waste," I explained, more honest than I probably should have been.

He seemed to ponder that, swirling the drink in his cup. "How about this: for every question I answer of yours, you answer one of mine."

"I don't know what knowledge I could possibly have to offer you," I replied, my brows scrunched in confusion.

"You'd be surprised," he countered, taking a sip. I wished I didn't feel the need to watch his every movement. I just couldn't tear my eyes away. "So?"

"Deal."

"Look at us, two fae, bargaining," he mused. "How very natural."

"I'm only half fae," I reminded him, but he rolled his eyes.

"You bear the signs of your heritage, you're fae enough."

I nearly preened under the weight of his words. I'd spent so many years being told I wasn't dracon enough, I was almost afraid to claim my faerie blood.

"Go on. I'm waiting to hear why I concern you so deeply," Waelyn teased, but the look in his eyes was unwavering.

I shifted in my seat. "You are an all-powerful god. Do I need further reason to be wary of you?"

"You show no hesitancy with Drystan, and he is far older than I."

"He is not the God of Death. His arcane doesn't make the air thick."

"So, you fear power?"

"*No*," I replied pointedly. "Do you truly not understand why you are threatening?"

"Oh, I understand plenty. I just thought I'd soothed your worries. I've told you I will not hurt you, and you know lying pains us. What else could possibly unsettle you?"

Perhaps it was the strange pull I felt toward him. Or the way my eyes followed him like magnets. I'd dismissed it as morbid curiosity all those years I spent watching the world through his eyes, but now I worried it was something more. Something obsessive.

I couldn't admit any of that to him, though.

"If nothing else, you are a strange man who is keeping me in a realm I know far too little about," I finally answered, but we both knew that wasn't what I'd wanted to say.

Gingerly sipping the contents of my glass, I tried to ignore the burn as it slid down my throat.

He hummed. A deep, gravelly sound. "Is that not what this is for?"

He was right. This was my opportunity to ask everything I needed to know to quell the insatiable curiosity that swelled with each flicker of his shadows.

Unfortunately, I couldn't focus on any of my own thoughts over the ramblings of the thing that whispered the future. I rubbed my temples as I sorted its sentiments from my own.

"Are you feeling ill?" Waelyn asked.

I shook my head. "Just falling victim to my curse. That counts as one of your questions, by the way."

My attempt at a joke had the God of Death and Darkness pinching his brows together in confusion.

"Curse?"

"The priestess said my sight is a curse. Eventually, we all lose ourselves to it. The voice that speaks to me has just been a little louder since I arrived here," I explained. "And that's two you owe me, now."

"I'm good for it, don't worry," he assured me. "I've just never heard of a curse that affected those with the sight."

"Do you keep any oracles in your court? Perhaps there's someone I can ask about it."

"The gods that would know of such things have been asleep for turns, now," Waelyn said, sounding almost as disappointed as I felt.

"Shame," I muttered.

"I believe you have one more answer owed."

Overwhelmed with all of the possible questions to ask, I settled on the first thing that my eyes landed on.

"What do the runes on your rings mean?"

He looked down at the jewelry in surprise. "They're sigils. Some for power, others for protection. I'll have some made for you soon."

"The training, the runes… it's like you're expecting someone to hunt me down." It was intended to be a joke, but his expression grew grim.

"It never hurts to take precautions."

"But *what* are you afraid I'm going to encounter?" I pressed.

He held up his finger in a 'not-so-fast' kind of way. "That's a question answered, it's my turn to ask. Where did that scar on your stomach come from?"

I swallowed. "Which one?" I didn't bother asking when he'd seen it; he must have gotten a full view of everything when I'd nearly gotten myself killed by that wraith in the forest.

"The one that goes from here," Waelyn pointed to one side of his ribs, "to here." He dragged his finger to the other side.

"It happened when I was a whelp. I don't really remember anything but darkness," I explained. I'd never been asked about my scars. I didn't recall how I'd got most of them.

The god across from me leaned back in his chair. "That's not specific enough."

"You're being picky," I grumbled.

"You're not answering my question," Waelyn retorted, swallowing the contents of his glass in another gulp. He stood and refilled it before I was able to collect my thoughts.

When he found his seat again and I'd been able to prioritize my new questions, I spoke. "Has there been another godling with a Mark similar to mine?"

Waelyn thought for a long moment. "Once."

"What happened to them? Where are they now?" He'd sparked my curiosity. I was under the impression that I was the only one in existence with an ambiguous Mark.

He raised his brows at me. "You aren't very good at this game. Have you always had the sight?"

"No. It manifested well into my third turn."

He frowned. "That's quite late."

Was it? I'd never thought it was *that* strange. "It's rare, but not unheard of. It might have appeared before then, but I was in an accident when I was young that left me in the inbetween. When I woke, I had the sight."

"An accident?"

"It isn't your turn," I reminded him. I didn't like talking about the night the stars fell. It was the first time I'd lost everything.

"Still, the prophets I knew had visions when they were sprites. None reached arcane maturity without their sight." Waelyn looked contemplative. "Were you a late bloomer with your other arcane talents?"

"I have no other arcane talents," I told him, even though it was still my turn to ask a question. The words burned my tongue on the way out, fueled by the acid in the back of my throat.

His brows furrowed. "Stea, I can feel your arcane. It's stronger than that of a seer. Much stronger."

I faltered. "What do you mean? What— what are you saying?"

"You have other arcane abilities. Powerful ones, if I had to guess."

I stared at him. My lack of arcane had tormented me since the day I was old enough to realize I was different from the other fae. Now he was telling me he felt my arcane? Had anyone else? Had Verena? I doubted she would have avoided telling me such an important fact.

My head was spinning. I couldn't wrap my mind around what he was telling me, but I knew it had to be the truth. He looked far too relaxed. I downed the contents of my glass. Waelyn stood and refilled it with no hesitation.

"We can add it to your training, perhaps start seeing what your aptitudes are," he suggested once he sat in his chair again.

I simply nodded. I needed time to think. My stomach was knotted at the new information. "It's um… my turn."

He looked like he wanted to argue, but took a sip from his glass instead. "It is."

I swallowed, trying to think of something else to ask. "How often did you watch me through my mind? The way I visited you."

"Often," he admitted.

My cheeks warmed.

"Only after you'd visited me, though. It felt uninvited otherwise, and I didn't want to intrude."

"I didn't even know you were there. How is that possible?" I couldn't be angry. After all, I'd visited him nearly every night for centuries. It would have been hypocritical to be upset that he'd done the same.

Waelyn shrugged. "You haven't been trained to notice the signs. We can work on that." He paused. "My turn. How old are you? I know you aren't a sprite."

"Four hundred and ninety-two," I replied. "What do you feel when you look into my eyes?"

Waelyn hesitated. "What do you mean?"

I set the glass on the table at my side. "Everyone I've ever met—in the Mortal world, at least—has been unsettled when they look into my eyes. Even my closest friends. I've never understood why. So, what do you feel when you look at me?"

"I don't feel unsettled," he said, moving on quickly. "What did the former king of Kaedia do to earn your disdain? You were quite plain with your dislike of him."

"I should get to bed; it's quite late," I diverted, standing from the overstuffed chair that practically begged me to stay. The furniture in my temporary chambers wasn't nearly as comfortable as the pieces in here.

"Running so soon?" Waelyn asked.

If I hadn't trained myself to watch for the briefest signs of emotion, I would have missed the surprise that flitted across his face. It was gone the second I noticed it was there. He hadn't expected his question to end the conversation, but I wasn't willing to answer it.

"I'll see you at training tomorrow," I said, moving to the doors and closing them behind me before he had a chance to protest.

I woke the next morning to the sound of birds.

It seemed almost *wrong* against the starry night sky peeking in through the arched windows. The birds didn't know that, though. They chirped happily, singing unfamiliar tunes in their strange warbles. I supposed with time I could get used to it.

That was another strange thought. I had time. Immortality was at my fingertips; all I had to do was get strong enough to be useful to the Immortal world.

Speaking of which, Drystan hadn't pounded on my door. Usually, he retrieved me for whatever training Waelyn had planned for the day. It had been weeks since I'd woken up on my own accord. I ignored the oddity for the moment, deciding to enjoy the peaceful morning for as long as I could before my godly companions realized I was unsupervised.

I peeled back the blankets, bracing myself for the cold as my bare feet touched the stone floors. Getting dressed would be the first order of business. I crossed the room in a hurry, opening the dark wooden wardrobe doors and rifling through the fabric on hangers for something suitable. I assumed I'd be forced to train today, so I grabbed a long-sleeved black tunic and a pair of thick leggings. Long woolen socks and the new black boots that Waelyn had left outside my door a few days ago completed the outfit, and I felt ready to venture on.

My plan was to creep down the corridors until I made it back to the jaw-dropping library I'd spent far too little time in since its discovery. I made sure to tuck the new sketchbook from my desk into my pocket before heading out of my chamber and down the obsidian-decorated hallway that stretched on forever.

I'd barely made it two steps before the broad figure of Waelyn appeared, standing in front of me with a wry smile that made my stomach turn. When the priestess wore a smile like that, it never meant anything good.

CHAPTER EIGHTEEN

"Good morning," Waelyn said. "Or afternoon, I should say. You slept in quite late."

I frowned. "I didn't realize. Did I miss training?"

He shook his head. "No, we're taking the day off."

"What's the occasion?"

"You've been working hard lately; it's only fair you have a day to rest." He shrugged. It was a gesture that looked out of place for a god as powerful as he was.

Even in this realm, where everything seemed to have some kind of arcane affinity, Waelyn still radiated strength. I doubted he took many days off to rest.

I crossed my arms over my chest. "Seems suspicious. What's the catch?"

He chuckled at my words. "No catch. You've just been looking a little jaded lately."

I said nothing—what defense did I have?

"Come with me. I've made breakfast." He walked away without questioning my silence.

I let Waelyn lead the way to the kitchen. The mouthwatering scent of savory spices filtered through the air and caught my attention as soon as we rounded the corner. I spied two plates on the counter, filled to the brim with a variety of breakfast food.

Waelyn grabbed the plates and placed them in front of two chairs at the table positioned against a wall of windows. He gestured to one of them.

"Please, sit."

I moved to the table, trying to stop my jaw from dropping as he pulled the chair out for me. I sank into the seat, my muscles tense as he pushed it in, handing me a soft cloth napkin before settling into his own chair. He was making it easy to let my guard down, and that fact alone made me think I should stay on high alert. I couldn't afford to get too comfortable—I was in a realm of death, after all.

"Are you just going to stare at it?"

I speared an egg with my fork. "How do I know it isn't poisoned?"

He laughed dryly. "It's been weeks, Stea. If I wanted to, I would have by now."

"I suppose that's fair." I was starving; I would have eaten it whether or not it was poisoned. I just wanted to pester him a little bit. The ever-present soreness in my muscles demanded he pay the price, one way or another.

The first bite melted in my mouth, and I resisted the urge to sigh. I still hadn't gotten used to the food in the Night Realm. It was familiar, but so much better than what I'd eaten during my time in Dreka. Waelyn put the royal cooks to shame. Halfway through my plate, I had to remind myself to breathe between bites. It wasn't the most graceful I'd ever looked, I was sure, but if Waelyn noticed he didn't comment on it. He ate his own plate, smiling down at the ceramic dish as he did so.

"So," I said when my stomach was full and I was almost sleepy again. "What now? What's on the agenda for my day off?"

"Well, I typically head to my office after breakfast," Waelyn said, wiping a cloth across his face as he settled into his chair.

It seemed I wasn't the only one feeling a bit sluggish after such a big meal.

"I can't imagine a god like you has much paperwork."

He shrugged. "Comes with the territory."

I squinted at him, but followed nonetheless as he made his way down to the decadent library housed beneath starry vaulted ceilings. An eternity could be spent *here*, I supposed. I'd fallen in love with this library.

"Don't you think this is all a bit extravagant for an office?" I teased, making my way to my favourite armchair in the corner.

"Perhaps I have extravagant taste."

I knew that wasn't true. Sure, his estate was elegant, but it wasn't over the top like Orien's gaudy decor. *Extravagant* wasn't a word I would use to describe Waelyn.

He walked across the room to a desk I had never noticed before. In the corner, it was almost hidden by the shadows that lurked there. I wondered if that was on purpose. Waelyn lowered himself into the large leather chair behind it. My eyes were glued to him as he rifled through the drawers for bits of parchment.

"Do you have a question?" he asked without looking up.

Was my stare that heavy?

"Not at the moment," I replied, shifting my focus to the pile of books Waelyn had gathered for me a couple of weeks ago. I still hadn't read through its entirety. I picked up the one on the top of the stack, flipping through the pages until I came across the thin strip of fabric I'd used as a bookmark the last time I was here.

"Don't hesitate to ask when one does come up," he said, smirking in that effortlessly subtle way of his.

"I never do," I assured him brightly.

He smiled at that, before shaking his head and focusing on the papers before him once again. I decided to follow his lead, turning my attention away from the messy dark curls that brushed his jaw and back to the text I'd been trying to get through for weeks now. I liked to think it wasn't my fault that I'd been so distracted lately, but I knew that wasn't true. I'd spent far too many nights staring out of my bedroom windows watching the Onyx City below when I should have been studying.

Gods, now I sounded like the priestess.

That thought made me smile to myself before I realized I'd been stuck on the same page for the last few minutes. Holding in the groan that tried to escape my lips, I tried for the umpteenth time to finish yet another text on the history of the four realms. It wasn't that it was boring, per se… it was just difficult to understand out of context. I hadn't seen enough of the realms to make sense of all the little details that were packed into this dusty tome. I had half a mind to ask Waelyn to take me out of the Night Realm to see the other three.

"Can gods cross into other realms?" I asked, breaking the comfortable silence that had settled over us.

Waelyn's eyes met mine as soon as I spoke, giving me his undivided attention.

"Powerful ones, when invited."

"Can you do it?" I pushed.

He grinned, showing off pointed incisors. "Of course I can."

"Hmm."

His answer wasn't particularly surprising. Arcane rolled off him even now. It filled the room and pressed against the walls like there was never enough space to contain it all. If anyone had the ability, it would be the ancient ruler of the Night Realm.

I wanted to ask exactly how old he was, but it felt rude, somehow, so I kept that question to myself, putting the tome I'd been struggling with aside in favor of one that outlined different types of flora that could be found in the Night Realm. It wasn't the most relevant reading I could be doing, but it was interesting, and that was what I needed in order to stay awake in this too-soft chair.

Hours passed that way. I fought to keep my eyelids open and pestered Waelyn with questions when they popped up. He worked at his desk in the corner, scratching out lines on parchment until a steady drizzle of rain started falling. Then he moved over to the sitting area I occupied, lighting a fire in the obsidian fireplace and settling into the armchair across from me. I couldn't help but watch him over the top of my book. He grabbed his own from the stack between our chairs and propped his legs up on the low table that rested in front of him.

Barely five minutes had passed when he broke the silence.

"I can see why you haven't made much progress here. These are rather boring," he said with disdain.

I scoffed. "That's putting it lightly."

"Indeed," he muttered to himself. "I may be able to spare some time to give you real lessons on the realms. If you still have the energy after training, that is."

"Yes. *Please*. Gods, that would help so much."

He chuckled. "Alright, I'll see what I can—"

Waelyn's words were cut short as the doors to the library swung open, clattering off the walls with a loud crash. In the entryway stood Drystan, panting and out of breath.

"You—" he took a breath, "have a visitor."

Waelyn frowned. "I'll see to them later, you're interrupting."

Drystan winced. "It's a messenger from the Light Realm."

Waelyn cursed under his breath. "Fine." He turned his focus to me. "I'm sorry, Stea. I'll be back as soon as I'm able. Drystan, stay with her while I'm gone."

Drystan gave Waelyn a casual salute, then the God of Death and Darkness was gone, disappearing into the shadows as if he belonged there. After a moment of disappointing silence, I realized Waelyn and our cozy afternoon had vanished into thin air. I turned to Drystan.

He held up a finger. "I'm not answering a single question, godling."

"I wasn't going to ask you a single question." I was going to ask multiple, starting with 'who is this messenger Waelyn is so stressed to see?' I wouldn't be able to find out stuck in this room, that was for sure. I doubted Drystan would give me the information if I asked, though. I had to be clever about this.

I wrapped an arm around my stomach, plastering a wince on my face. "I'm feeling… off today. Could you escort me back to my chambers?"

Drystan narrowed his eyes at me. Gods, he was onto me. Still, to my relief, he gestured toward the door. Perfect. We'd likely pass the main hall on the way to my room. If Waelyn had his guest there, I would be able to see exactly who had encroached on his private estate.

Part of me knew it was foolish; Orien had never taken important guests in the front hall. No, such conversations were almost always saved for his private office. Hence my surprise at the sight of a *very* pretty redhead fawning over Waelyn in the front hall. She was dressed in gold and white flowing fabric, though it did little to hide the curves I was sure drove her suitors wild. Even from where I stood down the corridor, I could see the stunning blue of her eyes. An acidic taste tickled at the back of my throat as her hand came up to rest on Waelyn's arm.

"Shit," Drystan muttered. "Let's go back to the library." He ushered me with godly strength, forcing me to take quick steps back down the hall to the room we'd just left.

"Who was that?" I asked, ignoring Drystan as he shushed me, closing the dark wooden doors behind us.

My stomach started to knot up, lending truth to the tale I'd woven for Drystan mere moments ago. Perhaps I *was* getting sick? I should visit a healer, if there were any in this realm.

"You weren't meant to see that," Drystan grumbled, collapsing into the chair Waelyn had occupied not so long ago.

They were a stark contrast, the two gods. Waelyn was kind, observant… intense. Drystan was more aloof, more casual, yet spiteful.

"See what? Waelyn's consort?" I asked, feigning nonchalance.

Drystan saw right through my act. He was good at that.

"It's not your business," he replied, shutting down the conversation.

I hated that he hadn't denied my accusations. But why? Why did I care? I barely knew Waelyn. It didn't matter what—or who—he got up to in his free time. He was an immortal being, he probably had scores of consorts. Orien had, that was for sure. It was naive of me to assume anything different from the God of Death.

"You're right," I conceded, hoping that if I pushed the memory of the woman far enough out of my mind, she would cease to exist.

Settling back into my chair, I found that I couldn't release the tension in my muscles. I picked up the book I'd been reading before, but my eyes were glued to the hands on the clock that hung on the back wall. They counted every minute that passed until Waelyn rejoined us.

Seventeen minutes and forty-six seconds later, Waelyn reappeared in the doorway of the library. I kept my gaze on the pages of my book, but I felt him arrive. Drystan shot to his feet almost immediately, but before he could speak, Waelyn gave one command.

"*Out,*" he said stiffly, shoving a piece of parchment into Drystan's hands as he walked by.

Almost instantly, the god was gone, as if his interruption had never happened.

When it was just the two of us again, Waelyn released a heavy sigh, lowering himself into the chair across from me once more. "So," he prompted when I did not speak, "I know you have questions."

"About what?" I feigned ignorance. It wasn't a good look on me and I knew it, but the toxic feeling bubbling in my stomach demanded nothing less.

"The woman you saw. I felt your arcane, Stea. I know you were in the front hall with us."

I wanted to ask how he had felt my energy, but I couldn't give him the satisfaction of being right. Besides, I could sense *his* power—maybe it was the same for him, just on a smaller scale.

I shrugged. "It's none of my business. It's been months since I arrived; I had assumed your lovers would start visiting at some point."

Waelyn scoffed. "That woman is not my *lover.*"

I pretended not to find joy in the way his lips curled in disgust. "No?"

"No," he said firmly.

"Alright then."

"Aren't you going to ask who she is?"

"Aren't you going to tell me?" I retorted.

He shook his head, the smallest of smirks tugging at his lips. "You're stubborn, you know that?"

I nodded. It ran in the family.

"I should have guessed she would turn up," Waelyn sighed, running a hand through his messy hair. "That was one of Lux's consorts. She was delivering an invitation to a peacekeeping event the Light Realm is hosting in a few weeks' time."

The relief that flooded my body was almost alarming.

"Ah… how exciting," I replied, though my tone lacked feeling.

"It could be. I'll make an appointment with Cara to get something made up for you."

"I'm attending?"

"Of course—you're the newest godling. It will be expected."

"I see… what else should I know?"

"Far too much. My greatest enemy will be there." Waelyn's tone suddenly became serious. "You'll need to be prepared to face him."

"Who?"

His green eyes met mine. "*Lux*." He said the name as if it burned. "Leader of the Temple of Light and God-King of the Immortal world."

CHAPTER NINETEEN

"*Focus*, godling," Drystan grumbled, rubbing his temples.

"I am focused," I snapped.

"Well then *try*."

"I am trying!"

"Try *harder*."

"Easy," Waelyn warned, always the peacekeeper between me and the brunet god I wanted to strangle.

"We've been at this all day," Drystan groaned, leaning back on the rug that lay in front of the library fireplace, his legs still crossed in front of him. The incense between us was nothing but ash now. "She clearly has no skill in the arcane."

Despite the fact that I'd agreed with his sentiment until Waelyn had suggested differently, his words stung. I wasn't foolish enough to fully believe Waelyn when he'd said I had arcane abilities, but I had started to hope. That hope was obliterated after one day of training with the gods.

"You can feel it too; you know that's not true," Waelyn argued. "We just have to figure out what it is."

"Maybe she's just got a strong connection with the sight," Drystan suggested, crossing his arms.

I shook my head. "I haven't had a single vision since I arrived here."

"You said your sight was noisy the other night," Waelyn pointed out.

"The thing that lives in the back of my mind and grants me

my sight was noisy, but I haven't had any visions."

"The *thing* in your mind?" Drystan echoed with a frown. "I've never heard the sight described that way."

I shrugged. "It's been there as long as I can remember. The priestess told me my seer abilities don't come from the Well, like the prophets' sight, so I had always assumed the thing was the source of my visions."

The gods were silent for a moment, pondering my words. The minutes ticked by; I counted the seconds to be sure. My head was killing me. Pain had blossomed behind my eyes hours ago, but Drystan had demanded we keep trying. The fact that he was throwing in the towel now meant he had truly given up on me.

"Perhaps you can't access your real arcane because you haven't been inducted yet," Waelyn mused.

I frowned. "I thought I couldn't be inducted until I'd been assigned to a realm."

"Typically, that is the case, but you may be an exception." He paused. "I would have to speak to the council, but it may be possible to induct you as a godling of the Immortal world as a whole, rather than a specific one of the four. Though your ascension will likely be delayed until you have selected a realm."

"Would my lack of induction really stop my arcane from manifesting?" It didn't make sense to me, but they would know more about it.

Drystan shrugged. "Maybe. The Immortal world is old and has rules that existed well before Waelyn or I occupied it. The gods old enough to explain why it exists this way are asleep or otherwise indisposed."

Waelyn had made the same remark the previous night.

"Asleep?"

Drystan sighed as Waelyn took over again. "Gods get bored,

just like ethereals. It takes them many turns, but eventually, they grow tired of living day after day. Some choose to hibernate."

It made sense, but I still wondered why a god would choose that for themselves.

"I'll assemble the council," Waelyn continued. "Try to relax, Asteria. I'll let you know when I have news."

I stifled my surprise at his use of my true name. It had been so long since he'd called me anything but Stea.

"Drystan, make sure she eats."

The god frowned. "Why am I the babysitter?"

"I can manage on my own," I added, wanting anything but Drystan's company.

"Perfect," Drystan replied, giving me a rare grin before disappearing with a surge of arcane and the scent of cinnamon.

Waelyn sighed in frustration, clenching his fists at his side. "I'll return as soon as possible," he promised, and then he too was gone, the shadows swallowing him whole.

I was alone. It wasn't a rare occurrence, but usually I was too tired from training to do anything with the lack of supervision. My head still ached, and I longed for the elixirs I had stockpiled in my room on the temple grounds in Dreka. I probably had something among them that could have cured the pain.

The Night Realm likely had supplies too; I just needed to venture out to the Onyx City to look for them. It was still early enough that the shops would be open. The only thing I needed was coin. Waelyn probably had plenty.

I started with his desk, pulling open the drawers until I spotted a bowl of shiny silver coins. I grabbed a handful, shoving them into a leather pouch that was in the drawer too. I didn't touch anything else; I already felt guilty enough for stealing his money.

I gathered the pouch and made sure my dagger was secure in

the holster on my thigh. I hoped the training I'd been doing with Drystan over the last few weeks was enough to protect me from whatever Waelyn feared in the city.

I took up a brisk pace through the estate, but despite the emptiness of the grounds, I felt eyes on me. I was probably just being paranoid. After all, Waelyn *had* drilled it into my head that it wasn't safe for me to be alone in the realm until I was inducted.

The streets were emptier than I'd ever seen them. Their party had finally ended, it seemed. The city looked different without the lights and music—more sinister somehow.

I needed to relax. I was being dramatic.

I scanned the names of the shops as I passed, stopping at the first sign of an herbalist.

There was no bell on the door, no ringing when I walked in. The store was quiet, the ceiling covered in crawling vines and shelves lining the walls with different-sized bottles and tinctures. In the center of the room, there were stands with jars of herbs, labels neatly scrawled onto the fronts.

Browsing through them, I found some familiar ingredients, but far more were foreign to me. I gathered the ones I knew I needed: alder, blessed thistle, cedarwood, cloves, along with some of the ones I hadn't heard of: echinacea, eyebright, feverfew. I wanted to experiment, and Waelyn had plenty of empty rooms if any attempts went poorly. I grabbed a few bottles and corks and made my way to the counter on the far side of the shop. There was still no sign of a shopkeeper, but there was a bell on the counter. I unloaded everything I'd gathered and rang the bell.

Minutes passed. I rang the bell again.

"Is someone there? I can't hear very well back here!" a feminine voice called out from beyond a doorway that was nearly covered with vines.

"Yes, my name is As— Aura. I just want to buy some herbs," I replied.

It felt odd to be yelling at someone I couldn't see, but that problem was solved as a brunette poked her head through the doorway.

She smiled, her teeth brilliantly white. "Hello! I'm Emrel."

The name swirled in my chest. People really should be more careful about offering their true names so easily.

However foolish, she was beautiful. Her hair was long, falling in shiny light brown ringlets. Her eyes were a vivid blue, not quite as bright as Verena's, but calm, like the sea off the coast of Itharene. I'd only ever seen the sea through Waelyn's eyes, but the memory was potent nonetheless. She was petite, but dressed in colorful layers that made her seem larger. Perhaps it was done on purpose.

The woman moved to stand behind the counter, and that was when I spotted the green translucent wings attached to her spine. They were thin, and fragile-looking. I was in the presence of a pixie.

"I don't recognize you," she said, tilting her head.

"Is that so odd? You aren't the first to say that to me."

She smiled. It was blinding the second time around too. "When you spend an eternity in one place, you remember all the faces. Yours is new. So, where ya from?"

I eyed her for a moment, trying to decide if she was trustworthy. "Kaedia."

"Oh, the Mortal world. I should have known—we don't get many visitors from the other realms," she sighed, like it was a truly depressing fact.

"Most don't cross between realms," I conceded.

"Most don't want to, even if they could! Who would want to visit a realm like this?"

Her words irked me, and I felt a strange urge to defend the realm I'd inhabited for the last few weeks. I stifled the words that bubbled up my throat, humming instead.

"I just wanted to get these; I'm not sure if I have enough coin, though." I pulled the pouch from my sheath, plopping it on the counter and untying it so she could see the contents.

Peering into the pouch, her eyes widened at the sight of the silver coins. "You have plenty. I'll get you rung up."

She swiftly organized the herbs and bottles before placing them into a thin fabric bag that would be sturdy enough to transport them back to the estate. I traded her three coins for the wares and headed for the door.

"Come back again!" she called out. "I promise I'll be at the counter next time."

"We'll see," I said in response.

She laughed like I had said something amusing, before disappearing through the vine-covered doorway.

I took that as my cue to leave, so I slipped through the doorway once again. The streets of the Onyx City remained oddly still, but I tried not to think about it too much as I made my way back to the estate. My boots clicked off the pavement, echoing down the alleys.

No, not echoing. There was another set of footsteps, coming from behind me. I tried to spot the being in the reflection of the shop windows, but whoever it was stayed just far enough back that I couldn't see them. I could feel their stare, though. Heavy and pressing. It pierced me.

Maybe I was worrying for no reason. They could just be following me because we were headed in the same direction. I was still in the city, after all. I tried to brush off the anxiety, but my hand kept drifting back to the dagger in my sheath. The voice in the back of my mind was whispering warnings I couldn't decipher, but I knew enough to move faster. I needed to get back to the estate; I'd be safe there.

"Oh, godling," the being behind me crooned. "I hate playing games. How much longer are you going to make me chase you?"

The hair on the back of my neck stood on end at the sound of the voice—like nails on a chalkboard. I started running, willing my legs to go faster than they ever had before. I hoped and prayed to the gods for some of the draconian agility of my bloodline.

I made it to the edge of the city when the being appeared in front of me. I stumbled to a stop, but the man only smiled. His teeth were pointed, daggers in rows, like the monsters that dwelled in the Black Sea.

"Caught you," he sang, tilting his head. "What are you doing out here all alone? Don't you know there are hundreds of beings just waiting to snap you up?"

Chills ran down my spine.

"I've been trained to defend myself," I warned, despite the apprehension that filled me. I *had* been trained, but I wasn't sure that I was capable of fending off this man. He was much larger than me, nearly as tall as Drystan, with biceps that were the size of my head. He had a number of knives tucked into a bandolier across his chest, and judging by the way his fingers twitched, he was itching to use them.

He laughed. "I'm terrified, godling," he said mockingly.

His rough fingers grabbed my chin, forcing me to look up at him, to look into his eyes. The moment he met my stare, he flinched as if I'd struck him. His brows furrowed, but I didn't look away. He didn't move. Just as Orien had been frozen in place under the weight of my stare, so it seemed was this man. I stepped back, out of his hold. He still didn't move.

"Caught you," I whispered.

His lips twitched into a snarl, and I knew the second I looked away he'd be on me, slicing me up with one of those wickedly sharp blades.

I stepped backward, much too slowly for my liking. I wanted to put as much distance between him and me as possible.

"What do we have here?" a familiar voice called out, somewhat smugly. "Did the godling get herself in trouble again?"

"Drystan!" I breathed. I couldn't even be annoyed at his tone—the relief I felt overpowered any of the irritation that normally sparked when he was around.

I made the mistake of looking at the god, and the man took his opportunity to attack. He lunged forward, his hands going to the daggers in his bandolier before I could even react.

Thankfully, Drystan was faster. Arcane surged around us, and the man cried out.

"Ah, ah, ah. I wouldn't do that if I were you," Drystan tutted. "Lord Nox would not be pleased." He turned his wrist, and the man yelped, dropping to his knees.

"I don't care what that god thinks. He is not my ruler." The man spat at Drystan's shoes, and the god's gaze darkened.

"Then you are not meant to live here, are you?" With a wave of his hand, the man was silenced, his neck snapped.

As his body slumped onto the paved streets, memories of the Veiled Night flashed in my mind. I blinked them away.

"You are beyond foolish, Asteria," Drystan sighed when he was sure the man was dead. "Are you injured?"

"I'm fine. How did you know I was here?" I asked, brushing off his concern. It was out of place, just like him using my name.

Drystan stared at me, giving me a once-over as if he didn't believe me. "Your arcane was calling out. I'm surprised the whole realm didn't feel the surge."

I frowned. "I didn't use any magick."

"Maybe not knowingly," he mused. "Let's go, I need to get you back to the estate before Nox comes home from his meeting with the council."

I nodded, following him through the streets, unsure why he didn't want Waelyn to know what had happened. Was Drystan protecting himself, or me?

"What were you doing out here in the first place?" Drystan asked as we walked through the estate gardens.

I held up the fabric bag. Vials clinked against each other. "I needed supplies."

He rolled his eyes. "You risked your life for..." He grabbed the bag, looking at its contents. "Herbs?"

"I had a headache," I said in defense. "And I didn't know someone was going to try and *murder* me. What's going to happen to his body?"

We'd just left the corpse in the city streets for anyone to find.

"It'll be taken care of, don't you worry." He sighed. "And no more questions. You're giving *me* a headache."

"Then we're even," I grumbled, following him through the estate until we came to the doors of the library. I breathed in deeply when the scent of smoke and pine made its way to me. The tension in my shoulders disappeared.

"Are you leaving?" I asked the brunet god as I dropped into one of the overstuffed chairs.

He scoffed. "You obviously need supervision. I'll be here until his godliness returns."

"Perfect," I said dryly.

Then, we waited.

CHAPTER TWENTY

Hours passed.

I watched each one tick by on the clock above Waelyn's desk. Drystan had dozed off in the chair across from mine and I'd ended up on the rug in front of the fireplace, trying to make it through a few chapters on the history of the Elemental Realm. I hadn't made much progress. Like the others, this one was also a slow read.

Zenir, Ruler of the Elemental Realm, was ancient, like Lux and Nox. He was the only elementalist who could wield all five. He was an angry god, fueled by the fire he controlled, and he had wreaked havoc on the Mortal world more than once. The kingdom the realm had founded, Itharene, west of Kaedia, was the only one spared these brutal attacks.

It seemed Nox wasn't the only one with a penchant for spilling the blood of mortals. He was just the one the mortals remembered.

I'd just moved on to the section regarding Itharene's rituals— the very thing that kept them safe from Zenir's rage—when the library doors creaked open.

"Drystan?"

The brunet shot up in his seat. "My lord." He swallowed. He must have been truly nervous to address Nox so respectfully. "The godling and I are here, safe and sound, as you can see." He gestured toward the spot where I sat with my legs crossed.

Waelyn glanced at me, meeting my eyes for a moment. When

he turned back to Drystan, he was squinting. "What happened?"

"Why do you assume something happened?" Drystan asked, staring at the wall behind the God of Death.

"I can smell the blood in the streets." Waelyn's shadows wriggled impatiently.

"It's a busy city, people bleed all the time," Drystan deflected.

"*Drystan*," Waelyn growled.

The other god said nothing, his lips pressed into a thin line.

Waelyn turned to me, crossing the library in half the number of steps it would have taken me. "Are you hurt?" he asked softly, scanning my frame to check for himself.

"I'm fine."

"Tell me what happened, Stea," he pressed, crouching in front of me with his hands on my arms.

I resisted the urge to relax into his hold and instead met his gaze. He didn't flinch.

"It was my fault," I admitted. Drystan shook his head. "I left the estate to get some herbs and vials, and a man followed me back from the shop. He was cornering me on the street when Drystan arrived. He saved me."

Waelyn's jaw clenched. "You left the grounds? Alone? Haven't I warned you about the dangers that are out there?"

"I thought that maybe I was strong enough for an errand. I didn't know the severity of what might be waiting for me." I sighed. "It was foolish, and it won't happen again."

Waelyn shook his head, turning toward Drystan. "How did you find her in time?"

"Her arcane was practically screaming. It wasn't hard to pinpoint her position."

Waelyn stood, pacing the room. He was agitated, like an animal in a cage. "You should have stayed here, like I *told* you to."

Drystan crossed his arms. "Agreed. Now, there are more pressing concerns we need to discuss."

"More pressing than Asteria's life being put at risk?" Waelyn snapped. "And for what? A few hours of alone time? Is an eternity not enough for you?"

Drystan didn't back down. "The man who attacked Asteria is part of the problem we've been dealing with on the outskirts." He spoke discreetly, glancing at me out of the corner of his eyes.

Waelyn waved a dismissive hand in response. "That group won't do anything. They're just a few grumbling beings who want the old ways back."

The old ways? What had changed? The man had said Waelyn wasn't his ruler… I'd assumed he was from a different realm, but perhaps not?

Drystan shook his head. "I wouldn't be so sure. These things can escalate quickly. I've seen it."

Waelyn paused, the two of them sharing an unspoken conversation.

"I hear you, Drystan," he eventually said. "Get home, get some rest. I'll see you in the morning."

The brunet god nodded before disappearing in a surge of arcane.

Waelyn seemed to have calmed some. His hands were loose at his sides, his face scrunched in thought, not anger. Whatever Drystan had been talking about was a bigger concern for the God of Death than my ambush in the city.

"Are you alright?" I asked, picking at my nails nervously. I didn't like the idea of him in turmoil.

He sighed heavily. "No. No, I'm not."

"What was Drystan talking about? Is there a problem in the city? Is that why you didn't want me to leave?" My questions were rapid-fire, but he didn't seem to mind.

He tilted his head back and forth, considering his answer. "There are some in the Onyx City who prefer the way the realm was ruled when the previous Nox was in power."

Wait.

The *previous* Nox?

There were *multiple*?

Suddenly, the memory of Drystan's smirk when I'd spoken of the murders Nox had committed came to mind. He'd known then that there had been another Nox, maybe even more than one. My mind was reeling. Were all the four rulers replaceable?

I began with the most pressing of my questions. "There's another Nox?"

Waelyn looked at me in confusion. "Of course. There have been many throughout the history of the realms. It is simply a title one inherits, along with the power associated with the name."

"What power?" What was Waelyn's and what was inherited?

"It's more… responsibility than power. The god that holds the title of Nox becomes the Reaper and gains the ability to travel between the worlds—Mortal and Immortal. Nox is always the God of Death." He moved to sit on the edge of the low table as he talked.

It felt better to have him close. His pacing had been making me nervous.

"But the darkness is yours? The shadows?"

He nodded. "Before I was Nox, the mortals called me Odros, the God of Shadows."

The name was one I remembered. Perhaps I'd come across it when I was studying back at the temples in Dreka. Odros, a god worshipped by thieves and rogues, blessed them with the shadows necessary to perform their duties. How had he ended up as Ruler of the Night Realm?

"So you were gifted the title? The power?" My fingers drew circles on the rug as my thoughts raced.

"No. I was destined for it. Others have held the title, but I am the true Nox."

Goosebumps appeared on my skin as his words sunk in. His shadows flickered around him, seeming to wriggle in agreement, and his expression was relaxed. I doubted he was lying.

"How old are you, Waelyn?" I asked.

He winced. "Six hundred and forty-three."

Barely older than I was.

That was why he remembered what it was like to join the Night Realm, what it was like to lack purpose here. It explained why he was more patient with my questions than Drystan and more willing to teach me.

"You left Edessa just before I was born."

He nodded. "I wasn't even two turns old when I was sacrificed, during the last Veiled Night."

My heart ached. He had been so young. "Were you… killed?" I almost didn't want to know.

He hesitated. "Yes. The gods saw it as an initiation of sorts."

"That's horrible."

"I don't think about it often," he said lightly, as if his nonchalance made what had happened to him less severe.

I shook my head. "I'm sorry, Waelyn." I knew I wasn't responsible for the crimes of the gods that brought him here, but I still felt nauseous thinking about how alone and confused he must have been.

"Don't be. I'm powerful now. I am the ruler of this realm. I changed things here, and that's why some don't see me as their leader." He shrugged. "They'll be dealt with sooner or later."

"You seem confident."

"I am. Those who lay a hand on you will die first. I'm glad

Drystan was there to save you tonight, but I won't deny I would have liked the satisfaction of killing that man myself."

The faraway look in his eyes should have scared me, but the warmth in my chest didn't seem to get the message, matching the flush on my cheeks.

I needed to change the subject. "How did your meeting with the council go?"

"They agreed. You'll stand before them tomorrow evening," he said, as though it were an afterthought, the least important part of his visit.

"That soon?" I murmured, apprehension filling me. I had known this would come eventually, but tomorrow felt too sudden. My entire life would be changed forever; from tomorrow, I would be a true immortal.

Waelyn shrugged. "Every other godling has been inducted the moment they arrive. You are already behind."

His words pierced my chest with a sobering pain.

I was already behind.

I'd been behind my whole life. I couldn't keep up with Verena, I never showed the same magical prowess as the other fae, I wasn't as useful as the prophets, socializing was painful for me, and now I was already behind in the life I hadn't known I was going to have. My chest burned with the overwhelming feeling of failure, and my shoulders wound tightly, as though readying me to fight off the pain. I swallowed, knowing I needed to be far from Waelyn's prying eyes before the tears came.

"Right, I should go then," I muttered, leaving the book on the floor and clambering to my feet.

I had barely taken a step before a rough hand closed around my wrist.

"Why are you upset?" Waelyn asked, his brows furrowed.

He was genuinely confused—how could he not understand?

I was being thrown into a world I hadn't expected to see until a few weeks ago, and everything was changing. I had just gotten used to my routine in the Night Realm, and now I was being inducted.

What bothered me more was the fact that Waelyn had been able to read me. I'd worked for nearly three centuries to become an unreadable mask under the priestess's instruction. How had he chipped away at that so effortlessly?

"What was it you said about assuming things?" I asked in response.

He narrowed his eyes at the deflection, but it was all I could really do. With lying off the table, I had to avoid his questions carefully when the answers were uncomfortable.

"I am not easily distracted, Stea." Waelyn's tone was almost a warning, his eerily glowing eyes burning into mine. Green on violet.

"I said nothing about your focus," I retorted. I couldn't handle his persistence. I would not be pressured into spilling my guts. "I must prepare. I'm sure the council wouldn't appreciate the first godling in centuries standing before them looking disheveled and with no knowledge of their customs."

A moment passed, the only sound being that of my footsteps walking towards the door.

"They'll be grateful you stand before them at all, Asteria. You needn't worry about their judgment." Waelyn's voice was softer now, the tone he reserved for the fleeting moments when we were completely alone.

His words eased some of the restlessness in my chest, but I was still suffocating. Every breath felt like my last.

"If you'll excuse me."

It wasn't the proper response, but I couldn't stand before him any longer. My breaths came in heaving gulps as I retraced my path back to my chambers.

Gods. I had less than a day before I became a permanent member of the Immortal world. I would belong to the gods and their domains.

I would officially be a godling.

It was several hours later when I found myself falling into old habits. I'd begun to miss the rituals on temple grounds, however tedious I'd believed them to be. They had kept me stable in the flurry of time, which I desperately needed here. Between the haze of grief, training, and learning everything I could about the Night Realm, and my impending induction, I felt beyond lost.

It was the desire for some normalcy that had me grinding a mix of herbs into small crumbs before tucking them into a mostly-dried petal. I rolled it tightly, whispering the words my father had taught me turns ago, and sealed it with incense smoke. It was a faerie ritual performed twice a year to smoke the blend I'd prepared while grounded to the earth. If my life hadn't completely changed during the last cycle, I would have been preparing a much larger offering for Haryk and Tolith.

Swallowing the pain that surfaced at the reminder of the fae twins, I gathered the freshly rolled cigarillo and a match, and ventured into the corridors of Waelyn's estate. The cold stone beneath my bare feet sent a chill through to my bones, but I didn't retreat. Maybe it would have been wise to have donned more than the cloth dress I'd changed into after bathing, but it was too late now. If I turned back, I would abandon the idea altogether. I already felt silly enough doing this alone.

The halls were quiet, void of the pressing arcane that usually lingered in the air when Waelyn was in his chambers. It didn't matter—I was headed to the gardens. I needed to stand with my feet touching the grass.

The outside air was brisk, and the stars sparkled overhead, scattered across the sky like crushed diamonds. I'd turned toward the path I'd walked a few times on the way to and from training when the scent of smoke wafted through the air. To the left, in a part of the gardens I hadn't yet ventured into, a thin haze of gray smoke danced in the air, beckoning me forward with its familiar savory scent.

I rounded the edge of the estate and spotted the source immediately: Waelyn, leaning against the dark stone of the estate, a lit cigarillo between his lips. The smoke was denser around him, tangling with the shadows that normally lurked.

I backpedaled, hoping to retreat down the path before he noticed I'd ever been there, but as soon as I turned, his eyes were on me.

"Stea," he said in greeting, plucking the cigarillo from his mouth with two fingers. "It's late, what are you doing out here?"

"I didn't mean to intrude." I held up the petal-wrapped parcel I'd prepared. "Just a small ritual." Hopefully that would be enough of an explanation, considering he was fae himself.

"You're never intruding on me. I'm just indulging a bad habit," he assured me, waving me closer.

I took a few tentative steps down the path.

"What ritual?" he asked.

"Honoring Lady Veryn," I explained. "It's always been a favorite."

Waelyn chuckled. "I can imagine why. I've smoked quite a few of those over the years. I can't say I've always been functional the next morning."

I cocked my head. "Really? Usually I just get the giggles."

"I'd pay good coin to see that." His eyebrows rose as he took another puff from his smoke. "Join me."

"For free?"

"Call it a favor."

A heartbeat passed as I drank in the striking image he painted. His hair was damp, like he'd just come from the baths, and he wore a loose tunic that rippled in the breeze. His green eyes, normally serious and intense, were calm and bright. He was relaxed here, more comfortable than I'd ever seen him. It was a good look on him.

"I could use the company," I admitted.

He smiled, showing off his rarely seen pointed incisors. "Come here, the wind won't get you behind the pillar."

I followed his instructions, moving to stand beside him in the shadow of the massive estate, an entirely different kind of shiver racing down my spine as his body heat permeated the air around me.

Lifting the roll of herbs to my lips, I raised the match to the stone just behind us to strike. Waelyn seized my hand in his before I had the chance, pulling the match from my fingers and striking it against his ring. He leaned in as the flame flickered to life, holding it against the edge of my cigarillo until it caught. His breath fanned over my face, his closeness unavoidable. I forgot to inhale for a moment. As he retreated, snuffing out the match, my senses returned.

I took a long pull on the cigarillo, fighting the urge to cough as the herb-infused smoke filled my lungs. Wiggling my toes in the grass, I exhaled, watching it dance in the air with the gray haze from Waelyn's own.

"Lady Veryn," the God of Death and Darkness mused. "I didn't realize the faeries in Dreka still worshipped the old deities."

"They don't," I replied, struggling to find the right words as the fuzziness from the herbs crept in. "My father taught me about her. He was a herbalist."

Lady Veryn was known for blessing farmers and growers throughout the seasons for very small offerings. She was popular with the fae on the outskirts of the kingdom, but not in the city.

"Was he the one that taught you alchemy?" Waelyn asked.

I snorted. "Gods, no. He nearly blew up our cottage on the occasions he tried. He found me a teacher when I showed an interest in elixirs, but that all went away when Orien joined the council and outlawed recreational alchemy."

"Of course." He crushed the remaining end of his cigarillo against the stone, smothering it. "May I?" he asked, holding a hand toward mine.

Wordlessly, I handed it over. I'd already had more of it than I should have. The fuzziness crept over me slowly, and then all at once, I sank into the grass.

"That's probably the right idea," Waelyn muttered, joining me on the ground as he breathed the herbs in. "I've spent hours out here," he confessed, his eyelids growing heavier as the effects of the herbs kicked in. "In Elirede, we tracked every shift of the stars, every one of their flickers. There was always some party, or banquet, or ritual, or whatever else my mother decided to do to honor the occasion. At the time, I hated all of the fanfare. After I got here…"

"Are you still homesick?" I asked, twisting a blade of grass around my finger.

He breathed deeply. "Not anymore. Even if I went back, everything would be different. I miss an Elirede that's long gone."

I knew what it was like to miss a moment in time. His words ached beneath my skin, pushing words I'd never spoken to another out.

"Sometimes, I miss Dreka. The *old* Dreka. Back when I was just a sprite and my father hadn't fled the city. Before Queen

Eletha was killed."

"Why did your father leave?"

For once, I let myself feel what it would be like to trust someone with my deepest secrets. "He was afraid of what it meant to be a faerie in Dreka when Orien and his lifebinders were gaining power. He knew the tides were turning well before they actually did."

"But he left you behind."

I shook my head. "He asked me to go with him—begged really."

He rolled onto his side, propping his head up with his elbow. "You said no?"

I sighed. "I was… *involved* with someone in the city. I couldn't leave him behind, and he didn't want to leave his home."

The shadows around Waelyn flickered with agitation. "Even though it wasn't safe for you to be there?"

"We didn't know that at the time. Queen Eletha was still in power. I thought my father was paranoid," I said, in defense of the man I hadn't spoken of in turns.

Waelyn pondered my words, unconvinced. "What became of your lover?"

"He died the day the stars fell," I said quietly, the memory of the occasion playing in front of my eyes.

Waelyn frowned. "I'm not familiar."

I turned to look at him. "How could you not be? It was an act of wrath from the Night Realm."

His face mirrored my confusion.

"Tell me about it," he prompted.

The words were stuck in my throat for a moment, but after reading the sincerity in his eyes, I chose to tell him.

"It was just like any other day, I guess. It was after my father fled, after Queen Eletha was killed. I was taking flowers to his cabin, and…"

'And I caught him with another', I wanted to say, but I couldn't. That was a secret I kept close to my chest. It carried too much shame to speak aloud.

"… and there was this darkness. It was everywhere. The sky went black and it swallowed everything whole. He died in the chaos of it all."

Waelyn's brows pinched, his gaze faraway as he no doubt racked his memory. "What happened to you during all of that?" he finally asked.

"Gods know. I don't remember anything. I woke up in the royal infirmary a turn later with more scars than I could count. I just considered myself lucky, I suppose."

He hummed.

"That really wasn't you? The Night Realm?" I pressed.

He shook his head. "Not unless I smoked too many of those cigarillos and forgot about committing a slaughter." He winced. "That was in poor taste. Truly, I am sorry for your loss, Stea. No one should have to lose a loved one."

I didn't know what to say. The mortal had lost all favor with me in the moments before he died, but it would seem heartless to say that aloud.

"Tell me about these parties your mother would throw," I prompted, changing the subject entirely.

Waelyn tilted his head back, a laugh pouring out from him. I was entranced by the sound.

"They were always outrageous. My mother never did anything halfway," he said, his eyes alight with the memory of his years in Edessa.

"Outrageous is fairly standard for Elirede, isn't it?"

"Not like this." He wagged a finger, launching into the details of the masquerades and events his mother had thrown over the years.

High on his company and the herbs we'd smoked, I hung onto every detail.

Hours passed under the stars, laughing and sharing stories of the easier days we'd lived. Before all the murder and grief and darkness. For a moment, the thing in the back of my mind was still.

Then, the morning came, and with it, my induction.

I stared into the mirror in my bathing chambers. Restless violet eyes and unruly silvery-white tendrils of hair stared back. The dark circles that had always rested under my eyes were impossible to conceal, acting as a prominent accessory to the dress I'd found laid across my settee when I'd woken from the short nap I'd managed after coming in from the garden.

It was a lovely gown, made from a velvety material that melded to my skin, following the curve of my waist up to the high collar around my neck. Two thin straps rested on my shoulders, and the bodice had a single line of tiny glittering jewels down the center. It was simple, subtle, and beautiful.

I'd finished tying the ribbons to keep the thin slippers on my feet and still had time to spare. That was never a good thing. The excess time equaled time to think, and that was the last thing I should have been doing before I was supposed to pledge my allegiance to the Immortal world.

I hadn't even known this was a possibility a month ago. I was resigned to living a mundane existence as a seer, serving the temples and mixing my elixirs—but no, a Mark *had* to find its way onto *my* skin.

My breaths were hard to draw in and didn't fill my chest.

My skin grew hotter by the minute. I wouldn't cry; not here. I couldn't afford to show that kind of weakness.

Two sharp knocks on the door forced me to sober completely. I inhaled one sharp breath and blinked the tears away before the door opened without my permission.

"Ah, well, don't you clean up nice?" Drystan smirked, leaning against the doorframe with his hands shoved into his trouser pockets.

Where was Waelyn? Why wasn't he the one collecting me?

"Well, except for that frown. Are you sure you even know *how* to smile?"

"I know how; it just seems to disappear in your presence," I retorted.

"So cold," he said mockingly, his hand over his heart.

"Frigid. Did you need something, or are you just here to bother me?"

Drystan frowned. "I'm here to escort you to the council; is it not obvious by my absolutely *dashing* attire?"

He did look more dressed up than the last time I'd seen him, but I assumed that was because we'd spent the day training. There was no need to dress extravagantly for that. His brown hair was styled neatly, pushed off to one side, and he wore black trousers and a navy tunic that fit him well, accentuating the bulge of his arms. He was an attractive god, but they all were. It came with the gig.

Still, one thought persisted.

"Where's Waelyn?" I asked. I tried not to sound distressed, but some of the traitorous emotion leaked into my tone anyway.

Drystan looked away. "He's busy this evening... and remember not to use that name outside these walls."

I couldn't even begin to process Drystan's words as my mind whirled with what the God of Death and Darkness could be doing that was more important than attending the induction of the first godling in turns. Maybe that was a conceited thought.

"Did you hear me?" Drystan asked when I didn't answer.

"Yes, I heard you. I'll only refer to him as Nox outside of the estate."

"You won't need to discuss him at all this evening, Asteria. This is about you and your service to the realm," Drystan assured me, though his words just fueled the raging void that swirled in my chest.

My service—right. I wasn't here to simply exist, I was here for a purpose. I was nothing if not useful to others. I'd nearly forgotten—I'd spent too much time here. Waelyn had allowed me to live however I wished, and that wasn't what my future entailed.

I was destined to serve, not to live.

CHAPTER TWENTY-ONE

"We should go, we're running behind—could you *try* to look a little less miserable, *please*?" Drystan grumbled with a wave of his hand, preparing to transport us to the council.

"Can't we get there some other way?" I asked.

The immediate look on his face told me the answer was no.

I gripped the crook of his elbow when he offered it to me, my body instantly contorting in a way that would make me sick if I thought about it too much.

The breath was sucked from my lungs as my body twisted and compressed in ways it definitely shouldn't. I clutched Drystan's arm tightly, showing more fear than I would have liked to, but he placed a reassuring hand on my bicep until the floor under us was solid again.

"I forgot about your fear of arcane travel," he said nonchalantly, brushing imaginary dust from his shoulders and straightening his tunic after I released him.

"It would be ridiculous to be *afraid* of arcane travel," I retorted, crossing my arms. Never mind the fact that I *was* quite anxious about it.

Drystan merely shook his head, and I took a moment to absorb our new surroundings. Obsidian pillars rose high above to create a huge room around us. The room was free from, well, anything really, besides six simple stone chairs that resembled small thrones toward one wall. The wind whipped through the open gaps between the dark, sparkling stone, and when I looked through the pillars, my stomach turned. We were at the peak of the Temple of Night, the giant obelisk that speared the forever starry sky of the Night Realm.

"I've never been this high up before." I hated the awe my voice held, and I hated the way Drystan laughed immediately.

"Aren't you a dracon?" he asked, disbelief clear in his tone.

I winced. "Half." I wasn't going to tell him I'd never been able to shift. I didn't know what it felt like to fly, unlike the rest of my kind. No magick from my fae side, and no dragon form from the dracon side—I was nearly mortal.

Suddenly, the wind blew harder, stinging with its force. I stumbled back in my silk slippers. I regretted wearing them over the trusty leather boots that were sitting at the bottom of my wardrobe.

"Are you ready?" Drystan called over the wind.

Before I could answer, he disappeared, and the whole room was cast into darkness. I froze, and the wind stilled completely. There was the sound of swishing robes and rustling parchment. I wanted to feel the space around me, but I feared what I would find.

"Hello?" I called into the darkness, but I heard only my own voice echoing in response. I didn't dare take a step—I'd seen how high up we were moments ago, and there were no railings to stop an unfortunate soul from plunging to the earth below.

A strike of a match cast a small circle of warm light across the room. There were several runes drawn on the floor around it, illuminated in the glowing blue that meant arcane. I took a step forward without telling my body to, and as I was forced to kneel in front of the runes, I realized they were likely the cause. My knee touched the cold stone, and the flame extinguished in front of me, instantly relighting near the pseudo-thrones I'd noticed earlier. Now, six dark-robed figures occupied them, watching me with hooded expressions I couldn't make out in the low light.

Without warning, the two occupying the center thrones rose, stepping toward me with unified movements. I didn't know how, but I knew I shouldn't speak. I wasn't sure if my mouth would open if I tried, considering the magick that held me to the floor now. I should have been afraid as they neared, but I wasn't.

A cool sense of calm washed over me, invading my senses like thick smoke. It was a foreign feeling, not one of my own, but I welcomed it. It slowed the rapid beating of my heart and the tension in my body, but most importantly, it made me feel safe.

"Marked for the gods, your destiny lies here."

They spoke in octaves, sending a shiver down my spine. I couldn't see their faces, even as they stood directly over me. My breath came quicker, in time with my pounding heartbeat, and once again that calming sensation rolled over me, leaving the air cooler than before. The pair in front of me stopped moving, reaching one hand each toward me. The spot above my shoulder blades burned—my Mark.

"Marked one, godling. We name you—Asteria of the Immortal world."

At the end of their unified chant, they reached forward, and my Mark grew painful. Their cold fingertips brushed my forehead, and darkness took me.

I was dancing.

An orchestra of strings played enchanting melodies off to one side of the massive gold-gilded ballroom. On the other side of the enormous room, table after table of food and drinks were laid out for the partygoers around me. There must have been hundreds in attendance, getting drunk from the endless fountains of what I guessed was arcwine, and dancing on the wooden floors where I swayed.

The party was… *lively*. Excited chatter and laughter bounced off the walls, keeping time with the merry waltz the strings were singing. It was almost enough to distract me from the warm pressure on my waist and the large frame guiding me to the beat. Tanned hands held me tightly to a chiseled frame clothed in white and beige, with golden accents around his fingers and wrists. My stomach lurched at his sandy blonde hair and chiseled cheekbones, but what unsettled me the most was the molten gold of his eyes.

I was looking into the eyes of a god.

More than that, I was *dancing* with him.

Who was he? He seemed familiar, but I couldn't quite place him. His eyes… I'd definitely seen that golden gaze before. I assumed he belonged to the Temple of Light, but that was just based on his appearance. He could originate from any of the four temples and I wouldn't know.

Why was I letting him hold me like this? I could feel the entirety of his body pressed against mine. Why was I here? I looked around the room for familiar faces, but I spotted no one I knew among the drunken crowd.

"Are you looking for help, little godling?" His voice was surprisingly icy for how warm he looked.

My skin prickled as I tensed in his arms.

"You won't find any here; I'm afraid your companions are occupied." There was amusement in his eyes and malice dripping from his tongue.

Companions? Who had come here with me? Where *was* here? I had a feeling this god wasn't going to be kind enough to answer my questions.

Something dark poked at the edge of my mind, foreign, but

at the same time oddly familiar. This whole situation felt that way, and it was starting to drive me mad. The god holding me dug his fingers into my waist as that darkness grew sharper, more present.

"*Asteria*," it called.

Was I meant to answer?

"*Asteria.*"

I jolted awake, taking in the scene around me. Dark curtains hung from the ceiling to the floor, covering rounded windows, and the scent of pine and dust filled the space around me. There were smooth silk sheets under me, but the god staring at me intensely, his lips parted as though he had been speaking, was what drew my attention.

"Where… where did the blond man go?" I asked, restarting when my voice was too hoarse to get the words out.

Waelyn's brow furrowed in confusion. "What are you talking about?"

"The man. The one from the ballroom with the…"

Waelyn's expression only grew more confused as I spoke, and that's when it hit me.

I'd had a vision.

"Did you hit your head during your induction?" he asked, pressing a finger to my temple. There was a surge of power, but it retracted as quickly as it had come.

"No. Well, I'm not sure. The last thing I remember was the council speaking my name."

"And what of this blond man?"

"I… I think it was a vision."

"I see. Well, I suppose that's a good thing, isn't it?" He didn't look so convinced. "How often did you have them before?"

I pulled the thick blanket up a little higher over my body, which was clad in a nightgown I didn't remember putting on. It had to have been Waelyn or Drystan who undressed me. I didn't want to think about which.

"Not often, and they never usually feel that real. Or last that long."

Waelyn's forehead creased and he tilted his head as he looked at me in that assessing, judging way of his.

"It worries you."

It wasn't a question, but he watched me for an answer anyway.

How could he tell? There had been a tightly twisted knot in my chest from the moment I'd woken, and it was dripping with molten gold. Something about that man felt… *wrong*. I could only hope it was some bizarre dream and I wasn't seeing the future.

"Do you know a god like that?"

"A blond male god?" Waelyn sighed, sitting on the edge of the bed I was tucked into. "That's a vague description, Stea."

I couldn't help but echo his sigh, leaning back against the velvety black headboard. The fabric was soft and plush against my bare shoulders, and I'd just started to relax when I remembered my bed was *not* covered in velvet like this.

I wasn't in my bed.

Where was I? The room around me was massive, with obsidian fixtures matching the rest of the castle. High, arched windows stretched up toward the rafters. The stained glass sparkled in alternating panes, portraying several different figures and temples. To my right, bookshelves stretched from wall to wall, stuffed to the gills with parchment, books, and tomes, much like the few in my chambers. To the left, a wardrobe, its doors flung open to reveal a smattering of gray and black fabric as well as a deadly assortment of weapons, hung neatly on hooks.

"Am I in your chambers?" I whispered to Waelyn, though I was sure my quiet words wouldn't keep him from noticing I was in his bed. Warmth radiated from him where he perched on the edge of the mattress. It took real effort not to lean into it.

He crossed his arms. "Yes. Is that a problem?"

A problem? I hardly knew this man and I was tucked into his sheets as if I slept there every night! "Do you bring all dazed godlings to your bed?" I retorted.

"Only when they're as charming as you," he said stiffly. My words had seemingly caught him off guard.

"I thought charm was your area of expertise."

"You find me charming?" he countered, amusement sparkling in his eyes.

"That's not what I said," I muttered, pushing the blankets away from me. The air was cold, but I needed to get out of Waelyn's bed. *Now.*

I'd just barely started toward the edge of the ridiculously large bed when his hand clamped down on my bare shin.

"Where are you going?"

"To my chambers," I responded, giving him a blank look.

He frowned. "No, you need to rest."

"I can rest in my room," I said pointedly, but he just shook his head.

"You won't, though. I need to keep an eye on you." He pulled the blanket back up over me, pushing my shoulder until I laid back onto his lush pillows. They smelled of pine and smoke.

"I don't need to be taken care of, Waelyn," I grumbled, feeling more defeated than I wanted to let on as he moved toward the arch that led to his main sitting room.

He let out a deep chuckle, the sound raspy. It left me craving more. "I doubt that very much, Stea."

He disappeared through the archway into the sitting room. A few seconds later, the double doors clicked shut. If leaving me alone was his idea of care, I supposed it didn't matter that I was in his room rather than mine.

I was too curious for my own good, that much was a known fact. I'd suffered at the hands of the priestess countless times for my curiosity, so much so that Verena had begged me one winter night when I was a whelp to give up on my exploratory endeavors. Of course, I hadn't listened. Perhaps that same spirit was what convinced me it was a good idea to poke through the countless pieces of parchment shoved into every nook and cranny on Waelyn's old bookshelves. I probably had enough time to be nosy without being caught.

Even if I were, what would he do? Kill me? I nearly laughed at the thought. I couldn't see a world where Waelyn actually hurt me.

The first piece of parchment I pulled from the shelf was covered in small phrases, some crossed out and rewritten, others scratched out beyond legibility. There were several heavily underlined, and one circled. Those were the ones I read first.

Made of starlight, an aura, a lie

Lost to time, lost to—

"It's rude to snoop, Asteria."

I jumped, dropping the parchment, but Waelyn was there in a flash, shoving the paper back into its spot. In the next second his hand was wrapped around my arm, followed shortly by the nauseating feeling that came with arcane travel.

When I opened my eyes, we stood in my chambers, just next door.

Had I upset him that much?

"Get your rest," he said coldly, releasing my arm as if it had burned him.

I stumbled slightly and took another step to right myself. I wouldn't embarrass myself in front of him. Gone was the somewhat kind Waelyn, and in his place, a god of Night. One that *really* didn't appreciate snooping, apparently.

I opened my mouth to protest, or maybe to apologize for going through his things, but he disappeared into the shadows before I got the chance, leaving only the scent of smoke behind.

CHAPTER TWENTY-TWO

The following day, it was Waelyn who knocked on my door to wake me for training.

"Is Drystan well?" I asked immediately. I hadn't expected the God of Death to speak to me after our abrupt parting last night.

Waelyn's brow scrunched, as if he couldn't understand why that would be on his list of things to wonder about.

"Yes," he said sharply. "Now hurry, we've got too much to cover and far too little time to do it well."

I scoffed at that.

"Get dressed," he instructed, leaving little room for argument as he closed the door to my chambers with a quick snap of his wrist.

He was being short with me this morning—perhaps he wasn't over our spat last night.

"Good morning to you, too," I grumbled, hoping he could hear me from where he likely lingered in the hall.

Rude awakening aside, I didn't have time to waste being upset at the god. I did as he said and hurried to get dressed, washing my face and brushing my teeth in the process. It would have taken a whole extra set of arms to tame the mess of white waves that curled in a bird's nest around my face, so I just used a ribbon to tie it back. I could do something more elegant later if I still cared. It was more likely that my arms would be nearly useless if Waelyn had decided to make our training even more difficult.

When I pulled open the door mere moments later, Waelyn's arm was raised as if he were just about to knock. A small surge of satisfaction rolled through me that our roles had reversed from a few weeks ago, but I doubted he felt any of the embarrassment now that I had when he caught me outside his door.

"Are you going to be warm enough? That looks light," he commented, his eyes tracing over my dark pants and long-sleeved tunic.

"The training room is always sticky," I said, frowning. "This should be plenty warm."

"We aren't going to the training room. Grab your cloak."

The look of impatience on his face sent me back into my chambers to retrieve the hooded garment. He seemed satisfied when I resurfaced with the black cloak in hand.

"Where are we going?" I asked, as he led the way through the twists and turns of his estate. When we made it outside, the crisp air brushed across my skin, leaving tiny bumps along my exposed arms. I tied the cloak a little tighter at my neck, pulling it around my body.

"There are a few different spots I want you to see," he replied vaguely.

He raked a hand through his hair, the sleeves on his dark gray tunic flexing as if under strain. He wore dark pants today too, but that wasn't unusual. Waelyn was almost always clothed in black or gray. The only odd thing about how he looked was his lack of rings. Normally, his fingers were weighed down with the heavy jewelry. Today, they were all bare. The only thing accenting his skin were the dark inked patterns that peeked out from beneath his sleeves.

"And the first is… " I surveyed the location he had taken me to. "An abandoned tower?"

We hadn't been walking for long; the tower was likely still

part of Waelyn's estate. The twisting stone structure jutted out of the earth, and it seemed to be leaning with time. It looked more like a hazard than a stop on Waelyn's tour.

"A jumping-off point," he corrected, stepping confidently through the doorway.

I took one last look at the cracking stones that seemed like they could turn to dust at any moment before following him inside. He was already halfway up the first flight of curved stairs that wrapped around the tower. I climbed after him in silence, waiting for him to explain himself.

Waelyn didn't say a word, even as we reached the top of the tower and stepped out onto the roof. It was in surprisingly good condition, given the state of the rest of the structure. The stones were laid evenly, still flat, and had no cracks, even after all the years they appeared to have endured. It was a wide platform, with no barriers to stop one from plummeting off the side.

"I hope you don't think I'm jumping off this tower," I joked.

To my surprise, he smirked. "And why not?"

Oh gods. Surely he was teasing? Godling or not, I was fairly certain my knees would shatter from the impact. To make matters worse, Waelyn had started to unbutton his shirt.

"C'mon, Stea, don't look so nervous. We're going to shift and take a tour of the Night Realm." He was almost laughing at me now.

The blood drained from my face. It was like my whole body had gone cold.

"You're dracon?" I ask, my voice hollow.

"Not by blood. All gods have a dracon form, though. Aren't you?" His brows were furrowed, and his fingers paused on the buttons.

I breathed in. It was a sharp sound. "*Partly.*"

His hands dropped from his tunic completely. Concern and

confusion washed over his features—so predictable, and yet, so genuine.

"What aren't you saying?" he asked, his voice soft in a way I couldn't take. It was full of pity, like he already knew what I was holding back. The not-quite secret that had plagued my existence and Verena's as long as we'd both lived in Kaedia.

I swallowed thickly. "I can't shift."

He's quick to follow up. "Can't, or have never?"

"Does it make a difference?" I snapped. I couldn't help it, even if he was being kind. The topic alone left a bitter taste in my mouth, and memories plagued my mind. I had been reminded of my failure as a draconian throughout my life, and it was all thanks to the fact that I'd never completed the rite of my kind. I had never shifted. I could never be equal to the others. I would always stand apart.

Even here, in my new home.

"Yes, it does," Waelyn replied, taking a few steps closer to me.

I hated how much I wanted him to touch me, to comfort me, desires that would have made the priestess see red.

"Just because you haven't shifted doesn't mean you are incapable. I've known plenty of late bloomers."

"That doesn't help us today, does it?" I retorted, still swimming in the anger that had swallowed me up like a raging sea. I could see his patience and his effort, but I could not make it to shore.

His hands came up, grabbing the edges of my cloak and pulling it tighter around my body. The wind was worse this high up, and our arguing only delayed us.

"Thank you for being honest with me, Stea," Waelyn murmured, his fingers brushing my arms before he took a few steps back to where his own cloak was thrown to the side. "Now, let's get going. We can't afford to lose any more time."

He moved quickly, undoing the buttons of his shirt, and then his pants. I did him the common courtesy of turning away, despite the burning desire to see what the intricate patterns of dark ink looked like as a whole.

"Have you ever flown before?" he asked.

I had. Verena had flown me up to a great height when we were whelps in an attempt to help me shift. I didn't remember the flying part as much as the plummeting to the earth. It wasn't a fond memory.

"Once," I said.

"I'll try to be gentle," he teased, and my body caught aflame, the warmth that had fled moments ago returning with force.

I fought to keep my expression even, to keep the burn from my cheeks, but I doubted I was successful.

"What are you doing?" I asked, fearing his nakedness too much to turn around.

"*I'm* going to shift, and *you're* going to let me fly you around the realm," he explained. "Any more questions? Because I think my *appendages* might freeze and fall off if we wait around any longer—"

"Go! Go! I don't want to hear any more!" I exclaimed, waving him off even though I wasn't sure he was watching me to begin with.

There were no more words, only a great surge of arcane flaring against my skin, taking up space across the sky. My teeth ground together with the effort it took not to combust under the pressure of such power. I hadn't been this close to a shifting dracon since the Veiled Night. I'd forgotten how much raw energy was expelled in the process. My skin tingled in the moments after, the smell of smoke lingering in the air.

I could hear the breathing of a much larger being. The edge of the tower I stood upon was cast in shadow by its great figure.

In the shadows, I could see the outline of spikes along what I assumed was his spine. I took a deep breath and convinced myself to turn around to face Waelyn's other form.

He was… *stunning.*

His draconian body was long and lean, nearly taking up the entire roof of the tower, and covered in charcoal-colored scales that shimmered silver in the starlight. I wanted to run my fingers along them. Dark spines did indeed coat his back, complementing the lethal point of the talon-like claws at the end of every limb. Like his fae form, he looked beautiful and dangerous.

I shouldn't have been surprised.

We stared at each other for a moment longer. His similar, but oddly different, piercing green eyes followed my every move as I hitched a leg over his back and tried to settle into place. My stomach turned as I realized what was going to happen in a matter of minutes.

"Don't kill me, please," I asked under my breath.

He snorted at that, shaking his large horned head. Seconds later, I felt his muscles tense below me. I took that as a sign we were about to be in the clouds and clenched my legs around him as best as I could. Before I could take another breath, he launched into the skies at incomprehensible speed. I swallowed the fear that lurched up my throat and pried my eyes open. They'd closed at some point during takeoff.

I had never been this high up before. Clouds left mist on my fingers as I stuck my arms out to touch them. I felt as if I could almost touch the stars, as ridiculous as it sounded. Waelyn had slowed to a coasting pace, allowing me the time to look down at the realm below us.

There was life down there. I could see it around the obsidian spire I knew was the Temple of Night. A city had formed around the structure, expanding in rings around it. Colorful shops, gardens, houses, and temples to the minor gods rested in those rings. People, though they looked more like ants at this height, milled around the streets. There were whole families and communities here, in this realm of death and darkness.

Past the lively city were orchards. How did anything grow without sunlight? Perhaps the magick was strong enough to supplement the sun? The rolling fields of lavender plants reminded me of the outskirts of Dreka. There had been similar fields around the city's edge, where a cottage lay that I hadn't visited in a few turns.

I expected to see mountains just past the field, like there were in Dreka, but that seemed to be where the similarities ended. The edges of the Night Realm were covered in an immeasurable distance of forests. They stretched on further than I could see.

After a few more moments spent coasting through the skies, Waelyn decided I'd had enough time to sightsee. He picked up the pace again, though this time I was prepared for it. I was beginning to enjoy the way the wind whipped through my hair and brushed my skin, leaving it tingly and chilled. I felt free in the air, like I belonged there. I swallowed the sharp pain that shot through my chest at the reminder that I'd never be able to achieve this feeling alone.

Waelyn kept true to his word, trying to land as gently as possible. Still, I slid off his draconian form as soon as I could, thankful to have my feet back on solid ground. Well, as solid as the damp grass beneath my boots was. I made my way across the patch of grass, trying to give him enough room to shift back into his fae form so that I wouldn't feel the burn of it all.

"Stea? Are you alright?" were Waelyn's first words.

"Yes. Are you clothed?" I replied, keeping my back turned while I waited for his answer.

He paused. There was a rustling of fabric. "Yes."

I turned, though I had half a mind to wait another moment to be sure. Thankfully, he was mostly dressed, just redoing the buttons on his shirt. His eyes looked me over in that assessing way of his. It was almost like he was checking things off a list, making sure every bit of me was in order. The priestess used to look at me in a similar way, but Waelyn's gaze was subtly different; warmer, despite him being a god of Night. His was full of concern, while hers had been brimming with disdain.

I wouldn't have trusted anyone else with the experience he had just given me. Even my own sister had to convince me to take flight with her, and I'd agreed to Waelyn's plans in mere minutes. He was… different, and I realized in that moment that he had come to mean more to me than I had expected. I had never had a connection with anyone else in my lifetime that felt like this.

Was I alone in that feeling?

"Come, I have much to show you," Waelyn said, gesturing for me to follow.

Without a second thought, I did.

CHAPTER TWENTY-THREE

"It's strange to think that there's been such a thriving society just through the veil this whole time," I said to break the silence that had settled over us.

"I used to think so too," Waelyn admitted.

"Are all four realms like the Night Realm? How did they get here? The first families, I mean. Not all of them are gods; surely it wasn't easy to convince ethereals to move to the Night Realm?"

He blinked at me. "They're all dead, Stea."

My jaw dropped. "What?"

"Your tutor must have worked hard to avoid that tiny detail. Everyone in the Immortal world has already died. Just as mortals become one with the arcane upon their death, ethereals are transported here."

Waelyn sighed, though his frustration was not directed at me. I was starting to share a similar sentiment toward the priestess. How could she teach me so much and so little at the same time?

"I'm not dead," I pointed out.

"Godlings, and therefore gods, are the exception. Though many of us died to come here. As you know, I was once ethereal too."

I pulled my cloak around my body. The chill of the wind was suddenly cold rather than refreshing. "Do they know? That they're dead, I mean?" Was that why everyone knew each other? It must be easy to keep track of all the other townspeople when no one new was being born.

"Yes. Most of them don't remember how they died, but they are aware."

"What about my friends? They were killed by Orien a few days before the Veiled Night." The words were quiet as they left my lips.

Waelyn frowned. "I saw them through your eyes often. You were quite fond of them, weren't you?"

"Yes." I hadn't shown it well enough, but I had cared for them deeply.

"I reaped their souls myself. They didn't suffer long at Orien's hand," he assured me.

"Are they here, then? In the Immortal world?"

He nodded.

I blinked away the wetness that pooled in my eyes. "Are they together?" My voice was barely a whisper.

"No," he murmured.

My heart sank.

"They are all unique, though I'm sure you know that already."

"I do, but it hurts to think of them alone."

"They aren't alone, Stea. Haryk is in the Arcane Realm, studying the magick he loves with others like him. Tolith is serving Zenir in the Elemental Realm, and you may see Sarya at the peacekeeping event soon."

"Sarya is in the Light Realm?"

Waelyn's lips pressed into a line and he nodded. "She is."

I couldn't think about them any longer and maintain my composure.

"Don't you find it morbid? To be around death all the time?"

He gave me a sad smile. "Not anymore."

I recognized that look. It was the expression of someone who'd been familiar with death their entire life. I knew it well, and I wore it often. I couldn't keep letting myself forget that he was a god of the Night Realm; a murderous, dark being. He wasn't the compassionate man I was making him out to be in my mind.

"How do you decide who goes to what realm when they pass through the veil? Aside from the Marked ones, I mean?"

He shook his head. "I wasn't a god when those rules were made. That has to do with magick far older than myself."

I frowned. "I keep forgetting you're young."

I'd been imagining Waelyn as some kind of ancient being, perhaps as old as death itself, but he was barely older than Verena.

"I'm nearly two turns older than you! You consider that young?" he scoffed.

Did he expect me to think he was *too* old? "Actually, yes. Orien was nearly seven turns and the council called him a whelp," I argued, defending my point.

"Councils are often made up of the oldest beings alive. I'm fairly certain that's one of the only requirements for involvement. It's biased."

"Verena was one of the youngest councilmembers in history, so your opinion may be flawed."

He smiled. "Perhaps."

I had to look away. His eyes were too intense, too enamoring.

I cleared my throat. "Are you going to tell me why we're standing in a patch of soggy grass, or should I wait until I've sunk to my knees in the mud?"

"That would be quite a sight," Waelyn mused. "I think I'll wait."

I narrowed my eyes at him. "Fine. Maybe you can answer some of my burning questions then."

"Oh, if they're *burning* then I must," he teased.

I swallowed, sifting around all the new information in my mind. There were a million things I wanted to ask, but something stood out. Waelyn was *fae*.

"Why did you give me your true name so soon after we met? That's the number one rule of our kind."

I watched the smirk drop from his features.

He averted his eyes. "Why wouldn't I? You gave me yours."

"It's considerably more dangerous for you. You're the ruler of the Night Realm; I am just an insignificant godling. I was practically a stranger when you gave me your name.".

"You forget, I've spent years in your company, Stea. You were hardly a stranger. I decided I could trust you."

His words hit me in the chest as if I'd been struck. Trust wasn't something that had been easy to come by in Kaedia. In fact, I could count the number of people I had trusted on one hand. He had given me his trust—his life even, if I'd had the power to use his name against him—without a thought. Suddenly, I saw him differently. He was vulnerable to me. Open.

It was too much. I swallowed the feelings.

"I suppose it doesn't matter that you know my true name. You use Stea all the time anyway."

"You don't like it?" he asked.

I shook my head. He laughed a little.

"It's ridiculous," I scoffed.

"It's not," he defended.

"It means 'star' doesn't it? That doesn't make any sense," I argued, crossing my arms. I decided to leave out the part where I'd spent hours combing through tomes to find reference to the term.

"It's what I thought when we met," he said sincerely. "You hadn't shared your true name with me yet and I didn't want to call you by anything else."

"So *star* was your best option?"

He shook his head. "*Stea* was my best option. It means more than star, it's… ethereal, almost."

I didn't have a witty retort for that.

He thought I was *ethereal* when we met? I had never been described as beautiful, let alone ethereal. Maybe Waelyn was delusional?

"Say something," he said when I'd been quiet too long.

"Where are we going next?" I asked, changing the subject. My boots were thoroughly coated in mud now.

Hurt flashed across his features and it made me wish I'd said something else, anything else. I'd never been good at this—at letting people in. It felt like I'd pushed him further away.

That wasn't true. I had been good at it when I was young. My life had twisted me beyond recognition. The old Asteria, the kind Asteria, was long gone, leaving an angry, awkward shell behind that shut things down when they got to be too intense. Too vulnerable.

"Just down this way. There's an old temple you should see," Waelyn said coldly, his tone far from the playful one he'd used just a few moments ago.

He started down the grassy hill without looking to see if I was following. I trailed after him, my thoughts swimming with regret.

I needed to focus. Now was not the time to be wallowing in self-pity. I was getting a rare chance to see the entire realm; I should be focusing on that and not the single chain I'd just noticed dangling from Waelyn's ear. Or the way his tunic flexed across his back as his body strained against the fabric.

Focus.

I chanted the word over and over in my mind. Alas, the beautiful god remained the focal point of my thoughts.

He led the way through a wooded area, the arcane trees swallowing us whole as we ventured further into the forest.

Eventually, he stopped in front of a large, crumbling structure. He seemed to have a thing for abandoned buildings. I tried to keep an open mind as he picked the door off its broken hinges and set it aside.

"In here," he said, before disappearing into the darkness.

I took a deep breath, trying to shrug off his bad mood as I stepped through the decrepit doorway.

Despite the temple's horrid appearance on the outside, the inside was relatively well maintained. Waelyn made his way around the large open room, lighting torches on the wall with his arcane. I ignored the familiar twinge of jealousy at the sight of magick so easily used, and decided to focus my attention on the strange markings on the wall that were being illuminated as Waelyn finished lighting the room.

Drawings. They were drawings. I moved closer to the cold stone walls, tracing my finger over a figure cloaked in darkness, portrayed in the darkest tones, and surrounded by other, smaller shadows. I knew instantly it was him. I followed the figure through different drawings—etchings, really—until his path converged with a much darker one. I thought Waelyn was drawn in black, but compared to the figure next to him, he was a deep gray.

The other figure... was pure night, and unlike the other drawings, it wasn't human-shaped. It was drawn as an erratic circle, energy uncontained. Even from the raw etches, I understood the artist was trying to convey *danger*. Following the new dark being from picture to picture, I found scenes of horror, massacres, and wars.

I turned, finding Waelyn's eyes already on me. He was watching, waiting for a reaction.

"Is this a prophecy?" I asked.

I'd seen something like this before in the caves of the

mountains surrounding Dreka. The images there were of golden-scaled dragons wreaking havoc over Kaedia. When I'd told Verena, she'd laughed. 'Lifebinders wouldn't cause such destruction, Asteria,' she'd said. I wondered if she still felt that way after a lifetime of serving Orien.

Waelyn tilted his head. "We aren't sure. Some think so, others think it's meaningless art."

"What do you think?"

He stared at me for a moment, debating whether or not to answer. "I don't think it should be ignored."

"What is this supposed to be?" I pointed to the dark, erratic shape I'd followed from frame to frame.

"More theories," he said noncommittally.

"Like what?"

He sighed. "Death, the Blackwell, the Old Gods... No one knows for certain. These events haven't happened yet." He gestured to the point in the timeline where the dark figure joined the God of Death and Darkness.

"What is the Blackwell?" I asked. I'd only ever heard of the Well, the source of arcane; where mortal souls went upon their death.

"If the Well is the source of arcane power, the Blackwell is what consumes it," Waelyn explained, the furrow in his brow slowly dissolving as he talked. "The Blackwell is an endless void of hunger. It swallows everything, without the balance of the Well. Or at least, that's the current theory. Some still say the Blackwell and the Well are one and the same."

I blinked, trying to take in all the information. "For an ancient realm, there sure are a lot of unsolved mysteries."

"The ruler of the realm hasn't always been focused on solving them."

"But you are?"

Waelyn nodded. "For the moment."

I shifted back to the wall to study the drawings. I was almost frustrated that our outing had generated more questions than answers about the realm. I had more than enough to think about for a century, and I had a feeling it was only going to get worse.

Waelyn let me inspect each drawing in the ancient temple until I was satisfied before he began to usher me along to the next spot on his tour. We didn't speak as we walked through the marsh-like field and got another layer of fresh mud caked onto our boots. I could feel Waelyn's annoyance in the air between us, an almost tangible tension. I hadn't realized my shutting down would turn his mood sour so quickly. I'd forgotten how sensitive he could be.

"We should eat," Waelyn said, and as if on cue, my stomach grumbled in agreement.

"Do gods need to eat?" I was half-joking, expecting him to say yes.

"Sometimes," he shrugged.

Another brisk flight through the skies and we were on the outskirts of the Onyx City. I averted my gaze while Waelyn redressed, and then he was leading the way through the weaving streets that bustled with citizens of the realm. Spirits? I wasn't sure what to think now that I knew they were dead. It was strange to brush arms with them and feel their warmth. Did their hearts beat?

Did it matter?

No, it didn't. This realm was full of life, regardless of whether or not its inhabitants were.

I took hurried steps to catch up with Waelyn. People seemed to jump out of his way in the street. They still smiled and waved at the god cloaked in darkness, but their eyes were full of awe and fear. I wondered what he was to them—beloved or hated?

Feared or respected?

I didn't have time to wonder as Waelyn's hand hooked around my elbow and tugged me into a short building tucked beside rows of shops. My protests died on the tip of my tongue as the scent of spice filled my nose and made my mouth water.

"I was starting to wonder when you were going to darken my doorstep again!" a feminine voice called out, directly before Waelyn was swatted with a dirty dishcloth.

"Oh, Syll, you can't beat him just yet, he'll never come back!" a booming male voice chastised.

I had to lean around Waelyn's large frame to take in our host. Syll was pretty in a motherly sense. Her honey-blonde hair was tied away from her heart-shaped face and her eyes were warm and brown.

"It's been a while," Waelyn conceded, his deep voice flat in comparison to the excitable couple standing in front of him.

I leaned to the side, trying to get a better look at the room beyond.

"And who's this?" the male voice asked.

Waelyn stepped to the side, allowing them a full view of me. I was suddenly self-conscious about the mud on my boots and the disheveled state of my windblown hair as their eyes traced over me. I wasn't in an ideal state to be meeting new people— especially people who meant something to Waelyn.

"This is Aura, she's a godling," Waelyn introduced me, using the fake name as he'd done once before.

I offered a tight-lipped smile to the brunet man staring me down. His dark skin was shiny with sweat. What had we interrupted when we'd arrived? I looked around the room, realizing we stood in the doorway of a restaurant. It was packed full of people who were happily spooning food into their mouths and chatting loudly. It was a warm environment, much like the couple before us.

"Godling, eh? It's been a long time since we've met one of those," the man said. "I'm Erlan, and this is my wife Syllia." He extended a large, calloused hand.

I shook it once, my fingers incredibly cold by comparison.

"It's nice to meet you both," I said, thankful that the words rolled off my tongue with ease.

"Well, let's get you two out of the doorway and over to a table, hm?" Syllia said, before an awkward silence could settle over us.

"Is this your restaurant?" I asked as she led the way to a more secluded room to the side of the main restaurant. It was quieter, calmer. There were fewer eyes watching my every move.

"Yes! We opened a few years ago and haven't been able to close it since." She laughed, wiping her hands on her apron. As she snapped her fingers, two menus appeared. She left them on the table as we took our seats. "I'll grab some of the good stuff for you," she said to Waelyn. "Is there something you like to drink?" she asked me.

"Arcwine, if you have it," I said, though I hadn't been much of a drinker in the last hundred years or so. Like all whelps, I'd had my bouts with recreational elixirs and powders. I'd discovered I loved it *too* much; I had to give it up or face the priestess's wrath.

"By the gallon. I'll be back in a minute." She nodded before flitting away through the set of swinging doors Erlan had gone through moments ago. Assumedly they led to the kitchen.

With Waelyn and I left alone again, a tense silence settled between us.

"Seems like you're pretty familiar with the owners," I said, hoping to strike up a conversation.

Green eyes met mine.

"I am."

Okay then… had I annoyed him that much when I'd brushed him off? It seemed ridiculous that a god as powerful as he was would be frustrated by a being like me. I was insignificant in comparison; it should be impossible for me to bother Waelyn.

"Alright, we'll just have a lovely awkward lunch in silence, then." I sniffed, turning my attention to the rest of the room.

The walls were painted in bright colors, alternating from yellow to red, to blue, to green. The tables and chairs all seemed to come from different sets, none quite matching the others. There were photos and art pieces hung on the walls, and even though we weren't sitting with the rest of the patrons, their laughter was filtering into the room. It was homey.

"What would you like me to say?" Waelyn asked.

"Drystan told me it's been five turns since the Night Realm got a new godling. Is that true?" I had to ask him questions, otherwise he wouldn't speak.

He nodded. "Before that, it was a millennium."

"Why so long?" If Waelyn was the most recent godling, until I came along, and he held *this* much power… what did that mean for me?

He frowned. "There's been a drought. None of the realms have had new godlings in ages."

"What? But I thought… what about the Marked?" There certainly hadn't been a drought of Marked ones. We were paraded around Edessa every Veiled Night.

"We only collect the Marked who are godlings with potential."

That sparked a whole other line of questions. "There are Marked who don't have the ability to ascend? I thought that was the whole point."

Before Waelyn could explain, Syllia reappeared with two glasses. One was filled to the brim with arcwine, a bitter fruit scent wafting off the top, and the other was a short glass half-filled with red liquid. It was the same liquor Waelyn often enjoyed in the library or his chambers. It must be a favorite of his.

"Are you hungry?" she asked.

"Starving," I replied.

She smiled and wrinkles formed around her eyes. She reminded me of Mags. My heart squeezed at the thought. I couldn't let myself go down the path of missing people from Kaedia. I'd been pushing down my grief, but if I let it simmer to the surface, I wouldn't be able to hold back.

I picked up the menu, but Waelyn beat me to it.

"Two of my usual, please," he ordered, and Syllia smiled, nodding.

"Of course. I should have known." With another snap of her fingers, the menus disappeared. She followed suit, making her way back to the kitchen where I assumed Erlan was hard at work cooking.

"What's the usual?" I asked when she was out of earshot.

Waelyn shrugged my question off. "You'll like it."

"Fine. I believe you were about to tell me more about the Marked." I tried to redirect him back to our previous conversation. I'd lived my whole life assuming that all Marked were sacrificed to the gods. Now, I knew that wasn't true. But if they didn't all become godlings like me, what happened to them?

He cleared his throat. "Not all Marked will be gods."

"So what does the Mark mean?"

"A variety of things," he said noncommittally.

I rolled my eyes. "Are you going to make me beg?"

For the first time in an hour, he smirked. "Don't tempt me."

I crossed my arms, meeting his intense stare. He shook his head at my insistence, taking a sip from his glass before he spoke.

"The Marks appear on those who could be potential godling candidates, but the Mark alone does not determine whether or not someone ascends. That comes down to power, to arcane connection."

"Oh," I said lamely, a strange surge of disappointment filling me.

I knew what his words meant.

Though I may have been inducted into the Immortal world, I would never ascend.

I would never be a god.

CHAPTER TWENTY-FOUR

"Asteria," a voice reminiscent of nails on a chalkboard hissed my name.

Darkness surrounded me, thick and suffocating. It swallowed me whole. I couldn't see my hands in front of my face. Where was I?

I listened, trying to rely on my other senses. There was no wind, no sound other than the grating voices whispering my name. They chanted it over and over until it was nonsense in my mind. Intense pressure pushed on my body until I was gasping for air. My legs were moving, but I couldn't escape the darkness.

"Hello?" I called out. My voice echoed around me, getting louder as it mingled with the screeching whispers calling out to me. I had to get out of here.

My legs pushed harder. I was running without seeing. I had to get away.

"Come to me," the voice instructed.

My body moved of its own accord, following the direction of some internal compass.

"No, please. I can't."

It called out, yelling my name over and over and over and over. I clasped my hands over my ears, but it was no use.

"Asteria. Asteria. Asteria. Asteria. Asteria. Asteria. Asteria."

It was all a jumbled sound, invading my brain and echoing around my skull. It was too loud, pounding against my temples. The darkness invaded me, taking control.

I was drowning. I was drowning. I was drowning.

"Asteria!" Warm hands, *real* hands, grabbed my arms.

My eyes snapped open. I was in the main hall of Waelyn's estate, the doors flung open as if blown by a great wind. They still swung on their hinges, revealing the endless night sky outside.

How did I get here?

The god himself stood in front of me, his hands locked onto my arms, holding me in place, as his piercing gaze studied my face. His hair was disheveled, and he only wore a pair of loose pants. Had he been sleeping? I wore a silk nightgown, the wind blowing through the open doors nipping at my legs and sending shivers through my body.

"What's going on?" I asked, my voice coming out softer than I had intended.

"I'm not sure." His frowned. "Are you alright?"

"I think so," I said through chattering teeth.

Waelyn nodded his head toward the doors and they slammed shut. "You're cold, let's get you something warm."

He wrapped his arm around my shoulder and led me back to my chambers. I didn't pull away—it was for warmth, or at least, that's what I told myself. I was shaking, but I wasn't sure if it was the cold or the memory of the darkness that lingered at the edge of my thoughts, even now that I was awake.

He ushered me into my room, leading me to sit down on the bed before he turned to rifle through my wardrobe. I normally would have argued, but I couldn't be bothered to care with the inky tendrils still gripping at my mind and whispering in my ear.

'*Asteria*,' it called.

I couldn't answer.

Waelyn was in front of me seconds later, kneeling to pull a pair of thick wool socks onto my feet. He did so without a word, his eyes finding mine every few seconds, filled with concern. I didn't know what to say to reassure him. I didn't know what had happened in the first place. How had I ended up in the main hall in my nightdress?

Waelyn produced a thick robe from gods-knew-where, wrapping it around my shoulders. It had appeared in his hands as if he had willed it to. I put my arms through the sleeves, and he tied it closed at the front. It smelled like smoke; a familiar, comforting scent.

He kneeled in front of me again, his hands resting lightly on my knees. "Stea? Are you with me?"

I must have looked like a ghost. Anxiety was clear in his eyes. The priestess would have a field day with Waelyn. He was far too open with his emotions.

"Yes," I whispered, my voice hoarse.

"Can you tell me what happened?" he asked softly.

I opened my mouth to speak, but a cough racked through my chest instead. I covered my mouth with my hand, and it came away covered in black liquid.

Waelyn's eyes grew wide at the color staining my fingers. With a wave of his hand, it was gone, magically cleaned.

"Let's get some tea," he said, as if trying to brush off what had just happened.

Was I dying? My insides felt wrong.

He didn't wait for me to respond, pulling me to my feet and wrapping that same arm around my shoulders to lead me back to the kitchen. I was in a daze. The halls passed by, and my feet moved on their own. Waelyn might have asked me a question, but I didn't hear it. I could only focus on the echoes of that terrifying voice and the flashes of darkness it left behind.

Waelyn guided me to a chair in the kitchen, making sure I was steady before he started rummaging through the cupboards for whatever he needed to make tea. A silence settled over us, thick and uncomfortable. Waelyn's eyes kept drifting back to me while he worked. He must have been worried. A few minutes later—or more, I wasn't really keeping track of the time—Waelyn placed a steaming mug in front of me.

"Drink up," he encouraged, nodding toward the cup. "It helps, I promise."

I didn't ask any questions. I would take all the help I could get to quiet my mind. I took a deep sip, burning my tongue in the process, but I barely felt it. My body didn't feel like my own. Still, the tea was warm in my stomach, soothing some of the iciness eating away at my skin.

Waelyn folded and then unfolded his hands, placing his palms flat on the table. "Do you know how you got to the main hall?"

I swallowed hard. "No. I was having a… dream." I couldn't call it a vision—I'd seen nothing but black.

"What kind of dream?"

"I've never seen… *felt* anything like it," I managed to get out, the words becoming harder as the memory of that voice pulled at me.

Waelyn's hand came up to brush my cheek, swiping away wetness I hadn't realized was there. When had I started crying?

"It's okay, Asteria, you're safe."

I hated the tears that rushed to flood my cheeks at his words. I didn't cry in front of people, let alone powerful gods who could kill me with a flick of their wrists. It was embarrassing to be so weak in front of Waelyn.

"You were probably just sleepwalking. It's somewhat common." He tried to explain the situation away, but I knew that wasn't it.

"I've never sleepwalked before," I said, shaking my head. "It felt real."

"What did?"

"There were these voices." I swallowed. "Or one voice, I'm not sure."

"What did it say?"

I closed my eyes tightly, trying to remember the words without the sensation of claws in my mind. "It asked me to come to it. My legs were moving on their own," I recalled, pulling the robe tighter around my body.

He hummed, staring out through the windows, lost in thought. Did he know something I didn't?

"There's something we can try," he said after a long silence.

I nodded. "I'll do anything to make it stop."

He looked unnerved by my answer.

"I wouldn't speak so soon."

"You have to relax. Take deep breaths, or it's going to hurt," Waelyn instructed, eyeing my tense posture.

I sat cross-legged in the middle of the plush rug that sat before the fireplace in the library. We'd moved all the furniture out of the way for this arcane work. I was nervous—but who wouldn't be?

Waelyn had explained the plan last night before ushering me back to my chambers to get some sleep. He would enter my mind and try to witness the memory of the dream I'd had the night before. He thought he might be able to identify the being that haunted me; I just had to risk my inner self to see if it was true. I wanted to be embarrassed about what else he might see in my thoughts, but I was too desperate to keep that *thing* out of my mind.

Drystan was with us. He lingered at the edge of the rug, his arms crossed and a frown firmly plastered on his face. "I don't like this," he said for the hundredth time.

"Shh." Waelyn waved him off, but I didn't miss the anxiety that flickered across his features.

I couldn't blame Drystan—of all the schools of arcane, mind magick was some of the most notoriously difficult. There were very few who could navigate the inner workings of someone's being with ease. There was a chance this would go horribly wrong for both me and Waelyn, hence the supervisor, though he wasn't happy about it. Drystan had made a point to vehemently disagree with Waelyn's plan as soon as he was briefed. Waelyn had insisted that it was necessary for my safety. So, here we were, sitting in the library with tens of candles lighting the space and sigils drawn on the stone floor.

I had asked Waelyn how this was different from the way we used to visit each other's minds over the years. He'd told me they were entirely separate schools of magick. My dream draughts opened my mind to astral projection, and he had returned the favor. He had only been able to see my present, not my thoughts or memories. Actually *entering* the mind and looking for something specific carried a whole other level of risk.

Waelyn tied a piece of twine around a bundle of herbs, sitting across from me on the ground. He placed the bundle in a small glass ceremonial bowl Drystan had brought.

"Are you sure this is going to work? That we'll both be okay?" I asked, unable to keep the question from leaving my lips.

"I'm doing everything I can to keep you safe."

I recognized the roundabout language, the faerie lie. He *wasn't* sure, and that fact made my stomach turn.

"Come here," he murmured, gesturing for me to move closer to where he was sitting.

I tried not to jump when one of his hands came up to hold my jaw while the other hovered over my forehead covered in black dust. We were only inches apart now, if that. His breath was warm on my face as he drew a simple sigil where my third eye would be. He whispered a few words in the ancient tongue and the sigil grew warm on my skin.

"What's it for?" I whispered. It felt strange to speak out loud when we were so close.

"To stop him from scrambling your mind when he picks through your thoughts," Drystan drawled.

Almost like a bubble had popped, the force that pulled me closer to Waelyn was gone. He released his hold on me and I shifted back to where I'd originally been sitting.

"That's reassuring," I murmured, earning an eye roll from Drystan.

"I don't understand why we're risking so much to stop her from sleepwalking," he grumbled.

Waelyn turned to him with a sharp look. "You know it's not just that."

"What else is it?" I pried, sensing words unsaid between the two gods.

"I'll explain if my suspicions are correct. Are you ready, Stea?" His hand hovered over the bowl filled with the spell's ingredients. I knew as soon as I said yes, he would light it.

I was terrified.

He winced as if he could feel it.

"Yes."

He conjured a single black flame, igniting the herbs in the bowl and filling the room with a cloud of hazy smoke. He whispered a few words in that same language as he had spoken when he saved me from the wraith, and my vision went black.

Darkness.

It chanted my name and surrounded me. Circling like I was its prey.

Asteria. Asteria. Asteria. Asteria. Asteria.

Clawing, suffocating darkness. I was drowning, I was dying. It was consuming me alive. I couldn't breathe, I couldn't think.

And then… a different kind of black. A comforting night, thick like smoke, enveloped me. Protected me from the thing that called out my name.

Waelyn.

I recognized his arcane in the shadows. He put himself between me and the thing. I could see nothing, but I knew he fought to keep it at bay.

I could feel it.

"Godling."

A different voice; it didn't belong to the thing. It echoed around my mind, foreign and out of place. The darkness quickly filled the room it left in my thoughts. It pressed, pulling at my skin, trying to get inside my very being. It wanted to corrupt, to consume. It was so hard to fight. I wanted to let go.

The smoke-like night around me pushed back against that thought, against the darkness.

"Godling."

The voice came with a sharp pain in my forehead. I winced at the feeling before I realized it meant I could feel my body again. Was it over already?

"Asteria. Open your eyes."

I tried to do as Waelyn had instructed, but they were heavy. Slowly, I pried them open. He was close; I could feel the heat from his body. He watched me intently, his face filled with concern. Drystan had even taken a few more steps onto the rug, staring at me with hesitation. He must have been the voice I'd heard—Waelyn had never called me 'godling'.

"Do you know where you are?" Waelyn asked, guiding my attention back to him.

"We're in the library of your castle."

"It's an estate," he corrected. "But yes."

His thumbs brushed my cheeks almost too quickly for me to register the contact. All I felt was a smear of wetness left behind. Was I crying again?

"I felt you in my mind," I told him. "You kept the *thing* away from me."

He nodded. "I tried. I'm afraid it won't be enough."

"Is it what we feared?" Drystan asked.

Waelyn furrowed his brow, looking away from me. "Yes."

CHAPTER TWENTY-FIVE

"What is it?" I asked. I hated being the only clueless one.

"Do you remember what I told you about the Blackwell?" Waelyn asked.

I nodded.

"There have been a number of godlings throughout history that have heard its call. It invaded their minds, whispering to them, corrupting them. They existed in a trancelike state, unable to be woken."

I swallowed. "What happened to them?" I asked, though I wasn't sure I wanted to know.

Waelyn hesitated.

"They were driven mad by it. Lost to their own minds," Drystan said.

What had the priestess said to me? That I would eventually be driven mad by my visions? Perhaps this was what she had been referring to. Perhaps the Blackwell and the *thing* in my mind were one and the same...

Drystan shuddered. "It's terrible and gruesome."

It sounded like he was speaking from firsthand experience. I wanted to ask, but I bit my tongue.

"Is that my fate?" I asked instead.

"Perhaps," Drystan mused.

Waelyn frowned. "I won't let it."

Drystan scoffed. "You can't promise that."

The air around Waelyn darkened, the shadowy tendrils

becoming agitated as he glared at Drystan. "Do you really intend to tell me what I can't do?"

The brunet god waved him off. "You know exactly what I'm saying. There's no way to guarantee she won't end up like the others."

Waelyn festered for a moment, considering his words. I could pinpoint the exact moment he realized Drystan was right, as dread set into his features and a resigned understanding filled his gaze.

I waited for the silence to become suffocating before I spoke. "So, what's the plan?"

"What?" Drystan asked, scrunching his brows.

"Clearly we can't stop this from happening, so how do we fight it? What can we do to try to protect my mind?" I elaborated.

Waelyn met my eyes. "I noticed something in your mind—"

"Oh, gods."

"Something odd," he continued. "It was like a sigil, but not one I could see."

"Then how do you know it was there?" Drystan asked, crossing his arms.

"I felt it. It was like a seal, but I'm not sure what it could be holding back."

Drystan turned to me. "Do you have any traumatic memories someone might have sealed away?"

Traumatic memories? *Tons.* Powerful people who cared enough about my mind to seal them away? *Zero.*

I shook my head. "I don't think that's it."

Drystan sighed.

Tense silence settled over the three of us once again, but my mind was anything but quiet. What could possibly be sealed away in the deepest depths of my being? It took incredibly powerful magic to manipulate the mind—who could have done such a thing to me? The possibilities would drive me crazy.

"There's nothing we can do about it tonight, and you need to rest," Waelyn insisted. "Drystan, can you come back in the morning? I need your help to figure this out."

"Of course, your godliness." Drystan nodded his head at Waelyn, and then disappeared from the library in a flash of arcane.

Waelyn released a sigh as soon as he was gone, running a hand across his face and raking it through his hair. He tugged at the roots of the strands like they'd done something wrong to him. His stress rubbed off on me, nausea finding its place in my stomach. The library grew darker around us, ebbing with his frustration.

Eventually, he stood, holding his hand out for me to take. "Let me walk you back to your chambers."

Against my better judgment, I placed my hand in his, letting him pull me up. My head still spun, or at least, that was the excuse I told myself. How else was I supposed to explain how much I enjoyed his closeness?

I let myself indulge in the feeling a little bit as he escorted me back to the room I'd been living in since I arrived here. I tried to avoid thinking about the fact that I was about to go to bed, where I was most vulnerable to the *thing*. I had never feared it as much as I did now.

"I know it's hard, but try not to worry," Waelyn said as we approached my doors.

"Are you still in my mind?" I asked, teasing.

"I don't have to be. It's all over your face."

"I'm normally better at hiding it."

He nodded in agreement. "You are. I'm just better."

"I'll have to start practicing again," I replied, letting out a mock sigh.

"You don't have to hide anything here, Stea. You're safe with me," Waelyn protested, with a softness in his eyes that made my chest tight.

I faltered, unsure of what to say. He gestured toward the door.

"Get some sleep. I'll come get you in the morning."

With my hand on the doorknob, I hesitated. "What if it happens again?"

"I'll be awake. I won't let you walk off a cliff," he joked, but there was something genuine in his eyes. He felt my anxiety.

"You aren't sleeping?" I was stringing the conversation along. I didn't want to be alone.

He shook his head. "I have work to do. I've been neglecting my duties as of late."

I didn't need to ask why. I'd shown up and disrupted his life. I was only adding to his list of things to worry about now. That thought gave me the strength to push the door open.

"I won't keep you, then. Goodnight," I said, stepping into the room.

"Goodnight," he replied, disappearing into the shadows seconds later.

Breathing deeply, I tried to calm my mind and prepare for the darkness I knew was coming to meet me.

"Asteria?" Three knocks followed. "Open the door."

I blinked, rubbing the sleep from my eyes. It had been a fairly uneventful night. Dreams plagued me more than the *thing* did. In fact, I hadn't heard its terrible whispers since Waelyn had entered my mind the night before. Maybe his presence alone was enough to scare it off.

"Asteria!" the man on the other side yelled, shaking the door handle.

I couldn't remember locking it. He sounded panicked enough that I yanked back the covers and rushed to the door.

"What's going on?"

My question went unanswered as warm, rough hands framed my face, forcing me to look up into piercing green eyes. The calluses on his hands scraped my cheeks, the shadows at the edge of his figure flickering angrily, anxiously, as he stared into my eyes with an assessing glare. He panted, out of breath as if he had sprinted to my room. There were dark bags under his eyes.

"Waelyn?" My voice came out in a whisper.

"Where are you right now?" he asked gruffly.

"Are you kidding?"

"Answer me."

"I'm in my chambers in your estate."

"How old are you?"

I blinked. "I'm almost five turns old." He already knew that.

"Does your head hurt?"

There's a little twinge near my temple. "Barely."

He frowned at that; it wasn't the answer he wanted to hear. "You need to wake up."

"What?"

"It's been a day and a half, you need to wake up," he repeated. "Seriously, I'm worried."

"I'm sleeping?" This felt real—*I* felt real—but Waelyn wouldn't lie about this. He couldn't.

Before he could elaborate, he disappeared, shut out by a great force that wasn't of my own making. The pressure of his hold left with him. I felt cold; stranded. How was I supposed to wake up?

I took a deep breath.

One.

The darkness crept in at the edges of the room, pushing until it enveloped me. It clawed at my skin, trying to worm its way into every pore, every fiber of my being. My throat was tight, and I gasped for air.

Two.

Breathing deeply, I tried to center myself, to find that eerie calm that had settled over me when Waelyn visited my mind. It was a shaky silence, but it was good enough.

Three.

All my energy buzzed around that central point in my mind, the one place the darkness couldn't touch. The very center of my being. I pushed at it until the frenzied hum became so intense it burned. I was starving for air, my body disintegrating around me as I gave myself to it completely.

Shooting up with a sharp gasp, my chest rose and fell in heaves. I was drenched in sweat and my legs were tangled in the bedsheets.

"Thank arcane," a deep voice breathed.

Turning toward the sound, I met the sharp gaze of shadow incarnate.

"You were—you were just in my mind," I panted, my thoughts scrambled. Nothing that had happened in the last ten minutes made sense. Was I losing my mind already?

"Yes. Are you alright?" His hands gripped my shoulders, as though he was afraid to let me go.

"You didn't use any runes? No spellwork?" The air was distinctly void of that burning herb smell I'd woken to the last time he visited my mind.

"There wasn't time. I could feel *it* around you, it was latching onto your mind."

I let out a disbelieving gasp. "That is *so* incredibly risky."

"It had to be done." He was resigned to his choices, no matter what the outcome would have been.

I thanked the gods we were both intact.

"What if you'd been hurt?"

He faltered as if those weren't the words he expected to hear. "I'm fine, Stea."

I shook my head, looking away from him. It could have been so easy for Waelyn to make a mistake and lose himself. I couldn't understand why I was worth that risk. His success in the matter did speak to his power, though. He was strong. I'd nearly forgotten.

He sat on the edge of my bed, his fingers absentmindedly running anxious patterns over the bare skin of my arms. His touch was comforting… *warm*.

I looked at him for a moment, blanketed under the easy quiet that settled over us. The dark circles under his eyes had worsened, and his choppy hair was even messier than usual. He was wearing the same clothes from when I'd last seen him, but now there were crimson dots splattered along his sleeves. I didn't have to use my imagination to figure out what he'd been doing all night.

"Thank you," I murmured, allowing a rare moment of vulnerability to reach the surface.

Waelyn's brow furrowed as he met my gaze. He was close enough to touch, warmth radiating from him.

"For saving me from that *thing*. Again," I clarified.

"I swore I wouldn't let anything happen to you. I intend to keep that promise."

His stare was intense, but there was nothing new about that. I was starting to grow comfortable under the weight of it. The fuzzy feeling in my chest at his words was *not* comfortable, though. *Strange*.

"You look tired. You should try to rest," I suggested, though the idea of me looking after a god such as Waelyn was almost laughable. Maybe the fact that we were so close in age made it easier to contemplate.

He smiled, shaking his head. "There's much to do yet, Stea. Come, let's get you ready for training."

I ignored my stomach turning and placed my hand in his outstretched palm. He pulled me to my feet.

"Is Drystan meeting us?" I asked as I shuffled toward the wardrobe, stifling the yawn that pushed its way through my lips.

"He's waiting in the main hall, probably rather impatiently by now," Waelyn said, making his way toward the doors. "Meet us there."

"Okay."

Seconds later, he was gone.

I started rummaging through the drawers in my wardrobe for something suitable to wear. I wasn't exactly sure what was appropriate attire for a day of mind magick, but I assumed it was best to be comfortable when risking insanity. I found a tunic and a pair of thick leggings that would work, and began getting dressed.

I tried to ignore the cacophony of thoughts swirling around my mind, but it was proving to be difficult. What I hated the most was the fear that crept in with every bit of darkness that got closer. That *thing* was always just at the edge of my thoughts, waiting for a moment to pounce. It prowled in the darkness, sizing me up. The black that surrounded it was so different from the shadows that served Waelyn, and there was no escape from it. It was in this realm *and* my mind, and the gods had no explanation or solution. There was a very real possibility it would overcome me, and I had no power to combat it. I was foolish to think I'd have a life here. It was too good to be true.

My spiral was interrupted as shadowy darkness pushed at my mind. Waelyn. I must have been taking too long to get ready;

they were growing impatient. I laced my boots quickly and left my chambers.

CHAPTER TWENTY-SIX

Waelyn and Drystan were in the middle of a hushed conversation when I joined them in the main hall. Drystan's expression was terse, and he shook his head at whatever Waelyn was saying. Waelyn's back was to me, but I could see the stress in his frame.

"What's going on?" I asked for what felt like the hundredth time in the last few days.

"We're determining our course of action," Waelyn informed me.

Drystan rolled his eyes. "He's suggesting dangerous spellwork," he clarified as I joined their circle.

"What's new?" I scoffed.

"Drystan needs to see what I did. To figure out what the seal is. I think he should see it," Waelyn explained.

I winced. Another visitor in my mind would only add to the probability of me losing myself. Not to mention the risk it imposed on Drystan.

"If he doesn't want to risk entering my mind then—"

"He's not suggesting I look into your mind," Drystan cut me off. "He wants me to peer into his."

"What? That's unnecessary."

"It's not. He needs to see it," Waelyn argued.

"There's no need for you to put yourself at risk again, and surely my mind is safer for Drystan than yours. Besides, shouldn't he see the seal at the source?"

"Exactly the point I was making," Drystan said proudly,

agreeing with me for the first time since we'd met.

"Seems you're outvoted," I mused.

Waelyn glared at Drystan. "I don't like this."

"Now you sound like me." Drystan smirked. "Let's set up in the great room today. It's stuffy in that library."

I bit my tongue as defenses for the library flooded through me, focusing instead on the task at hand.

Thanks to Drystan's magick, the work didn't take long. He summoned candles and herbs while Waelyn made space in the great room, which I'd quickly learned just meant 'throne room'. A grand black throne sat on a raised dais at one end—an intimidating piece, to say the least. Pointed spikes shot out at irregular angles, promising to slice anyone who came close. Like the rest of the estate, it had a dark feel. It was a sharp contrast to the gaudy golden throne Orien had brought into the throne room in Dreka.

I caught Waelyn's heavy stare as I looked away from the dais. Had he watched me take it all in? What emotions did he see when he looked at me? He looked nervous, like his stomach was in the same knots as mine.

"Godling, come here. I need to put this sigil on you," Drystan called from the rug in the center of the room.

"Oh, okay." I moved to where he was, sitting down across from him, trying not to flinch when he dragged his fingers across my skin. His touch was rougher than Waelyn's, and far colder. I'd taken the shadow god's gentleness for granted, that much was obvious.

Speaking of Waelyn, he stood at the edge of the rug, arms crossed over his chest. It was nearly the same image as when Drystan had observed the ritual last night. They must have spent many years together to have adopted so many similar mannerisms.

"Are you okay, Stea?" Waelyn's voice interrupted my train of thought.

I nodded, words unable to leave my lips. My skin was crawling at the thought of another being in my mind.

"You look pale," he continued.

"She's always pale. Let's get this started, I'm ready for it to be done." Drystan clapped his hands together as he settled in across from me. The bowl between us was filled with the same dizzying concoction of herbs from last night, already aromatic despite the fact that it wasn't burning yet. "Ready?" he asked, his hand hovering over the bowl.

Again, I nodded.

"Be careful," Waelyn warned.

Drystan lit the bowl, and everything faded to black.

"Easy, easy."

The words were hushed, warbled, as if I were underwater. I blinked, the room coming into focus around me. Drystan sat off to the side, rubbing his temples with a harrowed look on his face. Waelyn crouched in front of me, his hands on my arms to hold me steady.

"Is he okay?" I asked, watching as Drystan took two deep breaths.

"He'll be fine. He ran into the *thing* in your mind, and it rattled him a bit," Waelyn explained, easing my nerves.

"I should have warned him that it lurks."

"Can you feel it always?"

"Most of the time. It's been there as long as I can remember, even in the Mortal world, but it's never acted like this before. It always used to feel like it was just… watching, somehow. But now it feels more restless… urgent. That sounds crazy.”

“It doesn't,” Waelyn assured me, before moving to check on Drystan's recovery.

Relief flooded through me as they talked and Drystan seemed to be behaving normally. How many more times were we going to be lucky before one of us faced permanent consequences for using this kind of magick?

“Any ideas?” Waelyn asked Drystan after handing him a glass of water.

Drystan shook his head. “Nothing good, that's for sure.”

“That's what I thought.” Waelyn sighed.

“The seal's not impenetrable.” Drystan was pacing now, walking the length of the rug back and forth as he thought.

“It's quite sloppy work from what I remember,” Waelyn added.

Drystan nodded. “But if we remove it, whatever it is holding back becomes our problem.”

“It's a gamble,” Waelyn conceded.

“What are the odds it's blocking something good?” I chimed in.

“Do you know something we don't?” Drystan asked.

“I wish.” The curiosity might drive me insane before the *thing* did. What if whatever the seal was holding back simply exacerbated the *thing* and made matters ten times worse?

The two gods thought for a moment.

“Who in Kaedia would have enough power to perform mind magick?” Drystan mused.

“The king perhaps.” Waelyn threw a wary glance my way at the mention of my enemy.

“There's the boy—the new archmage,” Drystan offered.

I knew him. Haryk had been miffed when he was brought in to replace the arcanist teacher.

"Not him," I interjected. "Atlas wouldn't do that to me." He was rude, but he wasn't cruel. "Perhaps the previous archmage?"

"*Atlas*," Waelyn echoed.

It wasn't a question.

"The new archmage," I clarified anyway.

"If not one of them, then who? I doubt a lifebinder is capable of this," Drystan commented. "On their own, at least. We have to hope it wasn't the king, considering he's dead now. He wouldn't be able to remove the seal anyway."

"It would have to be someone powerful. The options are slim if the strongest residents of Kaedia were present at the last Veiled Night. There were only a handful of beings that could even attempt magick like this," Waelyn muttered, his brows furrowed in thought.

"Are we sure it's someone within Kaedia?" Drystan asked, turning to me.

"I haven't traveled outside of the kingdom. I doubt anyone out there would have reason to do this."

Who would work with Orien against me? Who would have the power? Only one person came to mind, the only family I had left. I didn't want to believe it, but the *thing* in my mind thrummed.

"Verena," I whispered.

Waelyn frowned. "The queen?"

"And my half-sister. Stormkeeper, and most recently, challenger for the throne."

"Why would your sister do something like this to you?" Drystan asked skeptically.

I shook my head. "Gods know. Maybe she didn't, but she's my best guess if it comes down to power."

Waelyn looked unsure. "I truly hope that isn't the case."

Drystan shrugged. "It's the only lead we have, though. We

should follow it."

"You're right. Let me get my things together. We can be in Kaedia by early afternoon," Waelyn said, wasting no time at all as he waved his hand and the spell materials disappeared.

"What?" I scoffed. "You just expect to walk into Castle Dreka and get a confession from the queen? The archmage? That's insane."

Drystan smirked. "We're gods."

"That doesn't mean they'll admit anything."

Waelyn smiled wickedly at that. "I have ways of making people talk, Stea, don't you worry."

Suddenly, I was terrified that I'd made a huge mistake mentioning Verena's name.

"Hurry and gather your things." Drystan ushered me along.

"Bring a cloak. It's winter in the Mortal world now," Waelyn instructed, before disappearing into the shadows.

I turned to ask Drystan where we were supposed to meet, but he too had evaporated into thin air.

Gods.

I tried to breathe deeply as I made my way back to my chambers. I was going back to Kaedia, back to the kingdom that had given me nothing but sorrow during the first part of my life. Back to the sister who cast me off whenever things got messy. I was going back to the city I'd grown to hate.

I hadn't expected to feel at home in the Night Realm, but the dread in my chest at the thought of leaving it proved otherwise. Still, I had no choice but to collect my thoughts and prepare to return to Dreka.

It was strange to be back in Kaedia.

I'd only spent a few cycles or so in the Night Realm, but it may as well have been years. The Bones remained the same, the black sand of the Scorch still shifted unsteadily beneath my boots, but it felt different now.

This place was the same, but I was not.

"Ugh," Drystan grunted as he took heavy steps through the sand. "Remind me why you couldn't get us closer?"

"Because every dracon on the isle would feel my power," Waelyn explained, making his way to my side much more gracefully than the other god. "We don't need to alert them to our arrival just yet."

"What's the plan?" I asked, my body humming in anticipation.

"Right now, we need to focus on getting to the castle unseen."

"How can we be sure the one who made the seal is in the castle?" Drystan interjected.

"We can't." Waelyn shrugged. "If you have a better idea, I'm listening."

We trudged onward through the dead trees of the Bones, stopping only for water or to orient ourselves. Miles later, we broke through the tree line, the shimmering city of Dreka glistening in the late afternoon sun.

I'd expected to miss its warm glow after the endless night of my new home, but I clung to the cover of the shadows, hiding from its rays.

Waelyn was right; I *had* grown fond of the darkness in the Night Realm.

"Do you miss it?" he asked tentatively, as though he didn't want to know my answer.

"No," I said, tearing my gaze away from Dreka and continuing.

Soon we reached the fields of lavender that separated the city from the mountains beyond. Their scent was thick in the air, perfumy in a way I'd never noticed before. It was almost choking me, burning my nose with overwhelming florals. I was so consumed by the scent I almost overlooked the abandoned cottage Drystan had crouched behind as he chugged water from his flask.

"Stea? Are you alright?" Waelyn asked immediately.

Had he felt my emotions shift? Or was I wearing my feelings on my face?

I didn't answer; I didn't have the words. Instead, I rounded the corner to the front of the cottage.

It was the same as I remembered, simple wooden door, tarnished brass knocker, and planters beneath the windowsill that overflowed with weeds. *He* would die all over again if he knew how bad his garden looked now.

I didn't knock, I just pushed the door open and let myself inside, like I had countless times before. Like I had the day he died.

I froze in the doorway, reliving that memory. Glass crunched beneath my feet. No, not glass—*bones*. They were brittle after all the years that had passed, but I knew whose they were.

There was a shadow at my back—Waelyn. He was likely craving an explanation I could not give, so I ventured further into the cottage.

In the kitchen drawers, I found three vials with a black seal. My signature. I pocketed them all. It wasn't smart to leave my handiwork lying around for anyone to find.

"What is this… *hut?*" Drystan asked from the doorway.

I fought to keep the grimace from my lips as he too crunched over the bones.

Waelyn stood in one corner, looking over the room, deep in thought. I didn't want to tell either of them the truth of what had happened here. Knowing what happened and seeing the details of the betrayal were two different things. I kept those secrets close to my chest. I hadn't even spoken *his* name in decades. I wouldn't start now.

"It's abandoned. We should move on," I said, ignoring the knowing look Waelyn wore.

To my surprise, neither of them argued, allowing me to lead the way to the edge of the city.

The streets of Dreka were packed full of partying citizens. They were drunk on arcwine that sloshed from their cups when they danced and cheered. They crowded around musicians and fought when they grew bored. They were barbaric compared to the Night Realm citizens. Mortal, through and through.

"Draw your hoods; we don't want to be recognized," I murmured, though there wasn't much risk for the gods.

I was the one avoiding extra eyes. The kingdom's seer had died on the Veiled Night; she didn't need to be revived today. Thankfully, the gods heeded my words, pulling their dark cloaks up over their heads without a word. We moved like shadows through the city. I did not stop to admire the temples or the grove. I felt called to none of it.

We stopped at the servants' entrance to the castle. They hadn't added any security, making it easy to slip in undetected. I didn't know which feeling flooded me faster; disappointment that they hadn't bothered to protect the faeries that served them, or rage in my chest because I couldn't expect anything else from the Kaedian royals. I had wanted Verena to be different.

Faeries bustled around, entering and exiting the corridors without sparing the three of us a second glance. Even I thought we looked suspicious, but no one questioned us as we made our way to the main corridor system of the castle.

"Where are we going?" Drystan asked from the back of our line of three.

"Verena will be easier to persuade than the old archmage. I wouldn't even know where to find him. The room I occupied is just ahead. We can stop there to make a plan."

Neither god protested, so I led the way to the hallway I'd spent a brief period in. A strange sense of familiarity washed over me as I turned the handle to my room, but I pushed it away. This wasn't my life anymore.

The room was practically untouched, left exactly the same as it had been the day of the sacrifice. It smelled of grief and grime. The last time I had been here I was mourning my family. The image of their hanging bodies assaulted my mind with every moment spent here.

The memories were so strong I almost didn't notice the fae woman whose head turned toward us as we stepped through the doorway.

Her jaw dropped as her gaze met mine. "What are you doing here, cursed girl?" Mags grunted.

"I missed you too," I grumbled.

"You shouldn't have come," she said earnestly. "You were free."

"I need to see Verena," I replied, my brows scrunched. Her hands were clenched and her eyes wide. What was Mags afraid of?

She shook her head. "Lost all sense, that one."

"What happened?" I asked, turning to Waelyn for answers, but he shook his head.

Mags didn't answer my question. "Who have you brought to this realm of calamity?"

"Friends," I replied, and she eyed the two gods like she didn't believe me. She stared as though they were the enemy. I was sure, to her, the gods were intimidating. I'd just seen past their steely exteriors.

"Why do you need Verena?" she asked eventually.

"It's a long story," I deflected. "Do you know where she is now?"

She frowned. "Her office, likely. She's jumpy as of late."

"That's on the other side of the castle," I said to the gods. "It'll be tricky to get there unseen."

"What wing?" Waelyn asked. "I can get us closer."

"You'll expose us," Drystan hissed.

"We'll be quicker than any knight," Waelyn insisted.

"You'd have to know the area to transport us there," I pointed out.

Waelyn gave me an odd look. "I've seen it through your eyes; that will be good enough."

My cheeks warmed with the intimate reminder of all we'd shared.

"Her office is in the east wing," I told him.

Waelyn held his hand out to me. I placed mine in his without much thought, until I saw the strange look on Mags's face at the action.

"I will see you again," I said to the faerie woman.

I wanted to know if the conditions for the fae had gotten better, or if Verena was full of false promises like her predecessor had been, but I didn't want to keep the gods waiting with my questions.

Mags pressed her lips together. "We'll see."

CHAPTER TWENTY-SEVEN

Drystan placed his hand on Waelyn's shoulder, and three dizzying seconds later, I was being pushed through the inbetween. My stomach turned. We were in another long hallway of Castle Dreka.

"Are you well?" Waelyn's fingers squeezed mine.

I nodded, swallowing the nausea away. "Her office is a few doors down."

I hadn't been in this part of the castle more than a handful of times, but it was easy to spot Verena's office. Hers was the only door trimmed with deep blue, the color of stormkeepers. She was one of a kind, a fact that had inflated her pride throughout our whelp years. It had only made me envious of my older sister, in a worrying way that festered beneath my skin with every blithe comparison the other draconians made between us.

My feet were frozen to the floor of the corridor, but Waelyn and Drystan didn't have seconds to waste. Waelyn stepped forward, pushed the door open, and entered the office with Drystan close behind.

"Excuse me, what are you—*Asteria?*" Verena's tone changed entirely when she spotted my figure behind the two hulking gods in front of her desk.

I calmly closed the door behind me.

"The godling? That's the most exciting part of this? We're gods, for arcane's sake," Drystan muttered to himself.

Waelyn put a hand on his shoulder, shaking his head and

silencing the brunet.

"Sister," I said.

Verena seemed to be in the midst of paperwork, her quill in one hand and a piece of parchment in the other. There were tens more like it on her desk, but they weren't neatly stacked like I would've expected. They sprawled across her messy office, half-finished and tossed aside. Perhaps she *was* lost, as Mags had claimed.

She wore her shock plainly on her face. "You're alive?"

Had she sent me off with Nox with the belief that he'd been lying when he said he would not kill me?

"I am," I confirmed.

She looked royal today, dressed in a similar shade of blue to that which accented her office. Her dark brown hair was pinned back into a bun that showed off the warm glow of her bronze skin. She was beautiful, just like I remembered, even with the blooming dark circles under her eyes. Jealousy panged in my stomach.

"How are you here?" she asked, looking between the three of us for an answer. "The thinning of the veil has long passed."

A dry smile found its way to Waelyn's lips. "Those rules are for minor gods, Queen Verena. Can't you feel the power you're in the presence of?"

She swallowed. "What is this?"

"You're not going to ask how I am?" I tilted my head to the side.

Verena scoffed. "We hardly exchanged pleasantries before, sister, why would that change now?"

I sighed in understanding. The emotion she'd shown me during her challenge with Orien had been out of fear. I was one of the only people in her corner that night, and so I'd been her lifeline. Now that she had the throne, I was useless to her again.

She could go back to pretending I didn't exist.

Her lips pressed into a firm line as she waited for me to explain what was going on. I watched with fire in my chest as her eyes traced over Drystan first, then Waelyn. She took her time soaking in their figures, a heat filling her gaze that contradicted the shiny ring on her third finger.

"Congratulations on your engagement," I offered. "When do I get to meet your betrothed?"

She scowled. "What have you come for?"

Not a happy union, it would seem.

"What do you know of arcane seals?" I asked, getting to the point.

"It's tricky magic to pull off, so I assume very little," Waelyn goaded.

Verena bristled against his words, but her tone was polite when she spoke. "I know some."

"Is there anyone in Kaedia who knows more?" Waelyn pushed.

She narrowed her eyes. "The archmage."

He was smart to play against her ego. She was practically an open book when challenged. Maybe he'd learned that through our visits over the years?

"As we suspected," Drystan muttered, nudging me with his elbow.

"What is this, Asteria?" Verena repeated, growing more agitated by the minute.

"Did you put a seal on me? On my mind?"

Waelyn shot me a look that said he hadn't been planning on jumping straight to the point, but it was too late now.

Her eyes widened. "What are you talking about?"

"It wouldn't have been done alone," Waelyn added. "It seems there were two poking around her mind. The first was…

sloppier. I'd assume that was you, and the archmage came to clean up your mess, yes?"

Verena's cheeks reddened, her chest heaving with every breath. Her fingers clenched the parchment she held, creasing it beyond remedy.

"You don't know what you're talking about."

Drystan sighed. "Fill in the details, then. I'm getting bored."

Verena stared down at her desk for a moment, then she took a shaky breath. "There's too much to explain. You wouldn't understand unless you were there."

"I *was* there, Verena. I deserve to know what happened. What did you do to me?"

She shook her head.

"If you want there to be any chance for us to have a relationship after this, you'll tell me everything."

For a long time, I was worried she would keep her secrets. Eventually, she sighed, her shoulders sagging as if unloading a great burden.

"You're... so unlike the rest of us. You always have been. When you were young, we thought maybe your power was uncomfortable. Awkward. Everyone thought you'd grow into it. And then things started... dying around you. All the time. A plant you touched, a bird you watched too closely. Anything that had the misfortune of crossing your path."

No. That couldn't be true. "I don't remember that."

She winced. "You got older, and it became more dangerous. Your father kept you home often, but a mortal man entranced you. I put the seal on your mind to stop you from hurting him. You cared deeply for him, Asteria."

"I remember him... he died the day the stars fell..." My voice shook in the air between us, crumbling under the weight of her story.

Verena winced. "After Eletha passed, you… you were upset. Your father had left town, and…" She swallowed thickly. "And the mortal, he upset you. You… *snapped.* The seal I had made failed. Hundreds died. The damage was… incredible."

"What… what are you saying?"

"*You* were the reason the stars fell that day your lover died. *You* brought the darkness."

Me?

My mouth opened and closed as I searched for the words, any words to explain myself. None came.

"She's a murderer," she said gravely, turning to the gods behind me.

All the air left my lungs.

Verena and I had never been close, but to hear those words spoken from her lips shattered my heart. Breathing in sharply, I tried to fight past the twisting wound in my chest. Pine and smoke washed over me as Waelyn shifted closer. He was calming, grounding me despite the anger that pinched his brows as he stared Verena down.

Drystan crossed his arms. "That's not a very good explanation for such a violation."

"She's a *killer.* With no remorse—what do you call that?" Verena persisted. "She murdered hundreds of mortals—her *lover,* even!"

Hundreds of mortals? I had no memory of committing such acts, but the *thing* in my mind swirled with familiarity.

It remembered.

I closed my eyes in the hope it would stop me from experiencing Drystan and Waelyn's reactions. I waited for them to agree with her, to denounce me, to banish me from the Night Realm, but there was only silence in the office. Waelyn did not shift away from me; I could still feel the heat emanating from his side.

Slowly, I pried my eyes open.

Both gods stared at Verena with blank expressions, waiting for her to go on with her story. Had they not heard her words? I'd murdered the man who was supposed to mean everything to me. How could they brush that off so easily?

"Get to the part where you put a second seal on her mind. Or better yet, tell us what it's blocking."

I stared at Drystan in shock. He had never advocated for me before; I hadn't even thought he liked me, yet here he stood, arguing with the storm itself in my defense.

Verena seemed to rage at their lack of reaction. "When I discovered the slaughter, I knew what had to be done to protect Kaedia from her. I enlisted the archmage to put a better seal on her mind to lock her power away."

My knees went weak beneath me.

My *power?*

"And then?" Drystan prompted, as Waelyn gripped my arm in a steadying hold.

I was thankful; without it, I would have fallen straight to the floor.

Verena clenched her fingers into fists. "She committed a great crime, she wreaked havoc over the entire city. That kind of thing doesn't go unnoticed."

"The king found out," Drystan suggested.

"Of course he did. Orien had a vendetta against me from the moment lightning sparked from my fingertips. He was all too thrilled that a member of my family had ruined the capital." Verena sighed, rubbing a hand across her forehead. "She was tried and sentenced under his rule, just like everyone else in Kaedia. She served her time and took her punishments. When it was done, the archmage made it so she would remember none of it, as a favor to me."

I had been imprisoned? Was that where the scars littering my body had come from? The one that had almost disemboweled me—had that been at Orien's hand, and not the flight accident Verena had always claimed?

How many of my memories were fabricated?

Cool fog washed over me, invading my senses and easing the racing beat of my heart as it hammered against my chest.

Waelyn.

I needed to stop panicking, that was what he was telling me. We would figure it out together, I wasn't alone anymore. I repeated the thought over and over until I could stomach Verena's betrayal. When it no longer made me gag, I looked at the dark-haired woman who claimed to be my family, my blood. She stared back at me.

The darkness pushed at the edge of my mind, the *thing* pulsing as she spoke. Even if I didn't know the details, it did.

"Why didn't you just execute her if she was so dangerous?" Drystan asked.

Verena shook her head. "She is my sister. I couldn't do that."

"That isn't the full story, is it?" Waelyn pressed, his voice shaking. He was more Nox than Waelyn now, the room growing darker as his shadows expanded.

She frowned at him, then as if remembering who he was— *what* he was—she nodded her head. "My lord?"

"She was a stain on the Taranis name—one you had worked hard to build up," he suggested, crossing his arms over his chest. "You were hungry to make a name for yourself, to prove yourself as an asset to the kingdom, weren't you? A younger sister with power so uncontrollably strong was a threat. Or was it that executing her would force you to admit that there was shame within the Taranis bloodline?"

Verena flinched at his words. "No! That's not what happened. We just *fixed* her. Made it so that she remembered very little of her first few turns of life."

"Fantastic," Drystan said dryly. "My lord, what shall we do next?" He directed the question to Waelyn, who was quietly seething beside me. The shadows in the corners of the room were festering, filling the space with gauzy darkness that seemed to stress Verena as it calmed me.

Waelyn didn't hesitate. "Collect the dracon, we'll find the archmage. We'll need them both to remove the seals."

Verena jumped to her feet. "You can't! She's too dangerous to have access to her arcane!"

Waelyn turned to her with a murderous glare, the visage that concealed his god form slipping away as the shadows surrounded him and filled his gaze. "You do not have the authority to make that decision, *whelp*," he snarled.

She flinched and I smiled.

"Take her to the throne room. I'll be along with the mage shortly," Waelyn instructed, and Drystan nodded without argument.

"Let's go, Taranis."

Verena clenched her fists as though she was going to fight back.

Drystan sighed. "Alright, we'll do this the hard way, then." With a wave of his hand, Verena was unconscious, falling back into the oversized chair behind her desk. He moved to gather her up, throwing her over his shoulder before they both disappeared from the room in a flash of arcane.

Once, long ago, I would have worried for her. Now I hoped Drystan ran her into a corner or two on his way to the throne room.

Waelyn and I were alone. The room was suddenly much

more comfortable without the presence of my half-sister.

"What are you thinking?" Waelyn asked, his tone soft and holding none of the anger he'd had for Verena just moments ago.

"Too much," I said with a wince.

He brushed his thumb along my brow, smoothing it out where it creased in concern. "We'll handle this in the Night Realm, okay? I'm sorry this is happening, Stea," he said, looking at me earnestly, his hand drifting down to squeeze my arm reassuringly.

I nodded, deciding to trust him. He hadn't given me a reason not to, and it was so exhausting keeping the walls around me so tall. Besides, I'd clearly chosen the ones I trusted incorrectly, given Verena's admissions. Maybe I wasn't a good judge of character.

I would take my chances with Waelyn.

CHAPTER TWENTY-EIGHT

When we arrived in the Great Hall, Drystan was lounging lazily on the golden throne, one of his legs draped over an arm. Verena paced angrily along one side of the room, eyeing him with contempt. It seemed to amuse the brunet god each time she scowled at him.

The castle had recovered from the fight between Verena and Orien. The windows were repaired, and the walls were rebuilt. If I had been told no such thing happened here, I would believe it.

Waelyn had made quick work of the royal guards, incapacitating the new archmage—Atlas—in mere seconds. He'd barely even glanced at the mortal and he became unconscious. Waelyn didn't touch him, instead letting his magick carry the sorcerer to the throne room, where he was unceremoniously dumped onto the tiled floor. It was at that precise moment that Waelyn lifted the magick keeping him unconscious, and the mage woke in the midst of a tantrum.

"What is the meaning of this!" he yelled, throwing his arms up in a rage. "I haven't done anything!"

Atlas would be considered attractive by mortal standards, despite his lean stature. His dark brown hair was long, falling over his shoulders and down his back, but he kept it pushed away from his face, just like he had when we first met. His eyes were blue, but not as clear as Drystan's. They were darker; murkier. Like Waelyn, his skin was heavily tattooed, but he didn't wear art. No, his markings represented bargains.

"Maybe not, but you're going to undo something for me," Waelyn informed him.

"You animal! You—*You...*" Atlas faltered, the rage falling from his features as realization hit.

"Oh, you remember me, do you?" Waelyn smirked menacingly. "I remember you, too. I'd obey our instructions to the letter if I were you."

Atlas and Waelyn knew each other? How? I was learning too many things that I hadn't had the opportunity to ask about yet. It was driving me crazy. Well, that and the voice in my head that was *literally* trying to drive me mad. It was impossible to put any pieces together when neither Waelyn nor Atlas chose to elaborate on their obviously complicated history.

Atlas's gaze traveled around the room, spotting Verena and bristling at the sight of Drystan on the throne. He and Verena must have grown close over the last month or so. When his eyes finally landed on me, they were swimming with recognition.

We'd only met a handful of times, but each one had left a worse impression than the last. He'd visited the temples ever since he was a boy, but had always been rejected by the arcanists. The old archmage had denied the mortal's requests to join them, to learn from them, and he'd grown bitter. When the previous archmage disappeared under suspicious circumstances, and the council voted to appoint a mortal, I should have suspected something more was at play.

"Why am I not surprised you're involved in this?" he hissed at me.

"Do not speak to her, or I will rip each of your limbs from your body, and I will take my time doing it."

Atlas's lip twitched at Waelyn's threat, like he was fighting the urge to speak, but he said nothing.

"As much as I love a good torture session, I'd really like to get home. Shall we move things along?" Drystan clapped his hands together, announcing in a voice thick with sarcasm, "Oh, great Archmage, we require your services."

"As if I would help the likes of her," Atlas scoffed.

"You don't have much of a choice," Drystan drawled. "You'll help us, or my friend here will burn this castle to the ground. Doesn't she look like she wants to?"

They all looked at me. I tried to keep the shock from my face at the fact Drystan had referred to me as his *friend*. I just had to hope that Atlas didn't know about my inability to access my dracon form… and that Verena would keep her mouth shut.

Atlas scowled at the reminder of my presence.

"Good. It seems we're on the same page." Drystan smiled as he looked between the dracon and the mage we'd taken captive in their own castle. "Now, you're both going to remove the seals you put on her mind, no questions asked, and we *might* just leave your kingdom unscathed."

Verena opened her mouth to protest, but Drystan wagged his finger at her.

"No questions. I'd also like to remind you that we'll be inside your minds as… insurance. So don't do anything rash."

I didn't like the idea of Drystan and Waelyn risking the state of their minds yet again to ensure my protection, but there wasn't much I could say to convince them otherwise. With a snap of Drystan's fingers, there was a ritual set up on the floor of the throne room. The smell of the herbs in the burning bowl was becoming familiar to me. My only solace was that this would be over soon, as long as Atlas and Verena played their parts.

I couldn't consider the possibility of them wreaking havoc on my mind, despite the look in the archmage's eyes that said that was exactly what he wanted to do. I hoped Drystan's threats were enough to motivate them to help instead of hurt.

Waelyn kept a tight leash on Atlas as they finished preparing. He only broke his intense supervision to paint the protection sigil on my forehead with gentle, steady fingers.

Verena didn't fight the gods as they brought her to the circle Atlas and I already occupied. Maybe she realized what kind of power she was up against. I had no doubt that Waelyn could ruin both her and the sorcerer in a matter of seconds.

"Are you ready?" Waelyn asked me, green eyes searching mine for hesitation.

I swallowed the fear swelling up my throat. The words wouldn't come, so I nodded.

Drystan lit the herbs, and the world around me succumbed to darkness.

There was nothing but black around me. Intense, painful pressure started behind my eyes and bloomed throughout my skull. My head pounded, throbbing in time with the beat of my heart. I could feel their energy; two distinct beings, their arcane poking around in my mind. I had never felt more vulnerable.

The *thing* was there too, but it didn't seem to be moving to that exposed part of my being. It wasn't preying on me now. No, it was lurking, looking over the two beings working on my inner depths. It was a threat to them at this moment, protecting me. Perhaps it was because I was its host, but for the first time, I was thankful for it.

The first seal gave with a shocking burst of energy. Flashes of light blinded me, but they were immediately swallowed by the *thing*. I was burning up, consumed by pain so intense I was sure flames were licking at my skin. I was dying.

The second seal broke, and the fire erased me. There were no thoughts, no feelings.

I ceased to exist.

I woke wrapped in satin. I was cold, but there were swathes of black and gray fabric enveloping me—someone had clearly anticipated my drop in temperature. My eyelids felt weighed down by stones, but with heavy effort, I pried them open.

Squinting into the dark room, I spotted a full bookcase, gray bedding, and high-arched windows. It seemed I was back in the Night Realm, in my chambers. I didn't remember the journey. My mind was blank after the spellwork in the Drekkan throne room. My head didn't hurt though—a good sign, I supposed.

Where was Waelyn?

My curiosity drove me out from under the blankets. I found the robe he'd lent me a few days prior tossed over the back of my desk chair and pulled it around me. I shivered as my bare feet padded across the stone floor, but that did not stop my pursuit of the green-eyed god. I had too many questions and not enough answers.

When I entered the corridor outside of my chambers, I planned to knock on Waelyn's door. I hadn't expected Drystan to be leaning on the opposite wall, a lazy expression on his face.

"Oh, you're finally awake. Terrible timing."

"What's going on?" I asked. "Why is this a bad time?"

"Because Waelyn isn't here, so you're going to ask *me* a million questions." He sighed dramatically. "Come, let's wait for him in that dusty library you so adore."

I followed him down the endless hallways, biting my tongue to stop my questions from spilling out and proving him right. Still, I couldn't contain one.

"Where is he?"

Drystan shrugged. "Working. He'll probably be back soon. He's hardly left your side for the last few days."

Days? Had I been out for *days?* I hoped that meant good things, and not that the corruption lingering at the edge of my mind was winning.

"It was a success, by the way. In case you were worried about that," Drystan added as an afterthought as we approached the grand double doors of the library. He opened them and the smell of smoke washed over me, easing some of my nerves. "Your memories and arcane might take some time to return, but the seal was successfully broken."

"Good," I affirmed, moving to sit in one of the overstuffed velvet chairs to combat the chill that had settled in my bones. "Is Kaedia intact?"

Drystan shrugged. "Mostly."

I raised my eyebrows in question as he dropped into the chair across from me.

"Waelyn cut the archmage's left hand off, but he lived," he explained, as if the fact disappointed him.

"Why?"

He shrugged again. "I was still in your sister's mind when it happened. I woke to a bloody mess."

More questions I'd have to save for Waelyn. I was getting antsy as I waited for his return.

Hours seemed to tick by in silence. Drystan got up to fill a glass with red liquor more than once. I might have dozed off in the chair's warm embrace—I didn't understand how I could still be tired after days of rest, but I didn't have the energy to question it.

Eventually, when Drystan thoroughly reeked of alcohol, Waelyn appeared in the doorway of the library.

"Well, hello! Took you long enough!" Drystan said, stifling a hiccup.

"I was somewhat behind," Waelyn's deep voice rumbled in response. He looked exhausted, slouching against the doorframe.

"Asteria's awake," Drystan trilled, and Waelyn's head snapped in my direction.

"How are you feeling?" he asked, any sign of tiredness disappearing from his voice entirely.

"Fine." I shrugged. "You look a little worse for wear though."

He chuckled at that, raking a hand through his hair. "I am rather tired," he admitted.

"Ought to sleep, then," Drystan chimed in.

"Ought to," Waelyn agreed, but he didn't move from his spot. His stare was trained on me. "Why don't you take one of the spare chambers tonight, Drystan? I can't imagine you making it home successfully in your state."

"Good idea, my lord," Drystan gushed before gathering his glass and bumbling out of the library, leaving us alone.

The God of Death and Darkness moved into the room, taking Drystan's seat.

"I heard you cut Atlas's hand off," I said nonchalantly, as if it were casual gossip and not torture we were discussing.

"You heard true."

I tilted my head at him, a small smile on my lips. "Your restraint is admirable."

He smirked. "I thought so too."

Though all I wanted was to grill him with questions, the exhaustion on his face when he'd first arrived made me hesitate. Instead, we enjoyed each other's company in comfortable silence for a while, watching the flames in the fireplace dwindle into embers. I wasn't sure what time it was, but exhaustion pulled at my eyelids.

"Aren't you going to ask about the seal?" Waelyn asked after some time.

"Drystan said it was a success. I assumed there weren't many more details," I replied, pulling the robe tighter around me as a chill racked through my bones. I'd been relying on the fire for heat more than I realized.

He raised an eyebrow. "Are you sure you're well? I expected more questions."

"Oh, I have hundreds," I assured him. "But I can hardly ask when you look as exhausted as you do."

"Ask away." He waved his hand, but his eyelids were closing further and further with each passing moment.

I shook my head, standing from the chair with a stretch. I stood in front of him, holding my hand out for him to take. "Allow me to escort you back to your chambers."

Waelyn gave me an exasperated look, though beneath it lay something else. A warmth I was slowly becoming increasingly familiar with when it came to him.

"Fine," he grumbled, "but you owe me a hundred questions in the morning."

Waelyn took my hand and stood, allowing me to lead the way down the twisting corridors of his estate. I tried to ignore how warm he felt, how gently he held me. My cheeks burned; I was sure they were bright red. I couldn't recall when I'd stopped thinking of him as a murderous god and instead as… *something else*.

All too soon, and yet not soon enough, we were at his door.

"Goodnight, your godliness," I teased, releasing my hold on him.

He stared at me for a moment, green eyes full of an intensity that had once made me squirm, but now drew me in.

"Goodnight, Stea," he said softly, disappearing into his

chambers, leaving only the lingering scent of smoke and pine behind.

The night was especially dark around me, the air cold as it nipped at my exposed skin. I wore only the silk nightgown I had fallen asleep in mere hours ago, and the twigs that littered the forest floor stabbed the soles of my bare feet. I couldn't remember how I'd got here, just like I couldn't stop my legs from charging forward into the darkness.

The *thing*, the darkness in my mind, chanted my name, calling me to it. My body, the betrayer, obeyed. I couldn't see a thing in front of me, and I shivered against the frigid wind. My chest swirled with fervor, a frenzy I couldn't tame as I got closer and closer to wherever I was being led.

Asteria. Kin of Night. Asteria. Marked by the Stars. Asteria. Incarnate of the Old Gods. Asteria.

The voices, the words, they all overlapped, echoing around my mind and dissolving into a cacophony of sounds. I scratched at my ears, at my temples, trying to get it out. Out. *Out!*

Wetness streamed down my face, coating my nails and cheeks. The *thing* was going to kill me, I was sure of it.

I nearly tripped as the ground beneath me ceased to be dirt and became cold, wet, smooth stone. The voices wrapped around me, expelling every other thought from my mind as my arms moved of their own accord, reaching for the bottom hem of my nightgown. In one swoop, it was pulled from my body and discarded to an unseen place.

Asteria. Mother of the Void. Asteria. Servant of Darkness. Asteria. Matron of Insanity.

My legs took another step, plunging into a freezing pool.

Water sloshed around my calves as I took another step and the icy grip of panic seized me. I willed my legs to stop moving, but it was no use. The water was up to my ribs, and my body wasn't stopping. It was going to pull me under, to hold me there until every last gasp of air left my lungs.

Where was Waelyn?

That was the only thought circulating in my mind above the voices as the water lapped at my chin.

When my head went under the chilling depths, the voices went silent.

CHAPTER TWENTY-NINE

It was cold.

Dark.

Quiet.

But I could see the stars.

"Asteria? Look at me." That voice, usually so strong, wavered as it spoke.

I looked toward the source of the sound.

Waelyn kneeled upon dark stone, black as night yet shimmering like glass. There was a puddle of dark liquid around me. Blood? No, I wasn't bleeding. I was soaking wet. Drenched and naked.

"I'm cold," I croaked. As I coughed, black water spilled from my lips.

Waelyn untied the cloak from around his throat, draping it over my body and tucking it around me. It was warm and smelled like him. He gently lifted me into his arms, making sure the fabric covered all my exposed extremities. I wanted to be embarrassed that I was so vulnerable, but I didn't have the energy to be.

Waelyn felt safe.

"I'm going to get us back to the estate, okay? It'll be over soon," he assured me.

Just before we dissolved into gauzy darkness, I caught a glimpse of the black pool behind him.

The memories came rushing back. The voices, the *thing*

calling to me, being dragged into the water. I knew in my very being that I had bathed in the Blackwell; that it had swallowed me whole. I wanted to ask what that meant for me, for the realm, but the sensation of arcane travel flooded my body and stole my words.

Seconds later, we stood in a dark room lit only by candlelight. There were black silk sheets on the bed and an armoire filled to the teeth with clothing and weapons. We were in Waelyn's chamber. He laid me down on his bed before turning to rummage through his wardrobe. He returned with a long-sleeved shirt and a pair of cotton shorts. Patiently, silently, he helped me dress.

"I'm just... so sorry, Asteria," he murmured when I was clothed again.

I kept his cloak pulled around me for warmth as I sat on his bed. "For what?"

None of this was his fault. Gods, I didn't even fully understand what had happened in the first place.

He shook his head, fury in his gaze. "I was supposed to protect you from this. Drystan was drunk; I shouldn't have gone to bed."

I frowned. "I told you to go to bed."

"I shouldn't have listened. I knew better. I knew this *thing* wouldn't rest until it had you."

"What's going to happen to me?" I asked. I wasn't going to be able to convince him this wasn't his fault.

"I don't know, Stea. We're in uncharted waters. Very few have seen the Blackwell, let alone bathed in it. We know very little about it. I just don't understand..." Waelyn ran a hand through his shaggy hair, tugging at his roots in frustration. "Perhaps Drystan might know more."

"I wasn't looking for it," I explained, though I was sure he already knew that much. "I just woke up in the middle of the woods. I could barely see. I don't know how I got there. I thought it was just a dream…"

Waelyn's brow furrowed and he crossed the room to his bathing chambers. Moments later, he reappeared with bandages and a wet cloth.

"It sounds frightening," he said as he kneeled before me.

"It was too loud in my mind. The voices wouldn't let me feel scared. They wouldn't let me think."

I was trying to reassure him, but he pressed his lips into a tight line. His rage was barely contained, yet he touched me with care.

He was gentle as he pressed the cloth to the bottom of my feet, which were bloody and raw from hiking through the forest. He put some kind of salve on before he bandaged them up. It stung, but in a medicinal way that I knew would help. Once satisfied, he found a pair of thick socks and pulled them on.

"Thank you," I whispered. "I should have done that myself."

He shook his head. "It is the least I can do after I've failed you so horribly."

"You didn't fail me," I said firmly. "You said it yourself; these are uncharted waters."

"I'm the god of this realm, I should have anticipated that coming here might put you in danger."

Gods, he truly felt that this was his fault. His doing. I wasn't sure anything I said would make him see otherwise.

Moments passed in silence. Total silence. The voice in my head was gone, but the darkness remained. It swirled in my chest, no longer pushing at the edges of my mind. It was as if a missing piece had clicked into place; things were comfortable now. Whole.

"You need to rest," Waelyn insisted.

I was sure he was right, in some way, though I couldn't

imagine sleeping now. I always seemed to need rest lately. I wondered if this was how the remainder of my life would be; traumatic experiences and weeks spent sleeping them away. I hoped not.

"Will you stay with me?" I tried to ignore the weight of those words on my tongue; the implications they carried.

Waelyn hesitated. "I will stay here, but I will not sleep."

"That is all I ask."

I released my grip on his cloak in favor of the thick blankets on his bed. Weeks ago, I'd balked at the idea of sleeping in his chambers, but now the smell of pine and smoke was comforting enough to lull me to sleep.

I settled into his silk and velvet-covered bed, and he dropped into a chair at the side of it. There was a book in his lap, but judging by the intensity of his stare, I doubted he would get much reading done.

I fell asleep to the sound of his quill scratching against the paper and the sight of shadows dancing against the walls.

"I'm worried, Drystan."

Waelyn's voice broke through my groggy haze. He spoke in tense murmurs somewhere nearby. My eyes were too heavy to open.

There was a sigh.

"You said she spoke to you, right? She remembered what had happened?"

That voice belonged to Drystan. He sounded stressed too.

"Yes, but she's been sleeping for hours now. She's barely moved."

"I imagine it's quite an exhausting experience. Kharis slept for days after…" Drystan's voice was tinged with something distant, something solemn.

Waelyn was quiet. "She can't end up like that."

"You don't have much say in the matter now. What's done is done."

I could practically see Drystan's shrug.

There was a long silence. I almost fell asleep again, but then Waelyn spoke.

"I should have been there. I should have stopped it."

"You know there's nothing you could have done. It would have gotten to her eventually."

"Still…"

Another stretch of silence weighed on the room.

"Have you considered the prophecy?" Drystan asked.

"Of course I have."

"And?"

"*And* nothing. We won't know anything until she wakes," Waelyn grumbled.

I wanted to see him. I had questions.

Prying my eyes open, I was met with darkness. The windows were open, revealing the night sky beyond. I was warm now; Waelyn's cloak lay over the top of the blankets that covered my body. I felt too weak to move, but I didn't have to in order to spot the gods standing at the foot of the bed. They were close, which explained their low tones. Were they trying not to wake me?

"What prophecy?" I asked, my voice scratchy.

Both of their eyes snapped to me.

"Stea? How long have you been awake?" Waelyn asked, moving to the side of the bed immediately.

He lowered himself into the chair he'd occupied when I'd fallen asleep last night, holding one of my hands in his. My face suddenly felt much warmer.

"A while. I couldn't get my eyes to open."

"You're interrupting a private conversation, godling," Drystan said, leaning on one of the bed posts.

"Don't discuss cryptic prophecies and strange people in the same room as me and I won't interject," I retorted, glaring at him. "How's your hangover, by the way?"

"Oh, it's wonderful," he drawled, frowning at me. "Made worse when Waelyn came pounding on my door this morning."

"You likely deserved it," I sniffed, moving to sit up. My body groaned in response.

Drystan turned to the God of Death. "I think she's fine. She's as rude as she's always been."

Waelyn frowned. "You're sure?"

"I am not rude," I grumbled, but neither god acknowledged the words.

Drystan nodded. "With Kharis, it was different. They were silent for months, and when they did speak, it was incoherent. I would say the godling's mind is intact."

"Kharis?" I asked.

Drystan glanced at me. "An old friend," he said, offering no more explanation. The look in his eye kept me from pressing further.

Waelyn squeezed my hand. "Are you hungry? You must be."

I didn't know if he was genuinely concerned about my state of hunger or if he was redirecting attention away from Drystan and the line of questions I'd started. It was easy to assume that whatever had happened to Kharis was a sensitive subject for the brunet god. I had enough tact not to push.

"I'm starving," Drystan said when I didn't answer. "I'll be in the kitchen if you need me."

The god disappeared in a surge of arcane, on the hunt for breakfast. Was it morning? It seemed to be; I could hear the faint chirp of birds through the closed glass panes of the windows.

Waelyn stood, pulling me along with him by the hand still holding mine. "Can you walk?" he asked, his brow creased.

"I think so."

His hands came up to my arms, holding me steady as I rose on shaky legs.

"I'm fine, really," I said, though I didn't really want him to stop holding me. His touch was soothing.

"I know you are." His hold didn't loosen. "Tell me what's on your mind; I know you have questions," he added as he pulled a robe around my shoulders.

It was the same one he'd given me before. It smelled like him. I resisted the urge to take a deep breath.

"I've asked my question already. What prophecy were you and Drystan discussing?"

Waelyn shook his head. "We aren't sure it applies to you, Stea."

"What if it does? I should be informed."

He was quiet for a moment, guiding me toward the chamber doors and down the hall. "There's an old prophecy—it's really more of a story; you can't put much stock in it—that there will come a godling who will bathe in the Blackwell. That godling will hold the fate of the Immortal world in their hands. They will be responsible for keeping the balance across all realms."

"Seems... intense."

Was that my fate? Waelyn had said I was one of the few who had found the Blackwell, who had bathed in it. Was I the one meant to fulfil the prophecy?

The arm that was wrapped around my shoulder squeezed. "Get out of your head. It's not something you have to worry about right now."

I shook my head. "I don't know if that's true."

"I wouldn't say it if it wasn't. Right now, we're just trying to understand if anything has changed for you."

"Changed?"

"You had a seal removed from your mind and bathed in an ancient pool less than a day apart. There may be side effects, arcane abilities, or any number of new changes. We need to make sure you are alright before we think about anything else."

My chest warmed as his words sank in. It was strange to have someone care about me, to be truly concerned with my well-being above all else. My mind flickered back to my chosen family; the friends who had died in my stead. Perhaps I didn't deserve Waelyn's care. What had Verena said? That I was too dangerous with my power? What if I hurt Waeyln, after everything he had done for me?

"Who is Kharis? Truly?" I asked, changing the subject. I didn't want to entertain my spiraling thoughts just now.

The god frowned. "That is Drystan's story, I'm afraid."

"Were they a godling who heard the call of the Blackwell, like me?" I asked. It was the only thing I needed to know.

"Yes," Waelyn confirmed. "That is all I'll say."

We walked in silence for the rest of the journey, moving slowly since my legs couldn't keep up. I wondered what toll the Blackwell had taken on me, aside from the physical. My body was clearly in distress; what of my soul?

Waelyn stopped just outside of the corridor that led to the kitchen. "Stea?"

"Yes?" I turned to look up at him. Those bright green eyes stared into mine, seeing through to my very being.

He didn't say another word as he pulled me into him, bringing his other arm around my waist. The entirety of his body was pressed to mine, his breath against my neck as he rested his head on my shoulder. He held me tightly, long enough that I was able to recover from the shock and return his embrace.

"I thank arcane every minute that you survived," he whispered against my skin, sending shivers down my spine.

Then he pulled away, leaving me cold.

"You have such little faith in me?" I retorted, cursing myself for never knowing what to say in response to his displays of vulnerability. "I wouldn't die that easily."

He shook his head. "You're resilient, but everyone reaches their limit eventually. I worried."

I faltered. Did I need to reassure him? Thank him for worrying? I didn't know.

"Let's go. I'm sure Drystan is starving by now," he said, changing the subject before I could come up with an answer.

Unlike the day spent flying around the Night Realm, he didn't seem upset by my inability to meet his vulnerability with some of my own. Perhaps he understood.

Sure enough, Drystan was waiting for us, three plates of food on the counter in front of him.

"Took you long enough," he grumbled.

How many times had I heard that complaint from him?

"I'm moving slower than usual," I said, sitting down at the table with Waelyn's help. He moved to grab two plates, bringing them back to where I was sitting and taking the chair next to me.

He turned to Drystan as he picked up his silverware. "Thank you for cooking."

Drystan waved him away. "Your kitchen is much nicer than mine. Make sure to keep that in mind for the summer solstice."

"Noted." Waelyn smiled to himself. Then he turned to me. "Make sure you eat enough. We'll be spending the rest of the day in the library sifting through all the information that has ever been written on the Blackwell and that prophecy. There won't be rest until we have answers."

CHAPTER THIRTY

"Pass me the bottle, godling," Drystan groaned, holding his arm out. His other hand held a dusty tome that hadn't seen light in several turns.

I rolled the bottle of arcwine across the floor. I couldn't reach to hand it to him with my share of heavy books stacked in my lap. Drystan lunged for the bottle, shooting me a glare when it brushed past his fingertips. Waelyn stopped it with a flick of his wrist, sending it back toward the brunet god without looking up from the page he was focused on. He sat against one of the shelves further away from us, completing our little triangle.

"Thanks," Drystan slurred.

We had been drinking most of the afternoon, despite Waelyn's protests that it was too soon for me to be doing such a thing. I had to find a way to avoid dying of boredom as we thumbed through countless pages of ancient text, and arcwine seemed to be the answer. My head was growing fuzzy after more than a few glasses of the aged alcohol, but the gods seemed unfazed. I did my best to keep the hiccups stifled and the pink from my cheeks, though I had little control of the latter.

"Have you found anything?" I asked, looking for a distraction from the letters that had started to blur together.

Drystan sighed. "No, nothing has changed from when you asked ten minutes ago."

"It's been hours." I sighed, turning to another page that was nothing but nonsense. I hadn't spotted a single mention of the

Blackwell or the prophecy that spoke of it in the hours we'd been working. It was starting to feel hopeless.

"Stating the obvious, godling," Drystan drawled. He tossed his tome aside in favor of the bottle.

"What would this prophecy even say?" I huffed. "A godling who will maintain balance across the realms? How? Why?"

The brunet god rolled his eyes. "It's far too complex for you to understand."

I glared at him. "Try me."

"It wouldn't do me any good to waste my breath. Your greatest achievements are your little alchemy projects, and there you are a novice at best. I'll die long before you understand the threads of the universe."

"You're such a slug, do you know that?" I retorted, swallowing the sting of his words.

He put his hand to his chest. "You wound me, godling. Truly."

Waelyn spoke before I could tell Drystan just how much I cared about his wounds.

"Enough" he snapped. "I found something."

"Listen closely, godling," Drystan muttered.

"I thought we were on a first-name basis," I replied dryly.

Drystan scoffed, opening his mouth to retort, but Waelyn beat him to it.

"The prophecy refers to the being as someone capable of maintaining the balance across all worlds, Mortal and Immortal. An immortal ruler, one of the infinite, who answers to no one but the Void. The prophecy speaks of the Void as a living thing, all-encompassing and nothing in the same breath. It speaks of wars waged to gain the being's favor, their allegiance, and the destruction that comes before the balance. It says here that the prophecy should be considered a warning, against ever allowing this being to exist."

He dropped a tome in front of his lap, pointing to a passage on the page that was too far away for me to read. Clumsily, drunkenly, I scrambled to my feet, rushing over to the dusty book. Waelyn had found it, the proof was in the words pressed onto parchment, ancient and fading.

Written in a language I had never seen before.

Drystan whistled. "Been a long time since I've seen that." He peered over my shoulder to squint at the text. "I'm surprised you know the ancient tongue."

Waelyn shrugged. "Many important texts are written that way; it was a necessity to learn."

"Can you teach me?" I asked immediately. I wanted to read the prophecy with my own eyes.

Drystan chuckled. "I'm not sure you could learn if you tried."

"*Drystan*," Waelyn bit out. Green eyes found mine. "I'll show you, Stea. You'll catch on quickly."

He sounded sure, but it was hard not to believe him.

"Thank you," I mumbled.

"So, what now?" Drystan asked. "Because it sounds like we've made a colossal mistake by keeping the godling alive in the first place, not to mention removing that seal."

The arcane that pulsed through the room nearly burned, darkness surging around us.

"Careful how you proceed." Waelyn's voice was low. Intense.

Drystan didn't flinch. "If we hadn't removed that seal she likely wouldn't have found the Blackwell. If we'd shipped her off to another realm, the problem would have solved itself. She wouldn't have survived this long without us fixing every mistake she makes."

His words were sharp, cutting deeper than before. I worked to keep the wince from my lips. I hadn't possessed power like

Verena in the Mortal world, but I hadn't been *entirely* helpless. Here, I contributed nothing. Both Waelyn and Drystan were far more knowledgeable and powerful. I couldn't keep up. The training I'd been doing changed very little; I still couldn't access my arcane, and now that I'd bathed in the Blackwell, more problems had developed. I was a burden.

I wilted, but the feeling was pushed back by a thick smoke, calming every tense muscle in my body. It invaded my mind, but it wasn't like the *thing*. It was soothing. *Waelyn*.

"You're drunk, Drystan. Go home. I'll do something we'll both come to regret otherwise," Waelyn warned. His tone made the hair on the back of my neck stand on end.

"Very threatening, my lord," the brunet god drawled, before disappearing, leaving only the scent of cinnamon behind.

Waelyn sighed, shaking his head. "I swear on arcane…"

I stood on shaky legs, tidying up my stack of books and clearing away the glasses left on the rug. I was reaching for the bottle of arcwine when a rough hand wrapped around my wrist, holding me in place.

"Are you well?" he asked, his voice thick with something other than the anger he'd held for Drystan.

I paused. "He was being honest."

"That doesn't answer my question."

I breathed. It would take more work to avoid his questions than it would to answer them. "His words hurt, but I know there is truth to them."

"You are intelligent, Asteria. You know that, surely?" He stared at me.

I didn't have the urge to squirm under his gaze like I used to.

"That isn't the part of his sentiment that concerns me." I waved a dismissive hand. I was nearly five turns old; if I were still dim, it would be embarrassing.

"What is bothering you, then?" he asked, his words filled with concern.

Swallowing, I looked away. "He said it would have been better if I were dead. I can't help but believe that to be true, considering how much havoc I've wreaked since arriving in your realm."

Waelyn breathed in sharply, his jaw clenching. His fingers twitched until he laced them together.

"Do you regret bringing me here?" I whispered. If he couldn't hear my questions, he couldn't give an answer that would hurt far more than Drystan's intoxicated words. "Would it have been easier for you if I were in one of the other realms? If I were dead?"

"No," he said immediately. Firmly. "I regret none of my choices, Stea. Do you really not know that?"

I faltered. "I didn't want to assume."

"You know that I want you here in this realm. In my home. I've told you that much. Why would you wonder?" he asked, his brows furrowed.

No words left my mouth. I had nothing to say. It was clear that he had been fond of me before all this madness for reasons I couldn't decipher, but it didn't make sense to me that he still felt that way now after all that had happened. Surely I was more trouble than I was worth?

Waelyn took a deep breath, his chest rising and falling beneath the dark gray tunic that was unbuttoned enough to see the swirls of ink that covered his skin.

"I won't apologize for Drystan, that should come from him, but I will tell you his words are not genuine. He is hurt, though I doubt he has realized as much himself. Seeing you survive where others haven't been so lucky is hard for him."

He must be talking about Kharis, I thought. Had they lost themselves to the Blackwell?

"I understand." Drystan was prickly at the best of times, but struggling with something like that would make anyone sour.

Waelyn sighed. "Well, we've found what we were looking for. Why don't we get some dinner?"

"Sure," I agreed, and he led the way through the winding corridors of his estate, routing a path to the kitchen that was becoming comfortingly familiar to me.

We were nearing the Great Hall when I felt it—a surge of strong arcane that left the scent of cedar in the air. Seconds later, the doors slammed open, hitting the stone walls with a crack.

Waelyn's hand immediately found my waist, pushing me behind his large frame as he faced the open doorway.

"Lord Nox," a feminine voice rasped. "I have returned."

The God of Death and Darkness released the tension in his shoulders, shaking his head at whoever stood before him. Curiosity got the best of me, and I peeked out from behind him, taking in the tall, slender figure of a woman.

Her eyes glowed, a burning orange stare that reminded me of the bonfires that often accompanied temple celebrations. Her hair hung straight and dark around her face, framing the angular edges of her jaw and nose. Her lips were full, rounding out her beautiful features.

How did she know Waelyn?

"I can see that," he said plainly. Then he turned to me, stepping aside so that I was in full view. "Aura, this is Maeve."

Ah, so she wasn't in his inner circle.

"Hello," I said.

"It's a pleasure," she replied, smiling enough to show her white teeth—blinding, like Orien's had been. Her eyes scanned over my figure, taking stock. She wore no emotions on her face, but I felt the weight of her stare nonetheless. She held her side as she stood in the doorway, crimson dripping onto the floor.

"You're bleeding," I said calmly.

She looked down at the wound, then back up at me. "I am."

I expected Waelyn to take care of her, to use his arcane to heal her like he had done for me so many times, but he stayed planted where he stood, turning to look at me.

"Can you make a salve? I don't have any on hand," Waelyn asked.

"Um, sure. Let me go get my supplies."

"Maeve, you can take one of the guest rooms while Aura gets you patched up."

I left them in the Great Hall to collect the supplies I'd barely touched since buying them from that shop in the city. My chambers were still and quiet when I arrived. The silence that I once craved felt almost unsettling now. I'd gotten used to the whispers in the back of my mind, and now that they had found their rightful place, they were content. I grabbed the things I needed and made my way back through the corridors as quickly as I could.

Waelyn was waiting in the halls outside one of the rooms I'd never been in. For how little he hosted, he had far too many spare chambers.

"In here," he said, gesturing toward the open door.

Maeve lay on the bed, a spare blanket beneath her to stop the blood oozing out of her side from staining the linens. She inspected her wound as if it did not belong to her, poking and prodding as though she felt no pain.

"Stop that," I scolded, standing by the desk beside the bed as I unpacked my materials and got to work.

She gave me a dry look. "Were you a healer back home?"

"Back home?" I asked, crushing a bulb beneath my working knife and dropping the innards into a bowl.

"The Mortal world," she smiled. "I can smell it on you."

Perhaps I should bathe more.

"I was not a healer," I informed her, biting my tongue about the other part. I no longer considered the Mortal world my home, but she did not need to know that.

She sat up to watch as I poured water into the bowl before mixing thoroughly. Then I ground everything into a paste with my pestle.

"An alchemist, then?" she pushed.

"No, I just dabble," I replied. "Lie down." I doubted she was the type to take orders, but she obeyed, eyeing me suspiciously.

"That better not hurt," she said warily, as though she hadn't been picking at her wound mere moments ago.

"It won't," I assured her as I cleaned the wound.

Once the excess grime and blood were cleared, I dried her skin and smeared the salve over the bloody punctures.

"Were you bitten?" I asked.

"Stabbed," she replied. "Messy getaway." That part was directed at Waelyn, who leaned against the doorframe in a way that made it hard to focus on the task at hand. He didn't seem worried about her state. Perhaps this was a frequent occurrence.

I put a bandage over the wound and tied a piece of cloth around the woman's ribs to keep it in place. Then I scraped the excess salve into a little glass jar.

"Here," I said, handing it to her. "When it starts to hurt again, put that on and change your bandages."

She looked at the jar distastefully. "Thanks."

"You're welcome to stay here tonight and recover before our meeting tomorrow morning," Waelyn said, saving me from acknowledging her gratitude. "Was there anything urgent you had to report?"

She shook her head. "Nothing that can't wait. Will Aura be joining us tomorrow?"

I didn't miss the question in his gaze as he stared at her. "Yes."

She gave a tight-lipped smile. "Very well. I will see you both when the birds sing."

I didn't mean to kill my lover.

He was a kind man. Being in his presence had always reminded me of sitting in the sun. He had the kind of warmth that heated my skin until it burned. We met years ago, under the two moons of Kaedia. He'd asked for my hand, and when he smiled at me, I'd given it without a second thought. He was beautiful; no one could blame me for falling for a mortal.

I didn't mean to kill my lover.

We had spent hours in the very same cottage where I stood now. I'd explored more than his body; I knew his mind. That was how I knew he was kind; he was good. He was to be trusted.

My heart wrenched at the thought.

I didn't mean to kill my lover.

When I had arrived at the cottage in the early morning, the sun was barely peeking through the arcane trees that covered the mountains. I hadn't expected to find my lover in the arms of another. I'd been angry; I'd wanted to scare him. How dare a mortal cross me? How could he break my heart?

Still, I hadn't meant to murder him.

I didn't mean to kill my lover.

No, I'd wanted to kill his. The woman was pretty, with flushed skin and a shine to her long hair that I would never achieve. Had his betrayal been about beauty? It didn't matter now; she was hardly beautiful anymore—her skin was mangled and covered with the red blood only mortals could bleed.

I didn't mean to kill my lover.

Yet his body lay crumpled at my feet, his once handsome face permanently contorted in horror at my hand. I couldn't remember how it happened; it had been so fast. I still stood in the exact place where I'd frozen when I first saw them together, their limbs intertwined with frenzied lovemaking. I hadn't moved, yet they'd been brutally and destroyed in a flash of darkness.

It couldn't have been me; I didn't have power like that. Gods, I didn't have power at all. I was as useless as a mortal when it came to arcane, yet I couldn't deny that the darkness that enveloped the room before their screams felt familiar.

My hands… my hands were covered in blood. Fresh petals lay scattered at my feet, slowly being drowned in the red liquid that oozed from my lover's body. An hour ago, I'd been picking flowers to bring to him.

I wanted to laugh, but the movement brought bile up my throat. I turned and vomited as the room filled with static electricity.

Verena was here. I could feel it.

Sure enough, when I looked up, she stood in the center of the destruction. Her bright blue eyes were wide with shock as she surveyed the scene. When her gaze met mine, I saw the horror they had held before now drowned by confusion. She didn't understand how her younger sister could have created the bloody scene we stood in. I didn't have an explanation for it either.

Her mouth moved, but I never heard the words. My head was buzzing, and the sticky blood on my hands was driving me crazy. I wiped my palms on my dress over and over and over, but the feeling didn't go away, it just left streaks of red on the pale lavender dress that had been one of my favorites before this moment.

I didn't see her move, but then Verena's hands were clenched around my wrists, pulling my hands from my dress. They were rubbed raw now, my own blood seeping through the cracks. She was still trying to talk to me, but I couldn't hear anything over the *whispers in my ears.*

I didn't mean to kill my lover.

Did I say that out loud? It didn't matter, because then I was falling. Arcane enveloped me with a nauseating feeling—we were contorting our bodies through space.

Verena reappeared in front of me in an instant, her arm around my shoulder protectively as she guided me down the hall to a part of Castle Dreka I'd never been in before. It was all a blur as she pulled me through a set of chamber doors, and then through to the bathroom. The scent of her magick—rain, and something burning—filled the room around us, and then the tub was full of steaming water. In her next breath, she was pulling the ruined silk from my body and instructing me to get in the warm pool.

When I didn't move on my own, Verena pulled me into the tub, guiding one leg after another over the tall walls that caged the steaming water.

It was too hot, I tried to tell her, but my lips wouldn't move. I couldn't stop seeing his broken body, it plagued my thoughts.

In a matter of seconds, I was up to my chest in the bath. Verena had started pouring different soaps and elixirs into the water.

"How are you feeling?" she asked, and for the first time since she had arrived on the scene, I heard her words.

"I don't know," I whispered back, my voice suddenly too sore to be used.

She lathered a cloth with sweet-smelling soap before reaching for my hands. They were still coated in his blood.

"What happened?" she asked softly.

I'd never heard this tone from her before. Verena wasn't known for being soft. It must have looked horrid from her point of view.

How had I killed two people without lifting a finger? It wasn't possible. It just wasn't. Yet, somehow, I also knew that I had—it had been me. I just couldn't make sense of it.

"I don't know," I repeated. I was hollow, empty. There was nothing left for me to feel, for me to think.

"Whatever happened, it wasn't your fault," Verena said as she poured water down my back, wetting the strands of my hair that were caked in blood.

I tried to let her words sink in, but they didn't feel right.

"Yes, it was," I argued, but she just shook her head.

"How? I've never seen bodies so mangled, that's not something you're capable of," she replied. Her eyes were hard, a cold blue that reminded me of a storm as she lathered my hair.

"I don't know—there was this... darkness... and then they were dead." I was stammering, but Verena seemed to understand what I was saying.

"Asteria, you don't have any arcane abilities," she said, as if trying to convince herself and me.

I knew I wasn't strong; I didn't need a reminder. I'd been this way since birth, a disappointment.

"There's no way you could have done that," she persisted. "I'm going to help you out of this."

I couldn't convince her that I was responsible for the murder of two mortals, but I knew.

I knew that the darkness belonged to me. I was powerless, but I felt it swirling deep in my chest, even now. It festered, calling out for more. More blood. More destruction. More death.

But what scared me was that I wanted to obey its call.

I wanted the darkness.

CHAPTER THIRTY-ONE

Two sharp knocks on my chamber doors pulled me from sleep.

My head was pounding, a dull ache making its way through my skull. Was this the price of recovering memories?

The scene that had played out after I'd closed my eyes was familiar, as much as I didn't want to believe I had done something like that. My own lover, a mortal nonetheless, dead at my hand. I hardly remembered the man, though I supposed that was the purpose of the seal in the first place. I remembered loving him, though I didn't know why. I was young, when we were together. I didn't even know what love was back then. I wasn't sure I knew what it was now.

"Stea?" the voice on the other side of the door called.

Waelyn.

"Come in!" I called out, and within the second he was standing in my chambers. "Sorry, I was just thinking."

"Care to share?" he prompted, moving to the bedside. The mattress dipped as he perched on the edge.

The god was dressed in a black tunic and pants, his sleeves rolled up enough to show off the ink on his arms. His fingers were weighed down with silver rings, and there was a dagger I'd never noticed before sheathed at his waist.

Reminding myself not to stare, I answered his question. "Memories are returning, it's an odd feeling."

His magick pressed against my being, assessing, scanning. "You're in pain," he said.

It wasn't a question.

"It'll fade. Just a headache." I waved him off.

His hand came up anyway, his palm cradling my cheek for a brief moment before his fingers pressed against my temple. There was a rush of warmth and the ache was completely gone.

"Better?" he asked, pulling away reluctantly.

"Much." I nodded. "Thank you."

"There's nothing to thank me for, Stea. I can't sit here while you're in pain." He paused. "May I ask which memories plagued your sleep?"

I hesitated. Sure, he already knew about the incident, but telling him I had remembered it was like confirming that I truly had done such a thing. I stared at him, reminding myself that this was the Reaper sitting before me. He wouldn't shy away from a little bloodshed.

"I remembered killing the lover I had when I was a whelp."

"Ah." He seemed to tense. "Are you feeling alright? I imagine the grief can be strong when remembering the death of someone close to you."

I shook my head. "I'm fine. The hardest part is acknowledging that I did that, but I hardly know him. Knew him. I couldn't tell you anything about him, or about the time we spent together. I was hurt back then, seeing what I did. Hurt enough to kill him, but none of that is present now."

Waelyn's brows furrowed. "What did he do to you?"

I stared at my hands. "He had another with him. A woman I didn't know about. The betrayal was more than I could handle."

The god became as still as a statue. A long, tense silence settled over us, and the only thing I could focus on was Waelyn's fists, clenched so hard that his knuckles were white.

"That is unforgivable, Stea," he said, his eyes meeting mine with an intensity only he was capable of.

"That was the opinion I held too, considering I killed them both on the spot. It's like I can still feel their blood on my hands."

Waelyn nodded. "My first kill stays with me too. It's not something you easily forget."

I wanted to ask about it, to pry until he gave me every last detail of his early life, but the faraway look in his eyes kept my lips clamped shut. Instead of satiating my curiosity, I focused on the warmth radiating from the God of Death and Darkness. He was always warm, even when it was frigid in the estate, or when the wind was especially brisk in the Night Realm winter. It was a feat that impressed me, despite how mundane it seemed. It made it easy to want to be close to him—that, and the ever-present smell of smoke and pine.

Just seeing Waelyn was enough to put me at ease, to release the tension in my body and trust that everything would be all right. I nearly scoffed at the thought of a Night Realm god, let alone the ruler of the realm, being comforting. But he was. Waelyn was safe. I trusted him, even though that concept was practically foreign to me.

A warning that I shouldn't be so dependent on the god came to mind, and I did my best to stifle the thought. Sure, I had yet to see the other realms, to meet the other rulers and citizens of each, but surely none could compare to the dark-haired man at my side now. None could see me through what he had. None had spent centuries allowing me to see through their eyes. Waelyn had said it would be my choice which realm I ended up in, and back then I hadn't been confident which would be my home, but now I knew. I wanted to be wherever he was.

Besides, if my power really was death, the Night Realm was surely where I belonged.

"You should get dressed. We have much to discuss with Drystan and Maeve," Waelyn said, pulling me from my thoughts.

I'd nearly forgotten about the woman with ember eyes. "Of course. I just need a moment."

I slid out of the bed, despite the protest from my skin as it braced against the chilly air, and headed for the bathing chambers. The mirror above the sink showed a wild mane of white waves. My cheeks heated at the thought of Waelyn seeing me so disheveled. It was a foolish concern—he'd seen me in much worse shape—but the feeling persisted. I did what I could with some water and a comb, but it was a futile attempt and I gave up after a few minutes, letting the curls hang free rather than confining them to a ribbon like I often did. I was feeling generous today.

The eyes that stared back at me were odd. The same hue of lavender, as bright as always, but something had changed. I leaned over the sink to get a closer look and saw what I hadn't been able to from a few paces away. The black of my pupils spilled over into my irises with thin, inky tendrils. Not enough to be noticed by most, but I saw the difference. Was this because of my submersion in the Blackwell?

I blinked, pulling away from my reflection. That was something to worry about later.

My ablutions took a few minutes, and then I headed back into the bedchamber in search of something appropriate to wear. Waelyn had vacated the room, but I still felt his presence nearby. He was likely in the hall, giving me some privacy to dress.

How long had I been able to feel him by his arcane? I had always been aware of it when it was strong, but this was different. It was like I could pinpoint his whereabouts without thinking. Was it just Waelyn? Or could I do it with the others?

Drystan was supposed to be at the estate; I could try with him. Focusing, I attempted to zero in on the essence of the brunet god. I imagined the tingling sensation that his arcane left behind, the dull hum of power, and the scent of cinnamon.

It was as easy as breathing. He was waiting in the Great Hall with another. Maeve. I read his signature, then hers. Maeve's arcane was different, and spotty, unlike the gods'. It was as if her power ebbed. It was charred and burnt, different from the smoky essence that accompanied Waelyn's power.

I blinked, and the feeling was gone. That was definitely new. Did all arcane beings feel others like that? I'd have to ask Waelyn.

Absentmindedly gathering clothes, I dressed in dark pants and a black tunic with long sleeves. Finishing with my black boots, I strapped my sheath around my ribs, tucking the amethyst dagger into it, and opened the door to meet Waelyn.

"Perfect," he said as soon as his eyes found me. "Ready?"

I nodded. "They're in the Great Hall, yes?"

He looked at me oddly. "Yes. How did you know?"

"I can feel them. Or their arcane, at least. I've never been able to do that before," I revealed, unable to stop the tiniest of smiles from pulling at my lips.

His eyes lit up with amusement. "It seems your connection to the arcane is already changing, Stea."

Waelyn held his arm out to me, and I slipped my hand into the crook of his elbow without a second thought. Something in my chest always pulled me closer to him. I wouldn't resist the urge if he offered an opportunity. He guided me down the corridors to the Great Hall, where I could feel the dull hum of Drystan's presence.

The doors were open when we arrived, and Maeve's stare found me as soon as we darkened the doorway. Her eyes locked in on the point where my hand touched Waelyn, and I pulled away under the weight of her scrutiny. He looked at me with confusion etched into his features, a slight frown pulling at his lips. Drystan spoke before he could question me about the withdrawal.

"Good morning! I thought you were going to sleep the day away," the brunet god called out to me, his voice dripping in sarcasm.

"I'll never be on time as far as you're concerned. Why don't you act as my alarm clock from now on? Perhaps then you'll finally be satisfied," I retorted, following Waelyn as he moved toward the long oval table that was set up in the middle of the room. It hadn't been here the last time we used this space, but I imagined this was how his throne room typically looked. Was this where he held the council?

"And take the position from Lord Nox? I think not," he replied, shooting an odd look at the God of Death and Darkness, who shook his head in response.

"Shall we get started?" Maeve interjected, her tone stiff. She sat to the left of Drystan, across from me. Waelyn took the chair by my side.

He held up a finger to her. "Maeve is an informant who works for the Night Realm. She keeps an eye on anything happening in the other realms that may concern us," he explained.

"Do the other realms have informants too? Spies that visit Night?" I asked, looking between Maeve and Waelyn.

"No," Maeve spoke. "The Night Realm is in a unique position, having a ruler that is so young. The other realms aren't under the same pressure that we are. Now, may I begin?"

Waelyn nodded, though his features were tense.

"First things first—are either of you aware of the Light Realm's infiltration of the dissenter group that's been causing problems here?" She watched the two gods for any signs of surprise.

There were none.

"Of course," Drystan scoffed. "Lux is digging his own grave

sending them here."

"Aren't you worried that their presence will encourage the rebels?" Maeve pressed. "We should take care of this."

I had a feeling she didn't mean 'send them back to the Light Realm'. When people were killed in the Immortal world, where did they go?

"Lord Nox." Drystan turned toward the dark-haired god. "Will you please explain to Maeve that I'm right about this?"

"Surely Lord Nox cares more about the safety and security of his realm than using this against Lux," Maeve shot back.

Waelyn cleared his throat and they both fell silent. "The peacekeeping event is on the horizon. It will be wiser for us to address the god-king there when we have evidence. If we eliminate his citizens here and now, he will deny their presence completely."

Maeve's lips pressed into a thin line, and Drystan wore a smug smile. Were they always at odds? They almost seemed to be his advisors, giving opposite perspectives on the issues of his realm. If Maeve was as old as Drystan, their insight was likely invaluable to him.

"Is it safe to confront him there?" I chimed in. Three pairs of eyes turned to me. "From what I've heard of Lux, he is prideful, is he not? Wouldn't someone like that react poorly to having his peers hear negative claims about him?"

Waelyn shrugged. "Perhaps, but his reactions are not my concern."

"He is powerful, isn't he?" I pushed. The idea of Waelyn angering the ruler referred to as the 'god-king' made my stomach knot up.

The edge of his lip kicked into a smirk. "He is no match for me, Stea."

It was brief, but the arrogance that seeped into the air was tangible. His confidence melted the anxiety that had started creeping into my bones. Waelyn was young, but he was strong. I couldn't forget that.

"The worst that lifebinder can do is banish us from the realm, but even he couldn't keep that barrier active for long," Drystan scoffed in agreement.

Waelyn smiled at me. "Next item."

Maeve blinked. "Lord Rel is up to something. He's gathering hundreds of those terrible arcane monstrosities. They're organized and trained. I watched for weeks and couldn't get a sense of what they were preparing for, but it seemed big."

Lord Rel was Ruler of the Arcane Realm. There weren't many temples in Kaedia dedicated to him, as he was a god who predominantly blessed the fae. Orien had despised that fact and refused to honor him or the Kingdom of Elirede anywhere in Kaedia.

"Why would Rel be building an army of unkillable creatures?" Drystan mused, leaning back in his chair with a finger on his chin.

"Unkillable?" I echoed.

"Arcane is energy; it cannot be destroyed," Waelyn explained. "Those beings are pesky on the battlefield. Even when obliterated, they reform in a matter of seconds."

"Have you fought against them before?"

Both gods shook their heads.

"Rel has never been a foe. I wonder if that's changed," Waelyn mused.

Maeve steepled her hands. "Then there's Zenir. He seemed… agitated."

"Isn't he always?" Drystan drawled.

She shook her head, straight black hair swaying over her shoulders. "Not like this. He was nervous about something, and the streets were quiet in his realm."

Drystan dismissed her words with a wave. "He's been concerned about the dwindling population of the Elemental Realm for several turns."

She stared at him with fire in her gaze. "This is *different*. He was talking about the newly crowned King of Itharene—the boy. He didn't speak highly of him."

"What could the boy-king have done to lose his favor so quickly?" Waelyn asked, mostly to himself. "More importantly, what has Zenir *worried*?"

"I didn't stick around to ask," Maeve said.

"Right. Is that everything then?" Waelyn remarked, his hands on the arms of his chair as he prepared to stand.

"One last thing," the spy said, her ember stare finding me. "Lux knows about her. About what she is."

Waelyn tensed. "Elaborate."

There were many things Lux could know, starting with the fact that I was a seer or, more importantly, that I'd bathed in the Blackwell.

Maeve smiled, pleased to have his full attention now. "He's heard rumors of her days in the Mortal world. He's heard accounts of the effects of her odd eyes, the intensity of her visions. He suspects she will be the one to fulfill the Prophecy of Balance."

Waelyn's breath caught. "And?"

"And he wants her for himself."

CHAPTER THIRTY-TWO

"Ouch," I hissed as another pin stuck into my stomach.

"If you'd stop moving so much I wouldn't stab you as often!" Cara grumbled, beyond exasperated.

I looked down at her to respond, but she flinched when my eyes met hers. My mouth closed, the words on the tip of my tongue long gone. It had been so long since anyone had cowered under my gaze that I'd nearly forgotten how rare it had been for me to look someone in the eyes in the Mortal world.

Cara mumbled under her breath and moved on to another spot on the dress. Waelyn had escorted me to the shop early this morning, and I'd been standing on the pedestal in the center of the room for hours while Cara worked on a gown for the peacekeeping event that was happening in mere days. Customers came and went while she poked and prodded at me, leaving their coins on the counter when she was too involved in the layers of fabric draping my frame to tend to them.

The gown was black. At least, the layers Cara had started were. The color dominated my closet in the Immortal world, just as it had in Dreka. Part of me hoped it was Waelyn's subtle way of branding me with the Night Realm's colors. With the symbols of Nox.

Hours passed, ticking by on the clock above Cara's counter. My legs grew numb and stiff as she worked, but I knew better than to interrupt. Eventually, a familiar brunet appeared in the doorway of the shop.

"Oh! Lord Drystan, hello!" Cara exclaimed when she spotted his figure.

"Hello, Cara," he replied, his tone flat. "I'm here to collect the godling."

"I'm just finishing up this stitch, then you can have her," the seamstress replied, returning to threading her needle through the panel of fabric she was currently engaged with.

"Where's... Lord Nox?" I asked, stumbling over my words as I attempted to use his correct title.

Drystan smirked at my effort. "He and Maeve are discussing some of the finer details of her discoveries. Their meeting is running long."

The acid that bit the back of my throat was surprising and unwelcome. I swallowed, but the feeling didn't go away, and neither did the knot that was quickly forming in my stomach. Was this... *jealousy?*

I could only remember feeling this way toward Verena and the other whelps when their powers grew and mine didn't. When was the last time I'd been jealous when it concerned someone else's relationships? I couldn't recall.

That begged the question: *why* was I jealous that Maeve and Waelyn were spending time together?

The voice in the back of my mind was quiet these days, but even *it* told me not to be so dim. The fondness that warmed my chest when I saw him, the need to be close, the familiarity of his touch and his scent, and the safety I felt when he was around were all signs that my feelings for Waelyn had grown wild and uncontained. They were strong enough that the idea of him alone with Maeve, close enough that she could touch him—or worse, he could touch her—nearly made me sick.

"You've gone pale, godling," Drystan said, his brows furrowed in a rare gesture of concern.

I swallowed. "I've been standing here awhile." It was technically the truth.

"We need to get back to training if standing is making you ill," he scoffed.

"Seems we do," I replied noncommittally.

Cara finished her work and removed the mass of fabric from my body. I was free to move again. Stepping off the pedestal felt like soaking in a warm bath after a long day. Gathering my cloak from the hook near the door and fastening it around my neck, I called out a quick thanks to Cara, and we were on our way.

The wind howled through the streets of the Onyx City, even though it was only late afternoon. Winter here seemed brutal; were the other realms the same? As much as I'd grown to enjoy my time here, curiosity still burned at the back of my mind when it came to the rest of the Immortal world.

"It's quite cold this year," Drystan complained, pulling his jacket closed across his chest.

"Is it usually not this frigid?" I asked through chattering teeth.

"Occasionally. We've been lucky for the last few turns. I'd forgotten what a brutal winter felt like," he said, giving me a helpful explanation for once. Perhaps he was coming down with something.

"We were always buried in snow this time of year," I told him, remembering the times Tolith had dived into the banks of fluffy white flakes. He was like a sprite when it came to the snow. He loved it with the kind of awe one would regard the gods with.

"I hate the cold," Drystan muttered, his hands coming up to hold the pointed tips of his ears that were quickly turning red.

"You need a cloak."

"I have plenty," he shot back.

"None good enough to wear?" I looked at him pointedly. He

only wore pants and a tunic beneath his jacket, no wonder he was shivering.

He sighed and shook his head. "We're almost there, stop pestering me."

The estate was in view, the gardens coated in a dusting of snow. The wind was tossing it into the air, creating an icy mist that chilled my skin wherever it touched. Drystan stopped when another gust tore through us, cursing under his breath.

"What are you doing?" I asked, nodding toward the path that led back to the front doors of the estate. "We're so close."

He shook his head, reaching out to grab my arm. A surge of arcane pushed at my skin, and my being turned inside out before righting again. When the sensation cleared, we were standing in the Great Hall.

"Ugh," I groaned, holding my sides.

"Apologies, godling, I couldn't take the wind any longer," Drystan said, sounding sincere enough.

"I believe I told you no arcane travel," another voice rang out, silky and deep. He was displeased with the brunet god, that much was clear.

Waelyn's eyes were focused on me, full of concern as he moved across the room. Maeve stood at the table behind him, her brows pinched as she watched him abandon whatever they had been working on.

"It's ridiculously cold out there, Nox. I was saving her from freezing to death," Drystan said in defense.

Waelyn shot him a look that said he didn't believe him for a minute. "Are you alright?" he asked me.

I nodded. "Apologies for the interruption," I said, before he could reach me. Before he could touch me and melt the knot in my stomach that only grew tighter when I saw Maeve.

He paused at my words, his eyes narrowing ever so slightly.

The shadows that cloaked him reached out toward me, but I did not relish in that fact.

He noticed.

"I'll find you after I'm done here," he said, his words a promise of questions to be asked.

I nodded, saying nothing as I turned back toward the doors that would lead me out of the room. I couldn't breathe in here under Maeve's pointed stare; the tiny smile on her lips as he returned to the table.

I couldn't watch.

Drystan lingered behind, speaking words I didn't hear as I let the doors shut behind me. I needed to take my mind off the unease that filled my body. I needed to get warm.

Making my way to my chambers, I tried to focus on anything but Maeve and Waelyn. I hated to admit it, but Drystan being there made me feel a little bit better.

Since when was I so obsessed? Waelyn could see whoever he wanted and be with whoever he wanted, though nausea did creep up my throat at that last thought.

My room was silent, untouched from this morning. An open sketchbook lay on my desk, the rough outline of roots drawn on the exposed page. A half-filled glass sat next to it, a thin paintbrush resting against the brim. The windows had an edge of frost coating them, and the room was chilly. I'd have to hunt down an extra blanket for my bed tonight or else I really would freeze to death.

Moving to the wardrobe, I secured a pair of thick leggings and socks, as well as a tunic that was lined with extra layers of fabric. I'd thought these pieces were much too thick when Waelyn had originally brought them back from Cara's shop, but now I saw their purpose. It got cold in his stone estate, much colder than the temple dorms. I was thankful for the clothes and their absurd thickness.

Once I had redressed in clothes that weren't damp, I padded through the corridors to the kitchen. I was sure I could find the cabinet where Waelyn kept his herbs for tea. I could still feel the three arcane beings in the Great Hall as I traveled through the estate, but I did my best to pay them no mind.

The kitchen was dark, the hanging lanterns void of any flame. I brushed my hands over the countertops in search of the matches I'd seen Waelyn use, but they were bare. Sighing, I stared up at the dark lanterns. As if I had willed it, they lit up, hungry flames flickering in the circles of glass.

Breathing in sharply, I looked at my hands, half expecting some type of physical change. My skin was as pale as ever, but my hands tingled. Was this what it felt like to use arcane? Was it even my doing? Perhaps Waelyn's estate was enchanted, magicked to sense the whims of its inhabitants. Though if that were true, why would he ever bother with matches?

Shaking the questions away, I found the kettle and the tea sachets in one cabinet, and a glass saucer in another. Within moments there was water bubbling on the stove. I poured the water into the cup, steeping the tea until it turned a dark color. I took a sip, hissing as it burned my tongue, then cleared the counters and cleaned my mess while I waited for it to cool. Once I was satisfied, I gathered my drink and headed for the library.

The fire was burnt down to embers, but with a little help, it was crackling once again, casting a warm glow on the overstuffed chairs I'd come to love. I settled into one of them, sipping my beverage and picking up where I'd left off in one of the hundreds of tomes detailing the Night Realm's history and customs.

An hour ticked by before I felt him enter the room. My entire body prickled with awareness as his smoke and pine scent filled the air.

"Stea." His footsteps echoed off the floor as he moved to the chair next to me. "What's going on?"

I marked the page I was on, putting the book aside as I looked up at him. "What do you mean?" I asked, trying not to focus on the way the ends of his hair brushed his brow or the way his eyes seemed to pin me in place.

"I can feel the… turmoil. It sits in your stomach, doesn't it?" he elaborated, his brows creasing.

I frowned. "How did you know that?"

He shook his head. "I can feel it. When you feel something strongly, I can too."

"Just me?"

Waelyn nodded. "Just you."

"Odd," I replied, no more words coming to mind. I had never heard of anything like what he was describing, and frankly, it made me feel insecure, knowing he felt what I did. How many times had he known exactly how overwhelmed I was when I was adjusting to the Immortal world?

More importantly, did he know how I felt about him?

"I ask again, Stea. What's going on?" he repeated firmly.

How did I even begin to explain? I couldn't. There was no way to justify why I was jealous of Maeve and the attention he gave her. I was acting like a foolish mortal, lovestruck and dumb. It was embarrassing.

"I was feeling sick earlier when Drystan brought me back to the estate. My stomach was turning." Technically true.

"That's not all," he insisted.

I swirled the dregs of my tea, breaking away from his stare. "You were busy. I didn't want to disturb you and Maeve."

Understanding flickered across his features as soon as her name left my mouth. That was a mistake. I shouldn't have mentioned her.

"Is this about her?"

Oh gods. I fought to contain the idiotic thoughts swirling in my mind, but it was no use.

"She doesn't like me, you know," I said, unwilling to answer his question directly.

"Then she's a fool," he retorted immediately. "But you should know Maeve takes a while to warm up to people. Her walls are tall—that much you should understand." His pointed stare made it no secret what he was trying to say.

It wasn't my fault I was guarded—I had to be in order to survive. It wasn't easy to keep the secret of my fae heritage in Dreka.

"How long did it take her to *warm up* to you?" I replied, unable to keep the bitter tone out of my voice.

Amusement twinkled in his eyes as he scoffed. "Decades. I'm still not sure she likes me."

I rolled my eyes. "She does, I promise."

"Now, Drystan… he got through to her in record time," Waelyn mused. "I never quite understood how that happened."

"Are they… involved?" I asked. It was the only explanation I could think of.

Waelyn tilted his head. "Perhaps. I've never asked."

"If I didn't know better, I would assume she was interested in you," I said knowingly, and the god's lips kicked up a fraction. He was enjoying this.

"You'll have to elaborate on that thought," he prompted.

"You aren't that oblivious."

He raised his eyebrows. "I might be."

I sighed, finding the right words. "Her eyes find you first in a group, and she smiles when she has your attention." It sounded silly when I said it out loud.

Waelyn smirked. "Is that not just because I am who I am?

Wouldn't she behave that way if she craved power or station here?" He posed good points, but that was because he didn't see himself the way I did.

"Sure, but you…" I took another breath. "You're kind and *compassionate*. You're intelligent and thoughtful, and charming when you want to be."

He stared at me, his mouth slightly agape. I couldn't stop the heat that burned my cheeks.

I cleared my throat. "Not to mention the fact that you're Nox, God of Death and Darkness, Ruler of the Night Realm. I'm sure she wouldn't be the first to be enamored with you."

There was a long moment of silence, and I was worried I'd said too much. Embarrassment burned through me, leaving a shameful scorch throughout my body. I'd all but confessed the thoughts that had filled my mind over the last few weeks. The feelings I'd harbored for the god next to me. Vulnerability had never been my strong suit, yet there I lay, exposed to his judgment.

"I can't say many have lined up to be courted," he finally said.

Disappointment and relief tore through me all at once that he hadn't acknowledged my words, and I wasn't sure which I felt more potently. Did he feel those emotions too?

"It hasn't happened, or you haven't noticed?" I shouldn't have been asking those questions, but I couldn't keep the words from spilling out.

"I haven't cared to take note."

"I see."

He stared at me curiously. "Stea, are you…" He frowned to himself. "Are you tired? I can escort you to your chambers."

I wanted to push, to know what he had been intending to say before he changed his mind, but I didn't. I couldn't. What if he asked me a question I couldn't bear to answer?

Part of me knew which words were on the tip of his tongue, which question he would ask.

Was *I* enamored with him?

The answer was yes.

CHAPTER THIRTY-THREE

Waelyn was silent for the entire walk back to my chambers. His arm brushed mine every so often, sending tiny shocks across my skin. My fingers twitched with the need to hold his, but I contained myself. He hadn't acknowledged my words—my compliments—so it was clear that he didn't feel what I did. The attention he paid me was because I was the first godling since his arrival in the realm, or maybe because I was suspected to be the one to fulfil some ancient prophecy.

He felt nothing more for me.

Sadness weighed heavily in my chest, pushing at my ribs and crushing my lungs. When had I gotten so attached?

Part of me missed the version of myself that had never allowed anyone to get close enough to make me feel this way. I'd lived almost four turns after the mortal; four turns spent keeping people at arm's length. Why had I allowed Waelyn to get close?

We arrived at my chambers too soon, yet not soon enough. Waelyn's brows were pinched, his gaze swimming with something I couldn't place. Did he feel the sorrow seeping into my bones?

"Stea, I—"

"I should sleep, I'll see you in the morning," I cut him off, slipping through the doors to my room and closing them behind me before I could hear what he had to say. I didn't want his pity.

I felt him linger for a moment, his presence on the other side of the door like a beacon calling out to me. I was relieved when he finally retreated to his chambers. I wasn't sure how much longer my self-control would last.

Too antsy to sleep, I drew a hot bath. The chill from the afternoon hadn't quite left my bones, and it was still early enough in the evening that I wouldn't be tired in the morning if I stayed up just a bit longer.

As soon as I was submerged in the steaming water, I felt a little better. The warmth slowed my racing thoughts and the beating of my heart. I could focus on what was important.

I cared for the God of Death and Darkness.

And I needed to quell it. I couldn't carry on this way, allowing his words and actions to make my chest flutter or my cheeks burn. It was embarrassing, especially now that I had spilled my guts to him.

I sank beneath the water, holding my breath. When my lungs burned, I resurfaced, breathing in gulps of cool air.

It was then that the world turned black, my eyes unseeing. The water in the tub was gone, and the air on my skin was no longer cool but humid and reeking of metal and rot.

Rough cloth pressed against my eyes, and my wrists burned where coarse rope bound them. I was stretched so far it was painful.

Groans filled the room, the sounds of the injured and dying. They echoed off the walls and invaded my every thought. The noise faded to nothing as thundering steps pounded off the stone floors. The silence was loud, and so was the fear that enveloped the space.

"My darling Asteria," a voice dripping in malice spoke.

Chills ran down my spine, and the hair on my arms stood on end. The king of Kaedia was speaking.

"How did you end up in this mess?" Orien crooned, his fingers rough as he yanked the blindfold away from my face.

My scalp stung as he ripped strands of hair with it. I swallowed a cry.

Words that weren't my own left my lips. "You tell me."

I was in a dungeon, crumbling stone walls encasing me. There were cells lining either side of the hall, thick bars imprisoning their occupants. To my right, there were several faeries in one filthy cell, the green tint of their skin nearly invisible beneath the grime that coated them. They clung to each other, two females and one younger male, protecting each other from the king's presence.

What horrors had they faced before?

He hummed, circling me. "What fun shall we get up to this evening?"

Aches trembled through my extended limbs, reminders of the fun he'd had every night for the last month. Skin sticky with blood; hair drenched in sweat plastered to my neck. I stared back at him. I would offer no suggestions for my own torture, even if his prodding gaze demanded so.

"You really shouldn't leave the decision to me, dear," he warned, waving his hand over a table of wicked instruments that were coated in crimson. "But if you insist on remaining silent…"

His hand hovered over a curved blade that would be able to gut me in one slice. His fingers twitched—he'd made his mind up. I looked away as his hand closed around the hilt. Watching would do nothing but make my stomach turn.

With my eyes squeezed shut, I had no warning when the tip of the blade broke my skin. I clamped my lips together, unwilling to give him the satisfaction of crying out.

"Doesn't that hurt?" he asked, digging the blade in deeper.

It was as if an iron-hot poker had pierced my stomach, just below my ribs. Pain spread through me like wildfire, and I twisted in an attempt to get away from the knife, but Orien just laughed as he thrust it through my skin.

Perhaps my reaction wasn't enough for him. Maybe that was why he pulled the blade across my stomach, slicing through me like I was nothing. I couldn't stop the scream that tore through my lips as the pain became so much more than a fire. An inferno was consuming me as blood poured down the front of me.

"That's better!" he cackled, watching with a crazed glint in his eyes as I gushed like a fountain.

Spots danced in my vision. Was this the end of me? Would this be the final blow?

I gasped, and the water in the tub sloshed around me. My heart pounded against my chest as I looked around the room, no longer confined in the dungeons of Castle Dreka. My fingers found my stomach beneath the water that was now cold, tracing over the angry raised line that stretched from one side of my ribs to the other. The scar that Orien had left behind when he'd nearly eviscerated me.

It seemed another memory had resurfaced.

Pulling the plug from the tub, I stood and found a towel as the water drained.

The images of the memory were stuck in my mind, playing on a loop. The sounds the imprisoned had made; the smell of rot; the fae clinging to each other… to life. The pain Orien had inflicted was secondary; I'd already healed from that.

How many years had I spent in that dank dungeon? How could Verena have left me there, knowing what Orien was doing to me?

I'd always assumed the scars littering my body were from misadventures in my whelp years that I'd forgotten as time passed, but now I knew better. Orien had inflicted them.

That was why he had been so familiar with me when I had moved into the castle. I'd resided there before, though in a very different context.

The pieces were clicking into place. Nausea bubbled up my throat. I swallowed hard, willing the sensation away. Moving to the wardrobe, I dressed quickly in the warmest clothes I could find, donning a cloak and my leather boots before creeping into the corridors with my sketchbook tucked under one arm. With all the foreign memories and feelings plaguing my being, I craved something familiar.

The estate's gardens were divided into several zones, each with a different theme for the topiary. There were beasts, blades, representations of the four realms, and my personal favorite, celestial beings. I wasn't sure who or what had managed to carve the shrubs in such a meticulous way, but this corner of the garden truly resembled a night sky. There were dark plants spotted with white surrounding every sculpture, and the figures themselves showcased a variety of planets and moons. Some of the taller trees were cut into a sprinkling of stars, letting through a swathe of real starlight from the never-changing sky above.

I nestled into the grass, thankful for whatever magick Waelyn had used to enchant the grounds to keep the snow from settling. There were inches of the white fluff just outside the garden, and the thought of sitting on it made me shiver. I pulled my sketchbook from under my arm, retrieving pencils and charcoal from the pocket of my pants.

My gaze fell on the sculptures of the two moons first. I drew, paying extra attention to the way the leaves fell against one another, hiding the branches within from the curious eye. The roots of the two shrubs tangled into each other, forever entwining the plants. I committed the image to the paper of my sketchbook, putting in as many details as I could before my fingers went completely numb.

Time passed. How much, I wasn't sure. Perhaps a few hours, maybe more. My breath came out in white puffs, and my fingers weren't moving when I told them to, but I was determined to finish. I had convinced myself that this would make the feeling of Orien's blade against my skin go away; that it would erase the image of the faeries clinging to each other.

Both remained.

Birds chirped above before I was satisfied with the image I'd created. Stretching my near-frozen limbs, I got to my feet. It had been more than a day since I'd last slept, but I was not tired. I *should* have been, but I wasn't.

The grass crunched under my boots as I walked back to the estate. The kitchen would be my first stop. Some tea would ease my restless body and bring the exhaustion I knew lurked in the depths of my bones to the surface. I'd rather make myself sleep now than collapse later.

The halls were quiet, as was the norm in Waelyn's estate. I reached out with my arcane in an attempt to find him in the winding halls and wings, but it was no use. His power was too strong, his presence overwhelming. He was everywhere. I'd only found him the other day because he'd let me. The realization of his strength was like being doused in ice water. Again, I'd let myself forget who he was. *What* he was.

I wasn't expecting to find Waelyn in the kitchen, holding two steaming cups. Too wrapped up in my thoughts, I hadn't noticed the arcane presence growing stronger as I moved through the estate.

"You look cold," he said.

I froze in the doorway. "It's cold outside," I replied hesitantly.

He hummed in agreement. "Would you like some tea? It's just finished steeping." He held a cup toward me.

The God of Death and Darkness had made me tea.

I blinked, taking it from him. "Thank you."

The words came out quieter than I'd intended, but he nodded nonetheless, leaning against the edge of the counter.

A moment of silence settled over us, and the reminder of our last conversation filled my thoughts. My body ached with shame. I pulled my cloak tighter around me, despite the warmth in the kitchen that demanded I remove it entirely.

"Were you out all night?" Waelyn asked before sipping from his cup. His rings clinked against the ceramic as he set it down on the counter.

"Most of it." I wasn't sure how long I'd been in the bath, stuck in a memory I'd never wanted to relive in the first place.

He nodded. "Well, I hope you aren't too tired. We're resuming training today."

"Really?"

"Unless you still need time to recover?" He regarded me with a furrowed brow.

I shook my head quickly. "No, no. I'm ready."

I'd been itching to get back to training ever since the seals had been removed from my mind. I wanted to know if anything had changed. Truthfully, I was hoping that I'd gained some kind of unnatural strength so I could repay Drystan for all the times he'd thrown me onto the training room floor.

"Good," Waelyn murmured. "Finish your tea and change. I'll escort you to the training room."

"Ugh, that felt like a rib," I groaned, laying back on the mat, my hands pressed to the side of my body that made a sickening crack just seconds ago.

It had been nearly four hours, but I was determined to beat Drystan before Waelyn made him back off. It certainly didn't seem like I'd gained anything by having my supposed 'power' released, or bathing in the Blackwell, but I still hoped that would change with every charge Drystan made.

The brunet god laughed, bending down to squeeze the aching spot.

I glared at him.

"You'll be fine," he assured me.

"*You* might not be," I grumbled, pushing off the floor and getting back on my feet.

He shook his head. "Get ready. I'm coming at you again."

"Be careful this time," Waelyn muttered from where he stood at the edge of the room with crossed arms.

Drystan gave no warning before launching forward, no familiarity in his eyes. He fought like a feral cat—graceful, yet deadly. I wouldn't want to be his opposition in a real fight. I was grateful for Waelyn's watchful eye as we sparred. Sometimes, Drystan got carried away, like he was lost in a moment far from this one.

I dodged his first swing, whirling to follow him as he dashed behind me. Drystan was smart, he stayed in my blind spots. In order to win, I had to keep my eyes on him. His fist shot out again, and I ducked too slowly. He clipped my shoulder, and I clamped my lips together to stop from crying out. He made a mistake then, shifting his weight to the foot nearest me as he tried to pivot. I kicked out, aiming for the leg that supported him. A cry of triumph left my lips as I connected with the back of his knee, and for the first time since we had started training, Drystan hit the mat with a dull thud.

I crouched, throwing my leg over his stomach like he'd done to me a million times before, pinning his arms down.

Drystan rolled his eyes. "Don't look at me like that. You got lucky."

My world spun and I hit the ground. Drystan stood over me, holding a hand out.

I laughed to myself. "It's progress."

Waelyn coughed. "I think that's enough for today."

I shook my head. "It's only been a few hours. I can keep going."

"We've had this conversation before, Stea," Waelyn sighed, moving to grab my cloak from the hook it hung on.

"So overprotective," Drystan crooned.

Waelyn glared. "For good reason."

"Sure," Drystan replied. He gathered his cloak and made for the door. "Get some rest, godling. The next time you see me, we'll be headed to the Light Realm."

CHAPTER THIRTY-FOUR

"Stea?" Waelyn's voice was muffled through the door, but I heard him call out nonetheless. "Are you clothed?"

I stared into the mirror. A polished version of me stared back.

The dress Waelyn had commissioned from Cara had arrived a few nights ago, and had been sitting in the corner of my chambers since, a looming threat and constant reminder of the peacekeeping event. Earlier in the afternoon, a set of hair pins, shaped in the crescents of the two moons of Edessa, were laid on the dressing table next to the gown. Though I doubted Waelyn had snuck into my chambers, I suspected he was responsible for their sudden appearance.

"Yes," I replied.

The knob of my door squeaked as it turned. Within seconds, Waelyn stood behind me, his gaze meeting mine in the mirror.

"You look…"

The gown *was* lovely. It was clear why he went to Cara for projects like this. It was black, with a full skirt of fabric made of the same gauzy darkness Waelyn's shadows seemed to be. It trailed behind me, a tad longer than necessary, but it was dramatic. The bodice was a corset, which I hadn't fully finished lacing up. The top arced over my breasts, accented with black jewels that sparkled in the light. The same material that made up the skirt draped over my shoulders, nearly as long as the dress itself. Finely strung jewels hung over the draped fabric, weighing it down and holding it in place. The same jewels lay against my back in sparkling swoops that made quiet tinkling sounds when I walked.

"I don't have the words." He sounded as surprised as I felt. "Seven turns alive and I can't find the right words."

How was I supposed to stop my heart racing when he said things like that!

Waelyn's fingers came up to trace the metal of the pins in my hair. He was gentle, as if he was worried I'd disintegrate beneath his touch. The warmth in my cheeks was threatening to burn me to ash, so perhaps he was onto something.

The God of Death and Darkness was dressed in black from head to toe. A finely tailored suit, no doubt also made by Cara, hugged his frame like a second skin. The fabric was dark, accented with black constellations that were somehow even darker. A cloak hung from his shoulders, though it wasn't the usual one he wore when we were training or traveling. This one was finer, plush, like velvet. Swirls of ink poked out from the collar of his jacket, reaching upward to his face. I traced his features with my eyes, noting every curve of his lips and the sharp edge of his jaw. His dark hair was choppy and shaggy as always, curling at the nape of his neck and brushing his brow, but the obsidian crown on his head was new. It matched his throne, made of sharp points that threatened to spear anything that got close. When I met his eyes, they were already on mine. A bright green that conflicted with the darkness that shrouded him.

Beautiful.

I swallowed. "I'm not quite dressed. The corset is hard to lace up alone."

His lips parted, but no words came for a moment. Then, he blinked, finally regaining control of himself. "I can help."

Nodding, I braced myself on the edge of the sink, avoiding

his gaze in the mirror. I'd worn my fair share of corsets in the near five turns I'd existed, and none were easy to tighten. I'd been yanked around by an uptight seamstress more than once. The last thing I had expected was the gentleness with which Waelyn approached the task. He moved surely, as if he had experience in such matters, but was tentative when it came time to pull on the laces that crossed my back. His fingers brushed against the exposed skin, sending shivers down my spine.

I hoped he wouldn't notice.

The small smile on his lips suggested he had.

"You're kinder than I expected," I said when the silence became too much for me to bear. His touch almost made me forget the ache in my chest that I couldn't seem to shake.

He stilled, but only for a second before he continued lacing. "Are you still operating on assumptions, Stea?"

"Habits are hard to break," I replied. "It's rare to find someone in the Mortal world that speaks plainly and acts with their true intentions in mind."

He smiled at that.

I traced every one of his features in the mirror.

"Immortals have more time to make amends when things go awry. It's easier to be honest that way."

I hummed. There was truth in his words. I'd only met a handful of gods and deceased ethereals in the month or so I'd spent in the Night Realm, but they were more direct than most I'd encountered in the Mortal world. Even the ones who had wanted to kill me were forthright about it here. The same couldn't be said for the people of Kaedia.

Orien was sneaky, Verena even more so. I'd expected Orien to be cruel. Several turns of power like he possessed were bound to corrupt a man with a weak will. Verena was strong—or at least, I'd thought she was. It was still hard to wrap my mind around the fact that she had sealed my memories—my power; my life—away.

Though, I supposed there had been a silver lining to that act. Sarya, Tolith, and Haryk flashed through my mind. Not their ending, of course, but other memories. The turns we had spent in each other's company. The warmth in Sarya's smile; the wit from Tolith's mind; the quiet understanding Haryk met us with. I would accept permanent estrangement from my arcane for the chance to experience their companionship again.

"Why is it that I'm always waiting on the two of you?" Drystan huffed as Waelyn and I arrived in the Great Hall.

The brunet god was dashing in a navy suit that complimented the blue of his eyes. He wore no cloak, but had a train from the bottom of his jacket that trailed on the floor behind him.

"Because you're annoyingly punctual," Waelyn grumbled back.

"Most would say that's a positive trait," Drystan retorted.

Waelyn rolled his eyes, but said nothing in reply. He was too focused on the shimmering mass near the front doors of his estate.

"We're taking a portal?" I asked.

"Don't get too excited, godling," Drystan teased.

"Is it that obvious?"

Waelyn frowned at our bickering. "I'm sorry, Stea, I know this isn't easy for you."

I waved a hand. "What better first impression than spilling my guts all over the floor of Lux's ballroom?"

The corner of his lips tilted up, and a surge of accomplishment filled my chest.

Waelyn's focus returned to the portal. "It's ready. Lux has granted us access to his realm."

"How gracious," Drystan drawled. "Come on, let's get this over with."

Drystan held the crook of his elbow out to me, and I placed my hand on his arm without a thought. He had become a sort of friend during my time in the Night Realm, one that I found oddly comforting, despite our regular disagreements.

Waelyn's eyes were hard as he noticed our intertwined limbs, but I didn't think too much of it.

I couldn't.

The brunet god nodded to the God of Death and Darkness, and we stepped through the portal, twisting and turning until my stomach sank to my feet.

Oh gods, Asteria, don't throw up.

I swallowed hard just as Drystan patted my hand. "We made it, you can stop being so dramatic."

"I'll puke on your shoes," I groaned, hoping it came across as a threat.

When the nausea passed, I took in my surroundings.

The pavement below us was flecked with white and gold, matching the opulent building paces away. It reminded me of the paintings I'd seen of Thelassan a few turns ago. Perhaps that kingdom was modeled after the Light Realm, just like Kaedia had been after Night. The structure was huge, probably as large as the entire inner circle of Dreka. Now I could understand why Waelyn referred to *his* home as an estate. *This* was a castle.

Complete with towers and no doubt too many wings to count, the tan, sand-like stone building sparkled as if made of crushed diamonds. It nearly hurt my eyes. There were spires topped with shimmering gold in every corner, glinting in the sun.

The *sun*. It was warm, despite the streaks of orange and pink in the sky announcing its descent. Did the Light Realm not experience eternal day as the Night Realm did night?

There was no time to consider, or even ask my companions. Whispers brought my attention to the other partygoers, milling around the pavement where we stood, watching us with sharp gazes. I'd nearly forgotten the Night Realm's reputation. Did these people think I was a monster?

"Pay them no mind," Waelyn murmured as he stepped closer. The shadows that surrounded him were darker now, more menacing. His eyes were a murky green instead of the bright tone I was used to.

He was Nox now.

"Let's get inside," Drystan said, straightening his tie. "This is where the commoners lurk."

Waelyn nodded, leading the way to the grand entrance, where tens of guards stood, checking every guest that dared to approach. Lux, it seemed, was desperate to keep something out.

"Lord Nox," the first guard acknowledged.

Waelyn simply looked at him, but it was enough for the guards to stand a little straighter as we passed their line. The god radiated power. Authority. I'd never been in the presence of another like him.

Once inside the extravagant castle, it was clear that Lux liked to flaunt his wealth. If the outside wasn't telling enough, the inside was covered with decadent fabrics hung like tapestries along the corridors in varying shades of sunset. The walls themselves were made of the same crushed diamond material the outside was, reflecting every beam of light coming from the tens of chandeliers that hung from the tall ceilings. A dracon or two could fit in the main hall—it was excessive.

A fair-haired woman clothed in maroon stood just inside the

Great Hall with a tray of glass flutes, filled to the rim with an opaque orange liquid.

"Care for a drink, Lord Nox?" the woman asked, leaning in as close as was appropriate to the dark-haired god.

He waved her off, scanning the crowded room. Drystan stepped in front of me to grab a glass from her tray. Curiosity filled me, so I took one too.

As quickly as I'd picked it up, Waelyn plucked it from my grasp and placed it back on the tray.

"That's a powerful psychedelic, my lady," he warned.

The woman raised her eyebrows as he addressed me, her scrutinizing stare scanning the length of my figure. She no doubt wanted to know what made me deserving of his respect. I didn't have the answer.

"I see," I replied, unsure how much to say in front of strangers. I couldn't be as familiar as I normally was with the God of Death and Darkness. Not here in this foreign realm.

"Your seats are at the head table," another being dressed in maroon said curtly.

Waelyn did not reply, but Drystan nodded.

"Are they all consorts?" I asked in a hushed tone as we moved further into the ballroom. Further into the enemy's lair.

"Servants," he corrected.

The thought hadn't occurred to me; I had become far too familiar with Waelyn's lack of staff. I'd forgotten he was the exception, not the rule.

"Right," I muttered, looking around. There were so many of them, dressed in that same dark red. Were they treated like the fae in Dreka? Worse?

"The consorts are in white," Drystan leaned forward to whisper in my ear just before he took a long sip from his glass.

There were tens of them, too. Maybe even more than the

servants. Male and female, distributed around the room like furniture, carefully placed. Was that Lux's way of bragging?

I quickly spotted the redhead who had visited the Night Realm, laughing where she sat on the edge of a drink table. She was surrounded by men hanging onto her every word. I moved on; she wasn't who I was looking for.

I scanned so many faces that they started to blur. They were all the same, pretty and smiling. Blissfully unaware that their leader had sent dissenters to the Night Realm to overthrow the God of Death and Darkness. That very act would be enough to start a war if Lux wasn't the god-king.

Speaking of the ruler of the Light Realm, he sat at the front of the room, surveying the crowd with a stare of molten gold. I'd seen those eyes before—once—in a vision. We had been dancing, in this very room, but Drystan and Waelyn had been absent. He wore the same white suit I'd envisioned back then, his blond hair falling in waves around his face. He met my eyes and a shiver ran down my spine. Orien's face flashed in my mind.

As if he could sense my discomfort, Lux smiled. I couldn't focus on him though, not when another consort dressed in white perched on the edge of his throne.

A consort with auburn hair and a golden circlet that was all too familiar.

Sarya.

CHAPTER THIRTY-FIVE

Led by the pounding in my chest, I was pulled across the ballroom toward Sarya, toward the god-king.

Drystan's hand clamped down on my arm, halting me. "Where do you think you're going?"

I turned to him, meeting his icy blue eyes with a rage that stemmed from deep within my being. I couldn't let him stop me. For the first time, Drystan flinched when I met his eyes.

"Godling," he warned, "not here."

"What?" I just wanted to get to Sarya—I *needed* to get to Sarya. To apologize. To tell her how much I missed her.

A hush fell over the room, hundreds of immortal beings falling quiet.

"Stea." Waelyn's voice was low and commanding. His eyes were dark as he looked at me. "Your arcane is flaring. They can all feel it."

How? I couldn't even feel it myself. Then, I realized the darkness that had once echoed in my mind now swirled in my chest, making my skin tingle. Was this what my power felt like?

I tried to stifle the feeling, to quiet the hum, but it was no use. Not with Sarya so close, not with all those eyes on me. The anxiety antagonized the arcane, making it fester.

Thick smoke pushed at the edge of my mind, my being. It was too late to calm me. Lux's molten gold eyes met mine from across the room, a dangerous smirk on his lips. He stood from his throne, clearing his throat. The eyes left me in favor of him.

"My dear friends and colleagues, it would seem our esteemed guest has arrived," his voice boomed through the room like the brass instruments used to announce noble comings and goings back in Castle Dreka.

His words were welcoming, but the look in his eyes sent shivers down my spine.

He was cold, calculating, dangerous. That much was clear.

Lux held his hand out toward me. "Please, come."

It was seemingly an invitation, but I knew better. There was no choice here. I would meet him on his dais, or I would be punished.

I stepped toward the man of gold, but Waelyn and Drystan blocked my path, standing shoulder to shoulder as they stared down the ruler of the Light Realm.

"Why don't we save the pleasantries for dinner? Rel and Zenir haven't arrived yet," Waelyn suggested, his tone deceptively calm considering the darkness in his eyes.

Lux raised an eyebrow, staring at him incredulously. Waelyn was bold to disagree with him, especially in front of all these people. Fear squeezed in my chest at the thought of the consequences he might face for such an action, my memories of my time in Orien's dungeon flashing through my mind. The same thick smoke from earlier pushed the thoughts away, easing the tension in my frame. Waelyn wasn't worried.

The god-king smirked, nodding to the two bulky guards who stood in front of his throne. They stepped toward my companions, but neither of the Night Realm gods moved an inch.

"Don't be rude, *Lord* Nox. Allow me to dance with your pet. As the *king. Your* king." Lux's voice dripped with malice: a final warning.

Waelyn didn't budge.

Lux sighed. "You forget you're in my realm. We'll see you for dinner."

With a wave of Lux's hand, Drystan and Waelyn disappeared, leaving no trace of their existence behind. The smell of citrus, tangy and sour, hung in the air as proof that Lux had used his arcane.

"Where did you take them?" I asked, as panic coursed through me. I knew better than to show it, but it leaked out anyway.

Lux smiled. He could sense it. "Worried your god will find another toy to play with? Don't fret, little godling. I'm here to take care of you."

He cut across the ballroom to where I stood. His presence was overwhelming, but not in the way Waelyn's was. Lux was too close, his cologne too strong, his touch too firm as he grabbed my hands. Perhaps it was to make up for the distinct lack of arcane coming from his being? I was sure he must be strong, but his magick felt nothing like Waelyn's. Lux's arcane was a wispy cloud, both there and yet not.

"I don't need to be taken care of," I snapped, stepping back as his hands found my waist.

He didn't appreciate the move, pulling me in closer to him. The front of his body pressed against mine as he gestured for the band to continue playing. The musicians hesitated, but with another glare from the god-king, they were playing lilting tunes once more. He guided me around the dancefloor, pushing and pulling my body when I resisted.

"Tell me about yourself, pet," Lux prompted, as though we were merely courting.

I wouldn't entertain the notion. "How did you send Nox away? He's powerful."

As we turned, I tried to get a glimpse of Sarya over his

shoulder, but he shifted to block my line of sight.

Lux laughed. "Is that what he told you? He's rather full of himself."

"Are you saying he isn't strong?" I wasn't sure I'd believe the god-king either way. Waelyn's power was tangible, an all-encompassing force.

"I'm saying it doesn't matter how strong you are when you're in another god's realm," Lux said smugly. "He should know better than to pick a fight he can't win."

A thousand more questions came to mind, but I pushed them away, focusing on keeping as much space between my body and his as possible. Lux, sensing my aversion to his touch, pulled me closer, a wicked smirk gracing his lips.

"Why do you scurry so far away? Is it because I speak poorly of your god?" Lux asked. "You must not be very bright to have aligned yourself with him so soon. You have yet to meet the rest of the rulers." He scowled, nodding toward the gown draped over my frame. "Perhaps you show him your loyalty because he has branded you. What a fool."

Lux wanted me to argue with him, that much was obvious. I had to choose my words carefully.

"It's wise to keep one's options open," I said, erring on the side of vagueness rather than spewing the insults that coated my tongue. He wanted to get a rise out of me, but why, I didn't know.

"Diplomatic," he commented, guiding me in an elaborate spin before pulling me back to his chest.

Lux was beautiful, or at least, I would have thought so had I not known his nature. His hair was long enough to brush his jaw, but was pushed away from his face, showcasing his high cheekbones and strong features. His nose was straight, his jawline sharp, but the soft shape of his lips lessened the angles of his expression. He was tall and broad like Waelyn, but his hold was demanding and tight. He evidently wasn't told 'no' often.

He leaned in. "You're far too smart to be stuck in Nox's dungeon of a realm. You'd fare much better here, pet."

"A generous offer, though I doubt Lord Zenir and Lord Rel would agree with your words."

Another smirk. "I'm the king, I don't need their agreement."

"Fair enough." I caught a glimpse of Sarya as he spun me once more. She watched with wide eyes as I danced with her king. "How do you choose your consorts?" I asked, changing the subject.

"Are you interested in the position?" he mused, his gaze raking over my body. "Or is this about your friend?"

"You know of mine and Sarya's history?" I tilted my head. Had she told him how I'd gotten her killed?

He rolled his eyes. "The whole realm likely knows. She wailed for weeks about how you were to be killed by my chosen."

Sarya had worried for me? It was just like her to focus on everyone else but herself. More concerning, however, was his admission of support for Orien.

"Orien was your chosen? An odd choice for a God of Light."

His fingers tightened on my waist. "I am *the* God of Light, pet. My choices are never *odd*."

I frowned. "He murdered several Marked during his reign. Is that not a crime against the gods?"

Lux narrowed his eyes at me, confirming what I had begun to piece together. He knew of Orien's attacks on the Marked—he'd likely orchestrated them himself—but to what end? I thought of Waelyn's words shortly after he'd taken me from the Mortal world: there hadn't been a new godling for the Night Realm in many turns. Was Lux the cause of that drought?

"You ask far too many questions," he scowled.

Drystan's face flashed in my mind, wearing an annoyed expression that wasn't dissimilar from the god-king's. "I've heard that a few times."

"It matters not. You'll have all the answers you'll need after you spend a few turns in my realm," Lux said dismissively.

"I don't believe I've accepted an invitation for such a stay."

He smiled deviously. "You don't need to. You are the one who will fulfill the Prophecy of Balance, are you not?"

Word traveled fast in the Immortal world.

"There's little reason to believe that," I scoffed, sure that Waelyn wouldn't want the details of my visit to the Blackwell to be shared with the god before me.

"But there *is* reason still. You'll make your rounds to all the realms, in due time. Such is customary."

"I know little of your customs, I'm afraid," I admitted. I'd spent far more time studying the Night Realm.

Lux sighed. "What is that god of yours teaching you? Nothing useful, it would seem."

Again, I bit back my defenses of Waelyn. It would help neither of us to deal in matters of petty pride.

Where had Lux sent the God of Darkness? The stress that had been lying in wait since his disappearance seized my chest again, forcing my breaths in and out in shallow puffs. He could handle himself, but I wasn't naive enough to dismiss the disdain the God of Light held for him. Lux was dangerous, if everything Waelyn had told me was true.

"I tire of talking about that buffoon. I want to hear about you, pet," Lux prompted.

"What could I tell you that you don't already know?"

"Plenty. Starting with the incidents in your whelp years—the ones that inspired my chosen to despise you so."

My blood turned cold then, the darkness in my chest

festering. "I have no memories of such incidents. Your *chosen* made sure of that."

Lux smiled. "Your arcane feels different. It flares at the mere thought of those days of carnage."

"My arcane is likely responding to the memory of years spent in a torture chamber under the instruction of your pawn," I snapped. Chills covered my skin as I felt the blade against my stomach all over again.

"That's neither here nor there," Lux said dismissively.

I fought the urge to roll my eyes, following as Lux guided me in an arc around the dancefloor, depositing me on the edge of the crowd

"Why don't you socialize? I'll make sure your god is receiving the *best* treatment," he purred, releasing me from his too-tight grip. In a puff of citrus, he was gone.

Lux's words were meant to antagonize me, nothing more. I swallowed my concerns, scanning the room for Sarya. She was perched on the edge of the dais near Lux's throne, her eyes wide and locked on me.

I crossed the room quickly; no one dared stand in my way. They'd seen the attention their king gave me. Sarya stood as I approached, her arms open and waiting. Flinging mine around her, I pulled her close to me, breathing in the warm vanilla scent I'd never appreciated in the Mortal world.

"Asteria," she gasped, her grip tightening. "I can't believe you're here."

"I'm so sorry," I said immediately, blinking away the tears that pooled in the corners of my eyes.

She shook her head, her chin mussing my hair ever so slightly. "You have nothing to be sorry for."

"I got you *killed*, Sarya."

"King Orien killed me. Not you," she insisted, pulling back

to squeeze my shoulders.

She couldn't understand, not without the two turns of memories that had been stolen from me. I would tell her everything later, when we were safe in the Night Realm.

"Never mind that. We have to get you out of here," I murmured, looking around for listening ears.

Sarya's brow furrowed. "What? Why?"

I mirrored her expression. "You can't stay here with Lux. He's *evil*, Sarya. Orien was *his* chosen."

She laughed as if I'd made a joke. "I *love* Lux, Asteria. He is my king. My god. He isn't some villain. He's kind, and quite generous. Whatever choices he made, they were for the good of all the realms."

She had to be brainwashed. Or perhaps Lux had pulled a thick wool over her eyes?

There was, of course, a third option—that Waelyn had lied to me—but given Lux's general demeanor during our dance, I refused to consider it.

"We can talk about everything later. Come with me after the ball."

Cologne permeated the air, filling my lungs with an artificial spice that nearly had me coughing.

"I hope you aren't propositioning my consort so blatantly, pet," Lux's too-smooth voice murmured from just behind me.

Sarya's eyes softened at the sight of him. My stomach turned. His arm snaked around my waist, turning me to face him. There was barely any space between us as he guided me away from Sarya.

"Excuse me, dear," he called out in passing.

She stared after him with a dreamy expression.

"What lies have you told her?" I hissed at the god-king as soon as I could bare to pull my focus from my friend.

Lux rolled his eyes. "You think so little of me. Perhaps I should ask what lies *your* god has told *you*?"

I opened my mouth to respond, but he beat me to it.

"Never mind, pet, I shouldn't have asked. He isn't familiar enough with this world to craft clever tales." Lux tilted his head, studying me with an assessing stare. "There are things Nox can't tell you about yourself, about your power. Things he doesn't know. It would be advantageous for you to reside here. I could educate you."

I faltered at that, and would have stumbled had Lux not anticipated my shock. He held me upright, his grip tightening as he supported my weight.

He smirked. "An intriguing offer?"

I met his molten gaze. "What do you know?"

"More than he does. Do you know why your god spends his days buried away in his books? Why he wastes immortality learning every excruciating detail of the past? He has had the losing hand in a battle that has gone on for tens of turns now. He will forever be behind, always chasing an advantage that doesn't exist. Why don't you join the winning side for once, Asteria?"

I blinked, absorbing his words. The damned picture they painted.

"My pet, you look at me so differently now," he crooned. "Just in time for your god to see."

Waelyn had returned? I scanned the room, looking for the god whose power I couldn't feel. He stood in a doorway behind Lux's throne, his brow furrowed and his gaze dark as he followed the two of us around the room with his eyes.

Lux leaned lower to whisper in my ear, his breath warm against my neck. "He knows I'm persuading you. I don't think he's happy."

I started to argue, but Lux released me from his hold as

Waelyn appeared just paces away. His normal pine and smoke scent was smothered with a floral perfume—lilies. The top button of his shirt was undone.

Where had Lux sent him?

"Oh good, you're back in time for dinner!" Lux exclaimed with false cheeriness and a goading look in his eyes.

The orchestra stopped playing, and the guests resumed their hushed conversations. Lux grabbed my hand in his, pulling me up to his dais. Once in front of his throne, he raised his arms, and with a surge of acidic arcane, the dance floor was replaced with a long dining table. Not large enough to fit all the guests present, but the partygoers already seemed aware of that fact. Some took places at the table, others filtered through doorways at the edge of the ballroom, perhaps to other accommodations. Sarya was in that group, following the herd of white-robed beings out of the ballroom.

"Please, join us," Lux said to Waelyn. "Pet, your seat is here, just beside mine," he added, guiding me by the hand he still held to a seat at the right of the head of the table.

I moved stiffly as he pulled the chair out for me, gesturing for me to sit. I obeyed, but my eyes were on Waelyn. The God of Death and Darkness followed my every movement, his jaw clenched as Lux pushed the chair in.

"What's the matter?" Lux asked his counterpart. "Oh! Of course!" He snapped his fingers, and Drystan reappeared, seated in a chair across from me.

"This is the worst trip I've ever had," he grumbled, his pupils large black pits.

Relief flooded me now that both of my companions were in the room again, even though Drystan was clearly under the effects of the drink he'd had earlier, and Waelyn looked ready to turn this entire palace to dust.

"Please join us, Lord Nox," Lux repeated, gesturing to the chair next to Drystan. "We have much to discuss."

CHAPTER THIRTY-SIX

An eternity ticked by before Lux or Waelyn spoke a word. There was a standoff between the gods, an unwillingness to break the tense silence that had settled over us. The other guests spoke in easy tones, chatting about nothing of substance. A closer look would show that their eyes flickered from the gods to their plates, doing more eavesdropping than fraternizing. They were all actors on Lux's great stage, creating the illusion of a party.

This was an ambush.

Lord Rel and Lord Zenir were never coming, and all the partygoers seemed to originate from the Light Realm, judging purely by their attire and complete submission to Lux's every order. That fact should have raised alarms earlier, but I had been distracted.

Across from me, Drystan nudged Waelyn's elbow with his, eyes trailing down to the floor. There, beneath our chairs, were large spell circles, enchanted to trap whoever was unfortunate enough to come across them. They were orange, nearly the same color as the stone that made up the ballroom. It was an excellent form of camouflage and didn't bode well for us. If Lux was smart, he was all the more dangerous.

"Am I to make the gracious assumption that the wards beneath our chairs are mere coincidence?" Waelyn nonchalantly asked the god-king as he reached for the empty glass tumbler in front of his plate.

"You may assume what you like, but I'm afraid there is no

coincidence here, Lord Nox." Lux sighed. "I need all of you to stay put until I've said my piece. Afterwards, whoever wishes to shall leave my realm whole."

"Ominous," Drystan muttered under his breath, using his fork to spear the air above his empty plate. He put the fork in his mouth, pressing his lips closed to savor the bite of whatever he thought he was eating.

What exactly was in that elixir?

"Before we begin, I have one more special guest," Lux announced, turning toward the large arch that led to the castle interior.

There, through the golden light, emerged a tall, broad man, with hair the color of sand, amber eyes, and an oily grin.

Orien. In the flesh.

Lux said more, but there was only static in my ears, broken up by thunderous heartbeats. I stood, my body moving independently of my thoughts, driven by the murderous rage that had arcane buzzing at my fingertips.

I *needed* to kill him.

Waelyn subtly pressed the hilt of his silver dagger into the palm of my hand. I had his approval to kill the god-king's chosen—and that was what I would do. In the next breath, I launched forward, crossing the table to take the shortest path to Orien.

At least, I tried.

The spell circle formed an invisible barrier that halted me halfway, straining against the force of my arcane, but refusing to give. The frenzy in me demanded death, but a vice made of pure light came down on me—on my magick—snuffing it out as if it had never existed.

At the head of the table, Lux smiled.

Was it his arcane that had stifled me? How? I hadn't felt

power like this the entire evening we were in his presence. Was this the advantage of a god being in his own realm?

"Don't be rude, Lady Asteria," Lux chided. "He's my guest."

Waelyn tensed, his lips pulled back in a silent snarl. "What is the meaning of this?" he demanded, pinning Lux with a murderous glare as his shadows writhed, growing denser and more agitated by the second.

Lux held up his hands. "Calm down, Lord Nox. This is an offering to the godling."

Fingers digging into the wooden table, I stared Orien down. "I want nothing to do with that monster."

Lux tutted. "Don't be so short-sighted. Think of all you could gain. Surely you want to know why he killed your friends, or why he tortured you himself for so many years?" He leaned forward, catching my gaze. "You could ask him about all of the memories you can't quite recall. Or, for all I care, exact your pound of flesh. Take your revenge."

Confusion flashed across Orien's features. He hadn't known his god would sacrifice him.

"Why would you make an offer like that?" I asked, brows pinched as I straightened in front of my chair.

"Consider it a welcome gift, pet. I want you to thrive here."

My head spun, bouncing between emotions as they crashed over me in waves; rage, disbelief, and worst of all, *temptation*.

Lux had answers—knowledge I craved. Was this why Waelyn had tried so hard to convince me he was the enemy?

No, I was falling for Lux's scheme. Even from our brief interaction, I knew him to be a nasty piece of work. Besides, Waelyn wouldn't lie to me, not about this.

I repeated those thought until my breaths didn't stab my lungs with each inhale.

Sensing my conflict, Lux waved Orien over, gesturing to the

empty seat beside me.

"Join us, former King of the Mortal world. Asteria has much to consider."

I held my breath as he approached. A foul, traitorous, parasite of a man. He didn't deserve the beats his heart gave him. He deserved to suffer.

Waelyn cleared his throat. "Fill my glass before I spill blood on your marble floors," he growled, tilting his glass toward Lux.

Lux stared at him a moment, considering the thinly veiled threat. Then, he picked the bottle of arcwine up from the table, stretching to pour a healthy amount into the god's glass.

A glint of satisfaction flashed through Waelyn's black irises. He'd won. In this small interaction at least. We *were* still spelled to the floor.

"You're not a very nice guest," Lux nearly pouted. "I set all of this up for you."

Waelyn rolled his eyes. "Your servants set this up."

Lux squinted. "It's the same thing."

"It is not. Speak your mind quickly, *Your Highness*," Waelyn snarled. "My patience grows thin."

"I care not about your *patience*," Lux scoffed.

"Foo-lish," Drystan sang under his breath, taking another bite of air.

"Excuse me?" Lux raised an eyebrow as he turned to look at the brunet god, his pupils the size of gold coins.

Drystan burped. "Excused."

Lux's jaw clenched, and I waved my hand dismissively at Drystan.

"He had an elixir," I said knowingly to the god-king.

He looked at me for a moment longer before rolling his eyes. "This is the best and brightest from your realm, Nox? How disappointing." Lux shook his head as he regarded Drystan.

Waelyn looked at him dryly. "Best and brightest isn't how I'd put it, but yes. Drystan is my right hand."

"And what does that make our lovely Lady Asteria?" Lux nearly purred my name as his stare raked over me. "Surely she is an important fixture considering how secretive you've been since she arrived in the Immortal world."

Waelyn was as still as a statue, but his white-knuckle grip on his glass revealed that he was anything but calm. "We've never been especially conversational, Lux. I hardly think there's been a change on that front."

Lux smiled lazily, a dangerous expression. "Perhaps not. Still, I would have expected some communication from you as Lord of the Night Realm. Is it not your duty to inform a god when you kill one of their chosen?"

Waelyn scoffed. "I did not kill your worm, Lux. There was a challenge for the throne. You would know if you ever bothered to visit the Mortal world instead of sending a proxy."

A group of servants emerged from the doors behind Lux's throne, carrying tray after tray of steaming food. I paid it no mind, too entranced by the battle in front of me. I was listening, but I was also digging, looking for the meaning beneath their words. They were communicating in a language no one else spoke. The language of power.

Lux couldn't let Waelyn push too hard, or he would lose respect as the god-king. He was in a precarious position on those grounds alone. And Waelyn...

Well, he was more powerful than Lux, that much was clear from the arcane I sensed rolling off the two of them. Waelyn could say what he wanted as long as he could handle the fight that would surely be coming. Perhaps that was why Lux hadn't called on his guard? He knew he wouldn't win if left to a test of strength.

Neither of the gods touched the food placed in front of them. Drystan's eyes grew to the size of saucers as his fork dug into real food for the first time all evening. His mouth was agape as he inspected the morsel he'd expertly speared.

"You encouraged the whelp that challenged the king I chose, did you not?" Lux asked, crossing his leg over his knee and leaning back in his chair, a portrait of faux relaxation.

"Nox did not. Verena had plans to challenge Orien long before the Veiled Night," I piped up, unable to stop myself from coming to his defense.

Lux turned to me. "And you know this how, pet?"

"Verena is my half-sister. I found her plans in her office weeks before the challenge."

Orien scowled at the mention of his successor. I gripped Waelyn's dagger with white knuckles, willing him to shift into the boundaries of my spell circle.

The god-king placed a finger over his lips as he considered my words. "There was a shift of power, nonetheless. Kaedia was dedicated to the Light Realm for several turns until your sister intervened."

"Verena is determined to bring back the Kaedia that existed before Orien's reign—the one that worshiped Night," I said earnestly. "The way things were when Edessa was formed. Balanced."

Lux scoffed. "Balance means nothing in this world. It is all about power, my dear."

"Of which you have plenty," Waelyn said.

"Of which I want more," Lux retorted. "Hence, my irritation that you did not inform me your realm was housing the being destined to fulfill a world-altering prophecy."

"That is *not* confirmed," Drystan hiccupped. "I'm not convinced she's that special."

"Thanks," I muttered back.

"The whispers speak of the Blackwell. Are you to tell me that information is false?" Lux asked.

"There is much to be discovered yet, Lux," Waelyn replied. "And I have not unlawfully kept Lady Asteria in my realm. She is not Marked in a traditional sense."

Lux buzzed with curiosity. "I'd heard as much. Show me your Mark, pet."

I tensed, looking to Waelyn for help. He was still as stone, staring at Lux with fire in his eyes. If looks could kill, Lux would have been a pile of dust on the floor.

With no guidance from the God of Death and Darkness, I turned in my chair so that my back was toward Lux. I pulled my hair over my shoulder, revealing the pale skin with a perfect black circle at the base of my neck.

When his eyes fell on my Mark, Lux burst into laughter, loud, echoing guffaws that bounced off the ballroom walls and silenced every bit of performative conversation happening down the table. He clapped his hands together with glee as he stared us down, his gaze focusing on Waelyn.

"It all makes sense now, brother."

"What?"

Lux raised his brows at my question. "She doesn't know?" The god looked shocked as he turned to Waelyn. "You haven't told her?"

The God of Death and Darkness looked at me, black pupils swimming with something I couldn't place. "I was going to, in due time. Now is *not* that time."

My stomach felt hollow. "What... what's going on?"

"Stea, I—"

"Do you know what those Marks mean, pet?" Lux asked, interrupting.

"They mean you are destined to serve the gods in the realm you are Marked for," I replied, reciting the passages every sprite in Kaedia knew.

Lux nodded. "Among other things. I wonder… did you also know that finding another with a Mark that… *matches* your own is a symbol that your souls are intertwined?"

"Souls intertwined? Like a prophecy?"

"Not quite. More like soulmates. Fated by the arcane," Lux explained.

"What does that have to do with me?"

Lux smirked. "Your Mark is… peculiar. A rare occurrence."

I nodded.

"Brother, why don't you… let us all in on your little secret, hm? Lady Asteria deserves the truth, does she not?"

My brows pinched together as I took in the implications of Lux's words. Did he mean…

I looked at Waelyn, truly looked, and I saw the truth in his eyes, in the way his head hung. He hadn't wanted me to know. He hadn't wanted to be whatever our Marks meant we were.

"*Come on*, don't disappoint my guests," Lux pressed.

Waelyn said nothing. He simply slid his jacket from his shoulders, his eyes on mine as he unbuttoned the top few clasps of his shirt. Only when he turned to show his Mark did his gaze leave me.

All the air in my lungs evaporated.

An empty circle, the perfect match to my full one, lay between his shoulder blades, at the base of his neck.

"They complement each other nicely, wouldn't you say?"

Waelyn ignored Lux's words, turning back to face me. "I was going to tell you—"

"But you didn't." My throat felt tight. Acid churned in my stomach. But worse than any physical feeling, any emotion I felt, was the darkness stirring in my chest.

I felt betrayed. Waelyn had known how much I longed for the truth, for answers about my future in the Immortal world. He'd seen through my eyes and felt my emotions—I'd spoken more of my inner thoughts to him than any other soul. There was a tear in my chest and an ache that resonated in the very core of my being. He had publicly humiliated me, rejected me, and allowed Lux to make a spectacle of it in front of his court.

Waelyn leaned forward, and the smell of lilies washed over me. He *had* been with another before; Lux had practically warned me. Of course he hadn't wanted to tell me about the Mark—he had a lover.

"Stea—"

"Don't call me that," I said bitterly. The hum of arcane was at my fingertips, begging to be used.

"Ah, seems I've inspired a lovers' quarrel," Lux chuckled to himself. "My dear, is it time we revisit our conversation about you becoming one of my consorts?"

I didn't answer. I couldn't.

What else had Waelyn kept from me? Orien cackled beside me, full of glee at my despair. It was all too much. I couldn't breathe.

I couldn't breathe.

I couldn't breathe.

I couldn't breathe.

I'd trusted the wrong person again. I'd been a fool. The shadows that had pressed into my mind recoiled as if they had been struck.

There wasn't time to blink before the ballroom exploded into darkness. Thick, gauzy black that could only have one source. I heard Waelyn's roar, but saw nothing. There was only the crash of furniture and the shattering of glass. Another male yelled. He had attacked the god-king.

There were sounds of a fight, shouts from both gods, and potent magick in the air. The ballroom was illuminated in a flash of light, but it was quickly suffocated by the rich darkness that filled every inch of the room.

Still, the split second was enough for me to see the blood coating the floor of the ballroom. Who was bleeding? I didn't know, but it didn't matter. The arcane that had been festering all night ripped its way out of me like a taloned beast, the *thing* that had plagued me for so long finally flooding the room. Screams echoed off the walls, but they were just music to the monster within. It raged, wreaking havoc and leaving carnage in its wake. I was nothing but a vessel.

My skin was wet, with sweat or blood, I didn't know. All that existed was the darkness inside me, threatening to disintegrate Lux's entire realm. I saw nothing but destruction and knew nothing but terror. The Void took the room, snapping bones and cutting skin. Their cries meant nothing, not to the darkness.

I was the darkness.

Smoke pushed at my mind, begging me to stop, but the Void clamped down, pushing it out. Pushing *him* out.

Verena was right. She had tried to warn them. I was a monster; the thing that lived in me, consumed me, *was* me. I was the Void the prophecy spoke of. The Blackwell too, perhaps. We were all one and the same. She had been saving everyone by locking me away, rewriting my memories. I could see now that it *was* for the greater good.

Suddenly, Drystan's words from moons ago came to my mind.

We made a mistake allowing the godling to live.

He was right. They had made a mistake. Perhaps blinded by curiosity or greed for the power that rampaged in my being.

Either way, I knew there was only one way to stop it.

The second the thought crossed my mind, my fingers twitched toward the dagger that was strapped to my leg. From within the darkness came a yell. Not the same cries that came from the helpless party guests. No, this was a scream of rage, of will. From the gauzy night he appeared, his hands gripping my arms tightly. His eyes were green like they were *supposed* to be, as they bore into mine with a plea.

"No. Not like this." His voice was firm, unflinching in the midst of chaos as he begged me not to forfeit my life.

As if it knew his wicked touch was the cure, the darkness in me, the darkness that made me, stilled.

He breathed, as though the weight of the worlds was on his shoulders. Ever so gently, one of his hands came up to touch my face, his fingers ghosting across my cheek as though he wasn't sure I was real.

"I'm so sorry, Stea," he said quietly.

All at once, the night in the room was gone. The chandelier flickered back to life, the candles relit as if they had never been extinguished.

I looked around the ballroom, though I wished I hadn't. The wetness coating my body was sticky, the same dark shade that pooled beneath the bodies of the party guests, twisted and mangled beyond recognition. Only Drystan and Lux still stood, though the latter had blooming bruises and splotches of blood staining his white suit.

The god-king regarded me with something dark, more dangerous than curiosity or lust. He wanted me in a way that spelled trouble for the Immortal world. He wanted the power I possessed.

"I do believe this leaves no room for discussion," Lux stated, his eyes flickering gold as they glowed in the hazy room.

"Lux, no—"

With a wave of the god-king's hand, Waelyn's words were silenced.

"I allowed you your fun. You got your punches in, but now, I want what I am owed," Lux said lowly, dangerously.

Waelyn stood in front of me, protecting me despite the monster that lived within. Even though I was a partner he didn't want.

"You are owed nothing, Aedil," Drystan spat on the floor, holding his side as he stood. Had I hurt him? "The Light Realm has been running unchecked for far too long. You are not suited to house a being as strong as she."

Lux scoffed. "You are nothing but a bitter old man, *Drystan*, and you are not welcome here."

With another wave of his hand, Drystan was gone, banished from the realm.

"And *you…*"

There was a surge of arcane as the God of Death and Darkness was thrown across the room, crashing into one of the many marble pillars with a sickening crack.

I should have cried out; I should have run to him, but the wound of his betrayal kept me from doing either. I couldn't move, even as Lux approached, snaking an arm around me once more.

"What do you make of my offer now?" he murmured.

Waelyn got to his feet, arcane radiating from him as he realised that Lux held me.

"Stea, don't listen to him," he pleaded.

I didn't know who to believe, who to trust.

I decided then and there that I wouldn't trust anyone.

Never again.

To keep myself safe, I had to learn everything I could about the other realms. About my power. About the Immortal world. I had to talk to Sarya; find Tolith and Haryk.

But if I wanted to do any of those things, I had to stay in the Light Realm, where no one had any claim to me.

As if sensing my resolve, Waelyn made to attack the god-king.

It didn't matter. Before he could summon his power, Lux banished him.

My god, my friend, my betrayer—gone.

Lux breathed in deeply, his nose pressed to my hair. He sighed, a contented hum leaving his lips.

"You are *mine* now, pet."